DOUBTS AND DESIRES

Highfield Hall
Book One

Charlotte Wren

ARE YOU SIGNED UP FOR DRAGONBLADE'S BLOG?

You'll get the latest news and information on exclusive giveaways, exclusive excerpts, coming releases, sales, free books, cover reveals and more.

Check out our complete list of authors, too!

No spam, no junk. That's a promise!

Sign Up Here

www.dragonbladepublishing.com

Dearest Reader;

Thank you for your support of a small press. At Dragonblade Publishing, we strive to bring you the highest quality Historical Romance from some of the best authors in the business. Without your support, there is no 'us', so we sincerely hope you adore these stories and find some new favorite authors along the way.

Happy Reading!

CEO, Dragonblade Publishing

Additional Dragonblade books by Author Charlotte Wren

Highfield Hall Series
Doubts and Desires (Book 1)

The Highfield Chronicles
Of Christmas Past (Novella)
If the Fates Allow (Novella)
Loving Lysander (Novella)

The Lyon's Den Series
The Devilish Lyon

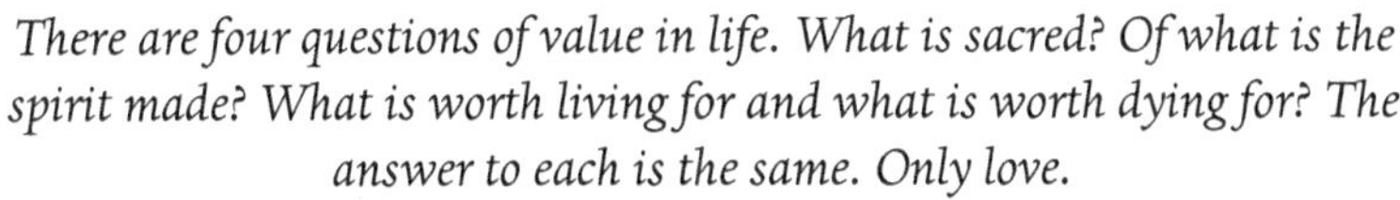

There are four questions of value in life. What is sacred? Of what is the spirit made? What is worth living for and what is worth dying for? The answer to each is the same. Only love.

Lord Byron

For Mrs. Corvinelli.

CHAPTER ONE

Yorkshire
February 1845

T HEY WERE NOTICEABLE simply by their presence on this deserted stretch of moorland. A distant dark figure astride an equally dark horse, standing motionless, like some obscure statue in a London park. Louisa gave them but a fleeting glimpse, due to the fact she had her own horse, Byron, hurtling along at a fine gallop. She didn't even slow when the wind snatched the hat from her head and whisked it away, pheasant feathers and all. Instead, she let out a shriek of laughter quite unbecoming a well-bred young lady. But then, propriety had little significance out here, where earth and sky met without the hindrance of man-made horizons. And this particular day, blessed by watery sunshine and a mild breeze that hinted at spring, was meant to be savored.

Which was why, despite strange men and airborne hats, the solid thud of Byron's powerful hooves continued unabated. Only when they reached the crest of Monk's Tor did Louisa finally rein her chestnut gelding to a halt, simultaneously parting with another unladylike whoop of delight. The mad dash had lit a fire in her cheeks and tugged several curls loose from their pins. And, since losing the veiled hat, she'd probably collected a muddy freckle or two, adding to those naturally bestowed.

Not that she much cared.

She leaned forward and gave Byron a few solid pats on his glossy brown neck. "Good boy," she said, chest heaving. "That was tremendous fun. You enjoyed it too, didn't you?" The gelding, withers trembling and damp with sweat, snorted a response.

Louisa lifted her face to the sky and filled her nostrils with the heady scent of marsh and meadow. "Magnificent," she muttered, shading her eyes with a gloved hand as her gaze roved over the wilderness. At best, it was a majestic but unforgiving landscape that mocked many an unwary traveler. At worst, it was… another word slid into her mind.

Bleak.

Especially now, at the tail end of winter.

A thick carpet of heather, bare and bedraggled, covered much of the firmer ground. Prickly tangles of gorse and rusty stands of bracken occupied the grassy, open spaces. Slender cotton-grass and heath-rushes served to warn travelers of boggy areas, where man and beast, if not heedful, might find themselves well and truly mired. Thickets of hawthorn, sculpted into bizarre shapes by the prevailing winds, might offer a small measure of shelter to those seeking it.

Bleak, indeed. But magnificent, nonetheless. Louisa's passion for these northern lands flowed through her veins as hotly as her blood.

Her gaze shifted to the big house nestling sedately, and in isolation, at the foot of the Tor. Northcott Manor belonged to her father, inherited from his Godfather, whose soul had departed the world nearly two decades before. The manor had since been leased out a number of times to a variety of well-shod tenants. The most recent of these had been a reclusive Tuscan aristocrat who, defeated by the Yorkshire climate, had returned to warmer climes the previous winter.

Consequently, for the last ten months, the manor had stood in empty silence with only a minimum of staff keeping the place in readiness while awaiting a new principal occupant. Louisa shifted in the saddle and considered heading down there to have a chat with Reuben Thornthwaite, the old gardener. She'd known him all her life and, in her eyes, he'd been forever ancient, with his weather-worn face and frosty-white curls poking out from beneath his cap. A natural storyteller, he was always willing to share tales of his life and experiences. Louisa could listen to him all day.

But even as she considered her visit, the breeze blew a little stronger, drawing her attention to an ominous gathering of clouds in the west. It did not do to be caught on the open moor when the rains came down, though she had hoped for a little more time. She patted Byron's neck again as she eyed the threatening skies. "I think we'd best be on our way back, boy."

The return journey began at a more sedate pace. An unwelcome awareness of the inevitable had replaced Louisa's euphoria. After this week, it would be a good while before she'd be able to ride out alone again, or to be overly concerned about her appearance or composure. This time next week, she'd be well on her way to London to commence her second Season, and another half-hearted search for a husband.

Half-hearted on her part, anyway.

She'd gazed upon a fair amount of handsome and not-so-handsome faces during her last Season as she'd been whisked around a variety of dance floors. She'd even enjoyed some appropriately pleasant interludes with several potential admirers, three of whom had hinted at marriage.

Their hints had been brushed respectfully aside.

She'd *liked* all of them, but only as much as one might like an inanimate object or a decorative piece. The thought of spending the rest of her life with any of them left her void of feeling. She had yet to meet a man who stirred her soul and made her heart quicken, someone who could addle her brain with a flattering comment or raise color to her cheeks with a simple smile. What if such a man didn't exist? Or worse, what if he did, but they were destined never to cross paths? Perhaps settling was something she'd have to consider. Maybe love would grow from like. But what if it didn't?

Perhaps she expected too much.

It didn't help, of course, that she'd been raised by parents whose love for each other formed the basis of legend. She knew, too, that she'd never be forced into an unwanted marriage. But she also knew her parents—and especially her mother—were keen to see their eldest daughter taken down from the proverbial shelf, settled and happy.

She heaved a sigh.

Byron, undoubtedly sensing his mistress's deflated mood, chomped at his bit and shook his head, apparently asking a silent question.

What are we waiting for?

Louisa shrugged off her apathy and trained her gaze on the distant horizon, where a solitary majestic oak stood beside a derelict medieval watchtower. Two ancient signposts pointed the way to Louisa's home and birthplace.

Highfield Hall.

She tugged Byron to a halt and leaned forward. "Ready for some more, my beauty?" she murmured, feeling the horse tremble beneath her. "Then let's go."

The beast needed no further encouragement, and Louisa parted with another whoop of delight as he surged forward. A mile or so later, chest heaving anew, she reined in beneath the oak and dismounted. She gazed up at the gnarled branches that were already tipped with buds. By the time she returned from London, they would all be in full leaf.

Clouds, skittering across the sky, created an illusion that the tree was toppling over. Giddy, Louisa stepped back, clutching at the stirrup leather to steady herself. On the opposite side of the track stood the medieval watchtower, its tumbledown roof partially open to the elements. As a child, Louisa had hidden her eyes rather than look at the ruin, convinced something evil lurked behind its bricked-up doorway. The childhood fear had long since surrendered to reason. Yet, even now, the blackness on the other side of the tower's narrow windows sent a prickle across the back of her neck.

She grabbed Byron's reins and set off down the lane toward Highfield. "A cup of tea," she murmured, conjuring up pleasant images in her mind. "And a slice of Mrs. Padley's gingerbread."

A short while later, she passed beneath Highfield's old gatehouse and crossed the courtyard to the stables, blinking as she entered the darker interior. The sound of men's voices drifted out of the shadows, one of them easily recognizable.

"Greetings, Papa, we're back!" She inhaled the agreeable smell of horses and hay. "It's simply glorious out there today. Or it was. It looks like the weather is changing for the worse. Is Willis with you? Byron is ready for a rub down. I'll settle for some tea."

The voices fell silent, followed by the sound of her father clearing his throat.

"Papa?" She tethered Byron by his stall and wandered farther into the stable.

"I'm here, Louisa," came the response. A moment later, he stepped out of a nearby stall, his eyes widening a little as he regarded her.

Louisa grinned and attempted to brush an errant curl from her brow. The curl ignored the attempt and returned to its previous location. "There you are! I...oh!" Her voice faltered as a man appeared at her father's side. A stranger, impressively tall and impeccably dressed, his facial features partially obscured by shadow. Louisa's stomach gave a queer little lurch, as if prodded from within. "I beg your pardon, Papa. I didn't realize you had a guest. I just assumed you were with Willis."

Captain Aldous Northcott, Louisa's father, cleared his throat again. "This is Mr. Harlow, Louisa. He'll be our guest at Highfield for the night. Mr. Harlow, allow me to introduce my eldest daughter, Miss Louisa Northcott."

The man inclined his head. "A pleasure to make your acquaintance, Miss Northcott."

His voice, rich and deep, had an educated timbre, edged by

the provocative hint of a regional accent. *Scottish?* Louisa's inherent curiosity flared. Who was he? Why was he here? She willed him to move into the light, so she might see him more clearly.

"Likewise, Mr. Harlow." She bobbed a slight curtsy, a movement that loosened several other loose curls that had been tucked haphazardly behind her ears. As they tumbled around her face, she was reminded of her less-than-stellar appearance. With a gasp of horror, she glanced down at the spattered hem of her skirts. "Oh, heavens, I'm such a disgrace!" She scraped the curls from her face again and made a futile effort to return them to her ruined chignon. "I gave Byron a good run across the moor and lost it somewhere. My hat, that is." The rebellious curls sprang free once more. "Then my hair came loose, so—"

"Please, Miss Northcott, think nothing of it." The mysterious Mr. Harlow stepped into a patch of pale sunlight that had sneaked through one of the windows. Light and shadow now played across the man's finely hewn features; a strong, clean-shaven jaw, neat sideburns, defined cheek bones, and eyes that slanted upwards ever so slightly. Dark brows and a firm mouth gave the impression of austerity, while his equally dark hair, falling in relaxed curls to just below his ears, hinted at the opposite. He was, in a word, utterly striking, and what remained of Louisa's wits scattered like a flock of startled birds. Then he arched one of those brows, a movement that made Louisa realize she was staring at him.

Blatantly.

Botheration!

"Go and tidy yourself, my dear," her father said. "Willis will be back in a few minutes. I'll make sure he sees to Byron."

She regarded her sire who, to her further embarrassment, wore a decidedly amused expression. "Um, yes, Papa, of course." She managed a smile and bobbed another curtsey. "It was nice meeting you, Mr. Harlow. Please excuse me."

And with that, she fled.

COULD IT HAVE been any worse?

"Hardly," Louisa announced, to her much-improved reflection.

Her earlier bedraggled appearance in the mirror had been more disastrous than she'd expected. So bad, in fact, that she'd actually laughed out loud at the sight of it. Had the muddy smear across her nose been there before she'd touched her face in the stable, or after? Before, she suspected. In any case, she looked like she'd been frolicking in a bog. And as for her silly rambling…

Oh, well.

Lamenting the hapless occasion served little purpose. The moment had come and gone, the first impression had been made, and Mr. Harlow—the only man to have *ever* made Louisa's heart beat faster—had seen her at her absolute worst.

Fate was cruel.

Then again, she mused optimistically, one could only improve on the *absolute worst*. Which is precisely what Dawkins, her mother's long-serving lady's maid, had set about doing.

First, the mud-spattered skirts had been discarded and the same spatter expunged from Louisa's flesh. Her abundance of rich, brown hair had been brushed till it shone and braided into a soft coil at the nape of her neck, except, of course, for the two perfectly styled ringlets that framed her face. Her dress of lavender taffeta complimented her complexion, although Dawkins had tut-tutted her disapproval of the natural blush on Louisa's cheeks and promptly tamed it with a touch of powder. A pair of amethyst earrings and matching pendant added a delicate finishing touch. Louisa, seated at her dressing table, now looked 'quite presentable' as Grandmama Hutton would say.

"Thank you, Dawkins," she said. "You've worked wonders."

"My pleasure, Miss Louisa," the woman replied, smiling at their reflections in the mirror. "I have to say, you're the absolute image of your mother at the same age. It's like looking back in time."

The maid left and Louisa rose to her feet, turning this way and that as she regarded her reflection. It occurred to her that she'd never been quite so critical about her appearance and wondered why it even mattered so much. The answer was immediate. It mattered, of course, because she wanted to impress her father's guest, although her extraordinary desire to do so had her flummoxed. She knew nothing of the fellow after all, not even his Christian name. He was *Mr.* Harlow, so no title. Maybe he was related to a peer. And maybe he was affianced or married.

The latter thought caused an unfamiliar flutter in Louisa's stomach that felt horribly like dismay. "You're being totally silly," she muttered, smoothing her scowl away as she dabbed a drop of rosewater behind each ear. "The man might turn out to be a total bore. Or an arrogant—"

She jumped as a drumroll of frantic knocks landed on her door. The door opened before she'd even had a chance to answer, and two identical female faces peered around it. "May we come in?" they chimed, in unison. A redundant request, since both girls stumbled into the room a moment later and closed the door behind them.

"No." Louisa scowled at her twin sisters. "It's polite to wait for a response."

"Too late," Clara said, grinning. "Gracious, Lou! You look absolutely splendid. Certain to make an impression."

"On whom?" Louisa asked, feigning ignorance.

"Are you telling me you haven't seen him yet?" Evie glanced at the door as if expecting someone to be listening behind it. "Our mysterious guest who happens to be staying overnight."

"He's a bit standoffish," Clara said, "but visually quite delicious."

Louisa regarded her younger siblings. With their own chestnut curls, wide brown eyes, and dainty appearance, the twins looked younger than their sixteen years. Their physical daintiness, however, utterly belied their tenacious personalities. As was often the case, their gowns were identically styled, but of differing colors. Today, Clara wore cerulean blue and Evie a pale green. "You both look rather splendid as well," Louisa replied. "And if you mean Mr. Harlow, then yes, I met him briefly when I returned from my ride. He was in the stables with Papa. And he didn't seem standoffish to me."

"Actually, that would be Mr. *Maxwell* Harlow of Harlow Industries, with business interests in Glasgow, South Shields, and Sheffield." Evie curtseyed and fluttered her eyelids. "Delighted to make your acquaintance, sir. Please excuse me while I sink gracefully into an adoring faint."

Maxwell.

Louisa absorbed the snippet of information and gave her sister a smile. "What sort of business is he in?" she asked, endeavoring to keep her tone casual.

"According to Julian, it has something to do with cutlery and trains. Quite an odd combination. He's well-educated too, apparently. Studied at Edinburgh University." Clara stepped over to the mirror, twirling around as she regarded her reflection. "In any case, though it appears he's rather well-shod, he is most decidedly—"

"Middle-class," Evie concluded, wrinkling her nose. "An industrialist."

"Half-Scottish," Clara continued. "Or half-English, whichever way you choose to look at it. He has a *wee* bit of a Scottish accent, though, which is rather charming."

"Yes, I noticed," Louisa said, trying to decide how she felt about the man's societal status. She'd always told herself such things were of no consequence. "I wonder why he's here. Did Julian say?"

"Apparently, he has purchased one of Papa's mares," Clara replied. "The dapple gray, I believe."

"He came to Highfield just to buy a horse?" Louisa frowned. Her father's interest in horse-breeding was more of a hobby than a serious venture. "Seems a little out of the way."

"I'm certain there's more to it than that." Evie tapped a finger against her lip, cocked her head, and gave Louisa a thoughtful look. "Maybe he's shopping for an aristocratic bride. You know, to elevate his social-standing? Being wed to the niece of an earl would be a fine feather to tuck into his tradesman's cap."

"Shopping for a bride in the wilds of Yorkshire? Surely not." A touch of warmth arose in Louisa's cheeks, and she silently thanked Dawkins for the powder. "That's even less likely than shopping for a horse."

"I have a suggestion." Clara leaned into the mirror to fix a loose strand of her hair. "How about we—"

"Go downstairs and find out precisely why he's here." Evie finished. "Are you ready, Lou?"

Louisa gave her reflection a final glance and shrugged off a vague sense of nervousness. "Yes," she replied, "I'm ready."

CHAPTER TWO

LOUISA HAD A special fondness for Highfield Hall's main parlor, which had been aptly described by her mother as *regally shabby*. Timeworn Turkish rugs softened mellowed oak floors. Antique cherry-wood furniture gleamed like vintage port. Ornate, gold-framed oil paintings of varying personages hung on creamy damask walls. A couple of leather armchairs and two large, well-stuffed settees provided a comfortable gathering place. The massive Jacobean fireplace anchored the room to its regal past in a majestic fashion, especially during the colder months when the hearth blazed with a welcoming fire.

As it did now.

Clara and Evie sat on one of the settees with Arthur, who, at fifteen, was the youngest of Louisa's siblings. Louisa settled herself on another of the settees between her eldest brother, Julian, and their mother, Grace.

All eyes were fixed upon the master of the household.

Dressed in black, tailored jacket and trousers, maroon waistcoat, and a white shirt and cravat, Aldous Northcott stood by the hearth nursing a glass in his right hand. Louisa felt a familiar swell of pride as she regarded her father, the man she adored above all others. A veteran of the Napoleonic war, and specifically the Battle of Waterloo, he had forever been a hero in her eyes. A tolerant man and a loving parent, he rarely raised his voice in anger, though it was not wise to test him.

His chin lifted slightly as he cleared his throat. "Although you have all met our guest casually, I believe a proper introduction is, nonetheless, merited."

Louisa shifted her attention to said guest, who met her gaze briefly, his mellow expression unchanged. Maxwell Harlow sat at apparent ease in one of the comfortable armchairs, right leg crossed over left, glass of what looked like whisky in one hand. Louisa guessed him to be not much older than Julian. In the latter end of his twenties. Perhaps a bit older. In any case, quite young to be so successful.

Although Clara's earlier observation had some merit, Louisa had decided that the man wasn't standoffish, he was merely serious in nature. If he did possess a frivolous side, he kept it in check. If anything, his quiet restraint only added to the enigma of him and continued to have an unsettling effect on Louisa's heart and stomach.

"As you know, Mr. Harlow, of Harlow Industries, will be staying at Highfield Hall this evening," her father continued. "His reason for being here is that he is looking for a home in this fair county of Yorkshire, and I may be able to provide one for him. Assuming, of course, he finds it suitable for his needs."

Louisa blinked. *A home?*

Arthur voiced the most obvious question. "You intend to take lodging at Highfield Hall, Mr. Harlow?"

"No, Master Northcott, not here," the man replied. "Possibly nearby, however. That's if your father and I can come to an agreement."

Louisa's sharp brain quickly figured out the riddle. "Northcott Manor," she said. "Is that it, Mr. Harlow? You're taking tenancy of Northcott Manor?"

He fixed her with his dark gaze. "Possibly," he repeated with emphasis. "So far, I've only seen the property from the outside, a situation to be remedied tomorrow."

Captain Northcott nodded. "Indeed."

"Oh, I'm sure you'll love it, sir," Louisa said. "It's a fine house, well deserving of an occupant. I was over that way today actually, while out riding, and thought it a shame that no one had lived there for a while."

The beginning of a smile appeared on the man's face. "My first impression of the manor is a positive one, Miss Northcott, but first impressions are just that. I have learned that one should not always judge by them."

"That is true," Louisa replied, wondering if she imagined the pointedness of his remark. "Though I'm sure your subsequent impression will be equally as positive as the first."

"Would it be a temporary tenancy?" Clara asked.

"It would be a year's lease initially," Mr. Harlow replied.

"And would it be just you living there?" Evie chimed in.

"Or do you have a wife?" Clara finished.

Louisa's mother gasped. "That will be *quite* enough from both of you," she said, glaring at the twins. "I do apologize for my daughters' rudeness, Mr. Harlow. They forget themselves."

Louisa exchanged a glance with her father, whose sober expression belied the amused twinkle in his eyes.

"The young ladies are curious, which is to be expected," Mr. Harlow replied, graciously. "In answer to your question, should I agree to lease the manor, it will be for myself and my younger brother Finlay, who assists me with my business affairs. The manor will also allow me to properly entertain business colleagues and shareholders. Once I marry, my wife will join me there as well. Indeed, she is the main reason I am seeking a more permanent home."

"Mr. Harlow recently became engaged to Viscount Dent's daughter, Miss Sybella Chessington," Aldous explained. "The dappled mare is a gift for her."

Louisa's heart didn't exactly plummet into her shoes, but it definitely deflated a little. So much for Evie's theory about Maxwell Harlow searching for an aristocratic bride. It seemed he'd already succeeded in that regard. Though she knew the name, she could not recall ever meeting Miss Sybella Chessington.

"Well, I'm sure the future Mrs. Harlow will love Northcott Manor," she said. "If you decide to take the lease, of course."

"We shall see," the man replied, just as the gong sounded out in the hall.

"It would seem dinner is served." Grace rose to her feet. "I hope you like roast pheasant, Mr. Harlow."

THE ROAST PHEASANT had been quite delicious, as had the entire meal, in fact. Afterwards, the ladies had excused themselves, and the men, with the exception of young Arthur, had retired to Captain Northcott's rather splendid study.

Maxwell, brandy snifter warming in his hand, was now installed in yet another leather armchair. So far, he could not fault the hospitality he'd been shown at Highfield Hall. The family had been nothing but gracious. Nor did their congeniality feel forced or contrived, especially given his reason for being there. It had been made quite clear that being a guest of the Northcott's in no way obligated Maxwell to take tenancy of the manor.

As for his societal status, well, that was another issue entirely.

Money—and Maxwell had plenty—did not an aristocrat make. Bloodline and title were the principal indicators on any noble barometer, with wealth and privilege being the inherent rewards going back generations.

If Maxwell had inherited any traits at all from his late father—who had been a successful wool merchant—they would include a knack for negotiation and a flair for business. Maxwell, however, had not embraced his father's trade. New and exciting prospects had driven him to explore Britain's evolving industrial landscape. Opportunity had a smell, and Maxwell had the nose for it.

"I can understand why you have chosen this area, Mr. Harlow." Julian Northcott's voice drew Maxwell from his musing. "It's well-placed for access to South Shields and Sheffield.

Manchester and Liverpool as well. I'm assuming that is largely what drew you to our little patch of moorland."

Maxwell regarded the eldest son and heir of Highfield Hall, who was only a couple of years younger than himself. A decent fellow, according to Maxwell's investigations, who had been educated at Rugby and Cambridge with no scandal or blemishes on record.

There was another son too, Maxwell knew. Josiah, the second eldest of the siblings. An artist, currently studying at the Royal Academy in London.

Six Northcott offspring in all, then. A nice balance of three boys and three girls. Louisa, the eldest daughter, was about to embark on her second Season, but didn't seem overly excited about it. Maxwell wondered that the lass had not been snatched up already, for she was a bonny wee thing, though apparently a little reckless, judging by what he'd witnessed that morning. He hadn't realized, at the time, that the wild woman charging across the moor on horseback was a Northcott. Only when she'd appeared in the stables, looking rather like she taken a lover's tumble through the heather, did he make the connection. Her embarrassment, due to her disheveled state, had amused him. The other sensation he experienced, which felt rather like intrigue, he decided to ignore. He did, however, have something in his possession that belonged to her, but intended to wait for the right moment to return it.

As for the Northcott's 'little patch', Maxwell knew it amounted to the nearby village of Morthwaite, the manor house in need of a tenant, as well as almost six hundred acres of pasture, moorland, and forest supported by a half-dozen tenant farmers. Not to mention the fine old house in which he now sat.

In fact, he likely knew as much about this branch of the Northcott family tree as anyone, including the family themselves. Learning about those with whom he did business—personal or otherwise—was all part of his process.

He addressed Julian's observations. "Indeed, Mr. Northcott,

the location is ideally situated for most of my business interests. I own a house in Glasgow, but otherwise I rent rooms whenever I travel. However, as I mentioned earlier, it is my engagement to Miss Chessington that has prompted my search for a suitable marital home. Northcott Manor will be the third property I've looked at in as many weeks."

"Then I hope a fourth will not be necessary," Julian responded. "However, with respect, sir, I wonder that you have not considered purchasing land and property and living off the income it brings, since you are surely in a position to do so."

Maxwell smiled. His future father-in-law, Lord Dent, had posed the same question not a fortnight earlier. In that case, a motive had been embedded in the viscount's query, prompted by nothing more than the sour taste of class distinction. With Julian Northcott, the question appeared to be benign. Still, Maxwell couldn't help but respond in a like manner. "Losing my trades-man's cap and becoming a gentleman, you mean? I'm afraid I cannot envisage such a pastoral existence. The world is changing, and I intend to be actively on the forefront of that change."

"I meant no offense, sir," Julian said, without malice. "On the contrary, I commend your ambition. As to being on the forefront of our nation's industrial progress, it seems apparent that you're already there."

Maxwell cleared his throat. "This entire northern area is one of the most important industrial hubs in the world and is all set to witness yet more growth and advancement."

"You're referring to the continued expansion of the railway system, I assume," Aldous said.

"Indeed, Captain." Maxwell swirled the remaining cognac in his glass and drank it down. "Mark my words, travel by rail is the way of the future."

"I don't doubt it." Aldous reached for the decanter. "Will you take a little more, Mr. Harlow?"

The rest of the evening passed with equal affability until, prompted by the sound of rain against the windows and the subsequent thought of a warm bed, Maxwell had taken his leave.

He was not, by nature, a covetous man, and he certainly didn't want for anything. Yet, making his way along the shadowed hallway, its ancient, paneled walls hung with ancestral portraits, he couldn't help but feel a slight tug of envy. Highfield Hall, like many old established houses, seemed to hold time in its grasp, safeguarding it for the ancestors long gone and the descendants yet to come.

"Too much brandy," he muttered, a corner of his mouth lifting at the foolish direction of his thoughts. He started up the exquisitely carved oak staircase, the ancient treads creaking beneath his feet. At the top, he paused a moment to regard the large rose window that graced the upper façade of Highfield Hall. There, at the foot of the circular portal, a large, solitary candle burned steadily, its bright flame reflecting in the glass. The placement of the candle, so close to the floor, appeared to be significant rather than useful. Maxwell wondered at it. On the opposite wall hung the portrait of a young man, his blue-eyed gaze fixed eternally on the window. Next to the portrait, a smaller frame, with a glass front, displayed a silver disc, hanging from a red and blue ribbon. Maxwell moved closer, recognizing it as the Waterloo Medal. Another significant placement, he thought. It felt almost like a shrine.

"We light a candle here every night in memory of my Uncle Julian," a female voice said, startling him. He turned to see Louisa Northcott moving out of the darker depths of the corridor. Garbed in a demure *robe de chambre* of fine, ivory-colored wool, the lass appeared almost ghostlike, her face half-hidden in shadow, a long, dark braid snaking over her left shoulder. She had a book clasped to her breast, he noticed.

"He was my mother's elder brother who died at Waterloo." She gestured to the painting. "That's his portrait. My brother is named for him."

As she'd spoken, she'd moved closer, and most of the darker shadows had fallen away to reveal the alluring vision that now stood before him. Maxwell's pulse quickened. Louisa Northcott was indeed bonny, with her high-cheekbones, large dark eyes, and full, soft lips. Bare feet at that moment, too, he noticed. Ten delightful toes peeking out from beneath her robe. An unbidden urge to discover what other delights lay hidden beneath that robe was acknowledged and then shoved aside. Even if Maxwell had been unattached, the lass was not to be tampered with. She was an innocent, first of all, and also happened to be the daughter of his potential landlord. But none of Maxwell's mental restraint could prevent his physical response.

His focus, however, remained on the topic at hand, and he saw no reason to feign ignorance about it. "I'm aware of your uncle's sad demise, Miss Northcott, though not about this nightly observance. It's a fine tribute to him."

"Yes, it is." She hugged her book tighter. "But the candle also serves as a sign of life, since its light can be seen from the outside. A beacon in the darkness, you see, should anyone find themselves lost on the moor and in need of help."

"Which makes the tribute to your uncle all the more special," he said.

"Indeed, it does." She inclined her head. "Well, if you'll excuse me, Mr. Harlow, I'm off to exchange this book for another."

Curiosity got the better of him. That, and perhaps a vague reluctance to bid the lass goodnight. Besides, he had another reason to delay her departure. "Would you consider it rude if I asked what you're reading?"

"Not at all." She showed him the book, a copy of Ainsworth's *Rookwood*. "It's wonderful. Have you read it?"

"I have not," he replied. "I confess, I find myself with little time for pleasurable reading."

Her eyes widened briefly. "Oh, I see. I was about to ask if you'd care to borrow it, but there's little point if you would never find the time to read it."

"A kind thought, nonetheless." He cleared his throat. "I wonder, Miss Northcott, if you would mind waiting here a moment. I believe I have something in my possession that belongs to you."

The eyes widened again. "You do?"

"Aye. It's all quite appropriate, I assure you." He inclined his head.

"I'll return in a few moments."

LOUISA STEPPED ASIDE as Maxwell Harlow moved past and watched him wander off down the dimly lit corridor. He glanced back as he reached the end and gave another nod before turning onto Highfield's east wing, where his bedroom lay.

Something that belongs to me?

Louisa couldn't begin to imagine what the object might be. Truth be told, she struggled to think clearly at all whenever Maxwell Harlow was nearby.

The wretched man.

At that moment, the candleflame in the window popped and spat, making her jump. "I have to stop this foolish infatuation, Uncle Julian," she whispered, gazing up at her uncle's portrait. "It's really quite silly and nothing will ever come of it."

The candle spat once more and then settled back into a steady burn.

Louisa heaved a sigh and plopped onto a nearby chair to wait. Shortly thereafter, a sound drew her attention back to the corridor, where she saw the shadowed figure of Maxwell Harlow returning, something clasped in his right hand.

She stood, anticipating.

"Though I didn't know who you were at the time, Miss Northcott," he said, "I happened to witness some of your ride across the moor this morning. In particular, the part where you misplaced a certain item." He handed her the hat that had been snatched by the wind. "I took the liberty of finding it with the hope of reuniting it with its owner. It seems to have survived its airborne journey quite well, despite landing in a gorse bush."

Louisa gasped. "My hat! Oh, my goodness, I would never have guessed. How kind of you, Mr. Harlow. I believed it gone forever." His words conjured up another memory from her morning's ride. "Actually, now you mention it, I think I saw you also. You and your horse, off in the distance. I suppose I should have stopped when my hat went flying, but Byron and I were having far too much fun."

"Aye, so it appeared." The man's eyes narrowed a little. "Byron? Would that be after the notorious lord himself?"

"Yes, it would. I confess to being fascinated by the fellow. I've read everything he's written."

"Hmm." Maxwell winced. "A character of note, certainly, though I daresay some of his choices were questionable."

Louisa shrugged. "Which makes him all the more interesting, I think. Then again, much of—"

A creak on the stair drew her attention.

"What's this?" Julian appeared at the top of the stairs, arching a single brow as he glanced from Maxwell to Louisa. "Am I interrupting something?"

"Not at all. We were just talking." Louisa, resenting the accusatory gist of her brother's remark, pinned him with a hard stare. "I was telling Mr. Harlow of the reason behind Uncle Julian's candle."

'It's a fine observance," Maxwell said.

"Yes, it is." Julian ran a quick gaze over Louisa's bedroom-attired form. "What the devil are you doing with that hat, Lou? You can't be going anywhere, surely. Not dressed like that."

"Of course not." She maintained her stare, and added a brief, forced smile. "I lost it on the moor this morning and Mr. Harlow found it. He returned it to me just now."

"Really? How extraordinary." Julian's brow lifted again as he regarded Maxwell. "Forgive me, but how on earth could you have known the hat belonged to my sister?"

"I didn't, at first," the man replied, unflinchingly. "I was on my way to Highfield Hall this morning when I noticed a young woman riding across the moor and saw the hat fly off."

"I had Byron at a full gallop when it happened," Louisa said, her eyes still hurling hypothetical daggers at her brother. "Mr. Harlow kindly retrieved it and only later realized it belonged to me."

"Ah, I see." Julian still looked unconvinced. "But why bother retrieving it if you did not know the identity of the person who lost it?"

"I'm sure Mr. Harlow is not obliged to explain his motives to you, Julian," Louisa said, making no effort to hide her irritation.

"Not obliged, no," Maxwell replied, "but if it means putting your mind at rest, good sir, I will happily do so. Given the remoteness of the location, and the fact that the young lady was unescorted, I dared to assume she lived locally, and therefore could be easily located. So, I collected the hat and placed it in my saddle bag, intending to enquire further upon my arrival at Highfield Hall, assuming someone here might know of the lady's identity. The incident completely slipped my mind till Miss Northcott returned from her ride and I saw her in the stables. I realized, then, to whom the hat belonged, but didn't mention it at the time because I felt it might cause her embarrassment with her father being present. Instead, I decided to wait for a more discreet opportunity, which presented itself a few minutes ago. That is all."

"A perfectly fine explanation, Mr. Harlow, thank you." Louisa threw another fierce glance at Julian. "Which I'm certain must now satisfy my brother's curiosity."

"It does, indeed," Julian replied. "I appreciate your frankness, sir."

"Of course." Maxell nodded. "Now, if you'll excuse me, Miss Northcott, Mr. Northcott, I'll bid you both a good night."

Julian returned the nod. "Goodnight to you too, sir."

"Goodnight, Mr. Harlow," Louisa said, managing a smile. "I hope you rest well. The gong will sound when breakfast is ready."

Gritting her teeth, Louisa waited till Maxwell Harlow had disappeared once more before turning on her brother. "What the bloody hell was all that about, Julian?" she demanded. "You embarrassed both him and me with your questions. We were simply having a conversation."

"Mind your language, Louisa, and yes, you were indeed having a conversation." Julian raised his chin and folded his arms. "Just you and Harlow, late at night, in near darkness, and you barefoot in your dressing gown. For God's sake, you should know better. *He* should know better."

She scoffed. "You're being quite ridiculous. We did nothing wrong."

Julian grunted. "It was the *potential* of wrong doing that bothered me. Papa would have been equally disapproving had he happened along. You know he would."

"Potential?" Louisa regarded her brother with undisguised shock. "You're suggesting what, exactly? Don't bother answering. I can guess. And I doubt Papa would harbor such a low opinion of me."

Julian's expression softened. "I'm not really suggesting anything like that, Lou. It's just that you seem quite taken with the fellow and, frankly, that bothers me. Harlow's not for you, you must know that, and I don't want to see you compromised. It would be disastrous."

"I'm not *taken* with him at all," she said, somewhat feebly. "And I think you're judging him unfairly. Being middle-class doesn't mean he lacks propriety. He's been nothing but gentlemanly since he got here."

Julian scratched his head. "Class has nothing to do with it, dear sister. It is simply that Maxwell Harlow is a man, and you're a reasonably pretty girl."

Louisa gasped, her eyes widening. *"Reasonably pretty?"*

His stern expression melted into a brotherly grin, one that indicated an end to their tiff. "You're not beyond catching a fellow's eye, Lou," he said. "Just make sure the eye belongs to an appropriate fellow, that's all. Right, I'm off to bed. Night-night."

Louisa couldn't help but return his smile. "You're so bloody infuriating at times, Jules," she said. "Will you be going to the manor with Papa and Mr. Harlow tomorrow?"

"You're so bloody impetuous at times, Lou," he replied. "And yes, I believe I will. Will you?"

She laughed and nodded. "Yes, I believe I will."

"See you at breakfast, then. Now, go and wash your mouth out with soap and get to bed." He tugged on her braid and headed off toward his bedroom. Louisa remained where she was for a moment, debating whether or not to go downstairs to the library and return the book. It could wait, she decided, and wandered back to her bedroom, where she placed the hat atop her dresser.

The itinerant headpiece had now acquired a certain esteem. Since it had, against the odds, found its way back to her, and despite its worn edges and slightly ruffled feathers, Louisa resolved to keep it. If nothing else, it would serve as a souvenir of a breathtaking day on the moor.

If nothing else.

CHAPTER THREE

O NE MIGHT, MAXWELL thought, as he toured Northcott Manor the next morning, be forgiven for imagining the place sheltered a resident ghost or two. With its shuttered windows, dark corridors, rooms filled with mysterious objects hidden beneath white dustcovers, the silent house had a haunted feel.

But Maxwell didn't believe in ghosts. He also knew the shutters could easily be flung open, sunlight would quickly chase the darkness from the corridors, and the dustcovers could be removed to expose the mysteries beneath. The silence, too, could easily be exorcised. That's if he took tenancy of the place, and so far, he liked what he'd seen.

The three-story house was a decent size without being rambling. In addition to a handsome main suite, it boasted seven additional bedrooms, a dining room with access to an outside terrace, two large parlors, a smaller, private sitting-room, a study, a library, and a games room. The servants' rooms occupied much of the third floor, while below-stairs the various utility rooms, including the kitchen, had been kept in spotless condition.

The outbuildings included a stable, a carriage house, a barn, and a row of three small cottages.

"The gardens are a little bare right now," Aldous said, as he, Julian, and Maxwell left the stable yard and walked around to the front of the house. "But they'll soon be filling in. There's a resident gardener who looks after them, with help from a couple of villagers. He lives in one of the little cottages."

"Reuben Thornthwaite," Julian added. "A grand old chap. Been here for years."

Maxwell looked across the gardens, admiring the symmetry of lawns and ornamental hedges that encircled a central pond and fountain. Then he squinted up at the manor's impressive Georgian façade. There was no denying that the house met all his requirements, but what of Sybella? So far, she'd shown little enthusiasm for living anywhere north of Cambridge, though she admitted to once visiting a cousin in Cumberland and had apparently found it 'quite pleasant'.

Still, as his wife, she'd have little choice but to live wherever he decided. And, since the majority of his business interests lay in the northern parts of the country, including Scotland, their marital home would absolutely be somewhere north of Cambridge. Well north.

"Do you think the future Mrs. Harlow would approve?" Aldous asked, as if he'd just read Maxwell's thoughts.

"Of the house? Aye, Captain, I'm sure she would," Maxwell replied. "It's the location that is something of a stumbling block for her. But it's hard to imagine anyone not liking the place. It's splendid."

"It is, indeed." Aldous gave a solemn smile. "The house holds lots of fond memories for me, and I don't like to see it standing empty. It needs someone to bring it back to life. And you must agree that the lease price is more than fair."

"More than fair," Maxwell repeated, as the pungent smell of burning vegetation wafted through the air. Seeking the source, he turned to see Louisa Northcott chatting to a fellow by a walled corner of the garden, where a small bonfire dispatched a thin spiral of smoke skyward. "The resident gardener, I presume?"

"Yes," Aldous replied. "My daughter has a fondness for him. He's quite the storyteller, apparently."

At that precise moment, any remaining doubts about leasing

Northcott Manor drifted away, much like the spiraling smoke. While not prone to fanciful notions, Maxwell nevertheless felt, for want of a better word, a sudden sense of *rightness* about the place. He put the feeling down to his well-honed business instinct. This was, after all, a business transaction.

"I've seen enough, Captain," he said, turning to look Aldous in the face. "I'll take a twelve-month lease beginning in April. As we've discussed, and as part of the agreement, I shall maintain the manor and cover all expenses for the duration, including the wages of those staff already here. Any additional staff will be interviewed and employed at my discretion, though you will be kept notified of any new hirings."

Smiling broadly, Aldous held out a hand. "Excellent, Mr. Harlow. I'm truly happy to hear it."

"As am I," Julian added, with genuine ardor. "Excellent, indeed."

Maxwell shook Aldous's hand for a prolonged moment, appreciating the solidity of the man's grip, something he recognized as a measure of sincerity. "I trust you'll send me the necessary documentation."

"I'll have my solicitor prepare the papers within the week," Aldous said. "To be sent to your Sheffield office, I presume?"

Maxwell nodded. "Aye, thank you. I look forward to having you as my landlord, Captain."

"Business agreements aside, Mr. Harlow," Aldous said, "I hope you and your future wife will come to look upon the Northcott family as friends and neighbors."

Louisa witnessed the handshake that affirmed Northcott Manor had acquired a new tenant. Reuben noticed it too.

"Getting a new master, it seems." The gardener piled more damp debris on the fire, invigorating the plume of smoke.

"Captain'll be happy, I reckon."

"Yes, I'm sure he will," Louisa replied, her heart beating just a little bit faster than it had a minute ago. Maxwell Harlow's decision was not, however, a great surprise. She'd had an inkling he'd take the lease, judging by his demeanor as his inspection of the manor progressed. "I'm sure you'll like Mr. Harlow, Reuben. He's a nice gentleman."

"I get along with most folk, Mistress, be they pleasant or otherwise." He leaned on the handle of his garden rake and gave her a wink. "But I only care to spend time with the pleasant ones."

Louisa laughed. "A good philosophy."

"Louisa," her father called. "We're leaving."

"All right, Papa," she replied and turned her attention back to Northcott's ancient gardener. "I'm leaving for London next week, Reuben, so I'll say goodbye for now. I'll see you in three months, or thereabouts."

"Don't rush into it, Miss," came the reply. "Be sure he's deserving of you."

She blinked "Who?"

"Whoever you decide to wed." The column of smoke faltered as he added fresh fodder to the fire. He gave her another wink. "Let him chase you till you catch him."

After the carriage ride back to Highfield, Maxwell Harlow bid farewell and left a little before noon, riding off on his big, black horse with the dapple-gray mare in tow. According to Louisa's father, by the time everyone returned from the Season, the new tenant of Northcott Manor would be in residence. And, since his marriage to Miss Chessington was due to take place at the end of April, the lady would undoubtedly be living there also.

After lunch, which she barely picked at, Louisa wandered into the library, grabbed a book, and curled up on one of the settees. She sought a distraction, something to steer her thoughts away from a man whose departure that morning had left her feeling irritatingly bereft.

Several hours later, if anyone had asked what her book was about, she would not have been able to answer with any great accuracy. She had merely turned the pages while her thoughts flitted about like bothersome flies.

If anything, meeting Maxwell Harlow, and saying farewell to him, had strengthened her resolve to find herself a husband before the end of the Season. It seemed unlikely she'd find someone who affected her quite the way Maxwell had. At least, not initially. But surely a slow blossoming of mutual attraction was better than this chaotic jumble of emotions that currently weighed upon her.

Dinner that evening had been something of a celebratory event, her father's delight at having secured a tenancy for the manor quite evident. His mood had been infectious, and by the time Louisa climbed the stairs with her mother to light Uncle Julian's candle, her melancholy had lifted somewhat.

She watched her mother light the wick and tried not to think about the previous night's conversation, in that exact same spot, with Maxwell Harlow.

"You've been very quiet today, my darling," her mother said. "Is everything all right?"

"Everything is fine, Mama," Louisa replied, smiling. "I'm just a bit tired, that's all."

"Are you nervous about the Season?"

"Not nervous, exactly." Louisa shrugged. "Well, maybe a little. You know I'm not terribly enthralled by all the parties and soirees. I find it all rather overwhelming."

"Yes, I do know, and I'm afraid you might have inherited that from me." She glanced about. "As it happens, I didn't have to endure it, since I met your father beneath this very roof."

"You were fortunate, Mama."

"I *am* fortunate, and I make sure to tell myself that every day."

"Today was definitely a good day," Louisa said. "Especially for Papa."

"Yes, I'm so happy for him. He's thrilled about the lease. It's a weight off his mind." She heaved a sigh and regarded the flickering candle. "It's a bit of a sad day on the calendar, though."

Louisa frowned. "Why?"

"Because it's the twentieth day of February."

Louisa gasped as the significance of the date dawned on her. "Oh, Mama, please forgive me. It completely slipped my mind."

"No need to apologize, dearest," she said. "I don't expect you or anyone else to remember. The date is only relevant to me, after all. Actually, it's been nice to have something positive to think about on what is usually a mournful day."

Louisa glanced up at her uncle's portrait and did a quick calculation. "He's been gone thirty years."

"Yes. Since this same day in 1815, except it was a Monday." Grace also regarded the portrait, her expression pensive. "It was snowing quite hard that day. Papa asked him to delay his departure, but he refused. He gave us both a kiss, got on his horse, and off he went, pausing at the gatehouse to give us a final wave. That final image of him has forever stayed clear in my mind. I never saw my father cry till the day he finally realized his only son-and-heir would not be coming home. I think a part of him died that day too, because he was never quite the same. He had a few gray hairs when Julian left. Several months later, his hair had turned completely white. The mind is a torturous thing when unenlightened. There's a gap where the truth should be, filled by terrible imaginings. There is no tomb to visit, no stone marking my brother's grave, but lighting the candle keeps the memory of him very much alive. I wonder about him every day, Louisa. Every single day."

Louisa nodded. She, and everyone else in the family had heard Uncle Julian's story many times, but no one ever complained about the repetition. They respected Grace's need to share it over and over. The tragedy, after all, was a part of their family history. Lighting a candle each night was not enough. The memory of how it came to be also needed to be kept alive.

A short while later, Louisa lay in her bed gazing up at the ceiling, the solitary candle on her bedside table creating a soft circle of light overhead. She felt calmer, as if the fresh outpouring of her mother's anguish had soothed her own unsettled emotions. Or maybe it had simply put things into perspective, allowing her to step back and take a breath. Twenty-four hours. It seemed longer.

But that's all it had been since a stranger on the moor had awakened something in Louisa that she'd never previously felt, that being a sense of attraction toward a man. And, dare she say, desire. Maxwell Harlow had an allure in the way he spoke, the way he moved, the way he thought. Certainly, he was somewhat solemn by nature. Staid, almost. Quite unlike herself. But Louisa had the impression there was more to the man than met the eye. There had to be, given his success. Perhaps he was merely guarded, allowing people to see only what he wanted them to see. That he was not of her world, but dared to enter it, only added to the intrigue.

And he was handsome. Dangerously so.

The twins still thought Mr. Harlow standoffish and absolutely middle-class. Julian, she suspected, hadn't quite made up his mind. Her parents genuinely liked him. More than that, her father trusted him, which said much. Arthur, as good-natured as they came, tended to echo the general sentiment, happy that the manor had been leased.

But, all other considerations aside, the sad reality remained. Louisa had found herself attracted to a man who would soon be married to someone else. And even if he wasn't, Maxwell Harlow was not for her, as Julian had taken pains to point out. Nor would he ever be for her. That was the cruel part; to feel something so profoundly, yet be denied the opportunity to express it, verbally or otherwise. She glanced at the hat, which still sat on her dresser. Maybe she would discard it, after all.

Heaving a sigh, she leaned over, and blew out her candle.

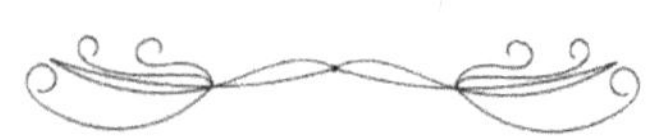

CHAPTER FOUR

London, March 1845

T HE DANCE ENDED after what seemed like an eternity. Louisa's resulting smile was genuine but stemmed from relief rather than courtesy.

"Thank you, my lord," she said, inclining her head.

"My pleasure, dear lady." Lord Milnthorpe took her hand and steered her from the dance floor. "Are you in need of refreshment, by chance? Might I fetch you something to drink?"

"Again, thank you, but I believe my brother has a drink waiting for me." Louisa tugged her gloved hand free of his and gestured to where Julian stood with their mother. She then scooted away before the man could answer. Something about him gave her goose bumps. The unpleasant kind.

"You scurried off the dance floor rather quickly, my dear," her mother said, as Louisa arrived. "Do you not like Lord Milnthorpe? He seems charming enough."

Julian snorted. "The man is about as interesting as nasal hair," he said. "I'm surprised Lou didn't fall asleep halfway through the dance."

"Nasal hair?" Louisa giggled. "Can't say I paid much attention to his nostrils, but yes, the man's personality is somewhat…"

"Absent," Julian finished, and held out a glass. "Lemonade, Lou?"

"Keep your voices down." Grace fanned herself and glanced about. "You're both adults, for heaven's sake. I shouldn't have to tell you to behave yourselves."

At that precise moment, the level of conversation in the room wavered slightly, like a ripple travelling through the crowd. A number of heads turning toward the doorway indicated that something—or someone—had caused the effect.

"What's going on?" Louisa asked, craning her neck and standing on tiptoes. "Has someone famous arrived?"

"Not precisely," Julian said, wryly, as he peered over the many heads. "Just our new tenant with his intended bride."

Louisa's heart did a flip. *Mr. Harlow is here?*

Her mother obviously had the same thought and voiced it. "Mr. Harlow is here?"

"Unless my eyes deceive me, yes." Julian replied, "and with Miss Sybella Chessington on his arm."

Louisa's stomach also did a flip.

"Goodness." Grace looked suitably surprised. "I had no idea he was even in London. I don't recall him mentioning he'd be here at this time. Then again, they're likely preparing for their wedding."

The hum of conversation picked up again and Julian snorted. "They're an object of curiosity, it seems. The daughter of a viscount engaged to a man who manufactures cutlery."

"I think he does a bit more than that, Julian," Louisa said.

"Yes, well, either way, I'm not sure whether to feel sorry for the fellow or commend him on his courage for daring to show up here. I'm surprised he was even invited. Lord and Lady Richmond are as pompous as they come."

"Lady Richmond is a cousin of Viscount Dent's," Grace said, "which is undoubtedly why Miss Chessington was invited, and they could hardly invite her and not her fiancé."

"By her fiancé, do you mean the proletarian who is probably wealthier than half the people at this party?" Julian remarked. "I'm sure most people here know why he's engaged to Miss Chessington. She has been bought and paid for."

"Julian, please," Grace said, glancing about, "keep your voice down."

Louisa gave her brother a withering glance. "Or you could say Miss Chessington has been saved from the shelf by a wealthy industrialist, because the *beau monde* turned their backs on one of their own."

Julian heaved a sigh. "There she goes again, defending the blasted fellow. It's becoming quite tedious."

"That's quite enough, both of you!" Grace echoed Julian's sigh. "You're acting like children tonight."

"We're acting like siblings, Mama, and always will," Julian replied, grinning. "Doesn't matter how old we get."

"Oh, here they are," Grace said. "What a handsome couple they make."

Louisa felt a tug on her heart as Maxwell Harlow escorted his fiancée onto the dance floor. If nobility was measured by physical magnetism, the dratted fellow surely outclassed everyone around him. Hair groomed to casual perfection, he wore his usual dark garb, with the exception of a stark white shirt and cravat, plus an intriguing glimmer of a ruby silk waistcoat beneath his jacket. He had to be aware of the attention he garnered but didn't appear to be discomforted by it. In fact, he didn't look out of place at all. Then again, given his many business dealings, Louisa suspected he'd developed a knack for blending into the environment wherever he went. Especially if it benefitted him to do so.

As for Miss Chessington, Maxwell's future wife...

The woman was too tall and too thin. Her nose was altogether too large. Her breasts? Why, they were hardly there at all. Her hair, a nondescript brown, had been styled in a fashion that left much to be desired. And as for her gown of fine pink muslin, edged in delicate ivory lace...

Louisa reined in her shameful malice and forced her eyes to see the actuality. Miss Chessington was, in fact, quite pretty, with a fine complexion and pleasant features. Statuesque and slender, rather than thin. Though not generous, her breasts were most definitely there. And her hair was actually a rich chestnut and perfectly styled. As for her gown... it was truly lovely. Acceptance tasted a bit sour, but Louisa could not deny, as her mother had already stated, that they made a handsome couple.

Her mother's voice intruded into her thoughts. "And if I'm not mistaken, Louisa, I believe your next dance partner is headed this way," she said. "Such a handsome man and from such a fine family! Enjoy yourself."

True. The youngest son of Baron Southersfield, the Honorable James Barclay, with his admirable physique and a wealth of reddish-blond curls, could well be considered handsome. He greeted Louisa with his usual politeness and escorted her onto the dance floor.

The orchestra stuck up a polka, one of Louisa's favorites, mostly because the liveliness of it hampered conversation. Mr. Barclay danced with his usual practiced ease, his expression kindly and pleasant. Louisa did her best to keep her focus on him, but couldn't help casting surreptitious glances around the room, seeking the face of another. A man who, while handsome in his own right, stood in stark contrast to Mr. Barclay in looks, demeanor, and social status.

The dance ended at last, with Louisa agreeing to a second dance with the gentleman later in the evening. She was not immune to Barclay's attraction to her. Indeed, had the evening not been punctuated by the arrival of a certain industrialist, she might have spent more time giving it serious consideration. As things were, anticipation played on her nerves as she wound her way through the guests, looked for her parents and Julian. She found them at last in the grand foyer, chatting with another couple; Lord and Lady Melrose, who had long been friends of the family.

And Maxwell Harlow was also there, with Miss Chessington.

Louisa assumed a cheery expression as she drew near.

"Louisa!" Her father, in his usual affectionate fashion, acknowledged her with his smile. "You know Lord and Lady Melrose and Mr. Harlow, of course."

Louisa bobbed a slight curtsy. "It's nice to see you again, my lord, my lady. And you too, Mr. Harlow." She regarded him, expecting, and feeling, the usual impact: the slight shortness of breath, the silly butterflies in her stomach.

Do not blush. Do not!

Maxwell inclined his head. "A pleasure to see you again, Miss Northcott. Allow me to introduce my fiancée, Miss Chessington."

Louisa summoned up her best smile. "Pleased to make your acquaintance, Miss Chessington."

Arching a single brow, Sybella Chessington tucked a hand into the crook of Maxwell's arm and gave Louisa an appraising look. "Likewise, Miss Northcott," she said. "What a darling dress. I must have the name of your *modèliste*."

Louisa glanced down at her gown. "Isn't it pretty? Her name is Francesca Corvinelli, and she has a charming shop in Knaresborough. I'll be happy to introduce you to her. And, please, you must call me Louisa. We're to be neighbors after all, and friends too, I hope."

The mild expression on Miss Chessington's face faltered. "Louisa," she repeated, and gave Maxwell a quick sideways glance. "Neighbors, yes, of course."

"I'm sure you'll come to love it in Yorkshire, Miss Chessington," Grace said. "It's a beautiful part of the country."

"But so terribly remote," Miss Chessington replied, "and such a long way from London."

There followed a moment of silence that threatened to stretch into awkwardness, made worse by the orchestra finishing its latest offering.

"Well, I believe we've been standing around talking for long enough," Julian said. "Would you care to dance, Miss Chessington? Assuming your fiancé has no objection, of course."

"I would be delighted," the lady replied, "and I'm sure he doesn't."

"No objection at all." Maxwell regarded Louisa. "Miss Northcott, unless you are otherwise promised, perhaps you would also do me the honor?"

"With pleasure," she replied, her traitorous cheeks rouging even as she spoke. Avoiding another glance at Miss Chessington, she placed her gloved fingers lightly into Maxwell's grasp as he accompanied her to the dance floor.

The orchestra struck up a waltz, and Louisa allowed herself to be taken into her partner's formal embrace. His right arm came gently around her, wrist set above the narrow of her waist, hand on her shoulder blade. Louisa placed her left arm atop his right, her hand resting lightly on his shoulder.

Their free hands joined, fingers folding around fingers. Maxwell's gaze, intense and unreadable, locked briefly with hers before looking past her, seeking his direction as the dance began. Louisa arched her spine a little and breathed in his intoxicating scent; hints of bergamot and mint and another that reminded her of warm summer nights. Then, with confidence and precision, Maxwell steered her smoothly around the floor. At once, the ballroom became a magical whirl of sparkles and light, and Louisa's spirit took flight.

If a person's heart was only allowed a predetermined number of beats, she mused, her lifetime supply was currently ebbing away with startling speed. But it was worth it to be given a chance to dance with this man. She wanted to laugh and cry at the same time. She had dreamed of this, never daring to believe the dream would come true. A feeling emanated from within. A joyful sensation that defied any real definition. Utter happiness, unique and sadly fleeting, for it was destined to be short-lived. While it lasted, however, she determined to revel in it.

"Are you enjoying the Season, Miss Northcott?"

An uninspired question borne from propriety. Louisa opened her mouth to respond as expected. *Yes, very much, Mr. Harlow. Thank you.*

She changed her mind and spoke the truth.

"Not particularly, no," she said, without looking at him. "Although there have been some enjoyable moments."

His fingers, wrapped around hers, tightened the tiniest bit. "I hope this is one of them."

"Yes, indeed," she replied, keeping her gaze on the shoulder-seam of his jacket, lest he noticed the sudden, foolish shimmer in her eyes. "You dance divinely, sir."

"As do you, Miss Northcott." His warm breath brushed across her forehead. "May I ask what has spoiled your enjoyment?"

"Nothing specific. Unlike Miss Chessington, I've never been terribly keen on the city. I'm afraid I find it somewhat… stifling."

He glanced at her. "It is not for everyone, certainly."

"It was a surprise, I must say, seeing you here tonight," she said.

"And not only to you, it seems," he replied, wryly, "judging by the response to our arrival."

"Yes, I noticed." She couldn't help but ask the question. "Did it bother you?"

"Only because it bothered my fiancée." His chest rose and fell. "I find it odd, frankly, that people who hold themselves in such high esteem can be so inconsiderate to one of their own."

"Not all of us are badly behaved, Mr. Harlow."

An easy smile appeared. "No, not all," he said. "In any case, it's something the lass will have to get used to."

Louisa smiled also. "I doubt it, sir, for we are as fickle as we are inconsiderate. It will soon become passé, and people will lose interest. Once Miss Chessington has settled into the manor, I'll be happy to introduce her to all the region has to offer, including Francesca's wonderful shop in Knaresborough. Shopping, I find, is one of the best tonics for *ennui*."

The smile almost appeared again. "That is very kind of you, Miss Northcott."

The music ended, and Maxwell Harlow released Louisa back into the reality of her life. She curtseyed in response to his bow, her fingers still bearing the warmth of his, even as her magical sense of joy had already cooled. The moment had come and gone. She doubted there would be another.

"It has been a pleasure, Miss Northcott," he said, escorting her from the dance floor.

"For me also," she replied, with more honesty than he would ever know. "Thank you, Mr. Harlow."

Almost immediately, Sybella Chessington swooped in like a bird of prey and clung onto Maxell's right arm. "I'm thirsty, Maxwell," she said, and dragged him away.

"She's jealous." Julian fell into step beside Louisa. "Couldn't keep her eyes off the both of you the entire dance."

Louisa huffed. "Don't be ridiculous."

"I'm not, and I think you know it." He gave her a sideways glance. "Given that you're looking so bloody pleased with yourself."

"I have no idea what you're talking about." She looped her arm through his. "Did Miss Chessington say anything?"

"About what?"

She shrugged. "About moving into the manor. I don't think she's too keen on the idea."

"No, she isn't," Julian replied.

"She told you that?"

"Alluded to it. She said, given a choice, she'd prefer to stay at this end of the country. I get the impression, however, that Harlow's not prepared to give her a choice. And quite right too, given his business interests."

Louisa pondered. "But if she's unhappy, it won't be pleasant for either of them."

"That's for them to sort out." Julian signaled to a footman who was passing by with a tray of drinks. "Are you thirsty, Lou?"

A short while later, thirst quenched, Louisa took to the dance floor twice more, with two different gentlemen who, though pleasant, left her decidedly unimpressed.

Then Mr. Barclay reappeared. The dance, this time, was a quadrille, another not ideally suited to discourse. Instead, Louisa surreptitiously studied the man who, of all those she'd met so far, impressed her the most. With the exception of one other, of course.

James Barclay really was quite charming. He stood as tall as Maxwell and danced equally as well. His blue eyes had a gentleness to them, and his mouth, when he wasn't speaking, always seemed to be on the verge of a smile.

He was, she conceded, just about perfect. Yet, for whatever reason, her heart chose to ignore him. While in his presence, it simply carried on with its usual rhythm, stoked merely by physical activity rather than by an intangible force. Certainly, the gentleman was better for her stomach, which, like her heart, remained noticeably quiet. Not a flutter to be felt.

Maybe their acquaintance needed cultivating. A chance to develop and strengthen over time. Should Mr. Barclay express a wish to call on her, Louisa would, she decided, allow him the opportunity to do so. Certainly, he gave the impression of being interested, for when the dance was over, he led her from the dance floor, thanking her with a delicate kiss on the back of her hand.

"I do believe you have found a potential suitor in Mr. Barclay, Louisa," her mother said, a short while later. "I wouldn't be surprised if he calls on you in the next day or two. Do you like him?"

"I do, Mama," she replied, sounding more convincing than she felt. "He's very nice."

Her mother heaved a distinctly relieved sigh. "Oh, I'm so glad to hear it. I've already made some discreet enquiries. Apparently, he's just completed his apprenticeship as a solicitor and is going into partnership with another gentlemen in Brighton this summer. Brighton! Can you imagine it, Louisa? The sea air will be wonderful."

A different kind of flutter arose in Louisa's stomach. "He hasn't proposed yet, Mama."

Her mother waved a hand. "I suspect it's just a matter of time, my darling. Oh, I had a feeling about this Season. Something told me it was going to be a successful one. Your father will be delighted as well. Do you know where he is?"

"No, Mama. I haven't seen him for a while."

Grace cocked her head. "Are you certain about Mr. Barclay, Louisa? If not, you must say so before anything else occurs. It wouldn't do to lead him on."

From the corner of her eye, Louisa noticed Maxwell Harlow and Miss Chessington nearby. They were talking to another couple who were vaguely familiar, although their name and title, if the latter applied, eluded her. At that moment, Maxwell said something, at the same time placing his hand in the hollow between Miss Chessington's shoulder blades.

And Louisa knew exactly how it would feel. How the heat of Maxwell Harlow's touch would traverse the thin fabric of the gown and warm the flesh beneath. And how, despite the heat, a shiver would then ensue, travelling up and down the spine in a delicious fashion.

"I'm certain, Mama," Louisa replied, smiling over a mild ache in her chest. "Quite certain."

Louisa opened the door to the ladies' retiring room, flinching as she met a barrage of florally scented air and a babble of female voices. No, this would not do. She'd be expected to smile and exchange niceties and felt like doing neither. All she needed were a few quiet minutes to herself. A little time to clear her head.

She stepped back into the hallway, barely closing the door before it opened again and two young women exited. They gave Louisa a cursory nod, linked arms, and then sauntered off, leaving a swirl of perfume and giggles in their wake.

Louisa glanced about and wandered farther down the hallway to another door, partially hidden in shadow. Her curiosity stirred. A parlor, perhaps? She glanced around, seeing no one, and then turned the handle, opening the door just wide enough to peer inside.

It appeared to be a large sitting-room or parlor, dimly lit, the chill air within tainted by the odor of stale tobacco and a more pleasurable hint of beeswax. Candles burned at each end of a carved black mantel, while another cast a circle of light across an ornate, leather-topped desk that stood near the door. A large damask settee and velvet *chaise-longue* monopolized the area around the unlit hearth. On the far wall, a cascade of plush, velvet curtains tumbled from ceiling to floor, closed against the winter's night. The rest of the room lingered in shadow, with a variety of furnishings forming intriguing silhouettes.

As Louisa looked about, something overhead caught her attention. A fresco of sorts, decorating the ceiling, the details not quite apparent. Intrigued, she opened the door wider and stepped over the threshold, an intrusion that stirred the air and caused the candles to flicker and dance. Standing directly beneath the artwork, she squinted up at it, her gloved hand stifling a subsequent gasp of shock.

Having spent time in Rome and Florence, she was no stranger to what might be termed as risqué artwork, specifically the naked human form, both sculpted and painted.

But she had never seen anything quite like this.

These men and women, depicted in a variety of sizes and shapes, were not only naked, but engaged in various acts of a blatantly carnal nature. The artistry, if one could call it that, was substantial, covering most of the ceiling.

Louisa was not entirely ignorant of the sexual act. Her brother, Josiah, had explained the basic process of conception to her several years before. She'd been horrified at the time and declared as much, shocked that their parents had obviously performed the appalling act six times. Josiah had laughed at that, assured her it really wasn't as terrible as it sounded, and sworn her to absolute secrecy. "If Papa or Mama find out I've told you, I'll be in serious trouble," he said. "And don't tell Julian either."

"Well, Josiah," Louisa muttered, craning her neck as she continued to examine the brazenly erotic display, "this goes way beyond what you described."

Turning her head this way and that, she studied the various depictions, not sure if she felt appalled or fascinated. Both, in truth. So absorbed was she, that a creak and a click from behind made her jump. Just the door, she realized, swinging gently shut. Given the nature of the indelicate display, Louisa wondered that the door had not been locked. She knew she was trespassing, but the room, though chilly, at least offered some peace.

A subdued buzz of conversation and merriment could still be heard, however. At that moment, the orchestra struck up their next tune. Galopede. Louisa's favorite country dance. She wondered if Maxwell was on the dance floor, and with whom. As if it mattered. In less than three weeks, he'd be married to Miss Chessington. Come summer, he and his new wife would be residing in Northcott Manor, the latter somewhat reluctantly, it seemed.

"For God's sake, Louisa," she muttered to herself, "stop it."

To continue like this was folly. Perhaps Mr. Barclay would end up stealing her heart after all, which would then take her mind off Maxwell Harlow.

Perhaps.

Shivering, she turned back toward the door, halting as a woman's voice could be heard in the hallway. Then the door handle turned, and the door opened several inches.

"This will do," the woman said. "It won't take a moment.

"This is obviously a private room, Sybella," came the masculine response. "Can't it wait, whatever it is?"

Maxwell?

Louisa's eyes widened in horror, her mind trying to decide whether to announce her presence, or to hide. To be discovered poking about in a room with a decidedly pornographic ceiling was, she decided, the greater of the two evils. She couldn't bear the thought of trying to explain to Mr. Harlow, and more especially, Sybella Chessington.

Looking about wildly, she sought refuge. The curtains! Holding her breath, she hurried over and quickly slid behind the velvet wall, gratified to discover a window seat. Trembling, she shuffled onto it, her petticoats and skirts all but filling the gap. Then she sat, still as a stone, hardly daring to breathe, her heart pounding like a bass drum in her ears.

Maxwell and Sybella. Of all people!

"What I have to say will not take long," Sybella said, and Louisa heard the door close with the same quiet click. "And it is simply this. I want you to stop telling everyone that we'll be living in Yorkshire after we're married."

"Why?" Maxwell replied. "Since that is where we will be living."

"No, we will *not*," came the petulant response. "At least, *I* will not. And especially if you're going to be absent all the time. You cannot possibly expect me to live alone in some dilapidated manor in a godforsaken part of England, away from my family and friends. It's unreasonable in the extreme."

"The manor is far from dilapidated, Sybella, and you won't be alone," Maxwell replied, his voice calm. "The Northcotts are a short carriage drive away at Highfield Hall and will be company for you when I'm gone. And I won't be absent *all* the time."

"Most of the time, then. Besides, having met her, I don't particularly like that Northcott girl. She seems a little unrefined. She's a bit too familiar with you, as well, I think. It's unseemly."

Louisa's eyes widened. *Unrefined? Unseemly? Why, of all the—*

"Miss Northcott is perhaps a little impetuous, but she's kind-hearted," Maxwell replied. "She's making an attempt to befriend you, Sybella, that's all. The Northcotts are fine people. You'll find them to be very welcoming."

A flush of guilty heat arose in Louisa's cheeks. Fine people did not eavesdrop on private conversations. Worse, the conversation had just become personal to her. She had made the wrong choice, she realized, squeezing her eyes shut. She should have made her presence known from the start and dealt with the consequences.

"Oh, yes, I'm sure we'll find them welcoming, Maxwell.

We're paying them all kinds of money to stay in their god-forsaken manor." Sybella released an audible breath. "It would be interesting to see how welcoming they'd be if that were not the case. Why can't you lease something down here? Or, better yet, do as Papa suggested. Buy some land, build a house for us, and have someone else do all the work. Give your brother more responsibility. I cannot fathom why you insist on working all the time when you can pay people to do it for you. It's ridiculous."

There followed a moment of silence before Maxwell spoke again. "I have always made it very clear, Sybella, that my work is important, and that I need to live close—"

"More important than *me*? More important than our *marriage*?"

Louisa winced at the outburst.

"And that I need to live close to my business interests, all of which lie in the north," Maxwell finished, his tone now a little harder around the edges. "Our marriage is important too, lass, of course, which is why I want you beneath my roof and in my bed."

A gasp followed. "Must you speak so crudely? And please refrain from calling me 'lass'. You know I don't like it. It's… it's common. And I simply will not be happy stuck in God-knows-where all summer. Besides, I've heard it rains there all the time."

"An exaggeration," Maxwell replied. "Look, I don't want you to be unhappy, so perhaps we can compromise. You can spend several weeks in Yorkshire, and then, if you wish, return to London for a while, or to your father's Hampshire estate. That way, we can both—"

A squeak cut into Maxwell's conversation. "Oh, my *heavens*. How utterly *disgusting*."

Louisa heard the sound of a fan snapping open and couldn't help but smile. It seemed Miss Chessington had noticed the indelicate decor.

"It's all over the ceiling," Sybella wailed. "How could anyone even *think* of allowing such depravity beneath their roof. I cannot remain here a moment longer. Not with all those unclothed bodies looking down at us."

"It's just a painting, Sybella. Don't look at it if it offends you. Let me finish what I—"

"It's filthy. An abomination. No, no, no, I cannot risk being discovered in here. What would people think? I swear I feel quite sick." There followed the sound of the door opening. "I'll be in the ladies' retiring room for a few minutes. Wait for me in the hallway, Maxwell. We'll finish this conversation later."

There followed the sound of a masculine sigh, and an unintelligible mumble.

Then silence. Then the sound of the door, clicking quietly closed again.

Had Maxwell gone?

The answer came by way of a throat being cleared, and Louisa, at that same moment, realized how chilled she was. The room had been cold enough, but behind the curtains, with only a thin pane of glass between her and a cold March night, it was close to freezing. Yet she didn't dare move. Not while Maxwell Harlow was still in the room.

Why hasn't he left?

She suppressed a shiver while silently cursing the fact that her nose had decided to run. But she didn't dare sniff either. She bit down to stop her teeth from chattering, willing Maxwell to leave before she caught her death of cold. But he was still there. Then, she heard sounds of movement and closed her eyes in relief. At last, he was leaving.

But then, "The show is over," he said, harshly, making her jump. "You can come out now."

She blinked. He didn't mean her, surely.

Did he?

"I'm talking to whoever is hiding behind those bloody curtains." His voice had hardened even more. "Either show yourself immediately, or I'll come over there and drag you out by the scruff of your damn neck."

Oh, dear lord!

Louisa gave a most unladylike sniff, got to her feet, and inched through the curtains like an actress with stage-fright. "Um, I do beg your pardon, Mr. Harlow." She swallowed and knotted her fingers at her waist. "I… I didn't mean any harm."

Maxwell, standing at the back of the settee, feet braced apart and hands on hips, stared at her for a moment, shock manifesting in his expression. Then he gave a soft, bitter laugh and looked down at the floor. "A woman," he muttered, "and a Northcott, for Christ's sake."

"You needn't worry, sir." Louisa gave her head a shake. "I promise I won't tell anyone about, er, about…"

Maxwell's head snapped up and he threw her a furious look that made her flinch. "About how you knowingly eavesdropped on a private conversation? Why the hell didn't you speak up? Were you enjoying the bloody performance too much?"

Heat arose in Louisa's cheeks, though it did little to stop her shivering. "Certainly not! And, with respect, if you knew I was there, why didn't *you* speak up?"

"Your *respect* is about five minutes late in showing itself," he replied, scowling. "And I didn't know you were there at first, whereas you undoubtedly knew you were no longer alone the moment you heard the door opening. Am I right?"

"Well, yes, that… that is true, but I…" Louisa searched for a defense. "But I didn't know who it was. For all I knew, it might have been some drunken rogue who, upon finding me alone, may have tried to harm me."

Maxwell scoffed. "Says little for the caliber of Lady Richmond's guest list, don't you think? No, Miss Northcott, that is far from being a reasonable explanation. Miss Chessington and I exchanged words as soon as the door closed behind us. You knew who we were within seconds of our arrival."

Without a valid rebuttal, Louisa's only option was to capitulate. Silently cursing her leaking nose, she sniffed as delicately as she could and released a pent-up sigh. "You're quite right, Mr.

Harlow. The truth is, I don't really know why I didn't speak up. Embarrassment, perhaps, at being caught in this, um," she glanced up at the ceiling, "in whatever this room is. All I can do is apologize sincerely and assure you that nothing I heard tonight will go beyond these walls. I swear it. My lips are sealed."

One dark brow lifted slightly as his gaze drifted to her mouth. "Why are you in here, Miss Northcott?"

"Completely by accident, I assure you! I mean, I thought it was just a parlor. I didn't know about…" without looking up, she jabbed a finger toward the ceiling, "about *that* at first."

"That doesn't really answer the question." He moved closer. "Are you hiding? Has someone upset you?"

"No. Yes. Well, not exactly. What gave me away?"

"Pardon?"

"My hiding place," Louisa replied. "I'm just wondering what gave me away."

Maxwell nodded toward to the window. "No self-respecting servant would have drawn those curtains without making sure the pleats were equally spaced on both sides."

Louisa blinked. "I don't understand."

He gave a slight shrug. "I noticed the curtain on the left had been disturbed. It was not hanging true."

She turned to look. "Goodness, you're awfully observant. I'm not sure I would have noticed such a thing." She regarded him once more. "But then, the curtain might have been disturbed accidentally, or perhaps moved by someone who simply wanted to look out of the window. It doesn't necessarily mean someone is—*was*—hiding behind it."

"Quite correct," he replied. "I didn't actually know for certain anyone was there till you emerged. And, given the nature of the room's décor, I never expected it to be a woman."

"But you threatened to physically drag me out! And by the scruff of my neck, no less."

"And the threat worked. If you'd ignored it and stayed quiet, I would have assumed myself to be mistaken and left without any further exchange." His eyes narrowed. "What did you mean by 'not exactly'?"

She regarded him blankly for a moment. "Oh! Nothing really. As I alluded to earlier, I've never been terribly enthusiastic about these society gatherings, and this is my third outing in less than a week. I told Mama I was going to the ladies retiring room for a rest, but I found it to be overly crowded, so I ended up in here instead." If he only knew the truth, she thought, and gave him a wry smile. "I just wanted a little time to myself, that's all."

"I see." He squinted at the ceiling. "Not exactly the most appropriate of sanctuaries, is it? Especially for a young lady. I'm surprised the door wasn't locked."

Louisa dared to approach him. "I thought the same thing once I realized what I was looking at." She breathed in his intoxicating scent, savoring it anew. Of course, he had no idea how much his presence at the ball had influenced her behavior that night and her subsequent desire for solitude. She suppressed a shiver. "I swear I was about to leave, Mr. Harlow. I simply panicked when I heard the door opening."

He frowned. "You look half-frozen, Miss Northcott. I'd offer you my jacket, but it would be more prudent of you to leave this somewhat scandalous room immediately and warm yourself elsewhere."

Louisa nodded. She should, of course, do exactly as propriety dictated; bid Maxwell Harlow a good evening and returned to the ballroom. It was asking for trouble to exploit this bizarre opportunity that fate had handed her. But to be alone with this man was a secret fantasy come true, one she wasn't quite ready to relinquish.

"I am truly sorry for what happened tonight, Mr. Harlow."

"You have already apologized," he said. "Think no more of it."

She shook her head. "I meant I'm sorry for what occurred between you and Miss Chessington."

"Ah." He shrugged. "Unfortunately, my fiancée considers

Northcott Manor to be situated at the farthest reaches of civilization. I must also apologize for her ungracious remark. I'm sure you know the one to which I'm referring."

"Yes, and I thank you for coming to my defense. You're right, though. I am horribly impetuous, and I believe this situation goes to prove that. But your apology is not necessary, sir. Miss Chessington's opinion of me is hardly your fault."

He huffed. "My *fault* is that I get out of bed every morning and go to work. If I were to buy land and then sit back and reap the benefits of it without lifting a finger, I'd be better received by people like y—" He hesitated. "Like most of those here tonight."

"Yourself," Louisa said. "You were going to say 'people like yourself' weren't you? Please do not include me or my family in your judgement."

His amused gaze raked over her. "Are you saying you and your family consider me an equal, Miss Northcott?"

A fraction of time passed. "I—

"Say nothing more," he said. "Your hesitation answered the question."

"No, it did not, sir," she countered. "I was considering my answer, since it is not one that can be qualified by a simple yes or no. It depends on one's perception of equality."

She half-expected a contradiction or an argument. Instead, the man's brow lifted once more. "And what is *your* perception of equality, Miss Northcott?" he asked.

"Not quite the same as yours, I suspect." She raised her chin. "You see, although I am the daughter of a captain and the niece of an earl, I also happen to be a woman. That being so, I must ask if you, as a man, see *me* as an equal."

He smiled his familiar sober smile and shook his head. "Sexual equality is another matter altogether," he replied, "and my answer in that case is no, I do not see you, or women in general, as being equal to men, nor will they ever be. In some aspects, of course, they are undoubtedly superior, but only in those which God—or nature—intended. Class distinction, to which I was initially referring, is a different beast entirely, one whose survival is currently being threatened by men like myself who have the audacity to believe they are worthy enough to share a dinner table with dukes and earls. I expect and ignore the disapproving looks and cold shoulders, but Syb—that is, Miss Chessington, is not quite as impervious."

Louisa tamped down the temptation to argue for her women-folk. Now was simply not the time for it, although if the opportunity ever did arise, she would be sure to exploit it.

"Well, I'm afraid I cannot agree with Miss Chessington's opinion of Yorkshire," she said. "Which begs another question, Mr. Harwell. Might this issue lead to the cancellation of your tenancy at Northcott Manor?"

He moved closer, his gaze momentarily settling on her mouth again. "Would that matter to you, Miss Northcott?"

His proximity seemed to suck the air from Louisa's lungs. "Well, of course it would," she managed. "The manor needs an occupant, and I'm sure my father will be terribly disappointed if you change your mind."

"Then allow me to reassure you," he said. "Despite what you overheard here tonight; I have no intention of—" Maxwell spun around as a key rattled in the lock. A moment later, the door opened, and a male voice spoke.

"That's odd. It's open," the voice said. "I keep it locked as a rule, and with good reason. I don't want just anyone wandering in here. You'll see why in a mo…" Lord Richmond's brows shot upwards as he regarded Louisa and Maxwell. "Good God! Miss Northcott, what the devil are you doing in here? And… Harlow? What is this?"

Louisa heard Maxwell part with a sigh, followed by the quiet utterance of a single word that barely made it to her ears.

"Fuck."

Shocked, she glanced at him. She didn't know what the word actually meant but understood it to be the vilest of curses. As she struggled to gather her wits, Lord Milnthorpe followed Lord

Richmond into the room. His gaze, at first, settled on Louisa, his expression of surprise evolving into one of relish, as if he'd just discovered a sweet little secret. His haughty perusal then switched to Maxwell. "Well, well, well," he muttered. "This beggars belief."

Lord Richmond's expression, meanwhile, had darkened visibly. "It certainly does," he said. "What is going on here, young lady? Has this man tried to take advantage of you?"

Louisa gasped. "Absolutely not, my lord. I'm appalled that you would even suggest such a thing."

"Then what, pray tell, are you doing in here? This is a private room. Off limits."

"But I did not realize that when I entered," she replied. "As you just mentioned, the door was unlocked."

"With respect, my lords," Maxwell said, his voice calm, "it is patently clear that you have misunderstood the situation."

"Yes, you most certainly have." Louisa, her heart banging against her ribs, looked from one man to the other. "Mr. Harlow speaks the truth. This is not at all as it might appear. I... I was actually looking for the ladies' retirement room and took a wrong turn. I found myself in here by mistake."

"And was Mr. Harlow already in here?"

"No." Louisa curled her hands into tight fists and prepared to confess. "My lords, the truth is, I—"

"The truth is, I *was* already here," Maxwell replied, "but Miss Northcott did not see me at first. The light is poor, and I was seated on the sofa."

Louisa threw him a puzzled glance. Why was he lying?

Lord Richmond looked unconvinced and Milnthorpe huffed. "A weak explanation," the latter remarked, "which I hesitate to believe. Scandalous situation. Utterly scandalous."

"I have to say, Harlow, I wasn't too happy with my wife when I heard she'd added you to the invitation list," Lord Richmond said, glaring at him. "Your behavior tonight serves to uphold my opinion that you do not belong here."

"Are you objecting to my presence in your house, my lord?" Maxwell replied, lifting his gaze to the ceiling. "Or just in this indecorous off-limits parlor of yours?"

Richmond sputtered. "How dare you question me, you insolent—"

"Mr. Harlow has done nothing wrong, Lord Richmond," Louisa cried. "This is all a misunderstanding. You see, I came in here because—

"Before anything else is said, Miss Northcott, you need to go and find your father and tell him what has happened." The resonance in Maxwell's voice sounded like a warning. "Trust me. You must also tell him that I shall be speaking with him shortly."

"My father? Why? What do you mean?" She glanced wildly from Maxwell to Lord Richmond and back again. "Nothing *has* happened. Please let me explain. This is all my faul—"

"I agree, it is a misunderstanding," Maxwell replied gently, "but your father must be made aware of it without delay. Just do as I ask, please."

"What on earth is going on?"

The question, to Louisa's utter dismay, came from Sybella Chessington, who appeared on the threshold but, with obvious intent, did not set foot in the room. Instead, she glanced down at her toes as if standing on the edge of a precipice.

"What is this, Maxwell?" Sybella demanded. "Why are you in here? Has something happened?"

"It is simply a misunderstanding, my dear, nothing more," he replied, "I came in here to wait while you were refreshing yourself."

Louisa gave Maxwell a sharp look as understanding dawned. Of course. No one knew that Sybella had been in the room just minutes before, nor was she ever likely to admit it, given the risqué decor. Even if the truth were told, it would serve no other purpose than to add fuel to a fire already smoldering.

No matter how it came to be, the fact remained. Louisa Northcott had been discovered alone with Maxwell Harlow in a room scandalous on its own merit. Fear churned in her stomach. Dear God, what had she done?

"This is all my fault," she whispered, hoping Maxwell would hear her.

Richmond cleared his throat. "I regret to inform you, Miss Chessington, that I discovered Mr. Harlow and Miss Northcott in here together, alone. Lord Milnthorpe bore witness also."

"I did indeed, sorry to say," Milnthorpe replied.

"Alone? In here?" Sybella's hand flew to her throat as she glanced, briefly, at the ceiling. "Oh, Maxwell, please tell me this isn't true."

"I'm afraid it is," Maxwell replied, "though the circumstances are entirely random."

Miss Chessington glared at Louisa. "Then what is she *doing* here?"

"It was a misunderstanding, Miss Chessington," Louisa replied, grasping at a final, feeble straw. "I mistakenly thought this was the retiring room and didn't realize it was otherwise occupied."

"That is a lie, Miss Northcott." The familiar figure of Lady Henrietta Chivers, the Duke of Whinfell's daughter, appeared beside Sybella. "You came into the retiring room a little while ago. I saw you with my own eyes. You stayed but a moment and then left. So, you cannot have mistaken this room for it at all."

Miss Chessington let out a soft cry and pressed a hand to her mouth.

Richmond's nostrils flared. "Is this true, Miss Northcott?"

Louisa met the man's gaze. "Well… yes, my lord, it is. But the reason I left the retiring room is because I found the atmosphere to be utterly *stifling*." She threw a scathing glance at Lady Henrietta. "So, I sought out a more agreeable retreat."

"Then why did you lie just now?" Lord Richmond demanded. "And why did you not leave immediately upon learning of Mr. Harlow's presence? And why was the door closed?"

"Because I…" Louisa swallowed over the tightness in the

throat and looked to Maxwell for support.

Lady Henrietta scoffed and snapped her fan open, a smug gleam in her eyes.

"As I explained, Miss Northcott did not see me at first," Maxwell said, "because I was seated on the settee."

"Yet when we entered, you were both on *this* side of the settee," Milnthorpe said. "And we saw no sign of either of you making haste to leave."

"I rose to my feet when I realized someone had entered, as courtesy demands," Maxell replied. "The fault lies entirely with me, my lords. I was remiss in taking the time to share a brief conversation with Miss Northcott. That is all."

Milnthorpe huffed. "With the door closed."

"It closed by itself," Louisa said, instantly aware of how desperate that sounded.

Sybella's responding huff implied a similar opinion. "Do not deem to defend her, Maxwell," she said. "It seems obvious she is playing some kind of game and has been caught out."

"That is not true, Miss Chessington." Louisa's voice sounded strange to her ears; shrill, edged in panic. "As Mr. Harlow stated, we shared a brief conversation. Nothing more than that."

"Utterly inappropriate, nonetheless," Lord Richmond said.

"And very possibly deceptive," Milnthorpe added. "Lady Henrietta has already testified to your previous lie."

Louisa gasped. "But I've already explained—"

"That is quite enough!" Maxwell's angry exclamation made her jump. "Say nothing else, Miss Northcott. The continuance of this argument is futile. These people have already made up their minds and may the truth be damned. You need to find your father and tell him what has occurred. Do you hear me?"

Louisa regarded him for a moment, seeing something in his eyes. A fleeting glimmer, there and gone. Sadness? No. Regret, possibly. "I am truly sorry, Mr. Harlow," she said, fighting tears.

"You are not to blame, lass." Fists clenched, he nodded toward the door, offering a barely perceptible smile. "Off you go."

Shivering uncontrollably, Louisa did as bid, stepping past Richmond and Milnthorpe, and obliged to push past Sybella Chessington and Lady Henrietta. Sybella followed her over the threshold. "I noticed how you looked at him when you were dancing," she muttered, grabbing at Louisa's arm. "Well, this sorry attempt at causing a scandal will fail. Our marriage agreement is signed and sealed, so your pathetic effort to lure him away will never succeed. I will *not* allow this to ruin me, but, by God, I'll make sure it's the ruination of you."

Louisa tugged her arm free and opened her mouth to defend herself but thought better of it. For one thing, several other ladies had now spilled out of the retiring room. Like wolves at a kill, they stood in a semi-circle as if awaiting an opportunity to join the feast. Maxwell Harlow was right. Things were ugly enough. Resorting to a further exchange of words would only make things worse.

Instead, Louisa lifted her chin and moved toward the female onlookers, who parted to let her pass as if she had some infectious disease. Shivering, she made her way along the corridor, her brave face merely a fragile façade. Shock and fear churned in her stomach as she navigated through the crowd, the potential repercussions of what had occurred biting into her like teeth. For the sake of a few selfishly stolen minutes, her life would never be the same. But what terrified her more were the possible consequences for those she loved. Scandal could attach itself to a family like a tick. And, despite what Maxwell Harlow had said, Louisa blamed herself.

Entirely.

For deep down in a private place, where she kept her innermost secrets, there sat a sour nugget of truth. That she had been in no hurry to leave Maxwell Harlow's side. That she had purposely engaged him in conversation for no other reason than she wanted to spend some time with a man she desired.

Regret had the bitterest taste.

So did guilt.

CHAPTER FIVE

ALONE WITH HIS thoughts, Aldous Northcott sat by the hearth, nursing a glass of his favorite Irish whiskey. The mantel clock had just struck midnight, the dying embers of the coal fire were turning to ash, and a gentle drumroll of rain played on the windows.

Grace and Louisa had gone to bed. Or, at least, they'd gone upstairs. Sleep, given what had occurred earlier that evening, would likely prove elusive. Julian, not quite sober, had also excused himself a half-hour since, filling his glass almost to the rim with whiskey and taking it upstairs. A necessary nightcap.

Aldous stared into the amber hues of his own drink and heaved a weary sigh. Two hours earlier, he'd been enjoying a glass of vintage port and a game of cards in the games-room at Lord and Lady Richmond's Westminster home. The orchestra had been playing in the background; a country dance. Aldous, meanwhile, had been holding the trump card, keeping his expression guarded, giving nothing away as he prepared to declare his first victory of the evening.

Then he'd felt a light tap on his shoulder, and Louisa—his beloved Louisa—had whispered in his ear. "Papa, I must speak with you. Something has happened."

Given her timing, he might have been justified in waving her away, irritated by the unwanted interruption. But something in her voice snared his attention. He turned to look at her, and what he saw stayed any disapproving remark he might have made.

A pale face, tight with anguish, brown eyes feverishly bright, and a tremble in her lower lip. His eldest daughter, usually amiable and happy, was clearly disturbed.

Aldous had set his winning card face down, excused himself, and risen from the table, ignoring the sputters of objection and displeasure. Without comment, he had allowed Louisa to lead him to a quiet spot at the end of the hallway. A place that lay in shadow, away from prying eyes.

And he had listened, without interruption, as she'd told him all that had occurred in Lord Richmond's private study; what she had overheard, what had been threatened, and what had been promised.

Everything.

"It's all my fault, Papa," she'd said at last, bottom lip quivering as tears streamed down her cheeks. "Entirely mine. I am so sorry."

Aldous had given her his clean handkerchief. "I want you to dry your eyes, Louisa," he'd said, his calm voice belying the churning pool of emotions within. "Then I want you to collect your things and wait by the front door while I find your Mama and Julian. Speak to no one, do you hear? No one."

Barely ten minutes later, they had been in a carriage on their way back to their own townhouse. Grace had sat beside Louisa and taken her hand, the physical contact saying more than words ever could. Only Julian had spoken, and with vehemence. "I'm going to kill the bastard," he muttered, which had prompted a quiet rejoinder from Louisa.

"Mr. Harlow is not to blame, Julian," she'd replied. "He did nothing wrong."

It was telling, Aldous mused, as his thoughts returned to the present, how Louisa had risen to Maxwell Harlow's defense that night, and more than once. That she was attracted to the man was, of course, no revelation. Aldous had been aware of it from the day they'd first met in the stables, but he'd never considered it to be anything more than a one-sided, hopeless infatuation. Certainly, Harlow had never shown any sign of reciprocation. The man was engaged to be married, for God's sake, and to a viscount's daughter at that. Though it appeared, according to what Louisa overheard, that the relationship was some way from idyllic.

But Aldous would sacrifice a limb before allowing his daughter to take the full brunt of whatever scandal emerged from this mess. Harlow would have to assume some responsibility for what had occurred. "If not all," Aldous mumbled and took a sip of whiskey, refusing to let his mind examine what the blasted fellow *should* have done in order avoid the entire debacle. It was too bloody late for that. The man had apparently promised he'd call, though for exactly what purpose remained to be seen. Given the hour, he probably wouldn't show his face till the morning.

The thought had no sooner slid through Aldous' mind than a knock came to the parlor door, and it opened. "Excuse me, Captain," a familiar voice said, "you have a caller."

Aldous twisted in his seat, surprised to see Barnes still awake. "Is it Mr. Harlow?"

"It is, Captain. He said he can come back in the morning if you prefer."

"No, send him in, Barnes." Aldous set his glass down and rose to his feet. "And then take yourself off to bed."

"Very well." The butler gave him what appeared to be a sympathetic smile. "Goodnight, sir."

Aldous responded with a nod. No doubt the events of the evening had already been dissected and examined below stairs. Servants' gossip, though discouraged, was as perennial as the tides and equally as impossible to control.

Maxwell Harlow strode into the room moments later, looking more than a little disheveled. "Captain Northcott." He inclined his head, the ends of his hair tipped with silver droplets of rain. "I suspected you'd still be up. I appreciate you seeing me at this late hour."

"My daughter told me you intended to call," Aldous replied, determined to keep a rein on his simmering disappointment, let alone his anger. He genuinely liked this man. Trusted him. Even admired him. Now he found himself questioning the validity of his judgment and couldn't resist a touch of intimidation. "You should know I've spent the last two hours trying to decide whether or not to put a bullet in your brain when you finally made your appearance."

Harlow didn't flinch. "And have you arrived at a decision, Captain?"

"Not yet," he replied, and lifted a decanter from its tray. "Whiskey? It's Irish, not Scottish."

"Thank you, aye," Harlow replied. "Especially if it's to be my last."

Aldous gave him a scathing look. "Well, now." He handed him the drink and gestured for him to sit. "That will depend on what you have to say."

Harlow sank into a nearby armchair. "How is Miss North-cott?"

Aldous gave a short, bitter laugh, took his seat, and met Harlow's gaze. "You may well ask," he replied. "She is frightened, and it breaks my heart to see it. And, for some reason, she is convinced this whole sorry mess is entirely her fault and will hear no argument to the contrary. That she behaved foolishly is irrefutable, but I have to lay the blame primarily at your feet, Harlow. You should have left the moment you realized my daughter was in the room. This damned incident has brought shame on the family and will undoubtedly affect her future."

"I'm fully aware of that, Captain, and despite Miss North-cott's protestations, I take full responsibility for what has occurred." Harlow took a mouthful of whiskey and then frowned into his glass. "It is up to me, therefore, to make things right."

Aldous raised a brow. "And just how do you plan to do that?"

The man lifted his gaze again. "By marrying your daughter, sir. With your permission, of course."

Aldous' glass paused on the way to his mouth. "Marriage?" He shook his head. "Marrying my daughter would mean calling off your engagement to Miss Chessington."

"Which has already been done, Captain."

Aldous gasped. "Good lord! The grass doesn't grow under your bloody feet, does it? You may be forgiven for being ruthless in your business affairs, but to be similarly affected in matters of the heart leaves me, frankly, dumbfounded. Are you telling me Miss Chessington must now bear the brunt of your mismanagement of this incident?"

Harlow's subsequent smile held no humor. "Miss Chessington is the one who broke our engagement, sir."

"Is that so? Odd, since she apparently told my daughter, in no uncertain terms, that she had no intention of doing such a thing."

"Nevertheless, our engagement is over."

"I see." Aldous sat back, a flush of fresh anger rising up his neck. "Then I must ask you this, sir. Had Miss Chessington not cast you aside, would you be here now offering to save my daughter from a scandal? One that could easily have been avoided had you applied some good sense, I might add. Or would you merely have left her to face the music? Right now, it appears to be the latter, in which case your audacity is quite remarkable, as is your ability to present yourself falsely."

Harlow opened his mouth as if to speak, and then apparently changed his mind. Instead, he downed his drink in one gulp and stared, for a moment, into his empty glass. "Your assessment of my conduct and my character is understandable, Captain, given what you've been told," he said at last, meeting Aldous' gaze once more. "Nevertheless, my offer of marriage to Miss Northcott remains, and whether you believe it or not, is made with the best of intentions."

Aldous studied him. "What aren't you telling me?"

Harlow raised both brows. "Captain?"

"You just said *given what you've been told*, which implies there are things that have not been said. If these things will prove my current assessment of you to be wrong, I should be heartily glad to hear them, and for my own sake rather than yours. Besides, if your offer of marriage to my daughter is as sincere as you say, you must allow her father to have few reservations when considering it."

"A fair point." Harlow regarded his empty glass once more. "This whiskey was surprisingly excellent. Not as good as the Scottish stuff, of course."

Aldous, understanding the man's intent, rose to his feet. "I take it you'll have another?"

"I believe I will," he replied, and handed the glass over. "And I must also beg your discretion, sir. I'd prefer that what I'm about to tell you remains within the confines of your family. For the time being, at least."

"Of course," Aldous said, filling both glasses once more.

"Thank you." Harlow took his drink, frowning as he appeared to ponder. "The wheels of gossip had begun to turn even before you left the party this evening," he said at last. "As a result, Miss Chessington broke our engagement at my insistence. The decision, being presented as her own, will hopefully allow her to maintain her dignity. Her pride is wounded, perhaps, but her reputation—and her heart—remain intact. And, in case you're wondering, I insisted she keep the mare. Otherwise, my regret at our parting is, I confess, somewhat benign. Ours was not a love match."

"Hmm, yes, I'm aware of that. My daughter told me about the argument she overheard."

Harlow gave a nod. "And the only way I can make reparation to Miss Northcott's reputation is by marriage. Hence my offer, which, I should also add, is free from any terms and conditions. I have no need of your daughter's dowry. She may keep that for herself. The only concern is that I travel a lot, so I'll be away much of the time, but the fact Miss Northcott will be living close to Highfield Hall means she will not be isolated. Other than my company, then, your daughter will lack for nothing. You have my word."

"I don't doubt your sincerity, Harlow, but to be frank," Aldous heaved a sigh, "this union is not quite what I envisaged for her."

The man's eyes narrowed slightly. "I'm certain that's understating it, Captain."

Aldous decided not to mitigate the remark. Given the circumstances, he'd already been more than lenient with the blasted fellow, influenced in large part by Louisa's refusal to place the blame at the man's feet. Instead, a different question slid into Aldous' brain, one borne from sheer curiosity. He took a sip of whiskey and then cleared his throat. "You're not obliged to answer, but I cannot help wondering about your financial agreement with Lord Dent. Does it still stand?"

Harlow gave a thin smile. "I should imagine there will be a few others asking that same question come morning, sir. The answer is yes, it still stands, but with an amendment. Lord Dent will now receive restricted company shares instead of the original lump sum, the dividends of which will allow him to pay off his debts over time."

"*Restricted* shares?"

"I'd rather not go into detail, Captain." The man downed the rest of his drink. "Suffice to say I'm just covering my own interests. Despite what has occurred, I don't owe the viscount any favors."

Aldous smiled inwardly at the man's implied shrewdness. If nothing else, having Maxwell Harlow as a husband would indeed mean that Louisa would want for nothing. At least, materially. He took a moment to reflect on what had already taken place and what would be the likely outcome of it all. He would do nothing till he had discussed everything with Grace. Isaac needed to be informed as well, and the sooner the better. As for Louisa, Aldous had little doubt she'd be disagreeable to the marriage, given her attraction to the confounded fellow.

But what kind of marriage will it be for our daughter? A lonely one,

I fear, empty of companionship. Maxwell Harlow has admitted to being at the beck-and-call of a demanding mistress, that being his business empire.

Yet the future of a young woman who bore a mark of disgrace was even less pleasing to think about. Aldous grimaced at the telltale beginnings of a heartburn attack. He felt weary all of a sudden, as if he'd walked into an invisible wall and been knocked flat.

"It's late, Captain." Harlow set his glass down and rose to his feet. "I'll leave you to consider my offer. No doubt you also wish to discuss everything with your family and Miss Northcott especially. I shall wait, then, to hear from you." He drew a card from his pocket. "This is where I'm staying for the next several days."

Aldous took the card. "Thank you. I sent the butler to bed, so I'll see you out. And yes, my family will need to be informed and consulted. That includes my brother, the earl. Gossip has a tendency to gather substance as it circulates. I need to make sure the real version of events is the one they hear first." He paused and regarded the man who, it seemed, would soon be his son-in-law, ignoring an inner whisper of regret. No, Maxwell Harlow was not the choice he'd have made for Louisa, but there it was. Better to look upon the union as a solution rather than a complication. "The damage is done, Harlow," he said. "The only thing we can do now is try to lessen its effects on those involved. I appreciate your efforts to do what is right, as far as possible, at least. I'll be in touch."

MAXWELL STEPPED OUT into the rain, pausing for a moment to draw a steadying breath before climbing into his carriage. The evening had been messy to say the least. Five minutes of negligence on his part had changed the direction of several lives, his own included. Whether it would be for the better, in his case, remained to be seen.

Since he'd agreed—with certain amendments—to uphold the financial arrangement with Lord Dent, losing Sybella had been costly solely from a financial standpoint. A cold perspective, perhaps, but Maxwell would not claim nostalgia where none existed. Sybella had merited his respect, but she'd never come anywhere near his heart. In a romantic sense, no woman ever had.

And, in truth, Sybella held him in the same regard. Even so, she'd refused, initially, to call off their engagement. Her protestations had not been due to a wounded heart, however, but wounded pride. She saw the annulment as a capitulation to Louisa Northcott, who, according to Sybella, had surely orchestrated the entire incident. Only when Maxwell had pointed out the potential ramifications of continuing with their alliance had she changed her tune.

By marrying Louisa Northcott, Maxwell might lessen the effects of a scandal, but he'd done her no great favor otherwise. The constraints of marriage had always been something he'd avoided due simply to his industrious lifestyle, which was not suited to the obligations of hearth and home. He feared the lass, with her romantic notions, would be even less amenable to it than Sybella.

That being so, and assuming his marriage proposal would be accepted, he'd have to make it quite clear from the outset that their relationship would not be without some challenges.

Otherwise, he saw no impediment at all.

CHAPTER SIX

"THAT, BASICALLY, IS the situation as it stands," Aldous said, "and also the reason we're here at this early hour. We wanted you to know the truth of what occurred last night before you hear any of the distorted versions. I have yet to speak with Louisa about Harlow's proposal, though I'm quite sure she'll accept."

"It's a bit of a mess, I must say." Isaac Northcott, seventh Earl of Hutton, and Aldous' eldest brother, wandered over to the sideboard and poured himself another coffee from the silver pot. "Then again, it could be worse. At least this Harlow chap is accepting responsibility and has offered to do right by Louisa. And it's not as if you know nothing of him. He's your tenant, after all."

Aldous grunted. "There's a bit of a difference between him being my tenant and being my son-in-law."

"Why? Because he's not a peer?" Isaac dropped a spoonful of sugar into his cup and stirred. "You surprise me, Aldous. I've always considered you to be more forward thinking than the rest of us. In fact, I recall a conversation we had not long ago. These industrialists will be the ones to shape this country's future, I believe you said."

"Hmm." Aldous frowned at the dregs in his cup. "I did say that didn't I."

"Assuming they do marry, it means Louisa will be living at

the manor," Eleanor, Lady Hutton, pointed out, "which in turn means she'll be close to Highfield. That is a good thing, surely."

"There is that, I suppose." Aldous exchanged a glance with Grace, whose bleary eyes gave testimony to a sleepless night. He conjured up a smile intended to soothe.

Grace returned the smile, though it held no joy. "Louisa's biggest fear is that the scandal will reflect on the entire family," she said. "She was inconsolable last night. Blames herself entirely."

"Oh, I doubt any of this will amount to much, especially with a marriage on the horizon." Isaac retook his seat. "Besides, there'll be a fresh scandal somewhere else tomorrow, or the day after that, or next week, and this incident will quickly become old news. In fact, I suspect people will be more outraged—and many falsely so—by the existence of this bawdy ceiling." He waggled a brow. "Richmond will be receiving a lot of private viewing requests over the next while, I should think."

"And the artist responsible will be likely to find himself with some new commissions," Eleanor said.

Isaac chuckled. "Indeed. In any case, I'll deal with anything that needs to be dealt with, including Mama."

"Ah, yes. Mama." Aldous grimaced. "I'm sure she'll have something to say about it. Should I not be the one telling her?"

"No, leave her to me." Isaac shrugged. "She'll be suitably appalled at Louisa but will lay all the blame solidly at Harlow's feet. You may tell my niece, however, that despite her lapse, we are not likely to become pariahs. And, in a show of support, we will, of course, attend her wedding."

"That might mean a journey to Yorkshire in the not-too-distant future," Aldous said. "I should imagine Louisa will want to marry at our village church."

"Then a journey to Yorkshire we will take," Isaac said. "Eh, Eleanor?"

"Unquestionably," Eleanor replied. "We wouldn't miss it."

"I'm sure that will greatly ease Louisa's mind," Grace said, a quiver in her voice. "Thank you, both."

Eleanor, who was seated beside Grace on the settee, took her hand. "Grace, my dear, we are family. You need never doubt or question our support. Now, will you have a drop more tea?"

CHAPTER SEVEN

MORNING SUN SLANTED through the leaded windows of Highfield's main parlor, teasing little glints of red and gold from Louisa Northcott's hair. Maxwell, seated opposite her, had not noticed them previously. Meanwhile, the light he'd oft times observed in her eyes appeared to have gone missing. Pale-faced, the lass sat in rigid silence on the settee, skirts of emerald-green perfectly arranged, slender hands resting in her lap.

She regarded Maxwell with an expression that surpassed solemn. If asked, he'd have guessed her disposition to be somewhere between wretched and remorseful.

A fine start to a potential lifelong union.

His marriage proposal had been accepted, and the legal processes, financial and otherwise, had already begun. The banns would be read at St. Paul's church in Morthwaite, on the Highfield estate, where the wedding date had been tentatively set for the seventh day of June that year, a Saturday.

Of course, due to her eavesdropping escapade, the lass already knew some of what marriage to Maxwell would mean. But he needed to reiterate. She had to understand, fully, that he had no intention of staying home to play lord of the manor. He had a business to run, an empire still in the process of being built.

Their meeting this morning was the first since Lady Richmond's party a week earlier. And it would be their last till the day of their wedding a little over two months hence. Maxwell was planning to leave London within the hour, heading for Scotland, and Glasgow specifically. Before he left, however, there were things to be said.

He'd already voiced his appreciation of Miss Northcott's time and given the weather its customary mention. She, in turn, had responded with expected decorum. Now, with the niceties out of the way, Maxwell needed to get to the crux of the matter. Parameters had to be laid out and expectations established.

He cleared his throat, which prompted the lass to lift her chin, as if she was preparing to hear what else he had to say.

"I have no regrets, Miss Northcott," he began. "That is to say, I see no reason why this marriage cannot be fulfilling for both of us. I believe you are already aware, however, that my business interests are likely to take me away from home frequently and for days at a time."

"Yes, I am aware of that, Mr. Harlow," she replied, "but since we'll be living close to Highfield, I doubt I shall lack for company."

"My thought also, but I simply want you to understand the way of things." He smiled. "That's assuming, of course, that my absences bother you at all. The opposite might be the case."

"I cannot imagine that to be so," she replied, her face brightening a little. "Despite the circumstances, or maybe because of them, I truly want this marriage to work."

"As do I," he replied, and allowed his gaze to briefly wander over her. Physically, he'd already compared her to Sybella—how could he not? Neither woman lacked appeal. The difference lay, primarily, in their character.

Sybella, fastidious to the point of priggish, took propriety to the limit. To begin, their arrangement had been purely financial. Little more than a true business agreement, in fact, suggested by a viscount burdened with debt. A widower who'd received no mercy from his peers and no wealthy suitors for his sole offspring, a dowerless daughter. Desperate, Lord Dent had lowered his sights and taken aim at a middle-class tradesman who had money to spare.

Most people assumed Maxwell had done the approaching, desperate to gain entry to some of the most prestigious parlors in the land. If that's what they wanted to believe, then let them. The truth was, Maxwell had initially refused the viscount's proposition. Marriage was nowhere near the top of his list of priorities. Certainly, he'd never expected to be *offered* a wife, and by an aristocrat, no less. But, after some consideration, Maxwell had signed the agreement. Sybella was a handsome lass after all, and her social status would certainly open doors that had previously been closed to him. He was under no illusion, however, that their marriage would be anything less than a challenge.

Louisa Northcott was a bird of a different feather. Though her blood was as blue as the Ceylonese sapphire currently sitting in his pocket, the lass had an impetuous streak that intrigued him. He recalled the first time he'd seen her riding pell-mell across the moor, when she'd sacrificed her hat to the wind. Her subsequent shriek of laughter had travelled the distance between them, the joyful sound infecting him in a like manner, making him smile.

If honest, he'd been attracted to the lass from the outset. And, given her inquisitive nature, he genuinely looked forward to introducing her to the more intimate aspects of marriage.

Unlike Sybella, Louisa had not balked at the sight of Richmond's erotic ceiling. To the contrary, she'd been curious about it, in no great hurry to leave. He suspected, therefore, that she'd be a willing participant between the sheets. The mere thought of taking her to bed after one of his hectic business trips was not in the least unappealing. His body responded accordingly, and he shifted his focus to collect himself. His gaze settled on a book that sat on the small table beside him.

The Poetical Works of Lord Byron.

"You should know that I am not a man given to flowery language or romantic notions," he said, regarding her once more. "That said, be assured I am not, by nature, unkind, and will never ill-treat you or give you cause to fear me. My expectations of you as my wife will always remain within the acceptable confines of marriage."

Louisa's brows lifted, and she looked down to where her hands lay in her lap. "I am not yet certain what your expectations of me are, Mr. Harlow," she said, regarding him once more, "nor am I familiar with the *acceptable confines* of marriage, though I'm sure you'll explain everything to me. For example, I wonder, as your wife, will I still be required to address you so formally?"

Maxwell frowned. It was a counter response, he realized, though gently expressed. "Did I prove my point even as I made it, Miss Northcott?"

The beginnings of a smile came to her lips. "Your delivery was obviously sincere, sir, but somewhat pragmatic."

"Then perhaps I can soften it a little." He went to her and held out a hand, which she took, allowing him to assist her to her feet. Her eyes were brown, he noticed, with tiny gold flecks that matched the ones in her hair. "I've never been married before," he said, "so, in that regard, much of this is as new to me as it is to you. But I can tell you that I am entering this union without reservation. I like you, Miss Northcott. I *admire* you and feel optimistic for our future. As for formality, let us dispense with it now. Please call me Maxwell. Or Max. Whichever you prefer or depending on your mood."

Her chin lifted again, and the smile appeared in full. "Then you will please call me Louisa," she said.

"Louisa," he repeated, and dug into his pocket, pulling out the small, blue leather box with a tiny, gold catch. "Well, Louisa, I made some discreet enquiries and discovered you were born in the month of September, which influenced my choice of stone. I hope you like it. If not, please tell me, and I'll have it changed."

He released the catch, and the lid opened to expose the ring that had been made for her. Nestled on a tiny cushion of white velvet, the oval cut sapphire shimmered a rich, cobalt blue, the depth of color enhanced further by a double cluster of diamonds, all set in yellow gold.

Somewhere in London, a couple of Garrard jewelers were currently catching up on their sleep, having spent much of the past week finishing the ring to Maxwell's specifications. And, judging by the look on Louisa's face and the renewed light in her eyes, it had been worth it.

She pressed a hand to the base of her throat. "Oh, Maxwell, it's beautiful!"

"I'm glad you approve." He took the ring, set the box down, and reached for her left hand, sliding the jewel onto her third finger. "I believe this means we are now officially engaged, my dear."

Fingers spread, Louisa held up her hand, eyes transfixed on the ring, which sparkled in the sunlight. "It fits perfectly," she said, bringing her hand closer for inspection. "How did you know my size?"

"I have my sources," he replied.

"My mother, I suspect," Louisa said, still gazing at the ring. "It's truly magnificent. I shall treasure it always. Thank you."

"You're welcome." He brought her right hand to his lips. "Now, I wish I could spend a little longer in your company, but my carriage is waiting. The next time we see each other will be the day we marry. But I shall write to you in the meantime, if that would please you."

"It would please me very much," she replied, a rosy flush staining her cheeks. "I have no reservations about our union either, Maxwell. I'm looking forward to it."

Minutes later, Maxwell clambered into his carriage, settled back, and endeavored to ignore what he felt at that moment. It was not an unpleasant sensation, but neither was it particularly welcome. There was no room for foolish sentiment in his life. This marriage was akin to a business partnership, its success dependent on each partner doing his or her part as agreed. He felt sure Louisa, in time, would come to see that.

CHAPTER EIGHT

Glasgow, April, 1845

GASLIGHT PUNCHED A hole in the night, exposing wet cobbles and smoke-stained sandstone. Maxwell gazed up, with some trepidation, at the three-story terraced house, its lower bay window lit by a soft glow from within, lace curtains providing an opaque screen of privacy.

He drew breath and mounted the half-dozen steps to the glossy black door, his hand hesitating over the brass knocker before he reached for it. The subsequent raps echoed down the street like gunshots.

Moments later, the door flew open, and a decidedly feminine squeal greeted him. "Heaven be praised, I was beginning to think you'd fallen off the face of the earth." A manicured hand reached for his and tugged him over the threshold. "Come in, quick, and close the door. You're letting all the heat out."

Maxwell stepped onto the chessboard-tiled floor of the hall-way and closed the door as bidden. Immediately, a blended odor of cuisine, coal fires and jasmine wrapped around him. Familiar. Comforting, even.

A measure of regret stirred in his gut.

By his calculations, it had been three months since he'd last set foot in this house, though it seemed longer. It appeared the lass had gained a little weight in the meantime, though it hadn't done her any harm. Her body was still the kind that made artists take up their brushes, and sculptors reach for hammer and chisel. Further blessed with an angelic face, strawberry-blond curls, and moss-green eyes, Flora MacNally was, inarguably, a real beauty. Maxwell had first met her in a private club in Glasgow and she'd become his mistress soon after, happy to move into the house he'd provided.

"How are you, Flora?" he asked, perturbed by the telltale glaze in her eyes and the smell of whisky on her breath.

"All the better for seeing you, my sweet." Rising up on tip-toes, she grabbed the collar of his coat, and pressed a kiss to his mouth, full lips moving eagerly over his, obviously seeking a reaction that never came. Frowning, she drew back. "What's wrong? Och, now, dinnae look at me like that, Max. I've only had a couple of wee drams, I swear. Helps me sleep better, y'ken?" She wormed a hand beneath his coat and gave his cock a gentle squeeze. "Not that I'll be doing much sleeping tonight."

Maxwell stepped back, removed his hat and gloves and placed them on the hallstand. "Wouldn't mind a wee dram myself," he said, shrugging off his coat and hanging it on the peg. "It's chilly out there."

"Right." Flora assumed a wary expression. "You are staying the night, aye?"

At that moment, given a choice, Maxwell would rather have been facing a factory full of hostile workers than this woman who'd been his mistress for the past five years. He drew a deep, quiet breath as he followed her into the cozy, lantern-lit parlor, where a coal fire flickered in the hearth. "No, Flora," he replied gently. "I'm afraid I can't."

She studied him for a moment as if trying to see inside his head, then went to the sideboard and filled a couple of glasses from a decanter. "Not the answer I hoped for," she said, her hand shaking a little as she handed a glass to Maxwell. She sat on the settee and patted the seat next to her. "But maybe I can change your mind afore you decide to put your coat back on. I can be very persuasive, as you well know."

Maxwell didn't give her the answer he knew she sought, nor did he sit beside her. Instead, he settled into the armchair by the fire and took a mouthful of whisky. There was no point delaying this. No point stalling. He'd come here for one reason, and there really wasn't any way to soften the impact of it. Nor would he tell her the whole story, for it served no purpose and didn't change the end result. She needed to know only one thing.

He leaned forward. "I'm getting married, Flora."

A look of surprise flitted across her face, and her eyes flicked to the fire for a moment. "Married," she repeated, regarding him once more.

"Aye."

She grimaced as if she'd just tasted something bitter. "I dinnae believe it, Max. Who'd be daft enough to marry you?"

He gave a soft laugh. "That's a fair question, I suppose."

Flora raised the glass to her mouth and proceeded to drain the contents in two gulps. "Then answer it," she said, licking her lips. "Who is she?"

"An English girl," Maxwell replied, frowning at what he'd just witnessed. "A captain's daughter."

"What's her name?"

"Her name shouldn't matter to you."

"It doesn't." She shrugged. "I'm just curious, that's all."

"Louisa." He took another sip of whisky. "Her name is Louisa."

"Is she bonny?"

"That's enough, Flora."

"Not as bonny as me, then." Flora toyed with one of her earrings. "Do you love her?"

He responded after a moment's hesitation. "No."

She frowned. "Then why are you marrying her? Is she carrying your bairn?"

"No, she is not. We're marrying because it suits us both to do so."

"Ah." Flora's brow relaxed. "I should have realized. A marriage of convenience. So, you'll still be visiting me."

"No, Flora, I won't."

She stiffened, visibly. "Why not? If you dinnae care for the lass, what difference will it make?"

"I didn't say I didn't care for her." Maxwell searched for the answer. "I just want… I want the marriage to work, and part of that means being faithful to her."

Flora's subsequent laugh held no mirth. Empty glass in hand, and with a little less grace than might be deemed normal, she got to her feet. "So, that's why you came here tonight, aye?" She wandered back to the sideboard and pulled the crystal stopper from the decanter. "To tell me I'm being cast aside in favor of some stuck-up English lass. Am I right?"

Maxwell heaved a sigh, set his glass on the hearth, and went to her. "No more," he said, his hand atop hers on the decanter. "You've had enough."

She jerked his hand away and turned to face him, pain evident in her eyes.

"Answer me, Maxwell. Am I right? The only reason you're here is to tell me we're finished?"

"I'm here to tell you that I'm getting married and wish to remain faithful to my wife. I could just as easily have abandoned you without a word."

She appeared to ponder for a moment and then shook her head. "But being married doesnae mean you have to shackle yourself to one woman. You can bed your Sassenach wife and still share nights with me. She need never know."

"But *I* would know," he countered. "Besides, it's not as though I'm the only man who shares your bed, and don't dare deny it. I wouldn't have been overly surprised to find someone here tonight."

"If I seek company elsewhere, it's only because you're away most of the bloody time," she said, scowling. "I get lonely."

"I'm sure you do," he replied, "which is why I've never insisted you stay faithful to me. I doubt you'd have done so anyway."

"Aye, I would, if you'd asked." She blew out a breath and cast her gaze around the room. "How long do I have, then?"

"Till when?"

"Till I need to find somewhere else to live. You're no' throwing me out right away, are you?"

"I'm not throwing you out at all," he said, putting the stopper back in the decanter. "The house is yours. I transferred ownership to you this morning."

She flinched as if she'd been slapped. "If that's meant as a jest, Max, it's a cruel one."

"It's not a jest," he said. "The house belongs to you, as well as a lump sum of money that will be dispatched to you in monthly increments, enough to cover your expenses for the next six months. After that, you're on your own, so get yourself sorted out and find yourself a job. There's no shortage of work in the city right now and it's not as if you'll have rent to pay. And go easy on the drink, Flora. I don't like what I've seen since I got here tonight. That stuff will ruin you."

The entire time he'd spoken, she'd merely gaped at him. "Bugger me," she muttered, and then hiccupped. "I own this house?"

"Aye." Maxwell sighed. "Did you hear any of what I just said?"

"My God, Max." Tears welled in her eyes. "I dinnae ken what to say."

"Flora, did you hear—?"

"Aye, I heard you. Get a job and dinnae drink so much, blah blah blah." She sniffed and slid her hand down to his cock again, caressing him through the fabric of his trousers. "But one final night, eh? For old time's sake. You're no' married yet, after all, and I've been burning for you since I saw you on the doorstep. Aye, there you go, my sweet, up and ready. You want it as much as I do. Have you even had any since our last meeting?"

Maxwell gritted his teeth as his traitorous cock stiffened. No, he hadn't had any and, for a moment, he considered capitulating to Flora's persuasive touch.

Only for a moment.

"Stop." He took hold of her wrist and kissed the smooth, pale skin on the inside of it, breathing in her familiar perfume. "Flora, listen to me. Do you know Alexander Blair and Sons, the solicitors on Bath Street?"

She snorted. "Och, aye. Alex and his sons are old friends of mine."

He gave her a withering look. "You know what I mean. You must go there tomorrow morning to sign some papers."

"What papers?"

"Legal papers regarding the ownership of the house and the terms of the expense coverage. Everything has been taken care of. All you have to do is sign."

"That's it?"

He nodded. "That's it."

The glaze in her eyes softened, shimmering in the lantern-light. "I cannae believe it, Max," she said.

"Just make something of it, Flora."

"That's not what I meant. I meant you and me. I cannae believe it's over." She cocked her head. "It doesn't have to be, mark you. If you find your Sassenach wife doesnae keep you topped up, you know where I am."

"I'll keep that in mind," he said. "I have to go. Come and see me out."

"But you only just got here." She pulled a sullen face. "You cannae even stay for a chat?"

A chat was the last thing she wanted from him. "I don't think that would be a good idea."

Pouting, she dragged her fingertips over her left breast. "Afraid I'll persuade you to stay the night?"

He'd allow her that. "Aye," he said, "I'm afraid you would, Flora MacNally."

She followed him into the hallway. "I'll miss you, Max."

He couldn't bring himself to return the sentiment, to give her hope where none existed. "Look on this as an opportunity and grab it with both hands," he said, shrugging on his coat. "Promise me you'll try."

"I hope this Sassenach is worth it."

"Promise me."

She wrinkled her nose. "Aye, I promise."

"Good lass." He opened the front door and paused for a moment on the threshold but did not look back. "Don't forget to lock it."

With that, he stepped out into the damp Glaswegian night and closed the door behind him, with only a single thought at the forefront of his mind.

Had he wed Sybella, would he still have let Flora go?

The answer eluded him.

CHAPTER NINE

L OUISA RECEIVED TEN letters from Maxwell all told, one for each week they were apart. Though not exactly romantic epistles, they were friendly and pleasant, as if she'd been sitting beside him, sharing light conversation. She had replied to each one, all, as per his request, addressed to his office in Sheffield.

The exchanges had allowed her to learn a little more about the man she was to marry, though much of the subject matter was fairly trivial. He always told her where he was; Glasgow, Sheffield, South Shields, and one time in Liverpool. Certainly, he seemed to travel a lot.

Each letter had been signed off with 'affectionately yours', a valediction that always provoked a little shiver of delight. That she had Maxwell Harlow's affection was enough for now. Love, she dared to believe, was simply waiting in the wings and would eventually make an appearance.

Ten weeks. Ten letters.

Today was the seventh day of June. Her wedding day. And it had begun with some advice from her mother. "Do not let nerves spoil your experience," she'd said, as Louisa began her ablutions that morning. "There is nothing to be nervous about, so set your fears aside and enjoy yourself. This is your wedding day. A day to be remembered in detail. Savor each moment, my darling. I enjoyed every minute of mine."

It had worked for the most part. At least, Louisa had managed to quell the horde of butterflies in her stomach, settling them down to a minor flutter. Consequently, the passing minutes were less of a blur, and she tried to take notice of everything, committing it all to memory.

First, she could not have been happier with her reflection in her bedroom mirror. Her gown of cream satin and lace, which had been made by Francesca Corvinelli, was stuff of fairy tales. The matching lace veil, held in place by a garland of myrtle, was romantic perfection. And her posy of delicately perfumed pink roses and sweet myrtle was exactly as she'd requested.

When the time came, she'd been driven to church in an open carriage beneath a cloudless June sky, hedgerows and gardens bursting with the first flush of summer. Evie and Clara, her bridesmaids, identically clad in pale pink silk and with similar garlands of myrtle crowning their heads, arranged her veil and train at the church door.

Walking down the aisle on her father's arm had been the proudest moment of Louisa's life. Bouquets of flowers, tied with flowing ribbons of white silk, adorned the ends of each pew, their fragrance sweetening the usually musty air. Sunlight, streaming through the stained-glass windows, had scattered iridescent jewels of light in their path.

Seeing the tears in her mother's eyes brought tears to her own. Seeing Maxwell waiting for her at the altar stoked those infernal butterflies into a frenzy again. He stood beside a man she assumed, by his likeness, to be Finlay, who also appeared to be his only guest.

Then her beloved father had lifted her veil, kissed her cheek, and given her to Maxwell, a poignant moment indeed. Yet, despite the beauty and ambience, Louisa couldn't help but be aware of the circumstances that had led to this day. If not for her foolishness, the man awaiting her at the altar should, in fact, have already been married to someone else.

Did he have regrets?

But then, "You look beautiful, Louisa," he'd whispered, as

she'd taken her place beside him. A warm blush had arisen in her cheeks, his words enough to settle her fears. She breathed in his familiar scent of bergamot and mint and spoke her vows with confidence. After the ring had been placed on her finger, and the vicar had made the final announcement, Maxwell had leaned in and placed a gentle kiss on her lips. The resulting tingle warmed Louisa's cheeks and set her heart racing.

She, Louisa Rose Northcott, was now the wife of Maxwell Benedict Harlow.

She could scarcely believe it. She'd expected to feel different, as if wearing a wedding ring would change her somehow. That, in becoming Mrs. Maxwell Harlow, what remained of Louisa the girl would be eradicated, leaving only the Louisa the woman behind. It hadn't. To her mild surprise, she felt no difference at all. Her status had changed, off course, but not her. Oddly, she took comfort from it.

Now, back at Highfield Hall for the wedding breakfast, introductions had been properly made, since most of the guests hadn't met Maxwell. Currently, he was chatting with Louisa's grandmother, Lady Hutton, the dowager countess. Well, not chatting, Louisa mused. Grandmama Hutton did not usually chat with anyone.

She conversed.

"Do you think he'll survive?" a male voice said, in Louisa's ear. "He's formidable when confronting a group of investors in a boardroom, but I get the feeling he might have met his match with her ladyship."

Louisa smiled up at Finlay, Maxwell's younger brother. They'd been introduced at the church, and she'd liked him immediately. The family resemblance manifested in little things; the similarity in height, the slight upward slant of the eyes when he smiled, as well as the smile itself, which seemed to come more easily to him than his older brother. His hair, a rich brown, was a shade lighter than Maxwell's, though he had the same dark eyes.

And the same charming accent.

"Well, they've been conversing for at least five minutes," Louisa replied, "and I don't believe Grandmama has huffed once."

"Huffing is bad?"

"Very."

"Then maybe he's giving her the sales talk. Before you know it, she'll be a shareholder in the company."

Louisa laughed. "Now, that would be an achievement."

Finlay glanced about. "This is a remarkable house, I must say. The stories it could tell."

Louisa nodded. "Endless, I should think. The site has been in use for about eight hundred years all told, although little remains of the original castle."

"Has it been in your family that entire time?"

She shook her head. "Just the past six hundred years, though it comes down through my mother's family, not my father's."

He laughed softly. "You make six hundred years sound like six months. Do you think I could have a tour of the place sometime? Not today, of course."

"By all means, and why not today? I'm sure Julian would be happy to oblige. He loves showing it off." Louisa looked about. "There he is. Follow me."

"Are you sure?" Finlay asked. "I don't want to impose."

She waved a nonchalant hand. "It's not an imposition at all."

Julian, as expected, cheerfully agreed to the request and went off with Finlay, leaving Louisa with Josiah.

Of all her siblings, Josiah was the one she saw the least. As an artist at the Royal Academy, he lived permanently in London, much preferring city life to that of rural Yorkshire. He'd always been a little bit *bohemién*, going his own way rather than moving with the crowd. Being the second-born sibling, he filled the gap between Julian and Louisa. Though he matched his elder brother in height, they shared little else in appearance. Josiah's tousled mass of tawny curls and striking blue eyes perfectly represented his artistic persona. Louisa adored him and secretly envied his unconventional approach to life.

"So, where are you going for your honeymoon, Lou?" he asked, eyeing the dessert table.

Louisa scoffed. "I can't tell you that."

"Why not? I won't tell anyone." Josiah shoved a sugared plum in his mouth, frowning as he chewed. "Florence, perhaps? Paris? Both?"

Louisa shook her head. "My lips are sealed."

"All right, how about this." Blue eyes twinkling, he cast a surreptitious glance around the room. "You tell me your secret and I'll tell you mine."

"You have a secret, Joe?"

"An absolute whopper." Josiah's eyes widened. "Ooh, marzipan."

Louisa chuckled. "You haven't stopped eating since we got back from the church. Do you not feed yourself in London?"

"I'm your cliché starving artist, dear sister." He waggled a brow. "Or, at least, I was. Sold a few pieces recently. Acquired several commissions as well, including a couple that should prove to be rather lucrative. Beginning to make a name for myself."

"Good for you, but even without those, you can't actually be starving. What on earth do you spend your allowance on?"

"That would be telling." He bit into the piece of marzipan. "Is it Switzerland?"

"Not exactly."

"Not exactly means I'm not even close." He pondered. "Venice."

"No. Why do you want to know?"

"Just curious, that's all. Keep your secret then, and I'll keep mine." He shrugged. "Thing is, I'll know about yours when you get back from wherever anyway, but you'll always be left wondering about mine."

Louisa made a face. "Oh, very well, just as long as you keep it to yourself."

"Of course." He drew an invisible cross over his heart. "I

don't have to ask if you'll keep mine, because I know you will. Ask me why."

Louisa laughed. "Why?"

"Because you wouldn't dare tell it to anyone else."

"Is it that bad?" Louisa glanced about making sure no one was in earshot. "All right, if you must know, we're going to the Lake District."

"The Lake District." Frowning, Josiah licked his sugary fingers. "I mean, it's a nice enough area and all, but I thought he'd be whisking you away somewhere a little more exotic than that."

Secretly, Louisa had thought so too. Or, at least, hoped so. "I don't think he likes to leave his business for too long," she explained. "Besides, it doesn't really matter where we go. We'll be together, which is what counts."

Josiah gave her a cynical look. "Bollocks," he said. "You hoped for gondolas and the *Piazza San Marco*, not cart tracks and sheep. I can see it written all over your face."

"Oh, be quiet," Louisa said, without malice. "And it's not all cart tracks and sheep. Actually, we're going for a ride on The Lady of the Lake steamer. She's just been launched on Windermere and is supposed to be quite the thing. Right. I've told you mine, now you tell me yours."

"I'll begin by giving you a clue." He lifted his gaze. "Ceilings."

Louisa looked up as well. "Ceilings."

"Yes. I paint them." He winked. "Under a pseudonym."

She blinked. "And that's your secret?"

He sighed. "Oh, come on, Lou. You're not normally this obtuse."

"What do you mean? What am I missing?"

"The fact that I use a pseudonym." He nibbled on a strawberry. "Why would I need to do that, do you think?"

She cocked her head, pondering. "Um, I suppose because you don't want people to know your real name?"

"Exactly."

"The reason being?"

He huffed. "Ye gods. All this marriage nonsense has obviously scrambled your brains. All right, one final clue." He popped the remainder of the strawberry in his mouth and winked again. "Richmond."

It took a moment or two, and then understanding hit Louisa with only a little less force than a cannonball. A hand flew to her mouth, stifling a squeak. "Oh, my heavens, Josiah, that wasn't you. Was it? You didn't. *Did* you?"

"Sshhh!" Grinning, he glanced about. "What did you think of it?"

Heat travelled up Louisa's throat. "Please tell me you're making this up."

"I'm not making it up. As a matter of fact, I'm very proud of the work. I've been studying life drawing and nude art for the past while. I thought you knew that."

"But these people weren't just *nude*, Josiah," she whispered. "They were…*occupied*."

He narrowed his eyes. "You obviously looked, then."

The heat flooded her cheeks. "Only for a moment."

The grin returned. "Your blush says otherwise."

"I'm blushing because I'm shocked. What if someone recognizes you?"

"Highly unlikely. I'm not often out in society and I'm always masked when I work on these things." He waggled a brow. "Which all adds to the erotic mystery of it."

"Oh, Josiah." She shook her head. "I can't believe it."

"What can't you believe, my dear?" Their Aunt Eleanor, Countess Hutton, came up to the table and regarded the offerings.

"Oh, um…" Louisa scrambled to find a response and looked over to where Maxwell stood with the dowager countess. "I can't believe how long Grandmama has been talking to Max. She was scowling at him over her spectacles when we first got back from the church. I can't imagine what they're talking about."

Her aunt's eyes widened. "Ooh, marzipan."

"Allow me, Aunt." Josiah lifted the plate and offered it, giving Louisa an amused sideways glance.

"Thank you, dear. And they're discussing the future," the countess replied, nibbling on her sweetmeat. "Rail travel, specifically. Your husband has dazzled her with his knowledge, it seems. Quite the achievement, especially considering she initially engaged him to reassure herself that he could actually converse using words of more than two syllables."

Louisa gasped. "Maxwell is very well-educated. He attended Edinburgh University."

"Oh, I know, my dear, but according to your grandmother, if it's not Oxford or Cambridge, it doesn't count." She regarded Josiah. "How are you enjoying the Royal Academy, Josiah? Are you working on anything of note?"

"I'm enjoying it immensely, Aunt Eleanor. And yes, I'm working on a couple of new projects at the moment, but sworn to secrecy, I'm afraid."

Having heard more than enough about Josiah's projects, Louisa quickly excused herself and left to wander around the room. She spent some time chatting to the twins and her cousins before ending up beside her parents and her uncle, Lord Hutton.

"Not that we're in a hurry to see you leave, dearest," Grace said, "but I believe you're scheduled to leave at two o'clock, and you've yet to change. We should perhaps start making preparations."

"I'm beginning to think I'll be setting off by myself," Louisa muttered, watching as Maxwell smiled at something her grandmother said, "since my husband appears to have turned his attentions elsewhere."

"It's quite the spectacle," Lord Hutton said. "I expected her to give him one of her renowned tongue lashings and leave him bleeding on the carpet. And instead, she's virtually flirting with the fellow."

Louisa giggled. "Maybe you should go and rescue him, Papa. He is your son-in-law, after all."

"No, I'm sorry, my dear." Aldous folded his arms. "He's on his own."

"Well, perhaps you could let him know that Louisa has gone upstairs to change into her travelling clothes." Grace took Louisa's hand. "Come along, my darling."

A half-hour later, Louisa surveyed a different reflection in her mirror, though it still pleased her. Her dress of shot-silk shimmered from green to blue as she moved, reminding her of peacock feathers. And her blue cashmere shawl, so soft to the touch, was light, yet warm. The combination was both comfortable yet fashionable.

"Absolutely perfect," Grace said, peering over Louisa's shoulder. "As indeed, the entire day has been. Have you enjoyed yourself?"

"Yes, Mama. Very much."

"My daughter." Grace drew a shaky breath. "Married."

Louisa drew a breath of her own. "But perhaps not quite the match you—"

"Hush. Actually, I think Maxwell is a fine match. I have no fear for your well-being at all." She appeared to ponder for a moment. "Are you worried about tonight, dearest?"

Louisa raised her brows. "Should I be?"

"Oh, no." A faint blush arose in her mother's cheeks. "That is, I'm sure Maxwell will be kind to you."

"I'm sure he will be too, Mama."

"If you have any questions about what will occur, you may ask them of me if you wish," her mother said, with a distinct lack of enthusiasm.

Louisa shrugged. "It's not necessary, Mama. Josiah explained it all to me when I was sixteen."

Her mother gasped and then her eyes narrowed. "I am going to kill your brother."

Louisa laughed. "To be fair, Mama, I pestered him about it. And besides, I was also witness to Lord Richmond's ceiling, remember?" She cringed inwardly. Josiah had not only explained it to her, he had illustrated it as well!

"Oh, gracious, so you were." Her mother blew out a breath and fanned herself with a hand. "I don't even want to think about that. I think it best we head downstairs, then."

The subsequent goodbyes were bitter-sweet. It occurred to Louisa that she was officially leaving her beloved home. She was excited about moving into the manor, of course, which also meant she'd be living close by.

But still.

"I understand you'll be moving into the manor as well," she said to Finlay a little later, as she prepared to climb into the carriage.

He cleared his throat and cast a glance at Maxwell. "Actually, I moved in two days ago. I trust there are no objections. I can take a room in the village if you prefer."

"Goodness, no, I have no objections at all," she replied. "I've been aware of the arrangements from the start."

"I'll be keeping an eye on things while you're away." He cocked his head at Maxwell. "I think my brother is worried his wee empire will founder without him at the helm."

"As long as we don't have any fires or workforce disruptions, there shouldn't be any problems, Fin," Maxwell said. "If something urgent crops up, you know where to find me."

Louisa tried to hide her surprise. What would Maxwell define as urgent enough to cut their honeymoon short? "I'm sure Finlay can deal with any crisis," she said.

"Quite possibly," Maxwell replied. "But I need to be kept informed of such things in order to make that judgement."

Finlay cleared his throat again. "I'm sure everything will be fine," he said. "Have a wonderful honeymoon."

"Thank you, Finlay," Louisa replied. "I'm sure we will, won't we Maxwell?" She looked at her new husband, willing him to assure her with a bold "yes".

But Maxwell merely smiled and helped her into the carriage.

CHAPTER TEN

THE ROOM AT the White Rose Hotel, where Louisa would be spending her first night as a bride, was certainly more luxurious than she'd expected. A large, canopied bed, already turned down, dominated the space. But the room also offered a cozy sitting area by the unlit fireplace as well as a table for two by the bay window. The general feeling was one of comfort and intimacy.

"It's a lovely room," she said, her fingers trembling a little as she untied her bonnet. Being alone in this bedchamber with Maxwell Harlow—with her *husband*—set her nerves tingling. The mere thought of his hands on her body, his mouth on her mouth, was more intoxicating than wine.

"I'm sure we'll be very comfortable," Maxwell replied. "Are you hungry? If so, I thought we might eat in here, unless you'd prefer to go down to the dining room."

"In here would be fine," she replied, doubting she'd be able to actually eat anything at all. "I'm not terribly hungry, though. Just something light, perhaps?"

"Shall I fetch a menu, or do you trust me to choose?"

"I trust you, of course."

"Leave it to me, then." He lifted her hand to his lips. "I'll be back shortly."

After he left, Louisa set her bonnet aside, shrugged off her cloak, and wandered over to the window to gaze out at the pastoral scene. The five-hour carriage ride, with one change of horses, meant they had arrived at the hotel with plenty of daylight to spare. It was a pretty place, the first of two stops on the way to their final destination: the Lakeview Hotel, on the shores of Lake Windermere, Westmorland, where they would be staying for a week. In the not-too-distant future, Maxwell had told her, the region would be serviced by rail. But for now, horse and carriage served as the only mode of transport.

Being ensconced in the carriage with Maxwell had allowed Louisa to get to know him a little better. One of the first things she'd asked was how he'd managed to beguile her grandmother.

"I wasn't aware I had beguiled her." he'd replied. "I didn't fawn or cower either, nor did I try to usurp her opinions or point of view. I simply conversed with her. She's an intelligent woman, needle sharp, and just a wee bit feisty, much like another lady I used to know."

Louisa pondered for a moment. "Your mother?"

He nodded. "Aye."

Louisa's smile expressed sympathy. "I should like to have met her. Did she live long enough to see your success?"

"Not quite. She died not long after I left university. She always told me I'd be successful, though." Maxwell shrugged. "My parents were strict, but not unkind. I have fond memories of both."

Other conversation had followed; shared tales of childhood and family, which mostly served to demonstrate the difference in their social statuses, and how little they knew of each other. There had been no animosity, but not too much lightheartedness either. Maxwell's sober personality had shown little sign of wavering.

Yet, despite that, or maybe because of it, he continued to affect Louisa in a way she couldn't quite fathom. It was not due to any single attribute, but rather a collection of things. His baritone voice, with its delicious accent, had the ability to lift the hair on her flesh. She liked how he gave her his full attention whenever she spoke. The way he moved, with purpose and confidence, excited her. And the rare bestowal of his smile—his *genuine* smile—made her feel as though she'd succeeded, somehow, in reaching a guarded part of him.

As for his eyes… at times, when he looked at her, they seemed to darken, as if reflecting on something she had yet to experience. As they had when he'd questioned her shortly before they'd arrived at the hotel.

"Do you know what will take place between us tonight, Louisa? Have you been told what to expect? What you will see and feel? I know what you saw in Richmond's study, but the sexual act depicted in a painting does not necessarily demonstrate the pleasure of it. Unless, of course, one has had previous experience."

The raw candor of his remarks sent her unprepared and innocent mind into a dither. "I'm aware of what *occurs*, Maxwell," she managed at last, her cheeks burning. "But I have no notion of what to expect from it. How could I?"

"Then it would appear you have never pleasured yourself," he replied, "which surprises me, frankly."

Her blush of modesty turned to one of indignation. "Should I be offended by that remark, sir?"

"Absolutely not, my dear." Amusement edged his voice. "It is simply that you are, by nature, curious, so I assumed, therefore, you'd be somewhat aware of what your body is capable of."

For reasons she couldn't begin to define, his response offended her even more. "Well, given the lack of my awareness," she said, "I trust I can depend on you to show me exactly what my body is capable of."

And then it appeared. The genuine smile, one generated by emotion rather than mere obligation. "Aye, lass," he replied, a slight huskiness to his voice, "I think I can manage that."

The sound of the bedroom door opening pulled Louisa from her reflections. Maxwell entered, followed by two young men, one carrying a tray of food, the other, a bottle of champagne, and two glasses.

"On the table, if you please," Maxwell said, and gave the lad a coin for his service.

LESS THAN AN hour later, the simple platter of local cheese, freshly churned butter, warm bread rolls, ripe strawberries, and succulent melon had been reasonably demolished. The champagne bottle had likewise been emptied of its cellar-chilled contents and Maxwell suspected his new bride, having consumed three glasses of the stuff in rapid succession, was just a teeny bit tipsy.

"That, Mr. Harlow—" Louisa sucked strawberry juice off her finger, making a deliciously provocative, if slightly indelicate, slurping sound as she did so—"was absolutely perfect."

Maxwell, who had endured numerous erections since leaving Highfield, groaned inwardly as his cock stirred anew. "I'm glad you enjoyed it, Mrs. Harlow." He rose to his feet and held out a hand. She took it, a blush rising in her cheeks as she stood.

"Mrs. Harlow." She giggled and hiccupped. "Oops, excuse me. I suppose I shall have to practice signing my new name."

"Aye, but not tonight." Maxwell traced the pad of his thumb along her jawline and then tipped her chin upward. "May I kiss you, Louisa?"

Surprise showed in the widened of her eyes, as if she had not expected to be asked for permission. His consideration was acknowledged by a subsequent appreciative smile. "Yes, Maxwell," she said, "you may kiss me, of course."

Keeping his touch light, he cupped her cheek with one hand and bent to caress her lips with his. He applied gentle pressure at first, moving his mouth tentatively over hers, barely controlling a growing desire to coax her mouth open. As desire grew, he coiled an arm around her waist and anchored her against him, while teasing the seam of her lips with his tongue.

To his delight, Louisa responded with enthusiasm. Her hands slid up his chest and over his shoulders, fingers burrowing into the curls at his nape as her lips parted. Maxwell deepened the kiss, tasting the sweetness of strawberry on Louisa's tongue. The little sound she made turned his cock rigid against her belly, their bodies shielded, of course, by several layers of clothing.

Unwanted clothing.

Still kissing her, Maxwell slid his other arm around her waist, both hands working in unison to unhook the fasteners on her gown. He frowned. *Silly, fiddly little hooks. Why so many of the damn things?* That would be something to invent, he thought, fasteners that took seconds to open and close, rather than bloody hours.

Louisa broke the kiss. "Wait," she said, and, with remarkable adeptness, proceeded to finish what Maxwell had begun, shrugging off both gown and petticoats and kicking them aside. Now, clad in only her stays and underclothes, she arched her brows and gazed up at him, innocent, yet brazen. "Shall I remove the rest of my clothing, Mr. Harlow, or will you?"

Maxwell regarded the woman he'd married and secretly thanked God for the blessed ramifications of scandal... and perhaps the three glasses of champagne she'd consumed. "I will," he said, casting off his jacket with all haste. "But you have to do the same for me."

An impish smile appeared, her top teeth digging into her bottom lip as she reached for his cravat.

Not even five minutes later, breathing hard, they stood naked amidst a careless scattering of clothes. Only one thing remained undisturbed, and Maxwell's deft fingers soon took care of that.

With a little bit of manipulation, the dispersal of a few hair-pins released a silky cascade of mahogany curls that fell to Louisa's waist. Silhouetted against the sunset's fiery glow, she looked not unlike some mythical goddess.

"Good Lord," Maxwell placed his hand on her left breast, the nipple pebble-hard against his palm, "you truly are beautiful."

Louisa glanced down at the scattered underclothes and wrinkled her nose. "I assume there's little point in unpacking my nightgown."

Maxwell bit back an urge to laugh. "No point at all, my dear."

"Mmm." Her gaze returned to Maxwell's face before descending slowly down his throat, over his chest and abdomen, and stopping at last where his cock protruded in stiff readiness from its nest of dark curls. Her blatant scrutiny was enough to make it twitch, and her eyes widened a little. Then she touched the tip of it.

Maxwell sucked in a quick breath and Louisa snatched her hand away, her gaze, now distraught, settling squarely back on his face. "Should I not—?"

"Aye, you most definitely *should*." He guided her hand back to his cock. "It took me by surprise, that's all."

"Oh," she said, and renewed her previous examination, tracing her fingertips from the tip to the base. Then she closed her hand around it.

Maxwell's throat went dry.

"It feels like silk," she said, moving her hand up and down its length. "Does it hurt, being hard like that?"

"No, lass, it does not," Maxwell said, through gritted teeth. "But, by God, what you're doing is torturous, nonetheless. Come here."

She let out a squeal of laughter as he hoisted her into his arms, carried her to the bed, and dropped her, rather unceremoniously, onto the mattress. Then he settled himself beside her, propped himself up on an elbow, and stroked a hand over her breast and down to the slight contour of her stomach.

Where it stayed.

His fingers itched to go further, to seek out the treasure hidden between her legs, to explore their untouched depths. He was eager to take her to a place she'd never been, to make her his. But he also wanted to take his time, to seduce and tease.

He half-covered her and claimed her mouth again, his hand returning to the swell of her breast to tug gently on the nipple. A sound of pleasure came from her throat, the vibration caressing his tongue as he continued to kiss her. As before, her arms wound themselves around his neck, her spine arching slightly, sealing flesh to flesh, her skin like cool satin against his. He inhaled, breathing in her essence; something floral, subtle and manufactured. It blended with another, this one less sweet, more sensuous, utterly natural and exquisitely feminine. Parting with another delicious little whimper, Louisa fidgeted in his arms, rubbing her outer thigh against his erection.

Bloody hell.

Had he ever been this hard? They'd barely begun, and he was close to spending already. So much for a slow seduction. His hand shifted back to the hollow of her waist as he eased a leg between hers, nudging them open. Then, leaving a trail of kisses on the pale flesh of her throat, his mouth moved to her breast and drew on the hard peak.

Louisa's soft intake of breath coincided with another arch of her spine, her fingers ploughing through his hair as he suckled. "Oh, Maxwell," she whispered on an exhale, the utterance one of sheer bliss.

He acknowledged it with a low groan and slid his hand between her legs, delighted to be met by the sultry heat of her arousal. At first, he merely stroked her, smiling against her breast as she parted with another sigh of obvious pleasure. Then his thumb sought out her most sensitive spot, manipulating and teasing as his fingers—first one, then two—penetrated her, probing gently, thrusting and withdrawing in a slow, sensuous rhythm. Louisa's hips lifted, pushing against his hand as she released an exquisite moan.

"Does it feel pleasurable, Louisa?" He licked and nibbled at her nipple as his busy hand moved a little faster, a little harder. "Being touched down there?"

"Oh, yes, yes, it does," she muttered, writhing beneath him.

"Please don't stop, Maxwell. Oh, God, it feels so... I want...oh, my...oh, my...*lord*."

He felt her inner muscles clench around his fingers and lifted his head to watch as she experienced her first climax. Eyes half-closed, lips parted, she issued a soft cry, her body shuddering against his. His cock strained and he bit down, using every ounce of his self-control not to follow her over that euphoric precipice.

"That was beautiful to watch," he murmured.

"Gracious, I didn't expect..." Chest still heaving, she shifted beneath him. "I mean, is that... does that happen every time?"

He gave a soft laugh. "I shall endeavor to make sure it does."

"Mmm." Her fingers trailed down his throat as she regarded him through half-closed eyelids. "I suppose this means I'm aware now."

"Not quite," he replied, and moved to cover her, easing her legs farther apart. His mouth found hers once more, his kiss more demanding as he rocked, gently, atop her, his cock gliding back and forth over her slick centre. He had not been wrong in his presumption that the lass would be a willing participant between the sheets. She was utterly without guile, not fettered by puritanical restraints, but eager to embrace the pleasures he could offer. Her trust in him was quite obviously absolute, which for reasons he couldn't quite fathom, was also incredibly arousing.

He reached down to position himself, watching Louisa's face as he finally claimed her, replacing innocence with awareness, her resistance slight and, thankfully, easily surpassed. She watched him too, eyes soft, cheeks flushed with the aftermath of ecstasy. As he seated himself fully inside her, she flinched and released a little gasp.

He stilled.

"Are you all right, lass?" he murmured, stroking her hair back from her face. "Did I hurt you?"

"Only for a moment, but no longer, and it is not... unpleas-ant." She shifted beneath him, an innocent yet highly sensual movement that caused him to suck in a soft breath.

"I'll be gentle," he said. And probably quick, he thought, as he began to move in a rhythm as old as time, seeking his own fulfillment. Louisa responded, writhing beneath him, driving him even more rapidly toward completion. Soon after, she arched her slender body, his name on her lips like a plea for mercy as she spiraled into ecstasy once more. And this time, he followed.

LATER THAT NIGHT, Louisa opened her eyes to candlelight and the sound of a quill scratching on paper. She blinked and lifted up on an elbow, squinting into the low light to see Maxwell, clad in his dressing-gown, seated at the table by the window, bent over a paper, pen in hand.

"Maxwell?" She rubbed her eyes, trying to ease a slight headache. "What are you doing?"

"Making a few notes," he said, still scribbling. "I didn't mean to wake you. I just needed to jot down some ideas while they were fresh in my mind."

"Oh." She stifled a yawn. "What is the hour?"

"A little after three."

"Goodness." She flopped back onto her pillow. "It's awfully early. Or maybe terribly late."

"Aye, I'm afraid I don't sleep much. But don't worry. We'll have separate bedrooms when we get back to Northcott. That way, I won't disturb you."

Louisa's foggy brain tried to make sense of what he'd said. "Separate bedrooms?"

"For sleeping, aye." His chair creaked as he turned to look at her. "*Only* for sleeping."

Her responding smile, which she aimed at the ceiling, was perfunctory. It was not at all uncommon, of course, for husbands and wives to have separate chambers. But, in Louisa's mind, it should perhaps not be quite so soon after their marriage. Her romantic ideal was falling asleep in her husband's arms and waking up in them as well. She pressed a hand to her forehead and suppressed a sigh.

Maxwell muttered something under his breath as he set his pen down and rose to his feet. Then he shrugged off his dressing gown and climbed back into bed, taking her into his arms. "I've upset you, haven't I? Damn it, Louisa. I'm sorry."

"No, I'm not upset." She trailed a fingertip over the light bristle on his jaw. "Well, all right, maybe just a *little* upset. But you did warn me, to be fair. No flowery or romantic notions, I believe you said."

"It seems my sense of timing is also abysmal," he said. "I apologize."

"No, it's all right." Her lips pursed as she pondered. "Besides, who knows? By the time we get back to Northcott, you might have become accustomed to sleeping with me."

"*Not* sleeping is the issue." He stroked her hair. "For some reason, I do my best thinking at night and tend to wander about."

"I see." Stifling another yawn, she snuggled into his chest and listened to the solid beat of his heart. "In that case, for the rest of our honeymoon, if you awaken me at some God-forsaken hour, I shall just roll over and go back to sleep."

"Ah, but what if there are occasions when I don't *want* you to go back to sleep?" His hand wandered down her back and caressed her bottom. "In fact, I believe this might be one of those occasions."

Louisa felt his arousal pressing against her and suppressed a shiver of excitement, but huffed, feigning nonchalance. "Well, I suppose I could make an exception in that case. Do you have something special in mind?"

He laughed softly. "I certainly do," he said, and lowered his mouth to hers.

CHAPTER ELEVEN

LOUISA SAT AT the writing desk in The Lakeview Hotel library and read over the latest entry in her new journal. The book, bound in fine, soft leather, had a been a gift from Maxwell, one of several that had been waiting for her when they'd arrived at their honeymoon destination. The journal had been accompanied by a gold fountain pen inscribed with her name, and a crystal inkwell. Her husband, while not a man given to poetic lines or public shows of affection, was certainly generous.

"I'm glad it pleases you," he'd said, when she'd expressed her delight and surprise at receiving the journal. "Given your love of the written word, I thought you might enjoy writing a few of your own."

It was an unexpected gift, one she could have neither imagined nor foreseen. Louisa loved to read, but journaling—keeping a diary—was something she had never done. Till now. And she'd since discovered that she loved it. The other gifts included a pretty pearl brooch and an ivory-and-lace fan. But the journal was Louisa's favorite. The most recent entry detailed this, their final day in the Lake District. There had not been much to tell. Apart from an after-luncheon stroll through the village, it had been a lazy day, spent mostly in their room or in the hotel's lounge.

Tomorrow, at an early hour, they would begin their three-day journey back to Northcott Manor. Louisa could quite easily have stayed a while longer, though she had the feeling Maxwell was keen to resume his industrious life. His nighttime restlessness had worsened as the days passed, though their larger suite at The Lakeview Hotel meant that he disturbed her less, since he could retire to their private sitting-room.

Pen in hand, she pondered over the composition of her closing sentence. How to sum it all up.

Everything had been practically perfect. Their hotel suite, with its beamed ceilings and soft carpets, blended rustic charm with luxurious comfort. The food had been excellent, and the views of the lake and surrounding hills were majestic, to say the least.

They had made love every night, often twice, sometimes in the morning, and on the occasional afternoon. While there had been no verbal expressions of love from either of them, Louisa refused to entertain any feelings of disappointment. That her husband found her desirable was not in any doubt at all. Besides, she told herself, they were still learning about each other. However, whether he knew it or not, Maxwell had already captured Louisa's heart.

With the exception of two soggy days, the weather had cooperated. Consequently, there had taken several outings to local places of interest, a picnic on the shores of Windermere, and an unforgettable trip on the newly launched steamer, The Lady of the Lake. A detailed account of that, and every other day, now existed in the pages of Louisa's journal. With one exception.

That particular day had been yet another surprise from Maxwell, and Louisa still didn't know how he'd managed to arrange it. She flipped the pages back to four days earlier: Tuesday, the twelfth of June, 1845.

The outing that day had been presented as a mystery, one prearranged by Maxwell who refused to give even a hint of what it entailed. "Bring your journal," he'd said. "I have a feeling you might need it."

The mystery deepened.

After a short carriage ride under sunny skies, they'd arrived at a magnificent old house tucked against a hillside, with an army of sweet-smelling roses clambering haphazardly over its white-washed walls. According to the sign at the gate, the house was called *Rydal Mount*. Louisa had never laid eyes on the house before, but she recognized its name. And she knew who lived there.

To her absolute surprise and delight, she and Maxwell had subsequently spent almost an hour in the owner's company; a precious measure of time with a man whose name was known worldwide and already assured a place in history.

The experience had been one of the most memorable in Louisa's life, yet she had written nothing about that day in her journal. First of all, it was hardly necessary. Each and every detail had been burned into her memory. Besides, it was an event that merited a verbal retelling, time and again; a tale to be passed down through the years. Mostly, though, she simply could not bring herself to write upon a page that had already been claimed by a master poet, even though he had written but two short lines: a grand total of eighteen words.

Plus, his signature.

Poetry is the first and last of all knowledge
It is as immortal as the heart of man.

William Wordsworth.

It was not every day that one had the privilege of taking tea with the Poet Laureate of the United Kingdom. True, the visit had been relatively brief, and Mr. Wordsworth had used part of it to voice his concerns to Maxwell about the encroachment of the railway into his beloved Lake District. But he'd also indulged Louisa with a tour of his wonderful gardens, including his 'writing-hut' with its spectacular views and where much of his poetry had been written.

It had been an unforgettable experience.

Louisa smiled and turned back to the current page in her

journal, the closure to that day's entry now set in her mind.

I was about to write that our honeymoon has been wonderful, but that would imply it is over. I much prefer to believe that it is only just beginning.

CHAPTER TWELVE

HARLOW INDUSTRIES HAD not been thrust into liquidation during Maxwell's absence. There had been a couple of issues, however. Something about a smelting-furnace failure in the South Shields plant and a warehouse fire in Glasgow, although the latter had been quickly contained and caused little damage. As a result, an exchange of words had taken place between Maxwell and Finlay, their clarity muffled by the closed door of Maxwell's office. Since then, his demeanor had hardened a little around the edges. Or perhaps, Louisa mused, it had simply returned to normal.

Finlay appeared nonplussed and remained as friendly as ever, but despite Louisa's protests, insisted on taking dinner in his room each evening. "You'll see me at breakfast, and you might see me at luncheon, but, unless my being there is absolutely necessary, the evenings are for you and Maxwell alone. I'm quite comfortable in my room, Louisa. It's no hardship at all."

Of course, Louisa's hope that her husband would become accustomed to sharing a bed with her all night had not material-ized. As alluded to, they each had their own chambers at Northcott, separated by an adjoining door, though Maxwell had again made it clear that the arrangement was simply a considera-tion for her, due to his insomnia. Their intimate relationship remained just as spirited, however, and the adjoining door usually stood open till well into the night.

Despite that, there had still been no verbal declarations of love from Maxwell. Louisa knew where her heart lay, but hesitated to speak from it, fearful that he would not reciprocate in kind, or worse, feel obliged to do so. She told herself words didn't really matter, that Maxwell showed his affection for her in other ways. At least, he did when he wasn't ensconced with Finlay in what had been the study but had now become his office. Apart from the evenings, Louisa hadn't seen much of her husband since returning from their honeymoon.

Not that she'd been idle either. Along with Northcott Manor's new, rosy-cheeked housekeeper, Mrs. Hartley, Louisa had been busy most of the week going through the manor from top to bottom, arranging and rearranging things. She'd also spent time getting to know the rest of the new staff as well as interviewing a couple of potential lady's maids.

"Out of the two, I think I prefer Mrs. Archer." Louisa sat at her dressing table, tilting her head as she put on her amethyst earrings. "Mrs. Talbot is a little too matronly for my tastes."

Maxwell, leaning nonchalantly against the mantel, frowned as he pondered. "Talbot's references are actually the most impressive of the two, although Archer's aren't too shoddy either. I want to verify both of them, though, before you make a decision. I like to know who I have living under my roof, and especially those working in close proximity to my wife. That being so, please do not ever hire anyone in my absence, Louisa. At least, not without checking with me first."

"Of course not." She held up her necklace, a delicate gold chain with an amethyst and diamond pendant. "Would you mind?"

He moved to stand behind her, took the necklace and placed it around her neck, a frown furrowing his brow as he fastened the delicate clasp. A tingle ran across Louisa's skin as his fingers brushed against her nape. "By the way," he said, "Finlay and I will be leaving for South Shields on Wednesday morning."

"Oh." She absorbed the information. "How long will you be away?"

"At least a week, I should think." Task completed, he straightened and regarded her in the mirror, his expression wary. "Maybe less if things go smoothly. Perhaps you could spend a night or two at Highfield while I'm gone?"

"Yes, I might do that." Determined not to validate his wariness, Louisa centered the pendant at her throat and summoned up a bright smile. "Actually, if you have no objection, I'd like to pay a visit to Francesca's in Knaresborough while you're away. Do a little bit of shopping."

"No objection at all," he said, his expression relaxing, "as long as you have McKinney drive you and have Francesca invoice me for your purchases."

Louisa shook her head. "I have my own money, Max."

"You'll not use any of it, my dear, I insist. Also, if your maid's employment hasn't been approved by then, you'll take one of the housemaids as a companion. All right?"

"Very well," she replied, rising to her feet as the gong sounded. "We're having lamb for dinner."

"Good, I'm starving." Maxwell took her into his arms and placed a gentle kiss on her mouth. "You look beautiful, Louisa, as always."

As PLANNED, MAXWELL and Finlay left on Thursday morning. And, since the references had been verified, Louisa's new lady's maid, Mrs. Archer, arrived on Friday afternoon. On Monday morning, having taken the weekend familiarizing her new maid with the way of things, Louisa had Byron saddled and set off to Highfield Hall, taking the shorter route over the moor.

The visit would be a surprise for her parents and siblings, whom she hadn't seen or spoken to since returning from her honeymoon. The warm and enthusiastic welcome she received made her realize how much she'd missed her family. To be living so close to them was, indeed, a blessing.

"Will you be staying the night, then?" Grace, her mother asked, upon learning that Maxwell wouldn't be back till the end of the week.

Louisa shook her head. "No, Mama, it's just a short visit this time, I'm afraid. I'm still sorting things out at the manor."

"Of course," Grace said. "Well, if you need any help or advice, dearest, be sure to let me know."

"I will, Mama. Thank you."

"But you are staying for luncheon, yes?" her father asked. "We want to hear all your news."

Louisa smiled. "I'd love to stay for luncheon, Papa. I have so much to tell you all. First of all, I suppose you should know where we went."

"Well, given the amount of time you've been away, I'm guessing it was probably somewhere in England," he said, "or maybe Scotland."

"Your first guess was correct," Louisa said. "We went to the Lake District."

"The Lake District?" Clara and Evie declared in unison.

"We thought Florence," Clara said, looking decidedly unimpressed.

Evie assumed a similar expression. "Or Venice."

"I thought Brighton," Arthur said.

"Well, I think it's nice that you stayed in England," Grace said. "We have plenty to offer here, and the Lake District is an exceptionally beautiful area. How was the weather, dear?"

"We had two rainy days, Mama, but otherwise it was fine."

"Lucky," Julian said. "Where did you stay?"

"The Lakeview Hotel," Louisa pulled a face at the twins. "And it was *lovely*, I'll have you know."

"One of the best hotels in the region," Aldous said, nodding. "I'm assuming you took a ride on the new steamer? I read about the launch."

"The Lady of the Lake. Yes, we did, and it was absolutely

splendid." Louisa reached into the cloth bag she'd brought with her. "But that was not the best part. I simply have to show you this. It's a journal, a gift from Maxwell, and I want you to read the entry I made on the twelfth. Here, Papa, you first."

She handed it to her father who turned to the appropriate page, where he blinked and blinked again as his brows lifted. "Good Lord," he said, gaping at Louisa. "Is this authentic?"

Louisa laughed. "It certainly is. It had all been pre-arranged, apparently. We spent almost an hour in the gentleman's company. He showed us around his beautiful garden, and I even sat in his writing-hut for a few minutes. I can still hardly believe it. He was quite charming, though a little sad too, I thought."

"Who are you talking about?" Grace asked, and Aldous passed her the book, resulting in a gasp of obvious amazement. Similar responses continued as the journal made the rounds.

"Very impressive, Lou," Julian handed the journal back to her. "How on earth did Maxwell manage it?"

"He wouldn't say," Louisa replied, hugging the book to her chest, "but it was one of the best days of my life."

The rest of the day was spent like so many others in Louisa's memory. Family chit-chat, friendly arguments, laughter over the lunch table, and afternoon games of cards and dominoes. Then, later in the afternoon, a stroll around Highfield's gardens.

"So, no regrets, Lou?" Julian asked, in a private moment.

She glanced up at him. "About what?"

"Marrying your industrialist."

"No, none." Louisa looped her arm through his. "Maxwell is very kind to me, and extremely generous."

"I'm glad to hear it, though it seems these absences of his will be a regular occurrence."

"Yes, but he made it quite clear how things would be, so I can't really complain."

"Well, at least we're nearby, so you don't have to feel abandoned."

To Louisa's dismay, her brother's remark hit a hidden, sensitive nerve. She swallowed over an unexpected rise of tears and glanced up at him. "I don't feel abandoned, Julian."

"Sorry, Lou," he said. "A bad choice of words. I simply meant that you don't have to stay at the manor by yourself. You know you can always come here whenever you feel the need."

She summoned up a smile. "I know. And, of course, you're always welcome to visit me. Or *us*, when Maxwell is home. In fact, I must arrange a family dinner party. Our cook is excellent."

Julian gave her arm a squeeze. "Just say when."

Louisa left a short while later, her saddlebag now holding another souvenir, that being a rather well-worn lady's hat, complete with pheasant feathers and the odd freckle of dried mud. Once back at Northcott Manor, she placed the hat atop the armoire in her bedroom.

EARLY WEDNESDAY MORNING saw Louisa and Archer on their way to Knaresborough, seated comfortably in the carriage with McKinney at the reins. The plan was to shop, have luncheon, and return to Northcott Manor with daylight to spare.

Francesca Corvinelli's dressmaking-enterprise was not the kind of place one might expect to find in a small Yorkshire town. But, despite its unassuming location on Knaresborough's High Street, the little shop possessed a reputation worthy of any London address.

Francesca Corvinelli's real name was actually Martha Swithenbank, who came, not from the *nobiltà* of Italy, but from a fine Yorkshire family of coopers. However, where her father, uncles, and brothers excelled in the manufacture of barrels and all manner of wooden implements, Martha excelled with a needle and thread and an eye for fashion. Due to demand, she also employed two seamstresses who worked under her close watch. Her patrons knew she didn't have a drop of Italian blood in her, but none of them cared. She was known to everyone as *Francesca*.

McKinney dropped Louisa and Archer off outside the shop mid-morning, with arrangements made to collect them from the Castle Tea Rooms at two o'clock, after luncheon.

"Your timing is absolutely perfect, ma'am," Francesca said, by way of welcome. "I have, only yesterday, received an order of some marvelous fabrics from Paris. Come through."

Almost an hour later, orders had been placed for three new dresses, two sets of underclothes, and a fur-trimmed jacket. "I think that might do for now," Louisa said. "If you could write up the invoice, Francesca."

"Oh, but this green silk is beautiful, ma'am." Archer gestured to the bolt of fabric. "I think it would look lovely on you. Maybe just one more outfit?"

"I agree. With your hair color, ma'am, it would be very flattering," Francesca said. "Perfect for evening attire, when entertaining your guests. May I suggest a layered skirt and matching bodice with a peplum, similar to this?" She turned to a page in her design book. "Perhaps some Brussels lace on the sleeves and collar?"

"Mmm, it is rather lovely." Louisa fingered the silk and surrendered to temptation. "Add it to the list, then. I'm not quite decided about the blue shawl, though. It looks almost violet in this light. I think I might change it for the darker indigo."

She took the shawl and wandered over to the shop window to better examine it in full daylight. No, it was definitely a lovely cornflower blue. She'd keep it, she decided, and turned her eyes, casually, to the street.

Her gaze fell upon a couple walking arm-in-arm on the other side of the narrow road. They appeared to be engrossed in conversation. The woman wore a becoming dress of pale blue, matched with a fringed, cream shawl. Her free hand, gloved in cream lace, gesticulated as she spoke, as if painting an invisible picture in the air. Then she laughed at something the man said. They were obviously quite familiar with each other. *Happy* with each other. Indeed, one might easily have assumed them to be man and wife.

The two continued on their way, quite oblivious to the fact they were being observed. Louisa had no idea who the woman was, though she appeared to be petite and pretty, with blonde ringlets peeking out from her straw bonnet.

Louisa knew who the man was, however. She'd recognized him instantly, but her brain had yet to fully grasp the truth of what, or who, she was looking at. The only thing she knew for certain was that, despite outward appearances, the couple were not married. At least, not to each other.

They couldn't possibly be.

"Ma'am?"

She flinched as someone touched her shoulder and spun round to see Archer's smiling face. The smile dissolved, replaced by a look of concern. "Are you quite well, Mrs. Harlow?"

Mrs. Harlow.

Louisa still wasn't used to hearing it. She blinked and turned her gaze back to the street, seeing only strangers going about their business. The man and woman had disappeared from sight.

But they had been no illusion.

Yes, I am Mrs. Harlow. Maxwell Harlow's wife of less than a month. The wife who is eagerly waiting for him to return from his business trip to South Shields. But you're not in South Shields are you, Maxwell? You're in Knaresborough, strolling through town with another woman on your arm.

You bastard!

"I'm fine, Archer, thank you." The response came without thinking. Louisa was far from fine, in truth. The next few words, however, were uttered with absolute aforethought. "But, upon consideration, I don't think I'm quite done shopping yet."

Later that day, back at Northcott Manor, she walked into Maxwell's office and put Francesca Corvinelli's invoice on his desk. Then she went upstairs to soak in the bath that had been prepared for her.

The warm, scented water helped to dispel the chill that had held her in its grip for the past few hours. She closed her eyes and settled back, silently commending herself on maintaining her dignity thus far, even as her tears demanded release. Hiding her shock and pain from Archer and Francesca had taken some effort. Indeed, she had decided against staying in town for luncheon. The prospect of sitting in a tearoom, nibbling on dainty sandwiches and little cakes, had been beyond her ability. She wanted to go home, to be alone with her thoughts and fears, to confront them in private. So, after leaving Francesca's, she'd declared a headache and sent Archer off to find McKinney.

For the entire way back, the image of Maxwell with the strange woman played out in Louisa's head, torturous in its implications. Mentally adrift, she reached for explanations, desperate to find something reasonable to cling onto. The woman couldn't have been a relative—Maxwell had no relatives. And how long had he been in Knaresborough? One day? Two? She had no way of knowing. Had he even been to South Shields? Yes, she decided, of that she had little doubt. He and Finlay had talked openly about the trip in front of her. But he obviously hadn't stayed there any longer than necessary. And instead of coming straight home to her—to his *wife*—he'd gone to Knaresborough to be with that woman.

Would he even be coming home that night?

There was nothing Louisa could do except wait and see.

A tap came to the door and Archer poked her head around it. "Are you feeling better, ma'am? It doesn't do to stay in the water too long. You'll get chilled. I have some warm towels here."

Louisa sat upright. "Warm towels sound wonderful, Archer. And I'd like to take dinner in my room this evening, and then get to bed early."

LOUISA OPENED HER eyes to darkness, pulled from sleep by an unsettling dream, the details of it already forgotten, though a feeling of despondency remained. She heaved a sigh and turned onto her back, wondering at the hour. No sooner had the question formed in her mind than the grand clock in the downstairs entrance-hall began to strike.

One. Two. Three.

The depth of night.

Her gaze drifted to the adjoining door. Had Maxwell returned? Did she dare investigate? She wanted to, yet dreaded what she might discover.

A need-to-know pulled her from the bed. She tiptoed to the door and pressed her ear to it, hearing nothing from the other side. Her fingers closed around the doorknob, turned it, and pushed. It opened with its usual soft creak. She held her breath and squinted into the darkness, her gaze trained on Maxwell's bed. Seeking. Hoping.

The bed was pristine. Undisturbed.

Empty.

Disappointment, in an agonizing form, pressed down like a weight on Louisa's chest. The ink on their marriage certificate was barely dry, and already, it seemed, Maxwell had cast his wedding vows aside.

Louisa shivered and moved back into her chamber, closing Maxwell's door quietly behind her. *Think, Louisa. How are you going to handle this? Ignore it? No. No, you cannot do that. But an offensive approach might only make things worse.*

"Make things worse?" She released a soft, bitter laugh, wandered over to the window, and pulled the curtain aside to gaze out, unseeing, into the night. Things could be worse, of course. Maxwell was an even-tempered man. Not willfully cruel, either, though the thought of him keeping a mistress—or maybe several of them—hurt Louisa more deeply than she'd ever openly admit.

Simply ask him to explain. Let him know you saw him. See what he says.

Her reflection in the glass stared back at her.

And then what?

"I don't know." She closed the curtain and scrubbed a tear away. "I really don't know."

Despite the hour, she had no desire to return to bed and tempt further unpleasant dreams. She needed a distraction. Something to shore up her crippled spirit. After lighting her lantern, she shrugged on her dressing gown, stepped into her slippers, and headed downstairs.

The East Parlor beckoned, specifically the bay window-seat, where one could curl up and watch the arrival of a new day, perchance to prepare for whatever challenges it might bring. Louisa padded her way through a silent house, aware of being watched by a dozen pairs of Northcott eyes, staring down at her from their ornately framed portraits.

The parlor door opened with a mere whisper, and Louisa paused briefly on the threshold, wondering if she'd imagined a hint of bergamot in the air. She filled her lungs through her nostrils, smelling only beeswax and turpentine. Folly, she thought, closing the door behind her. Lantern held aloft, she moved toward the window, its curtains drawn against the night. She set the lantern on a nearby occasional table and went to pull the curtains back.

"Louisa?"

Her name, though spoken softly, wrought a cry of alarm from her. She spun round to see a tall, shadowy shape rising up from one of the settees.

"Maxwell!" Her hand flew to the base of her throat as if to still the sudden, violent thud of her heart. "Oh, dear God, you startled me. I didn't know you were home."

"Why aren't you asleep?" He moved toward her. "Are you all right?"

No, not really. Not at all. I'm not ready to face you. Not yet.

"A little shaken, perhaps." Heat burned her cheeks. "I... I didn't expect anyone to be here. When did you get home?"

"A few hours ago." He placed a hand beneath her elbow. "I didn't mean to frighten you. You're trembling. Perhaps you should sit."

A few hours ago? So, late, then.

He wrongly assumed she was trembling from the fright he'd just given her. He couldn't know that she had just summoned up the image of him strolling down Knaresborough's Main Street with his female companion.

"No, I'm quite well, thank you." She folded her arms, effectively shrugging his hand away. "What are you doing in here?"

A slight frown appeared. "I might ask you the same."

"I asked first."

It was, she knew, a petulant response, one that resulted in a brief expression of surprise on Maxwell's face. "I have things on my mind," he said, "and sought a quiet place in which to consider them."

What things?

"I see." She held his gaze. "What of your meeting? Was it successful?"

"Very successful, aye," he replied, his tone wary. "Is something troubling you, Louisa?"

"I didn't expect...I mean..." Her heart rattled in her ears. "You said you'd be gone for at least a week."

"That's what I thought," he said, after a moment, "but things went better than expected, so we adjourned early."

"Yes, actually, I am fully aware of that."

'Oh?" A dark brow arched. "How come?"

She drew breath. "Because I was in Knaresborough yesterday, at Francesca's. And… and I saw you walking along Main Street. With a woman."

"Ah, I see." He cocked his head. "Is that the reason for this odd mood of yours?"

She ignored the question. "Do you deny you were there? With her?"

"Not at all. I have nothing to hide." He shrugged. "I spent

several hours in the lady's company, in fact."

"How nice for you." *How can he be so nonchalant?*

"Louisa, the woman is someone I've known for a number of years." He lifted a loose wisp of hair from her brow. "It's nothing you need to be concerned about."

She drew back from his touch. "But I am concerned, Maxwell. I object strongly to it. I hoped our marriage would not necessitate such behavior."

"What behavior is that?" His hand slowly clenched as it returned to his side. "What are you implying?"

"Well, I should think it's obvious." She took a breath, trying to calm her fraying nerves. "I realize this sort of situation is not unheard of in a marriage, but I want you to know that I'm not in the least happy about it. Not happy at all."

He looked perplexed. "To what *sort of situation* are you referring?"

Louisa barely stifled a gasp. Was he being purposely obtuse? "Keeping a mistress!"

"A mistress?" To Louisa's horror, the beginnings of a smile appeared on his face. "Is that what this is about?"

"Yes." Silently cursing a threat of tears, she raised her chin. "I realize, of course, that my objection will undoubtedly be disregarded in favor of your indulgences. It's just that I hoped for more from our union. I foolishly thought that I... I would be enough for you."

"*Enough* for me?" He gave a soft laugh and scrubbed a hand over his jaw. "Oh, Louisa."

"It saddens me that you appear to find this amusing, Maxwell," she said, glaring at him. "I'm reminded of a conversation we had not too long ago, when we touched upon the subject of sexual equality, or lack thereof. I wonder if you would be similarly amused if *I* was the one taking a lover. I doubt it, somehow. So, if you'll excuse me, I shall leave you to your mirth and return to my bed. I have said my part."

"You'll stay right where you are, lass, for I have not yet said mine." All traces of humor had now vanished from his expression. "First, let me assure you that your *objection* has been noted. That being so, I'm now compelled to make several things clear."

Louisa hugged herself, kept her eyes locked with his, and prepared for what would surely be an upbraiding. No matter her aristocratic background, when it came to the institution of marriage, she was the subordinate. If he wished to indulge in the company of a mistress, or even several mistresses, he would do so, spousal objections be damned. As his wife, she'd have little choice but to live with it. But she silently swore that she would never let him touch her again.

He moved closer—much closer—his tall form looming, shadows playing across his face and throat. He'd discarded his cravat somewhere and undone his collar, allowing Louisa a tantalizing glimpse of the dark hair that covered much of his chest. She breathed in his familiar scent of bergamot, which tonight blended with provocative hints of whisky and peppermint.

Damn you, Maxwell Harlow. Are you aware of your effect on me? The way you make me feel? The power you exercise over me? I felt it the first moment I saw you. And I fear that power is about to be my undoing, for being told I must share you with another will surely break my heart.

Maybe her heart had already broken, for something beneath her ribs felt as though it had been ripped in two.

"The lady's name is Jane Fairburn," he said. "Her husband's name was Bruce Cunningham. He and I attended Edinburgh University together and remained friends afterwards. He died of consumption five years ago. When he realized he was losing his battle, he wrote asking if I would provide help and protection to Jane should she ever need it. I gladly gave him my word, and consequently kept in touch with the lady. As it happens, she is now remarried, and happily so. Charles Fairburn is a clergyman—a good soul, well worthy of her. Between them, they run a charitable institution in Knaresborough, of which I am a patron. Yesterday's meeting with Jane was, I will admit, quite spontaneous. Our business in South Shields concluded earlier than expected. Finlay decided to go to Harrogate to visit friends, which prompted me to make a quick detour to Knaresborough, since I hadn't seen Charles or Jane in a good while. As it happened, Charles was away on business, but Jane and I lunched together in town, after which I visited the institution and made a donation to their cause. Then I came home, where I was advised that you had gone to bed early, so I decided not to disturb you. That is all."

Louisa stared at him, the fearful certainty in her mind sinking beneath a tide of cautious relief. "She… she is not your mistress?"

"No, she is not." A tic arose in Maxwell's jaw as he traced his thumb along the line of Louisa's lower lip. "I have no need of a mistress. I have a *wife*. And, God knows, she is more than enough for me. Indeed, I am well-pleased. Though, I confess there are times, like now, when I feel like shaking some damn sense into her."

"Oh, Max!" The relief became real, and a weight slid from her shoulders. "I don't know what to say. I'm so sor—"

His kiss interrupted her apology. He drew her hard against him, his lips grazing hers in an impassioned caress, while his tongue probed and explored her mouth with uninhibited boldness.

The world around her faded away. She clutched at his shirt and parted with a whimper of pleasure. He responded with a low moan and moved a hand from the small of her back to the swell of her breast. He squeezed, gently, stroking his thumb back and forth over the hardening nipple. Desire burned through Louisa like a fuse, igniting a fierce, demanding pulse between her legs.

She tore her mouth from his and gazed up at him. "Max, I want…" Her voice faltered at the ferocity—the *darkness*—she saw in his eyes. "What… what's wrong?"

"You will never again speak of taking a lover," he said, his voice barely above a whisper. "Do you understand?"

A shiver lifted the hair on the back of her neck. It did not come from fear, for she did not feel threatened by his words. If fear lingered anywhere at that moment, Louisa had the impression it rested, in some strange form, with him. "I didn't mean it, Max."

His eyes softened. "Not even in jest, Louisa."

"Not even in jest," she replied.

"Mmm." A dark brow lifted again. "Now, I believe you were about to ask me for something."

"More," she said. "I was about to ask you for more."

"Ah." A lazy smile appeared as his fingers crept down her thigh, scooping her flimsy nightclothes ever higher, till he was able to access what lay beneath the silk and lace. Louisa drew a sharp breath as his hand slid between her legs, his feather-light touch the ultimate tease. And an exquisite torture.

She shifted and opened her stance, giving him easy and full access. Yet still he maintained a frustratingly gentle touch. She wanted more yet. *Needed* more. She clutched his shirt tighter, raised up on her toes, and squirmed against him.

He nuzzled her ear. "What's wrong, lass?"

"Nothing's wrong. I just want…"

"What?"

"You're being too *gentle*, Maxwell. I'm not made of porcelain."

His quiet laugh brushed across her hair as he slid his fingers into her. As he probed and caressed, the mounting ripples of pleasure became almost unbearable. Louisa didn't want them to end, and yet gladly reached for her climax, eager to feel the ecstasy of release. She closed her eyes and approached the edge of what she sought.

And then Maxwell withdrew his hand.

Her eyes flew open. "Why did you stop?"

"Just a temporary pause, lass. I'm not nearly done with you yet." He took hold of her wrist and steered her around to the settee, where he sat and unbuttoned his fly, giving freedom to his straining erection. A ripple of sexual anticipation ran across Louisa's body.

"Come here," he said, and positioned her in front, facing him.

Then he hoisted her nightgown up to her waist and placed his hands on her bare hips. "Straddle me."

"*Straddle* you?" she squeaked, her eyes widening.

"Aye." He gave her a devilish smile. "Climb onto me. A knee on either side."

Giggling, and with as much grace as she could muster, Louisa eased herself over him.

"This is so *wicked*, Max."

"Not at all." A glimmer came to his eyes. "I've haven't shown you wicked yet. Lower yourself onto me, lass. Guide me in. Aye, that's it."

She sank down, taking every hard inch of him, gasping as he thrust upwards to seat himself fully inside her.

"So tight," he murmured, grinding his hips against her. "And so deliciously *wet*."

The softly uttered words raised a flush of embarrassed heat in Louisa's cheeks, yet excited her at the same time.

"Look." Maxwell nodded toward the wall by the fireplace, where their shadows had been cast by the lantern's warm light. "Move, Louisa. I want to see you move."

She did so, undulating her hips in a slow rhythm, increasingly entranced by the projected display of their lovemaking. The shadow couple seemed separate and apart, somehow. Like spiritual entities, perfectly emulating their human hosts.

"Arousing, is it not?"

She regarded her husband. "Yes, very."

For a moment, she imagined she saw something other than desire in his eyes. Something deeper. More profound.

"You are splendid," he murmured, and eased her back as his mouth latched onto a nipple, sucking and nipping through the thin fabric of her nightgown. Louisa moaned and tipped her head back, her body taut with pleasure as her husband continued his erotic onslaught. He moved his attention to her other nipple, at the same time pushing his fingers into the tight space between them, teasing and stroking as before. The additional stimulation, combined with the sheer fullness of him as she rode his upward thrusts, drove Louisa rapidly toward the brink.

"Oh, dear *God*."

She closed her eyes, aware of Maxwell's growing frenzy, his gradual loss of control as his thrusts increased. His obvious excitement burned through her final few threads of restraint. "Max, please... I have to..."

He drew a ragged breath, grasped her hips, and plunged hard and deep. "Then let it go, lass," he said, his voice strained. "Let it go."

Emitting a cry that she barely recognized as her own, Louisa arched her spine and surrendered to a dizzying wave of ecstasy. Somewhere beyond the rush of blood in her ears, she heard Maxwell's breath catch and felt him pulse inside her, filling her with his heat.

He fell back and Louisa collapsed into his arms, feeling the rise and fall of his chest and hearing the solid thud of his heart, loud in her ear. As she continued to drift on a cloud of sweet fulfillment, her weakened emotional defenses dropped and the words tumbled out before she could stop them.

"I love you, Max."

There followed a moment of silence in which she cursed her slip but dared to hope for an echoed response. The moment passed.

Then, "I'm a fortunate man," he murmured, and pressed a lingering kiss to her hair before easing her to his side, still folded in his embrace. "Very fortunate."

Not quite the response she'd hoped for. She lay still, unsure of what to say for fear of adding to her discomfort. Disappointment mingled with measures of regret and embarrassment. She grasped at reason, telling herself hope was not the same as expectation. That he'd declared his fidelity to her and demanded the same was enough for now. If—no, *when*—Maxwell finally declared his love for her, she knew it would be because he meant it. He undoubtedly cared for her and treated her more than kindly enough.

Indeed, except for his elusive declaration of love, she wanted for naught. And as for his administrations between the sheets—and in the middle of the night on damask settees—well, she had not a single complaint there.

There was time enough for those desirous little words to be spoken. Maybe she was placing too much importance on them. Still in his arms, she shifted to his side and lay still, hoping he wouldn't dispatch her off to bed with some excuse.

"You never answered my question," he said, adjusting his trousers to cover himself. "What brought you down here tonight?"

She took a moment to ponder her response. "I awoke for some reason and decided to come and watch the sunrise from the bay window. That's all. I didn't know you were here. I didn't even know you'd come home."

"You thought I was with her," he said, after a pause. "With Jane."

"Actually, yes, I did." She lifted her head to look him in the eye. "And before you interrupted me with your kiss, I was about to apologize for my false accusations. I'm truly sorry, Max. I assumed wrongly."

"It was a misunderstanding, now resolved." He touched her cheek. "One of these days, I'll take you to meet the lady. I think you'd like her."

"That would be nice."

"Perhaps you can wear one of your new outfits from Frances-ca's."

It was, quite obviously, a pointed remark, albeit spoken with a hint of levity. She cringed, inwardly. "You saw the invoice."

"Yes."

She winced. "I did spend rather a lot."

"A little more than expected, perhaps." He cleared his throat. "I'm curious. Did you finish shopping before you saw me with Jane? Or after?"

She couldn't lie. "After."

"Ah." He grimaced. "Well, that probably explains it."

"It was peevish of me, Max. I'll send a message and cancel—

He tightened his hold on her. "You most certainly will not. I trust you purchased some nice things?"

"Many." She wrinkled her nose. "I purchased many nice things."

He laughed. "And I shall look forward to seeing you in them. Now, if you'll excuse me, my dear, I'm going to take to my bed for a few hours."

Disappointment returned, this time succeeding in dampening her spirit. She'd have been quite happy to spend the rest of the night on the settee, in his arms. She sat up. "Yes, I'm sure must be tired. How long are you home for?"

"Till Monday, then off to Sheffield again for several days." He tugged gently on the braid hanging over her shoulder. "Perhaps, if the weather holds, we might go for a ride this afternoon."

"That would be nice."

"Are you still going to watch the sunrise?"

She nodded. "Will you not stay and watch it with me?"

"Another time, perhaps." He got to his feet and arranged his disheveled clothing.

The passionate lover had gone, and her sober husband had returned. Louisa smiled to hide her disappointment. "Of course."

He bent and kissed her cheek. "Till later, then."

After he left, Louisa wandering over to the window. She slid into the cold space behind the curtains and shivered, questioning her decision. Then she saw the folded blanket on the window-seat. Moments later, she sat cocooned in its woolen warmth, watching the eastern skies turn pale. It appeared, after all, that the day ahead would be quite pleasant. Certainly, better than she'd originally thought.

I have no need of a mistress. I have a wife. And, God knows, she is more than enough for me. Indeed, I am well pleased.

More reassuring than poetic, but that was his way. She had little choice, after all, but to accept it. Better that, she supposed, than a false declaration of love. And they still had the rest of their lives together. One day, she told herself, she would hear what she wanted to hear. And she would know it had been spoken from the heart.

CHAPTER THIRTEEN

THE DAYS MEANDERED gently into the depths of summer. On this particular August morning, sunlight slanted through the windows as Louisa settled at the desk in her sitting-room. She opened her journal to the previous day's date, the page still blank, the events yet to be recorded. Maxwell's return the previous evening, this time after a six-day absence, meant that the journal entry had been abandoned in favor of a more physical exercise. If there was a positive side to Maxwell's absences, it was surely the eager display of passion each time he returned home. Louisa's cheeks warmed as she recalled the details of their amorous evening.

"One would think he actually missed me," she muttered, without malice. He'd never said such a thing, of course. Whenever he went away, however, she missed him terribly. She had not become acclimated to his absences at all. If anything, each one became harder to bear, though she did her utmost not to show it. As for his declaration of love... that, too, remained noticeably absent.

Shrugging off a threat of melancholy, Louisa turned her thoughts to the more mundane events of the previous day and began to write. Not ten minutes into her account, the door opened, and Maxwell entered, waving a paper.

"A letter from Jane," he said, handing it to her. "We've been invited to luncheon with the Fairburns next Saturday and I'd like to accept. Providing nothing urgent crops up this week, it shouldn't be a problem."

Louisa scanned the letter. "Oh, yes. It sounds wonderful! I shall look forward to it. Which reminds me, while you were away last week, we also received an invitation to Uncle Isaac's eightieth birthday party. It's not till September the twentieth, but if you could make a note to keep that week free, I'd appreciate it."

"I'm sure that won't be a problem, my dear." He lifted her hand to his lips. "I'll see you at lunchtime. It's a fine day. Perhaps we can eat on the terrace."

"That would be nice," Louisa said, reading the letter again, admiring Jane's penmanship and the cordiality of the invitation.

As yet, she hadn't met any of Maxwell's friends or associates. More than anything, though, she was happy at the thought of spending some rare leisure time with a husband who tended to be more absent than present in her life. She prayed there wouldn't be any obstacles, such as a last-minute crisis somewhere in Maxwell's ever-expanding empire. And, as a second thought, she also uttered another prayer for fine weather.

Then, once again, she turned her attention to her journal.

AS IT HAPPENED, the week rolled by without mishap. Maxwell had been at home the entire time. Granted, he'd spent most of the daylight hours ensconced in his study with Finlay, but he'd been present for dinner each evening and in Louisa's bed most nights, though, true to form, he'd never stayed till morning. Still, it had almost been like a second honeymoon and Louisa had reveled in it. Even so, it wasn't till Friday evening that she dared to uncross her fingers. To her utter relief, there had been no last-minute summons from Maxwell's minions, and the weather looked promising.

"An early night might be in order," he said on the Friday

night, dabbing a kiss on her cheek. "I'd like to leave at sunrise."

Thusly dispatched, Louisa took to her bed and lost herself in some of Wordsworth's poetry before finally snuffing out her candle. She awoke before dawn, hurried to her window, threw back the curtains, and gazed out at a sky littered with stars. "Yes," she whispered, her subsequent sigh of relief clouding the glass. Unable to resist, she drew a heart in the misted patch and then laughed at her foolishness. A little over an hour later, following Archer's expert attentions, Louisa regarded her reflection with satisfaction. Her dress of white cotton muslin, printed with a delicate pink rose motif on the sleeves and around the hem, looked as fresh as the summer morning. Her rebellious hair had been tamed, but not severely so. The soft style framed her face and complimented the whimsical style of her outfit.

"Worth every penny," Maxwell said, rising to his feet as she entered the breakfast room.

Louisa blinked. "What is?'

"The small fortune you spent at Francesca's. At least, I'm assuming that's one of your new outfits. In any case, my dear, it's very becoming."

"Thank you. Yes, it is new." She regarded her husband, whose crisp white shirt and pale blue vest contrasted well with his dark looks. As always, a sweet ache of attraction rose beneath her ribs. She tussled with a desire to wander over and kiss him, to show him some simple affection. "You look rather splendid too, Maxwell."

He merely smiled. She took her seat, and he did likewise.

Not long after, they left Northcott Manor and set out under a golden sky, seated comfortably in Maxwell's barouche for the two-hour—or thereabouts—journey.

As the clip-clop of the horses' hooves merged with the crunch of carriage wheels upon the road, Louisa settled back against cushioned leather, savoring the sweetness of a perfect summer's day as the countryside passed by. The inimitable scent of fresh-cut hay blended with hints of wildflowers. Cattle shared emerald-green meadows with sheep. On occasion, the less pleasant offerings of a farmyard soured the air.

Conversation remained light and casual, no business, no politics. Louisa wanted to know more about her hosts, and Maxwell furnished the information. Charles Fairburn was apparently descended from landed gentry in Derbyshire, where his family still owned sizable tracts of farmland. And Jane's father had been a tutor at Edinburgh University.

"Which is where she met Bruce." Maxwell brushed a speck of lint from his trousers. "I believe she met Charles while visiting friends in York. He was a minister there before taking his current position."

"I'm looking forward to meeting them." Louisa shifted her gaze to the passing countryside once more, thankful for the movement of air as they travelled. The morning coolness had vanished as the sun had climbed higher. She breathed deep and released a contented sigh. This was, she realized, their first shared excursion since their honeymoon. "How fortunate we are. It's the perfect day for such an outing."

Maxwell took her hand and raised it to his mouth, sending a sweet little thrill down her spine. "Perfect, indeed," he muttered. "I guarantee they're looking forward to meeting you as well."

At last, the streets of Knaresborough rumbled beneath the wheels. The rectory, an elegant Georgian house surrounded by a capped stone wall, stood on the northwest edge of town, facing the road. The carriage halted in front of the black wrought-iron gate, and Maxwell helped Louisa down.

"Oh, how lovely!" She raised her parasol against the sun and cast an appreciative glance over the flower gardens surrounding the house. The air hung with an intoxicating fusion of floral scents, that of the rose being the most dominant, yet exquisitely delicate.

After giving the driver his instructions, Maxwell opened the gate, and gestured for Louisa to pass. "Jane enjoys gardening, as you can probably tell," he said, closing the gate behind them.

"She's something of an expert on roses."

A pinch of jealousy threatened Louisa's composure, but she immediately shoved it away. Maxwell had known the lady for several years. It only stood to reason that he'd know something about her likes and dislikes.

The front door opened before they reached it, and a man and woman—the latter with a straw bonnet clasped in her hand—appeared on the threshold.

"Here you are, at last!" The man's sermonic voice boomed over the garden. "I trust you had a pleasant journey?"

"Very pleasant, thank you," Maxwell replied and placed his hand in the small of Louisa's back. "Charles, Jane, allow me to introduce Louisa, my wife. Louisa, this is Charles and Jane Fairburn."

"A pleasure to meet you, Mrs. Harlow." The vicar inclined his head. "Welcome to our home."

Other than his white collar and cravat, the man was clad entirely in black. Though almost as tall as Maxwell, he had a softer physique, one that suggested a less vigorous lifestyle. An impressive set of eyebrows and sideburns adorned his features, their reddish hue similar to that of Yorkshire's beloved brown ale. His abundance of wavy hair, however, was a shade darker, and held firmly in place by a sheen of pomade. His brown eyes, while friendly in their assessment, seemed possessed of a perceptive light, able to see past any attempt at a counterfeit façade. He looked to be older than Maxwell, though not by much. And the man's deep, mellow voice had surely been created to deliver Sunday sermons.

"The pleasure is mine, Vicar," Louisa replied, "but please, both of you, address me as Louisa."

A smile crinkled his eyes. "Then you will address me as Charles from now on, my dear."

"And you will please address me as Jane." The lady extended a hand, which Louisa took. "I'm delighted to meet you at last, Louisa."

Jane's voice possessed a genuine warmth and her cornflower-blue eyes shone with unmistakable forthrightness. She was indeed pretty, with ringlets of wheat-gold hair framing a pale, heart-shaped face. The lady was also less robust than Louisa had originally perceived. Slender to the point of dainty, in fact, though the firm grip of her hand and the upward set of her chin implied strength of character. Louisa liked her immediately.

"Thank you, Jane," she replied. "I'm delighted to meet you also. You have such a charming home. The gardens are truly splendid!"

Jane's eyes brightened further. "They're at their peak right now. Would you care to take a stroll around them? It might be pleasant to walk a little after your carriage ride. We can have some lemonade on the terrace as well, if you like, since luncheon isn't going to be ready for about an hour. Our menfolk can put the world to rights while we get to know each other a little better."

Louisa smiled. "That sounds lovely."

"Excellent." Jane turned to her husband. "Dearest, would you ask Emmeline to take some lemonade out to the terrace?"

Charles nodded. "Of course."

Maxwell gave the small of Louisa's waist a gentle squeeze. "Enjoy, sweetheart," he said, and kissed her on the cheek.

Louisa drew in a soft breath as her heart sped up. Never had Maxwell used that term of endearment before. Nor had he ever shown such open affection while in the company of others.

"Come." Jane looped her arm through Louisa's and steered her into the gardens. "I grow all kinds of flowers, but roses are my favorite."

"Mine too," Louisa replied, her heart still skipping along. "Rose is my middle name, so I'm naturally drawn to them. Maxwell told me you were something of an expert."

Jane wrinkled her nose. "A bit of an exaggeration, perhaps. Like anything worthwhile they require some effort, but the results are so rewarding. I make my own rosewater from the petals. You must take a bottle of it back to Northcott with you."

"That's very kind. Thank you."

"You're welcome. But I shall speak no more of your departure. Our day together has just begun!"

Jane continued to chat animatedly, pointing out the different blooms and plants. She would have got along well with Reuben, Louisa thought. She listened to Jane with genuine interest, though a desire to don a pair of gardening-gloves and wield some pruning-shears never materialized.

"We have a good-sized vegetable plot across the road as well," Jane said, gesturing as they followed the gravel path through the garden. "A couple of local men tend to that. We only take what we require. The rest is distributed to local families. And back here…"

They turned the corner of the house, where a wooden gate nestled in a tall hedgerow of neatly trimmed yew, forming an intriguing barrier to whatever lay beyond. Smiling, Jane lifted the gate latch. "Back here is our private terrace and stable-yard."

The gate creaked as Jane pushed it open, and Louisa stepped onto a broad section of clipped grass that edged a large, cobbled courtyard. Here, the floral scent of the garden acquiesced to the less-delicate smells of horse and compost. A series of buildings, one of them obviously a stable, stood along the back wall of the courtyard, which was accessed by a large double gate.

A couple of Greylag geese, nibbling at the grass nearby, lifted their orange bills and honked.

Louisa chuckled. "Is that a welcome or a warning?"

"One can never be sure with Malcolm and Maud," Jane replied, with a smile. "They keep the lawn trim and would certainly alert us to any intruders. The stable and washhouse is over there, and here is the terrace, complete with refreshments as requested. Sit, Louisa, please, and have some lemonade."

The flagstone terrace ran the full length of the rear of the house. Potted ferns and shrubs, combined with a set of white, cast-iron furniture, made it a welcoming outdoor space. Shady, too. Louisa, feeling a little warm, sat in one of the cast-iron chairs and lowered her parasol.

"It really is quite lovely," she said, glancing about.

"It is." Jane poured a glass of lemonade and handed it to her. "We're very fortunate. Charles was based in York when we first met. We moved here after we married and much prefer it."

Louisa took a sip, allowing the bittersweetness of the drink to linger on her tongue a moment. "I'm glad you found some happiness. Maxwell told me a little of how he came to know you."

Jane also took a sip and appeared to ponder for a moment. "At the risk of being bold, I have to say that I'm delighted to see Maxwell so happy. He's obviously quite enamored of you."

He is? Louisa felt a rise of color in her cheeks. "We're well-suited, I think."

Jane set her glass down. "There. I've embarrassed you. Please forgive me, Louisa. I'm afraid I'm far too outspoken. It's just that I've known Maxwell for several years, and he's always been so…"

"Sedate?" Louisa offered.

"Well… yes, I suppose that might describe him. Certainly, a man possessed of a serious nature. Till recently, that is. At least, when we last met, he seemed more light-hearted."

"He spoke of me?"

"Of course! He spoke of you *and* your family. Mind you, he's always been discreet as well, so there was not much elaboration. But he had a hint of pride in his voice, and I'm convinced I noticed a sparkle in his eyes." She parted with a wistful sigh. "Then I saw the way he looked at you this morning. And as for that kiss on the cheek!"

Louisa's brows shot up. "The way he looked at me?"

"When he first introduced you." Jane frowned and cocked her head. "You seem surprised. Do you have reason to doubt his affection for you?"

"No, not specifically, though I confess the kiss was a surprise. He's not usually one for such displays." Louisa took another sip of lemonade. "I know he's fond of me."

"*Fond?*" Jane huffed. "A suitable epithet for a hobby or a dessert, and I doubt Maxwell sees you as either of those things."

Louisa giggled. "Well, perhaps dessert on occasion."

Jane's eyes widened. "My dear Mrs. Harlow, what an atrociously indelicate and delicious remark. Dare I hope to have found a friend who isn't dripping with false sanctimony?"

Louisa cleared her throat and pretended to primp her hair. "My dear Mrs. Fairburn, I'm not without propriety when it is called for, but being raised with brothers tends to open one's mind to different perspectives, and not all of them ladylike."

Jane laughed. "Oh, how wonderfully refreshing!" She leaned forward and lowered her voice. "I love Charles dearly but being married to a man of the cloth means being obliged to keep certain thoughts to oneself. Not always easy, I must admit. Bruce, in contrast, had a wicked sense of humor. Terribly *risqué*, in fact. But I enjoyed it. We laughed a lot in private."

"Did he make Maxwell laugh? He does so rarely, in my experience."

"Hmm." Jane tapped a finger on her chin. "I only saw them together a couple of times and do not recall him being anything other than pragmatic. That said, I cannot imagine he was totally impervious to Bruce's humor. It was highly infectious. They didn't see each other much after university, either, but kept in touch through letters. Bruce was an excellent judge of character and trusted Maxwell implicitly, which says much. He was also a cautious man. Shrewd. The epitome of a canny Scot." She released a soft sigh. "I consider it a blessing to have shared four years of my life with him."

Four years! Not long. Louisa wondered about the lack of children. Not that she would ever be so bold as to ask about that. "I'm sorry for your loss, Jane."

"Thank you. The grief will always be there, but I've learned to live with it. And it does not impede my love for Charles. He's a dear man, and I consider myself fortunate to have found happiness again. Indeed, it's what Bruce wanted for me."

"No doubt Charles considers himself fortunate as well."

Jane smiled. "As does Maxwell, I'm sure."

I'm a fortunate man. "Yes, he does," Louisa replied. "He has told me as much."

Jane cocked her head again, her eyes narrowing slightly. "Don't underestimate your worth to him, Louisa. I see a change in him. A positive change. And I believe you're the reason for it."

At that moment, the back door opened, and a maid indicated that luncheon was ready.

The subsequent gathering proved to be more than pleasant. The lighter fare leant itself to continued afternoon activities rather than the need for a nap. Maxwell appeared very much at ease. But then, Louisa realized, there was no one here who would judge him, surreptitiously or otherwise, on his perceived lack of societal status or his 'vulgar' wealth.

Her mind wandered, and she dared to imagine Grandmama Hutton seated at such a gathering. The grand old lady might have poked at a slice of ham and maybe even sampled a freshly picked tomato, but she wouldn't have gone anywhere near the pickled onions or the thickly sliced crusty bread. Given her sweet tooth, a slice of fruit cake might have tempted her. But the setting as a whole, despite its charming simplicity, would have resulted in a display of aristocratic huffing. Indeed, the imagined scenario made Louisa's mouth twitch.

"Would you care to share whatever it is you find amusing, my dear?"

Louisa blinked and regarded her husband, who was looking at her with an amused expression of his own. "Not really, no. I beg your pardon. My thoughts wandered for a moment. Did I miss something?"

"We were discussing our charitable venture," Charles said. "Your husband is a generous patron."

"Yes, so I understand." She gave Maxwell a smile and then addressed Charles. "How many children do you have in your care, Charles?"

"Children?" Charles looked perplexed. "I'm not quite sure I understand the question, my dear."

Bewildered, Louisa glanced around the table, noting similar expressions on Jane's and Maxwell's face. "It would appear I've misspoken, though I'm not certain why," she said. "I just wondered how many orphaned souls your charity cared for, that's all."

A collective mumble of comprehension followed.

"My fault, I fear," Maxwell said. "Obviously, I failed to fully explain the nature of the institution."

Louisa shook her head. "I don't understand."

"It's not an orphanage, Louisa." Jane set her napkin on the table. "St. Giles House is a refuge for cripples and invalids. Men, and specifically those who've been injured in the course of their work, rendering them unemployable and a physical burden on their families. We provide care for them and assistance for their kin, if required. We have fourteen residents at the moment. Is that right, Charles?"

He gave a nod. "Yes, that's right."

Louisa grimaced. "Forgive me, I assumed wrongly. Is it open to visitors? I should very much like to see it, if we have the time."

Charles shook his head. "I don't think that would be wise. It is not a place for the faint-of-heart."

Louisa's hackles bristled. "Who, here, is faint-of-heart?"

"I meant no offense, dear lady," he replied. "But you are gently-bred, and I fear you might find the experience difficult."

Maxwell cleared his throat. "I think Charles is simply concerned that you might be distressed by what you see there, my dear."

"Oh, but I'm certain I shall be," Louisa replied. "To witness suffering and *not* be distressed by it would be shameful. I assure you, however, I am not given to the vapors. Besides, if I should begin to feel overwhelmed, I shall simply seek the door."

"I must favor Louisa's argument," Jane said. "Her interest in the venture is understandable, after all."

"A bilateral female attack, Charles. We're done for." Maxwell sat back in his chair. "That being the case, would a visit be in order?"

"Certainly," Charles replied, amiably. "Would you still care to walk, or shall we take a carriage?"

Everyone agreed to the walk, which to Louisa's delight, meandered, for the most part, along the river. At one point, Jane and Charles had moved a little way ahead, leaving Louisa to speak to Maxwell with some privacy.

"It suits you, Max." Louisa, her arm looped through his, gazed up at her husband. "A day away from work, I mean. You look wonderfully at ease. Perhaps you should consider taking more time off in future."

A small frown came and went. "Would that I had that luxury, my dear. The business does not run itself."

"But you have Finlay. He seems more than capable of—"

"Not now, Louisa." He patted her hand. "Perhaps we can discuss it another time."

Not an unreasonable response, she supposed. And at least she'd broached the subject. Put the idea in his head. Whether or not he'd consider it remained to be seen. She nodded her agreement. "You're right, of course. Now isn't the time. It's been a lovely day so far. I've enjoyed it very much."

"You and Jane seemed to have forged a friendship," he said.

"Yes, we have. She's delightful. Perhaps we can return the invitation and have them come to Northcott for a few days."

"Perhaps," he said. "As long as I'm not called away on business, of course."

Which is very likely. The acerbic response remained in Louisa's head, though she tussled with a temptation to say it out loud. The sudden sound of ducks quacking shifted her attention to the river, where a passing rowboat had obviously disturbed the birds. The boat contained a young couple; the man at the oars, the woman facing him, her face shaded by a lacy, cream-colored parasol. The man said something, and the woman laughed, a sweet sound that made Louisa smile. "How romantic," she said. "It's a perfect day for such an outing."

"Are you sure you want to do this?" Maxwell asked.

She blinked. "Do what?"

His arm tightened against hers. "Visit the institution."

"Yes, I'm positive." Unable to resist, she voiced the wicked thought that had just slid into her head. "I'm not made of porcelain, Maxwell. I thought I made that clear to you that night in the East Parlor."

The suggestion of a smile appeared. "I'm just concerned you'll find the experience too disturbing."

"I've witnessed things on London streets that I found terribly disturbing. I cannot imagine this place to be any worse. Have you visited it often?"

"Twice only. The last time was when you saw me with Jane a few weeks ago. And I was also present when the institution was first opened. At that time, they had only a half-dozen residents. Obviously, that number has since grown."

"And it was all done with your help."

"Not only mine."

"Still, it's something to be proud of, Max. I can't help wondering why you never mention it."

He frowned. "I believe philanthropy should be practiced with modesty and discretion. Boasting about one's charitable activities is, in my opinion, an exercise in vanity, and also unwise. Discretion is essential if one wishes to keep the less-than-desirable wolves from the door. I didn't purposely hide the information from you, Louisa. I just never thought to mention it, that's all."

"I understand." She straightened a little and brightened her tone. "Look, Charles and Jane are waiting for us. We're laggards, both."

"A little bit of a climb," Charles said as they approached, and gestured to a lane leading away from the river. "But not too far."

St. Giles House—judging by the visible patchwork of repairs

and alterations—was a marriage of several buildings, with all but one of the doors having been bricked up. Hemmed in by a wall of similar red brick, the single-story house stood well back from the road, and was accessed by an adjacent rutted lane, barely wide enough for a carriage.

"It used to be a row of thatched farm cottages," Jane explained. "We simply converted the entire thing into one long building and put a slate roof on it. The single story is perfect for our needs, since many of our residents cannot manage stairs."

Despite its higgledy-piggledy exterior, or perhaps because of it, the house had a discernible, rural charm. Hefty oak lintels topped the row of white-paned windows. A rooftop weathervane, in the shape of a proud cockerel, stood atop the roof, pointing its arrow into the gentle, southern breeze.

The gardens consisted, primarily, of lawns dotted with purple clover and tiny, white daisies. A number of apple trees, likely remnants of the original farm orchard, provided shade for those who wanted it. A few of the residents were seated outside, taking advantage of the pleasant weather.

Charles explained that the institution employed two full-time assistants; one who worked during the day, the other at night. As well, they had several volunteers who donated whatever time they could to the venture. Food, clothing, and other supplies were also provided through donations.

"We try to make life for the residents as pleasant as we can." Charles opened the gate and gestured for them to enter. "None of this would be possible, however, without patrons like yourselves and those in the community who give freely of their time."

Louisa's attention was drawn to several men seated in the garden. They appeared to be of varying ages and disabilities. Some were obviously enjoying a nap in the pleasant afternoon air. A couple of them regarded the visitors with passive interest. One man, younger than the rest and seated in a bathchair, caught Louisa's eye and acknowledged her presence with a smile. She returned it.

"How do you decide who should come here?" she said to Jane, in hushed tones. "What are the criteria?"

"They're generally referred to us by the church or other charitable institutions," Jane replied. "But Charles always visits the family in question, if there is one, before making a decision. I confess we are quite selective."

"We have to be mindful of those who volunteer their time," Charles said. "Though a couple of our residents are mentally compromised, there's not a single man here who might be considered volatile. In that regard, you are quite safe."

"You would not be here otherwise, Louisa," Maxwell murmured, placing his hand on the small of her back.

"May we see inside?" she asked.

"Yes, of course," Charles replied. "I'm sure you must also be ready for some refreshment."

They stepped into the flagstone vestibule, and Louisa blinked several times, allowing her eyes to adjust to the darker interior. The air, though noticeably cooler, didn't smell nearly as fresh within. Her nostrils flared as they met the sour blend of medicinal, culinary, and other, less agreeable aromas.

They first went to the kitchen to quench their thirst before continuing with the tour. Charles explained that the residents adhered to a strict schedule of prayer, meal and bedtimes. The small dormitories were sparse in appearance but appeared to be clean and tidy. Where possible, Louisa learned, the men were encouraged to take care of their own hygiene, and some of the more capable even helped out those less adept. The activities varied, also depending on the severity of a person's disability. For those able to play, board games, such as chess and draughts, were allowed and even encouraged. Card games were acceptable, too, though gambling of any kind was forbidden. "We have volunteers who come and read to the men," Jane said. "I personally enjoying doing that. We read passages from the Bible, or an appropriate story. The serials from Mr. Dickens are always well-received. We even have a fiddle player who shows up once in a while and plays for them."

"And, of course, we hold a prayer service in the main dining room every Sunday, after church," Charles added. "If, for some reason, I cannot officiate, another parson volunteers his time."

Louisa, humbled by the reminder of how much she took for granted, said little as Charles continued to explain the ins-and-outs of the place. Not that she'd experienced a sudden epiphany. She'd always been cognizant of her family's societal status. Of *her* status. Being born to it, however, she didn't really give it much thought most of the time. It was simply the way of the world. *Her* world. But, as Maxwell had recently pointed out, the ways of the world were changing. He was proof of that.

Eventually, their tour took them back outside, where they chatted with some of the garden's occupants. Drawn by his cheerful demeanor, Louisa approached the young, fair-haired man she'd seen when she'd first arrived. His name, she discovered, was Tom Ellis, a quarryman who'd fallen and broken his back a year since. He wasn't married, but had a widowed mother who, despite her best efforts, had simply been unable to cope with a crippled son.

"I don't know where she'd be if not for this place," he said. "Don't know where I'd be, either. Pushing up the daisies, I should think."

"Does your mother ever come to visit?" Louisa asked.

"She's only been the once, ma'am, when I first was brought here. She lives in Pateley Bridge. Not easy to get here from there. I write to her every week, though." He held up his hands. "My legs mightn't work anymore, but these do."

"How long have you been here?"

"Ten months," he said. "And I thank God for my good fortune every day."

Good fortune? Tears pricked at the back of Louisa's eyes. "So, you haven't seen your mother in ten months?"

He shook his head. "Nay."

She felt a tap on her arm. "Louisa, dearest," Jane said, "we really should be going, or I fear you'll be driving back to Northcott in the dark."

"Very well." She smiled at the young man. "It was pleasure meeting you, Tom."

He bobbed his head. "You too, ma'am."

She moved away and touched Jane on the shoulder. "May I take a minute before we leave?" she asked, glancing over to where Maxwell and Charles stood waiting.

Jane, understanding the request, nodded. "Through the door, turn left, and go to the very end of the corridor. It's the blue door. Shall I come with you?"

Louisa shook her head. "No, I won't be long."

She entered the house again and paused for a moment, absorbing the silence, aware of the sudden thud of her heart. A peculiar feeling took hold of her, a strange sensation that set her nerves tingling and left her slightly breathless. Perhaps she'd had too much sun, she thought, as she made her way to the end of the hallway. Though she wore a bonnet and made use of her parasol, it had been a warm day and she'd been outside for much of it.

As before, many of the doors along the hallway were open, each leading to a small dormitory that held three or four beds. Currently, since most of the residents were outside, she knew the majority of the rooms were empty. And even if they weren't, she been assured she had nothing to fear.

She found the blue door with no trouble. A short while later, refreshed, and with her heart beating a little less frantically, she prepared to head back outside.

As she wandered along the corridor, a strange clatter from one of the rooms caught her attention. She halted by the door, which stood slightly ajar, and peeked around it. The room contained three beds, all neatly made, and was empty apart from a solitary man seated, in profile, at a small table by the window. The light behind him carved out his silhouette, obscuring detail. Still, Louisa could tell he was of thin build and apparently in possession of all his limbs. She wondered at his disability. He could obviously see, since he appeared to be arranging a set of dominoes atop the table, though the movements of his hands appeared a little clumsy. The clatter, Louisa realized, had been caused by several of the domino tiles tumbling to the floor, where they still lay. The man showed no apparent interest in retrieving them.

Strangely fascinated, Louisa continued to watch, but remained hesitant to enter the room unaccompanied. Since she could discern no visible disability, she feared he might be mentally compromised. Then Charles' assurance came back to her.

"…there's not a single man here who might be considered volatile. In that regard, you are quite safe."

Decided, and admittedly curious, Louisa pushed the door open. "May I help you, sir?" she asked, with more confidence than she felt. The man, however, appeared to neither see nor hear her. Absorbed in his task, he continued turning over the dominoes in readiness for a game. *With whom?* She moved toward him, now able to see more detail. He was elderly, judging by the lined, papery skin of his face and the fine, white curls adorning his head.

"My name is Louisa," she continued. "Are you aware that you've dropped some of your dominoes?"

Still no response. She assumed, then, he must be deaf, and thought to touch his shoulder to let him know of her presence but didn't dare be so bold.

Only when she bent to pick up the pieces did the man's hands halt their movements, as if he'd realized he was no longer alone. As Louisa rose to her feet, he at last turned to look at her.

Oh, dear God.

The shock of what her eyes beheld turned her blood to ice and froze the breath in her lungs. The dominoes, clutched in her right hand, dug into her palm as her fingers clenched. It took all she had not to drop them and back away from the dreadful sight. But she forced herself to breathe and tried desperately to gather

her scattered wits. It was, after all, a disfigurement. Nothing more.

At some time in his life, the man had sustained a terrible injury to the left side of his head. Part of his skull appeared to have been cleaved away. Or crushed, perhaps. His left eye surely had little or no function, judging by the drooped eyelid and the hideous fusion of scarred flesh above and below his brow. His right eye, however—a bright, brilliant blue—was currently regarding her with undeniable interest, widening as it did so. Then the man's mouth opened, and he made a sound. A groan of sorts.

Louisa swallowed. "You dropped these, sir," she said, her voice barely above a whisper. With a trembling hand, she placed the pieces on the table, aware of his continued regard. It almost seemed as if he was equally as shocked, though perhaps not nearly as horrified. He blinked at last, releasing a tear that trickled down his cheek. Then he raised a hand as if intending to touch her and uttered one word.

"Gray."

The tear fell from his chin, landing on the table with a tiny splash. And in that instant, Louisa's revulsion and fear vanished like smoke on the wind, replaced by a hard, throat-tightening swell of compassion. The man's deformity no longer mattered. It was nothing more than a façade, in no way representative of the human soul behind it.

"Please do not upset yourself, sir, there's no harm done!" She smiled. "Gray. Is that your name?"

He blinked again, and a second tear followed the first. "Play," he said, and looked down at the dominoes.

Louisa glanced briefly over her shoulder. "Well, I would love to, but—"

"Play," he repeated, touching the dominoes as if to clarify his demand. "Play gray."

Louisa sighed. How could she possibly refuse? *One game. It won't take long.* She glanced over her shoulder again, knowing

Maxwell would come looking for her when she didn't return.

"Very well, but only one quick game." She took the chair opposite. "Then I must go."

"Gray." He pulled a handkerchief from his pocket, wiped his good eye, and gave her a lopsided smile. "Gray."

"Yes, gray," Louisa repeated, not knowing how else to respond. She turned over a tile, a four-five combination. "Nine," she said.

The man then turned over his chosen tile, a three-two combination. He nodded, conveying his understanding that Louisa had won the right to begin. She chose her seven tiles, waited while he did likewise, and the game commenced.

It soon became apparent that the man's damaged brain worked well to a certain degree, since he never once faulted placing his dominoes. Though he didn't actually speak, he made odd little sounds as the game continued, usually when Louisa placed her tiles. It sounded, she thought, oddly like encouragement, as if he was praising her progress as one might praise a child.

"Who are you?" she asked. "What happened to you?"

But the answer, as expected, never came.

"AH, HERE SHE is," Jane said, with obvious relief. "Quite safe."

There had been few times in his life when Maxwell had actually been lost for words. In fact, at that precise moment, he couldn't recall a single time when the search for a pertinent remark or observation had failed him.

It failed him now.

His absent wife, in all her summer finery, had not accidentally locked herself in the latrine. She had not lost her way or been overcome by heat and fainted in the hallway. Nor had she, thank God, been the victim of a less-than-pleasant encounter with a resident of St. Giles House. This latter scenario, of course, contradicted Charles' assurance that none of the residents were dangerous. But the notion had danced on the periphery of Maxwell's brain. And he hadn't liked it one bit.

But no. It appeared Louisa had simply sat down to play a game of dominoes with a man. A complete stranger. And in that stranger's bedroom. Alone. Not only that the man appeared to be in possession of all his extremities, though he was obviously slow-witted. Still, while undoubtedly done with good intentions, Louisa's behavior was, nevertheless, totally imprudent.

Could she, just once perhaps, think before she acted?

"What are you doing, Louisa?" A rhetorical question asked before he could stop himself. He added to it. "You knew we were waiting for you."

And I was worried, damn it.

"Yes, and I beg your pardon, Maxwell." She threw him a brief glance before returning her attention to her pieces. "But I must also beg your understanding. I agreed to a game of dominoes with this nice gentleman. One game only, mind you. He asked me to play, and I simply couldn't refuse."

Jane gasped. "He *asked* you to play?"

"Yes." Louisa placed her domino and then looked at Jane. "Should I not have accepted?"

"Louisa, dear." Jane shook her head. "You must be mistaken. Samuel doesn't speak."

"With respect, Jane, I can assure you he does." Louisa regarded her opponent. "Samuel. Is that your name, sir?"

"I'm trying to understand why you would enter his room unaccompanied, Louisa," Maxwell said, tamping down a blend of relief and annoyance. "You must surely see the wrong of it. What would prompt you to do such a thing?"

"She was in no danger, Maxwell, I assure you," Jane said. "Samuel is a gentle soul. Quite harmless."

"Perhaps so." Maxwell ran a hand through his hair. "But he's a man, a stranger, and Louisa is, or was, unchaperoned."

"You don't have to speak around me." Louisa heaved a sigh. "I realize how it must seem to you, but there's actually a very simple explanation. As I was passing Samuel's door, I heard a clatter, and peeked in to see what had caused it. I saw that he'd dropped some of the dominoes on the floor, so I came in to help him retrieve them. Then, like I said, he asked me to play and something about his request touched my heart, especially when he shed a tear. I sincerely apologize for keeping you waiting, but I simply couldn't refuse him."

Jane frowned. "He shed a tear?"

"Yes. A couple of them, actually." She pointed to the wet spot on the table. "There, see? The remains of a teardrop."

"Forgive me, but I truly find this hard to believe." Jane shook her head again. "Samuel has been with us since last Christmas, and he's never spoken a word. Not a single one."

"Well, he did today," Louisa replied. "'Play', he said and repeated it twice more. He also said 'gray' a few times. I actually thought that was his name, but perhaps he's getting 'gray' and 'play' confused."

"Will you speak to me, Samuel?" Jane cocked her head and touched his shoulder. "Like you did to Louisa?"

He merely grunted and tapped a tile on the table.

"I believe he's telling me to stop dawdling," Louisa said, as she played her domino.

Somewhat appeased, Maxwell moved to her side. "I still say you should have fetched me before—oh, good Lord." The sight of Samuel's deformity momentarily stole his breath. "I didn't realize."

"I know, it is rather awful." Louisa said, without looking up. "It shocked me as well."

"And yet you stayed with him," Maxwell murmured, as much to himself as to Louisa. *Most women would have hoisted their skirts and fled. Or fainted on the spot.*

"Yes, indeed," Jane said. "You obviously have a strong constitution, Louisa."

"I think not, since my first reaction was to run." Louisa placed a domino. "But, as I said, something about him touched my heart. I now realize there is nothing to fear."

Maxwell gazed down at the woman he'd married and tried to imagine Sybella in her place, playing dominoes with a disfigured simpleton. He couldn't. Indeed, he doubted Sybella would have even consented to spending an afternoon at the rectory with Charles and Jane.

"What happened to him?" Maxwell asked. "How was he injured?"

"We have no idea," Jane replied. "He came here from a rather miserable asylum in York, referred to us by a pastor friend of Charles. Before that he was in Chester, I believe, in a church-run institution that burned down, which is how he ended up in York. Where he was before that is unknown, though we suspect he's spent most of his life in institutions, so it's remarkable he's lived this long. He's very calm and seems to enjoy his solitude. Never causes a fuss."

"Then he's all alone in the world." Louisa shook her head at Samuel to indicate she must miss a turn. "How sad."

"He has no blood relatives, but I wouldn't say he's lonely," Jane said. "Young Tom spends a lot of time with him. They play dominoes for hours. Tom reads to him as well, though I'm not sure Samuel understands any of what is said. I'm still puzzling over the fact that he spoke to you. I wish I could hear it for myself."

"Well, it seems I am defeated." Louisa turned over her remaining dominoes as Samuel placed his final piece. She pushed back her chair and stood. "I have to go now, sir, but—"

"Play," he said, and began to overturn the dominoes again.

Jane's hand went to her throat. "Oh, my heavens!"

"There you are, Jane, your wish has been granted." Louisa shook the creases from her skirts. "And no, Samuel, I'm afraid I cannot stay any longer. It's getting late, and we must—"

"What on earth are you all doing in here?" Charles' voice

boomed from the doorway. "Has something happened?"

"Yes, dearest, a miracle," Jane responded. "It seems Samuel is having a conversation with Louisa."

Charles flinched visibly. "That's not possible."

"Well, not a conversation, exactly," Louisa countered. "But he has spoken."

"Good heavens. What has he said?"

"Play," Samuel said again, his gaze still fixed on Louisa.

Charles' brows shot upward. "Well, I never!" he exclaimed. "This is quite remarkable. What prompted it?"

"I'm not certain." Louisa repeated the tale of how she'd retrieved the scattered dominoes. "I didn't realize he'd never spoken before."

"Play," Samuel reached out and took her hand. "Play gray."

Maxwell tensed. Conversation was one thing. Touching, quite another.

"I'm afraid I cannot, Samuel." Louisa pulled her hand free and drew a cross over her heart. "But I swear I'll come back and visit you again."

"'Play' I understand," Jane said. "But 'gray'? I wonder what it means."

"Only he can answer that." Charles stepped forward and squeezed Samuel's shoulder. "I always believed there was something going on behind that mangled face of yours, good sir. You're a wonderful mystery."

The man showed no awareness of Charles' contact. His gaze remained fixed, unflinchingly, on Louisa.

"Do you know how old he is?" Maxwell asked.

Charles shook his head. "We estimate he's at least in his sixties. Then again, with the life he's led, he could be a good bit younger than that."

"He's certainly taken with you, Louisa," Jane said. "I wish we could all spend some more time with him, but we really have to leave."

"Yes, we do." Charles patted Samuel's shoulder. "I'll have

Tom brought in to keep this gentleman company. They've struck up a friendship of sorts."

"Yes, Jane mentioned it." Louisa smiled at Samuel. "It was a pleasure to meet you, sir. I shall look forward to my next visit."

He blinked his blue eye and then looked down at the dominoes. "Play."

"Come, my dear, we must go." Maxwell placed a hand on Louisa's back. "It's getting late."

She nodded her assent and followed Jane and Charles into the hallway. They had barely taken a half-dozen steps when a clatter arose from behind them.

Louisa gasped and halted, looking back at Samuel's doorway. "Goodness! What was that?"

"Stay here." Charles exchanged a brief glance with Maxwell and went to investigate. He halted on the threshold and muttered something under his breath. Moments later, he rejoined them, a smile on his face.

"Is he all right?" Louisa asked.

"Oh, yes. Nothing to worry about. A few of the dominoes fell on the floor, that's all. Samuel does tend to be a little bit clumsy. I'll have someone pick them up when they bring Tom inside."

Louisa said little as they walked back to the rectory. They didn't there linger long. By the time they clambered into the carriage, the afternoon had almost gone. Louisa, clutching the promised bottle of Jane's rose water, settled at Maxwell's side, heaving a sigh as she tucked her arm through his.

"You must be fatigued," he said, as they set out. "It's been a long day."

Several moments passed in which he could almost hear the cogs turning in her mind. She fidgeted against him and spoke at last. "Papa once told me that some of the most precious things in life are the special memories we collect on the way. Unique little moments that stay with us as long as our memory serves. He calls them trinkets." She released a sigh. "I collected a trinket today, Max. Specifically, my game of dominoes with Samuel."

"You certainly made an impression on him," Maxwell replied.

"Yes, it would seem so. I wonder what his story is?"

"We'll never know."

"No, probably not." She stifled a yawn. "You have no objection to me returning for a visit?"

"None, just as long as you have a chaperone. Me, preferably."

"Samuel is harmless, Max. Besides, you're away so much, who knows when I might be able to return?"

"Nevertheless."

"Mmm, well." Another yawn materialized as she rested her head against his shoulder. "Frankly, I'm too tired to argue about it right now."

"There will be no argument." He glanced down at her and inhaled the soft scent of her hair. "Sleep if you wish, my dear. It'll be a while before we're home."

She fell silent, though her fidgeting told him she was still awake. Then, "I have something to ask you," she said.

"Go on."

"It's about Tom, the young man in the bathchair." She raised her head to look at him. "I'd like us to do something for him."

"What do you have in mind?"

"I wonder if we might arrange for his mother to visit St. Giles House. She's a widow with little means, so isn't able to make the journey but once a year."

Maxwell shifted in his seat. "Louisa, we can't provide for everyone."

"I'm not asking you to do so. Please, Max."

He sighed. "I'll consider it."

She nestled against him again. "Thank you."

As Louisa's breathing settled into the steady rhythm of sleep, Maxwell's mind pondered the events of the day. In particular, his young wife's newly acquired *trinket*. Her encounter with Samuel.

The man's reaction to Louisa had certainly been odd, though not particularly troubling. Such had been Maxwell's first impression, at least. That she had not fled or fainted at the gruesome sight of Samuel's face said much about her strength of character. She should not, however, have entered the man's room unaccompanied.

Maxwell would not prevent her from visiting St. Giles House in the future, but never again would she be left alone with Samuel. First impressions, it seemed, were not necessarily accurate, given what Charles had told him.

When they'd returned to the rectory that afternoon, the ladies had gone inside to refresh a little, while Maxwell and Charles waited outside for the carriage. That's when Charles related the strange truth about the clatter they'd heard. It had, indeed, been the sound of dominoes tumbling to the floor. But it had not been caused by clumsiness on Samuel's part. It had been deliberate.

The dominoes had been swept from the table. Every last one of them.

Samuel, however, was where they had left him. Seated at the table, unmoving and silent, staring at the empty chair opposite.

CHAPTER FOURTEEN

T HE FOLLOWING SATURDAY rolled around, bringing miserable weather and Clarence Ashbridge with it, the first of Maxwell's business colleagues to visit Northcott Manor. Louisa disliked the fellow from the moment of introduction, though if asked, she wouldn't have been able to say exactly why. It was just an overall impression. Tall and slight of build, the man regarded her with slate-grey eyes void of warmth.

"A pleasure to meet you, Mrs. Harlow." He smiled without revealing his teeth, lifted her hand with his gloved one, and bent over it in greeting. Louisa was met by the sight of his bald spot, which had been covered by combing long, threadlike strands of his remaining hair over it.

"Likewise, Mr. Ashbridge." Wearing a false smile, she removed her hand from his grasp as a chill settled on the spot between her shoulder blades. "Welcome to Northcott Manor. Osborne will show you to your room, if you'd care to refresh yourself."

"I DON'T LIKE him," she said, later that evening as she and Maxwell readied themselves for dinner. "He seems very cold-hearted to me."

She was rewarded with a frown. "I'll grant you he's not the

most charming of fellows," Maxwell replied, "but I don't necessarily do business with someone based on their grace and charm. Those attributes can easily be forged. At least Ashbridge speaks as he sees it."

Louisa decided not to pursue it further. This would be the first time she had played hostess to one of Maxwell's business colleagues, and she knew it was important to him. She simply told herself that she'd be glad when the evening was over.

Dinner was served at seven o'clock; the menu comprised of five courses. Louisa watched as their guest picked and poked at each one, her irritation growing each time he pushed his plate aside, having eaten little from it. At one point, she caught Finlay's eye, whose brow lifted a smidgen in obvious understanding. Maxwell seemed oblivious, but then, he and Ashbridge were chatting about the growing demand for coal, the preference for iron-ore from the Basque region of France, and the American demand for quality-made knives from Sheffield.

Louisa wasn't exactly stifling yawns, but any interest she showed in the conversation was totally fabricated.

"The output at my Durham colliery is down this month," Ashbridge said, pushing aside his main course, having barely touched it. "Bloody cholera outbreak. Dropping like flies, they are."

Louisa regarded the man's plate and simply couldn't help herself. "Is the beef not to your liking, Mr. Ashbridge?" she asked.

He regarded her and then glanced at his plate. "The beef is fine, Mrs. Harlow," he replied. "I've never had a particularly large appetite, I'm afraid."

Louisa smiled. "Ah, I see. Well, that explains it."

There followed a moment of silence and then Maxwell cleared his throat. "You were saying, Ashbridge? Cholera?"

"Aye. The deathrate is declining now, but the damage has been done."

"How awful," Louisa said.

"It could have been worse, Mrs. Harlow," the man replied.

"Output will pick up next month, I warrant."

She blinked. "I was talking about the people, Mr. Ashbridge. Your workers. How many did you lose?"

He huffed. "Enough to be inconvenient."

A flush of heat rose up Louisa's throat as she pushed her own plate aside. "Forgive me, sir, but I find your lack of compassion in the face of so much suffering to be somewhat ruthless."

"You might change your tune if you saw how these people live, dear lady," he replied. "They spend their wages on drink and live in filth."

"Might I suggest we halt this conversation immediately?" Maxwell regarded Ashbridge, but also gave Louisa a brief, telling look. "It is not appropriate for a woman's ears."

Louisa gave Maxwell a look of her own. "To casually dismiss the deaths of these poor people is not appropriate for anyone's ears, Maxwell."

"'Tis quite obvious you have led a sheltered life, Mrs. Harlow," Ashbridge said, his tone patronizing. "And your husband is correct. I should not have spoken as I did. I regret doing so and beg your pardon."

The expression on Maxwell's face stopped Louisa from continuing any further, though it took some effort to smooth out her ruffled feathers and summon up a smile. "Apology accepted, Mr. Ashbridge," she replied, the words souring her tongue. "It is true I am not intimately familiar with the hardships suffered by those less fortunate."

Ashbridge merely grunted and veered the conversation toward exports and imports. Louisa, however, sensed that the mood around the table had changed. Was it disappointment or irritation that now firmed Maxwell's jaw and tightened the skin around his eyes? As the meal progressed, Louisa said little else, but simply listened with half-an-ear to the complexities of business and politics. She felt, rather than saw, Maxwell's occasional glance cast her way.

At last, in an effort to make amends, she took advantage of a lull in the conversation. "Do you travel a lot on business, Mr. Ashbridge?" she asked.

"As needed, Mrs. Harlow." He pushed his half-finished dessert plate away and cleared his throat. "Thanks to innovators like your husband, travelling for everyone will soon be much easier. There'll come a day, in the not-too-distant future, when one will be able to hop on a train in York or Leeds and go all the way to London or Glasgow in a matter of hours."

"I can hardly imagine it." Louisa dabbed a corner of her mouth with a napkin and gave Maxwell a glance. He appeared not to notice.

Ashbridge grunted, leaning a little to the side as a maid cleared away his dessert plate. "There are those who continue to proclaim against it, dear lady, but they cannot stop progress. And Britain will be at the forefront, you mark my words. Which reminds me, Harlow, I've invited a German acquaintance to join us on the Glasgow visit next month. He expressed an interest in ordering some of our hardware, since none of theirs quite measures up. I have no qualms vouching for him. I trust you have no objection?"

"None at all," Maxwell replied, taking a sip of wine. "Always willing to consider foreign interests."

"Next month?" Louisa, still clutching her napkin, regarded her husband. "What are the dates of this visit, Maxwell?"

"I'll be leaving here on the fifteenth, I believe," he replied, somewhat warily. "Which is a—"

"Monday." Louisa gave a short, nervous laugh. "We're travelling to Myddleton that day, remember? It's Uncle Isaac's birthday on the twentieth, and the celebrations will be going most of the week."

Maxwell's face colored slightly. "Damnation! I confess it completely slipped my mind."

"That's quite all right. I'm sure you can change your plans." Anxiety shortened Louisa's breath. "You can change them, yes? Reschedule your meeting for a different date?"

Maxwell, looking rather like he'd swallowed a mouthful of vinegar, twirled his wine glass atop the table. "I'm sorry, my dear, I'm afraid I can't. Travel arrangements have already been made and hotel rooms booked. Changing everything now would inconvenience a lot of people."

Louisa's throat tightened. "Then I must insist you inconvenience them. This is a family occasion, Maxwell, and an important one. Everyone will be there."

"I know, my dear, and I apologize for my oversight." He shot a brief, telling glance at their guest, inferring the need for decorum. "I suggest we discuss it later, all right?"

Before Louisa could respond, Clarence Ashbridge cleared his throat in an exaggerated fashion that seemed to imply he favored Maxwell's suggestion.

"Can I not stand in for you, Maxwell?" Finlay asked.

"An excellent solution, Finlay, thank you," Louisa replied, still looking at Maxwell. "There. I believe the problem is solved."

"I appreciate the offer, Finlay," Maxwell said, holding Louisa's gaze unflinchingly, "but I absolutely *have* to be at this meeting. It's far too important to miss."

Louisa parted with another nervous laugh, though she felt more like crying. "Family is more important in this case, Maxwell," she said. "*I* am more important. I would ask, therefore, that you find an acceptable solution to this... this *oversight* of yours."

Maxwell's expression hardened, as did his voice. "And I would ask, my dear, that you remember where you are!"

The subsequent moment of silence seemed to amplify the futility of Louisa's argument. She inhaled and closed her eyes, seeking to control her anger and disappointment. But she could not stay there a moment longer. She opened her eyes and looked straight at their guest. "I do beg your pardon, Mr. Ashbridge. What must you think of me?" She rose to her feet and threw an icy glare at Maxwell. "I fear I'm not myself all of a sudden. That being so, I think it best if I leave you gentlemen to enjoy your port. If you'll excuse me."

The men stood as manners dictated.

"No need for an apology, Mrs. Harlow, I quite understand." Ashbridge inclined his head. "Thank you for a splendid evening. The meal was delicious."

Given that the man had hardly eaten anything, it took all Louisa had not to respond petulantly. Instead, she forced yet another smile. "I'm glad you enjoyed it, Mr. Ashbridge," she replied and glanced around the table. "I bid you all a goodnight, gentleman."

"Goodnight, Louisa," Finlay said, the cheer in his voice quite obviously forced.

Maxwell merely nodded but remained silent.

"Now you know why I never married," Ashbridge said, his remark following Louisa from the room. "I have never been able to fathom female hysterics."

Maxwell's reply could also be heard. "My wife's outburst was inappropriate, Ashbridge, and for that I apologize, but I wouldn't say she was hysterical."

"Only because you put her in her place," the odious man replied. "And quite right, too. Women are too easily influenced by foolish sentiment, which is why they are of little use in business and politics. They simply do not have the head for either one."

LOUISA SEETHED ALL the way to her bedroom and barely stopped short of slamming her door behind her. Couldn't they have waited till she'd gone out of earshot? Did they think she couldn't hear them? *Hysterics?* Hardly that.

At least Maxwell had somewhat defended her. As for putting her in her place… well, perhaps she had behaved in a less-than-appropriate fashion, but their guest had irritated her throughout the meal. She might have otherwise endured, but learning of Maxwell's so-called oversight, and his subsequent refusal to do anything about it, had been the final straw.

Something inside, already overburdened, had finally crumpled.

Flopping down at her dressing-table, she pondered her reflection as she removed her earrings. She thought about summoning Archer to help her prepare for bed but decided against it. Solitude suited her right now. Her bed had already been turned down, and a couple of flickering lanterns kept the deepening shadows at bay. Not that she had any intention of sleeping. She intended to hold Maxwell to his word and discuss the issue, no matter what time he came to bed. She opened the adjoining door and stood on the threshold, inhaling his familiar scent. Given that he was leaving early the next day, she didn't think he'd linger too long over his port. How long did he say he'd be gone this time? Was it four days? Five? They'd only been back from Knaresborough a week, and he'd spent three days of that ensconced in his study with Finlay.

Since she'd had foreknowledge of his frequent absences, it wouldn't be fair to complain about them. Besides, some wives, like those with husbands in the military, didn't see their husbands for months at a time.

But Maxwell wasn't in the military.

It was hardly unreasonable, then, to expect him to make an effort to accompany her on special occasions, such as family gatherings. He was her husband, after all. Obviously, he didn't give such things much consideration.

Still riled, she left the adjoining door open as she undressed and prepared for bed. Then she curled up in the chair by her window to watch the end of a less-than-happy day. Tears of frustration threatened more than once, but she blinked them away.

Almost an hour slid by before she heard the familiar sound of Maxwell's outer door opening and closing. Apprehension shortened her breath as she looked over to the adjoining door. A moment later, he appeared on the threshold, his expression impossible to read in the half-light. At the sight of him, Louisa's resolve faltered a little. Though their short marriage was not exactly a testimony to a fairytale romance, they had never once fought. They hadn't even argued. At least, not heatedly.

"I thought you'd be asleep," he said, frowning as he unfastened his cravat.

Thought? Or hoped?

"I'm too upset to sleep." Determined to state her case anew, Louisa slid from her chair and moved toward him, raising her chin. "You said we could discuss things later, so I'd like to discuss them."

By the subsequent look on his face, he wasn't so keen. "There's really nothing to discuss, my dear. I apologized for my oversight, and I meant it. The fault is mine entirely, and I don't blame you for being upset." A muscle twitched in his jaw. "Your behavior at dinner, however, was totally inappropriate. You embarrassed me."

"And I regret doing so," Louisa replied. "However, I don't like the man at all. He appears to be completely without compassion."

"Nevertheless, he's a potential investor. One who could allow me to expand my interests substantially."

Louisa huffed. "I'm frankly shocked that you'd have anything to do with a man who cares so little for the welfare of his workers."

Maxwell's eyes narrowed. "If his lack of principles bothers you, my dear, I suggest you take a good look at your own."

She gasped. "I beg your pardon?"

He pulled his cravat free. "There are still children as young as ten hauling buckets of coal from the depths of the earth, Louisa. Perhaps you should consider that the next time you warm yourself by the fire. And, while you're at it, be sure not to purchase any more wool, cotton or linen unless you can say, with certainty, that the millworkers are well-treated and being paid a decent wage." He sighed. "Doing business with men like Ashbridge offers opportunities to point out their failings, to suggest alternate methods and demonstrate how things might be improved for both master and worker. Changes are taking place, but there are more that need to be made, and there are those among us intent on making them. They aren't going to happen overnight, however, or next week, or probably even next year. For now, whether we like it or not, it is the way of things. I suggest, instead, you consider what would become of these families if they had no work at all."

"It is not much of a choice, though, is it? To risk death from making a living or to die from starvation."

"No, it isn't, and Ashbridge should not have breached the subject as he did. But your reaction to it was still inappropriate. As my wife, I expected better from you."

Louisa gave him a scathing look. "Well, since we're speaking of expectations, may I point out that, as my husband, I expect you to be at my side when our mutual attendance is required at important family events. Uncle Isaac's party is such an event, Maxwell. I don't want to be there without you. Please, you must reschedule!"

"I would if I could," he replied. "But I simply can't."

She folded her arms. "You absolutely have to be in Glasgow."

"Yes, I absolutely do." He tossed his cravat aside and undid his collar. "It's a very important gathering."

"More important than me?" Too late, Louisa's merciless memory hurled her back to a night when Sybella Chessington had uttered those very same words.

Maxwell's subsequent laughter held no mirth. "I'm not even going to dignify that ridiculous question with an answer."

"Then perhaps you should try to see things from my point of view. It's been a week since we got back from Knaresborough and, not including tonight, we've had dinner together twice in that time." She sighed. "Even when you're at home, you spend more time with Finlay than you do with me. You obviously prefer his company to mine."

He scowled. "Don't be absurd."

"Absurd?" Her pent-up emotions bubbled closer to the surface. "Fifteen days, Maxwell, to be precise, and that includes the two days this week. That's how much time we've had together since we got back from our honeymoon. Fifteen days."

"My God." Hands on hips, he looked away and parted with another humorless laugh. "You're actually keeping a tally."

"You gave me a journal, remember? It's easy to keep a tally when I spend time each day writing about my life." Louisa's bottom lip quivered. "When doing so reminds me that I am so often alone."

His angry gaze snapped back to her. "I told you how it would be, Louisa. I made it very clear, in fact."

"I know you did, which is why I've never complained. In truth, it makes me even more grateful for the time we *do* have together, and I've not once made a demand on you for more." She drew breath, endeavoring to shore up her crumbling emotions. "But I'm making a demand now, because this gathering is important to me. Can't you ask Finlay to act in your stead? I understand he has full authority to do so, and I'm sure he's more than capable."

Though still frowning, Maxwell's eyes assumed a pensive glimmer, and, for a moment, Louisa dared to hope. "You know, it occurs to me that you haven't been the same since we got back from Knaresborough last week," he said, at last. "I suspect the incident with that unfortunate fellow has affected you more than you realize, which might explain this emotional outburst."

Louisa gaped at him. "What happened at St. Giles House has absolutely bugger all to do with this."

He gave her a derisive look. "Vulgarity does not become you, madam."

"I do not care, sir! I just want…" Not wishing to give merit to Ashbridge's accusation of hysterics, she took another slow breath.

"I'm simply asking you for some consideration. Is it beyond you to provide it?"

He heaved a sigh. "Not usually, no. But in this case, there's no consideration to be made. I've apologized, Louisa, and that is all I can do. If bouquets of flowers and gifts of jewelry will further appease you, than I shall return from Sheffield laden with them."

She shook her head. "I have no need of either." *What I need, you cannot give me. Or you* will *not.*

He ran a hand through his hair. "Then I must declare this issue closed. Ashbridge and I are leaving at dawn, and I would like to get some rest. I suggest you do the same. Goodnight, my dear."

He turned away and closed the door with a resolute click.

Dumbfounded, Louisa stared at the barrier he had just placed between them, her frustration going from a barely controlled simmer to a rolling boil. "How dare you?" she muttered, through gritted teeth. Fists clenched, she stepped forward and put her mouth close to the door seam. "Since you consider my request for your presence at a family gathering to be an *emotional outburst*, I shall grant you another. For your future consideration, I do not like being called 'madam'. I find your tone to be patronizing and given our *social* inequality, quite inappropriate. Goodnight, *sir*."

Even as the words spilled from her tongue, she regretted them. She stepped back, pressed a hand over her mouth, and bit down against a sickening aftermath of remorse. *Oh, I should not have said that.*

She stepped forward again and lifted a hand to knock, intent on apologizing, wishing to make amends. *Wait,* an inner voice said. *Wait till morning. The light of day might offer a different perspective.*

True, enough had been said already, saturating the space between them with bitterness and regret. The air needed to clear. Of course, she'd have to be up early to catch him before he left. Shivering, she clambered into her bed, curled up in a ball, and mulled over what had been their first quarrel. Certainly not a milestone to be celebrated. It had been ugly.

Miserable to the core, Louisa at last gave freedom to her suppressed tears, her sobs erupting in hard silence. Sleep, when it came, was uneasy and filled with scattered, nonsensical dreams.

When she next awoke, the fading darkness and the song of a solitary blackbird beyond her window told her the night was almost over. Rubbing her eyes, she turned onto her back, straining her ears to listen for sounds of movement in the next room. But all was silent. She sat up, eyes widening in the gloom. Had he left already? Had she missed him?

As if in response, from somewhere outside came the mumble of men's voices, followed immediately by the sound of a carriage door closing and wheels on gravel.

With a cry, Louise scrambled out of bed, grabbed her dressing gown, and fled. Gown flying behind her like wings, she reached the bottom of the stairs just as Osborne began to close the front door.

"No!" she cried.

The butler spun around, eyes widening at the sight of her running toward him. "Er, good morning, ma'am. Is everything—?"

"I must speak with my husband." She brushed by him, hauled the front door open, and let out a shriek at the sight of the carriage pulling away. "Stop! Max, wait, *please.*"

The driver obviously heard her and reined the horses to a halt.

Oh, thank you, thank you, thank you!

Chest heaving, Louisa stepped out into the soft morning light, the stone-step hard and cold beneath her bare feet. For several moments, nothing happened. The carriage remained closed. Was Maxwell waiting for her to approach? Louisa eyed the gravel drive with trepidation. Then, to her relief, the carriage door opened, and he peered out. After saying something to the others, inaudible to Louisa, he stepped down and strode toward her.

Teeth chattering, Louisa tugged her dressing gown closed,

her stomach doing its customary flip at the sight of the man she had married. Only as he drew near did she see the dark shadows beneath his eyes. It appeared he had not slept at all, which only added weight to her conscience.

"What is it, Louisa?" He cast a critical gaze over her. "Are you unwell?"

"Yes." She swallowed and shook her head. "I mean, no. I just… I just wanted to apologize for what I said last night. Please forgive me. I didn't mean it."

A frown appeared. "Which part?"

"Pardon?"

"Which part didn't you mean?"

"Oh." She chewed on her lip. "The part about our social differences."

"Ah." He nodded. "Nothing to forgive, lass. I realized they were merely words spoken in anger. Is that it?"

"Well, um, yes."

"Right. I should be back on Friday." He moved closer still, dropped a kiss on her cheek, and then turned to leave. "Go and put some clothes on before you catch a chill."

"No, Max, wait, please!" She reached out, as if doing so might hold him in place.

He halted and turned to her again. "Louisa, I really have to go."

"But you're still angry, I can tell." Her hand dropped to her side. "Please don't be. My father says a man must never leave his home angry lest he might live to regret it."

"I'm not angry at all," he said. "I'm sure being married to me is not easy, and I've probably expected too much from you. We'll discuss it when I return. Now, if you'll excuse me, my dear, the carriage is waiting."

Expected too much? What did that mean, exactly? Had she failed him, then? Tears blurred her vision as he walked away. "Maxwell?"

He paused at the carriage door and turned back once more,

arching a brow in question. Louisa pushed a strand of hair from her eyes. "I love you," she called, and hugged herself.

Another frown appeared and he stared at her for a prolonged moment, hands slowly clenching at his sides. Then, "I have to go, Louisa. I'll be back on Friday evening."

"DID YOU SORT it out, Harlow?" Ashbridge asked, as Maxwell clambered back into the carriage.

"Nothing to sort out," Maxwell answered, feeling slightly ill as he settled back against the soft leather. "Everything is fine."

The man huffed. "Women," he muttered, and turned his gaze to the window. "Irrational creatures. Apologies if I fall asleep and start snoring."

Maxwell resisted an urge to look back at the manor, afraid it would be his undoing. He knew Louisa would still be there, barefoot on the steps, watching as the carriage drove away. Instead, he met Finlay's gaze and then switched his attention to the window, not willing to acknowledge the vague look of disapproval on his brother's face.

Even for Maxwell, who generally slept little, the night had been a long and restless exercise in self-recrimination. Although he hadn't actually heard her, he knew Louisa had cried herself to sleep. The mere thought of her doing so sickened him to the core, yet he'd clung doggedly to his pride. *I warned her*, he argued silently, seeking to lighten the lead weight on his conscience. *She knew, from the start, how the marriage would be.*

So why did he feel so bloody guilty?

Damn it.

He dared to look at Finlay again, and this time was granted with a sympathetic smile, which he actually found worse than the previous look of disapproval. He scowled at his brother and turned his attention back to the window, feigning interest in the passing countryside. His reflection stared back at him like a separate entity, critical and accusing.

He filled his lungs slowly and relaxed his expression, determinedly shifting his thoughts to the importance of the upcoming meeting. He needed a clear head. But a little voice at the back of his mind told him it was going to be a long week.

Then, from the opposite seat came a couple of snorts, followed by a sequence of snuffles, finishing off with a series of rhythmic, throaty snores. Maxwell exchanged yet another glance with his brother, both now sharing expressions of amusement.

It was also going to be a long trip.

Chapter Fifteen

A MUTED HUM of conversation permeated the smoky air of the hotel's dining-room. Male voices dominated, several of which emanated from Maxwell's dinner table. At that precise moment, however, Maxwell was paying them little attention. His mind had wandered onto another track, and not for the first time that week. It appeared his feelings toward his wife had undergone a change. It had been unexpected. Unforeseen. Unwanted, even.

He'd argued with himself constantly, trying to deny the truth of it. Louisa had, after all, been warned about his lifestyle prior to him placing the wedding ring on her finger. She'd been told what to expect. He'd taken great pains to clarify it, precisely because he didn't want to hear her complain about his frequent absences. Therefore, her tirade on Saturday night had surely been unreasonable. Except, when all things had been considered, it hadn't been unreasonable. Not really.

Not at all.

Unfortunately, he could not say the same about his response to it.

True, the lass had been a little out of sorts since returning from Knaresborough the previous week. He'd feared the visit to St. Giles House might have been upsetting for her, and indeed, it obviously had been. Not because of any snobbish revulsion or feminine fragility, but because of a simple game of dominoes with a pitiful soul who'd touched her heart. Maxwell had used that to make allowances for her emotional behavior at dinner that night, and later, when they argued in their chambers. But her arguments on both occasions, he had to admit, had teeth.

As she'd stated, up till that point she hadn't complained once about his business trips. To the contrary, she'd been fully supportive, wishing him a successful trip and a safe journey each time he'd left. Not a hint of melancholy or resentment to be seen. She'd made it easy for him.

In the beginning, at least.

As time went on, however, things changed. Louisa still never complained, but her cheery farewells had lost a little of their previous enthusiasm, her smiles hiding a truth she didn't think he could see. But Maxwell wasn't blind. He knew his frequent absences were increasingly hard on her.

At first, he'd ignored it, but it had become progressively difficult to do so. Lately, he found himself dreading every new departure, when he had to look in her eyes and see the sadness behind the smile. At the same time, he resented what he saw as a loss of control and an unwelcome shift in his priorities. It was a situation he hadn't bargained for, leaving him disconcerted.

Nor had he been prepared for Louisa's declaration of love, made during their passionate encounter in the East Parlor a few weeks before. Those three little words had knocked him off his pragmatic pedestal. At the time, he'd thought about responding in kind—till it occurred to him that having to actually think about it surely negated its sincerity.

An avowal of love should at least be truthful.

Such declarations were often made on impulse, and especially in moments of high passion. Consequently, he couldn't be certain Louisa had actually meant what she'd said either. It seemed unlikely. They hadn't been married very long, after all. And Maxwell had never declared his love to anyone before, in truth or falsehood. Quite simply, he'd never felt compelled to do so.

While he respected women and enjoyed their company, the concept of romantic love had always left him a little mystified. It had no clear definition. It could not be categorized. It seemed to be a cumulation of emotions, oft times spontaneous and unpredictable. Much like women, in truth.

Affection, admiration, satisfaction—these things he recognized. They could be cleanly applied to many aspects of life, together or individually. And Maxwell, without hesitation, applied all of them to his wife. Louisa had quickly gained his affection and his admiration. And, whether between the sheets or atop a silk-damask settee, she gave him great satisfaction. He considered himself a fortunate man and had said as much to her several times.

But, of late, none of the recognizable epithets seemed to sufficiently describe what he felt for his wife. Love, with all its mysterious depths and complexities, seemed to be far more fitting.

He'd been struggling with that reality since he'd left Louisa standing on the doorstep four days earlier. A sad apparition dressed all in white, face pale and drawn, feet naked upon the cold stone. The image still haunted him. Her parting words had been the second declaration of her love, and there could be no doubting the sincerity of it this time. The tearful glint in her eyes, the heartfelt tremble in her voice, had caused his throat to tighten.

At that point, he'd almost told Ashbridge to leave without him. The desire to take Louisa in his arms, to carry her back to bed and make love to her, had been close to overwhelming. He wanted to hold her, to tell her that her objections had been justified. That he'd misspoken and deeply regretted it. Instead, to his utter shame, he'd left her, tears and all. She had not failed him. He had failed her.

Miserably.

No, there was no getting away from it. After four days of exhaustive contemplation, he'd finally arrived at a couple of conclusions.

He'd behaved like an arse. And he'd fallen in love with his wife.

Yet, despite his conclusions, or perhaps because of them, doubt still plagued him. Did his heartless behavior mean he *didn't* love her? The thought wandered through his mind, seeking a definitive answer. Instead, it returned with a different question.

Could you live without her?

Aye, I could. An ache took hold of his heart. *But I wouldn't want to. In fact, I can't even bear to think of—*

"Will you be joining us in the bar, Harlow? If we stay here much longer, they'll be serving us breakfast." Ashbridge's strident voice snapped Maxwell's attention back to the dining room at the Crown Hotel. The dozen or so shareholders, including Finlay, who'd had been seated with him at the supper table, were rising to their feet. This being Wednesday evening, it had been a productive couple of days, with things going more smoothly than he'd anticipated. There were still a few minor issues to be ironed out, all fairly straightforward. By tomorrow night, everything would be officially signed and sealed, metaphorically and otherwise.

Finlay cleared his throat. "We're removing to the bar for a nightcap, Max."

"Yes, of course." Maxwell rose also. "Forgive me, gentlemen. I was elsewhere for a moment. If you'll excuse me, I believe I shall retire for the night. Fin, a quick word, if you please."

With parting mumbles, the others went off to the bar.

Finlay gave Maxwell an enquiring look. "What do you need, brother?"

"Nothing more tonight, but I'd like you to give my apologies to the others in the morning. I'd do it now, but I'm not in the mood for their questions."

Finlay's brows lifted. "You're leaving?"

He nodded. "Going back to the manor, first thing. You can finish up here."

The brows rose even more. "Me?"

"Aye, you."

Finlay shook his head. "Forgive me, Max. I don't understand.

You're leaving tomorrow morning."

"Correct."

"And you're asking me to finish up here."

"I am."

"Are you unwell?"

He shook his head. "No, I'm fine. I have a private matter needing my attention, that's all. Am I asking too much of you?"

"Of course not. It's the fact that you're asking that has me worried. It's an unusual request, to say the least." Fin narrowed his eyes. "Are you sure you're all right? You've been a little off kilter since we left Northcott."

Maxwell grimaced. "Has it been that noticeable?"

"Only to me, I'm sure. To the rest, you're just your usual ruthless self." He cocked his head. "A private matter, you say? Dare I ask if you've seen the light with regards to Louisa? If so, it's about bloody time. I was beginning to suspect my genius of a brother was, in reality, a complete arse."

Maxwell scowled. "I have no idea what you're talking about. And you're wrong. It's not an unusual request, it's bloody well unheard of. Just promise me you won't bugger things up."

Finlay smiled and drew a cross over his heart. "I promise I won't bugger things up, Max."

"Good." Maxwell tugged on his earlobe. "Actually, Fin, I might be relying on you more and more in the months to come. I'd like you to take over some of my business responsibilities, with the appropriate compensation, of course. I trust you'll be willing?"

The smile turned into a grin. "Bloody hell! You have seen the light, haven't you?"

"Just answer the damn question."

The grin remained. "Damn right, I'm willing."

"That's what I hoped to hear." And it was, though Maxwell couldn't help but feel a touch of angst. "In the meantime, I'll look forward to receiving your report when you return."

Finlay's expression sobered. "Louisa's a fine lady, Max. You're a fortunate man."

"I know I am." Maxwell gave his brother's shoulder a squeeze. "Enjoy your nightcap. Only the one, mind. You need to be clear-headed tomorrow, though I think we've covered everything of note. You might want to reiterate the legal requirements regarding the export—"

"*Goodnight*, Max." Finlay winked. "Give my regards to Louisa."

A short while later, Maxwell stood by his bedroom window and looked out over the wet, gaslit streets of Sheffield, waiting for something to happen. An earthquake, perhaps, splitting the ground apart. Or a host of thunderbolts, raining down like flaming arrows from cloudy skies. But no. The earth remained intact, and the skies remained empty. Obviously, then, he had no cause to worry. Asking Finlay to act on his behalf had not resulted in some kind of cataclysm. The world had not ended.

Indeed, for Maxwell, at that moment, it felt rather like a new beginning.

CHAPTER SIXTEEN

DESPITE THE BLUE skies and sunshine, the day of Maxwell's departure four days before had been a gloomy one for Louisa. After he left, she'd returned to her bed and, beset by misery, stayed there till noon. In her daydreams, Maxwell told Ashbridge to go to Sheffield without him. Then he'd returned to where she stood, hoisted her in his arms, and carried her back to bed, declaring she was the most important thing in his life, and that he'd reschedule the Glasgow meeting.

But daydreams they were. The reality was far different. Her spell of melancholy lasted till the afternoon, when she shrugged it off and allowed Archer to primp and pamper her. Feeling a little less wretched, she'd wandered out into the garden and had a chat with Reuben before spending the rest of the day with her nose buried in a book.

Tuesday and Wednesday brought ceaseless rain, effectively trapping Louisa indoors. By Thursday morning, she was ready to escape the confines of the house, no matter the weather. Fortunately, the rain had stopped, and by lunchtime, the sun had reappeared.

Louisa hurried out to the stable, waiting with some impatience as McKinney tacked Byron.

"I trust you'll be heading up onto the moor, ma'am," the man said, leading the horse to the mounting block.

"Yes." Louisa settled herself into the saddle and gathered up the reins. "I'm going to give this fellow a run and then spend a couple of hours at Highfield. I'll be back before dark."

"Might I have Henry ride with you, ma'am? For your own safety, that is. It put down a lot of rain these past two days. Ground'll be sopping-wet."

It was an obligatory suggestion. The stablemaster, familiar with Louisa's ways, undoubtedly knew what the response would be. She smiled. "I appreciate your concern, Mr. McKinney, but it's not necessary. I'm sure I'll be fine."

A short while later, she halted Byron at the crest of a rise and breathed deep of the pure air. Here, out in the open, away from the confines of walls and windows, she could think without hindrance or distraction.

Tomorrow, Maxwell would return. Louisa looked forward to it… and also dreaded it a little. Her ire had cooled substantially, though she still hoped to persuade him to change his mind about Uncle Isaac's birthday gathering. Maybe, since he'd been away, he'd also taken some time to think about it.

She patted Byron's neck. "Ideally, Byron, my husband will apologize sincerely and then make love to me." Blushing at the thought, she laughed and looked toward the distant horizon. "Ready for a run, my boy? Let's go."

"I WAS BEGINNING to think you'd forgotten about us, dear sister." Julian's scowl was belied by a twinkle in his eye. "It's been what… a whole fortnight since you were last here?"

"Almost three weeks, actually." Louisa wrinkled her nose. "And it's nice to know I've been so sorely missed, dear brother."

Julian grinned and settled back in his chair, the delicate china teacup looking quite lost in his large hand. He took a sip. "Where has your esteemed husband gone this time, and for how long?"

"He left for Sheffield on Sunday and should be back tomorrow," Louisa replied, deciding not to mention anything about their disagreement. "But we recently had a full week together. Actually, almost a week and a half."

"That long?" He reached for a biscuit. "Goodness. Things are markedly improving, then."

"I'm not sure they need to improve." She shrugged. "Have you ever heard me complain about his absences?"

"No, but the time I alluded to you being abandoned, you almost began to cry, so I assumed I'd rubbed salt into a hidden wound." He dipped the biscuit in his tea. "You do have a tendency to suffer in silence, Lou."

"Nonsense. It just wasn't a very nice thing to say."

"It was said lightly."

"Well, I didn't find it funny."

"Apparently not. Oh, bollocks!" Julian regarded the remains of his biscuit still clasped in his hand, the rest of it relegated to the soggy depths of his teacup.

"*That's* funny," Louisa said, giggling. "Serves you right for dipping, dear brother. It's terribly plebeian."

"Who cares? I've no one to impress." Julian shoved the remainder of his biscuit in his mouth.

"Oh? The last time I spoke with Mama, she hinted that you were corresponding with Miss…" Louisa frowned. "Haverley, is it? Baron Fitzwalter's daughter?"

Julian grabbed another biscuit. "Haverley, yes. Priscilla."

"Of course. Priscilla. I remember meeting her at a party in January. Has your correspondence ceased?"

"It has, probably because she has apparently accepted an offer from Cuthbertson."

Louisa's teacup paused on its way to her mouth. "As in Viscount?"

"Yes." He brushed crumbs from his waistcoat. "A little higher up the noble ladder than the son of an army captain."

"You're the nephew of an earl."

"And Cuthbertson is the son of one."

"You don't appear to be terribly heartbroken. Would you like my opinion?"

"No."

"She was too priggish for you."

"I thought I said no." Julian scowled into his teacup. "In fact, I'm sure I did."

"What did Mama have to say?"

"She didn't say much at all, actually."

"I'll wager she thinks as I do." Louisa sighed and cast a glance around the sitting-room. "It's a pity they aren't here. I should like to have seen them."

"They, and the demonic duplicates, are due back from Myddleton tonight. Why don't you stay over?"

Louisa laughed at Julian's reference to the twins. "Don't call them that!"

"Why not? It suits them. I simply cannot wait for their debut into society. Lord knows what kind of antics they'll get up to. I suspect they'll be in disgrace within a week of their arrival in London and the Northcott name will be forever tarnished. Your little episode in Richmond's salacious study will pale by comparison."

"Oh, I suspect Aunt Eleanor and Cousin Catherine will keep them in check." She took a sip of tea. "And thank you, but no, I can't stay. I told McKinney I'd be back before dark. If I don't show, he'll organize a search party. Besides, as much as I love it, Highfield is no longer my home."

Julian frowned. "Highfield will always be your home, Louisa."

"You know what I mean." Not liking the sudden lump in her throat, she changed the subject. "I must tell you! Maxwell and I recently had a lovely trip to Knaresborough." She then proceeded to describe their day and mentioned the visit to St. Giles House.

Julian looked unimpressed, perhaps even a little horrified. "What on earth would possess Harlow to take you to a place like that?"

"I wanted to see it. And it's quite a nice place, all things considered."

Julian huffed. "I still don't think he should have allowed it. Those institutions are breeding grounds for illness. What if you'd caught something?"

"Well, I didn't." She drew breath to steady herself before continuing with her account. Maxwell had not been wrong when he'd said the visit had affected her. "It's not your typical institution, Julian. Far from it. I did have a bit of an upsetting experience there, though. I can't stop thinking about it."

Julian sputtered and almost choked on his mouthful of biscuit. "Bloody hell, Louisa. Did one of them hurt you?"

"Oh, goodness, no, nothing like that. None of the residents are dangerous. Quite the contrary." She told him the story of Samuel. "It truly was the strangest thing. To weep as he did, and then to speak to me when he'd never spoken to anyone before. It defies explanation."

Julian pondered. "Do they get many female visitors at this place?"

She shrugged. "I'm not sure. I don't think so. Family members, perhaps. Some of the volunteers are women, I think. And Jane visits regularly."

"I suspect most of these women are well past their prime."

"Meaning what?"

"Meaning, you're probably the first attractive young woman he's seen in years. Hence his reaction."

Louisa shook her head. "I don't think that's it at all. He simply seemed happy to see me. There was no impropriety."

"You said he held your hand."

"Well, briefly, yes, but—"

"There you are then," Julian said. "The poor fellow was thrilled to have some attractive female company. So much so, he shed a tear of gratitude and found the wherewithal to utter his first word in years."

Louisa frowned at her brother's flippancy. "Two words,

actually."

"What was the other one?"

"Gray."

Julian set his cup down and brushed crumbs from his trousers. "Used in what context?"

She shrugged. "He just put both words together. Play *gray*."

"Makes no sense.

"No, it doesn't. As Charles said, Samuel is a wonderful mystery."

"So, it would seem." Julian narrowed his eyes. "I can tell the episode had quite the effect on you. Either that, or there's something else amiss. Tell me the truth, Lou. I get the distinct impression something is bothering you."

"Nothing is bothering me. I told you. Everything is fine." She smiled and switched the conversation to more comfortable territory, enquiring after Josiah and Arthur.

"They're both well, as far as I know," Julian replied. "Arthur's excelling in school and Josiah is, I expect, still happily wielding his brushes."

Louisa regarded him, looking for a sign that he was aware of Josiah's *risqué* ventures. She saw none.

"You'll see them at Uncle Isaac's party," Julian continued. "It'll be the first time the family has all been together since your wedding."

"Can't wait!" She almost told him about Maxwell's Glasgow meeting but decided against it. There was yet plenty of time to change Maxwell's mind. Instead, she glanced at the mantel clock and rose to her feet. "It's getting late, brother mine. I'd best be on my way."

He stood also. "Are you sure you won't stay the night?"

"I'm sure. Though in hindsight, I wished I'd told McKinney not to expect me. Maxwell won't be back till tomorrow night, so I could have stayed till the morning, at least."

Julian followed her out to the hallway and waited while she stood in front of the mirror and settled her hat atop her head.

"You look so much like Mama," he said, a touch of wistfulness in his voice.

Louisa smiled and turned to him. "Dawkins used to tell me that all the time. Be sure to give Mama and Papa my love. And the demonic duplicates as well, of course."

Julian grinned. "Will do. Shall I escort you back? Partway, at least?"

"Thank you, dearest, but it's not necessary." She raised up on tiptoes and kissed his cheek. "I love you, Jules."

"Love you too."

A short while later, Louisa halted Byron beneath the oak tree and looked back toward Highfield, feeling a familiar twinge of sentimentality. *Julian was right. It will always be my home.* As she urged Byron onward, she wondered if she'd ever feel the same about her marital home, no matter where it was. Perhaps she might when she had children, if and when they came. In any case, the visit with Julian had proven to be a much-needed boost to her spirits. Perhaps that's what she lacked more than anything—simple conversation and a sharing of thoughts and perspectives. Well, perhaps not *all* her thoughts, but enough to lighten the burden.

Feeling calmer than she had in days, Louisa kept Byron at a jaunty walk. A thin, patchy mist had drifted across the land while she'd been at Highfield, though it was nothing of any real concern. Consequently, she allowed her mind to wander through her memories of family, marriage, and recent events. She was brought back to the moment when a couple of grouse fluttered out of a nearby clump of heather. Byron danced on his hooves and whickered, tossing his head. Demanding.

"All right, my boy," Louisa muttered, shortening the reins. "Let's go."

CHAPTER SEVENTEEN

D USK HAD CREPT over the land by the time Maxwell alighted the carriage. He gazed up at Northcott Manor's impressive façade, where a couple of the windows glowed invitingly, and his gut tightened with anticipation. Undoubtedly, Louisa would be surprised to see him. He'd spent much of his journey home figuring out what he would say to her. In the end, he'd given up trying to memorize a script. He'd simply tell her the truth without any embellishment.

"Your trunk, Mr. Harlow," the driver said, setting it on the ground.

Maxwell muttered his thanks, stepped up to the door, and pushed it open to see Osborne hurrying toward him.

"Welcome back, Mr. Harlow. Is everything all right, sir? We weren't expecting you till tomorrow."

"Everything is fine, Osborne. Simply a change of plan." He removed his hat. "I trust all is well here?"

"It is indeed, sir," the man replied, taking the hat.

"Where might I find Mrs. Harlow?"

"I'm not sure where the mistress is at the moment, sir." He took Maxwell's coat as well. "She visited Highfield this afternoon, but I overheard Mr. McKinney saying she'd returned a short while ago."

"That's all right, I'll find her. Have my trunk taken upstairs, will you?"

The man nodded. "Of course, sir. Right away."

Maxwell first went to the sitting-room, expecting to see Louisa seated on the settee, her nose tucked into one of her beloved books. But the room was empty. Next, he checked the library and the east parlor. All empty.

Maybe she'd decided to retire early, he thought, and headed for the stairs, only to meet Archer on her way down.

"Mr. Harlow!" The maid failed to hide her surprise. "You're returned early, sir."

"It would seem so," he replied, tamping down an unreasonable flare of impatience at her stating the obvious. Since searching for Louisa, a strange sense of unease had settled in the back of his mind, inexplicable and unwelcome. "Mrs. Harlow is in her chamber, I take it?"

"Actually, sir, no, she isn't. I don't know where she is. I've been looking for her as well. She returned from Highfield an hour ago, apparently. I expected her to summon me, but she never did, which is why I came looking, just to make sure she was all right. I fear she's been a little… melancholic this week, sir."

Guilt lifted its sorry little head, but Maxwell ignored it, instead focusing on one word that had leapt out at him. "*Apparently?* What does that mean, Archer? Is Mrs. Harlow here or not?"

A faint blush arose in Archer's cheeks. "According to Mr. McKinney, she is, sir."

"Then where is she?" he muttered, a tingle of apprehension brushing across his nape. "Is McKinney downstairs?"

"I believe so, sir. In the staff dining room."

Maxwell nodded his thanks and turned away.

"Mr. Harlow?"

Arching a brow, he regarded her once more.

"Welcome back, sir."

He nodded again, aware of the relief in her statement, uncertain if it made him feel better or worse. He headed below stairs, drawn to the staffroom by the sounds of chit-chat and laughter.

His arrival on the threshold was noticed immediately and halted all conversation. In unison, all around the table rose to their feet, including McKinney.

Maxwell addressed him. "I understand Mrs. Harlow returned home some time ago, McKinney. Can you confirm that?"

The man blinked. "Yes, Mr. Harlow, about an hour ago, I believe."

"You *believe?*" He suppressed a sigh. "Did you actually see her?"

"Um, no sir," he replied, looking decidedly uneasy, "I haven't seen her yet."

"God, give me strength." Hands on hips, Maxwell cast his gaze over those present and raised his voice. "Has anyone here seen Mrs. Harlow since she returned?"

There followed a low chorus of denials and much shaking of heads.

"'Twas young George who told me she'd returned, sir," McKinney said, now looking rather pale. "I had no reason to doubt him."

"And where might I find young George?"

"He's likely seeing to your carriage horses, sir." McKinney moved toward the door. "I'll fetch him right away."

"No," Maxwell replied. "I'm coming with you."

A single lantern, hanging from a hook, cast a halo of light partway into the stable, where all but a couple of the stalls were occupied. The rest stood in near darkness, the silence disturbed by the rustle of hay and the subdued sounds of horses settling in for the night. A voice drifted out from one of the stalls, a low muttering, obviously meant only for a horse's ears.

"George." McKinney strode over to the stall. "Get out here, lad!"

The lad appeared a moment later, eyes wide. "Yes, Mr. McKinney?" His eyes widened ever further. "Mr. Harlow."

"The master has some questions for you, lad," McKinney said. "Pay attention."

The boy gave a nod. "Aye, sir."

"I understand you saw Mrs. Harlow earlier," Maxwell said. "Is that right?"

"Um." The boy frowned and scratched at his head, setting strands of his red hair on end. "Well, no, sir, I didn't actually see the lady. Just the lady's horse."

Maxwell's gut tightened. "Explain."

"Well, he—Byron, that is—weren't there when I left." The lad fidgeted and looked from one man to the other. "But when I got back, he were in his stall."

"Got back from where?" McKinney asked.

"From the barn, Mr. McKinney. I went to fetch some straw, and when I got back, there he were, large as life."

"Was he still tacked?" Maxwell demanded. "Saddled and bridled?"

"Aye, fully tacked, Mr. Harlow." The lad frowned. "He were a bit lathered as well, like he'd had a good run, but I know the mistress—Mrs. Harlow, that is—likes to give him his head. I gave him a good rub down, though."

McKinney frowned. "'Tisn't like the mistress to leave him like that."

"No, it isn't." Maxwell looked toward Byron's stall, now drenched in shadow, as a sickening suspicion slithered into his brain. He shifted his gaze to the open door of the stable, seeing nothing but gloom beyond. "Was the stable door left open when you went to fetch the straw, George?"

The lad followed Maxwell's gaze. "Aye, Mr. Harlow, it was."

Understanding, icy cold, passed through Maxwell like a ghost. "Jesus Christ," he muttered.

McKinney gasped. "Oh, nay, sir. Surely, you don't think…"

Maxwell braced a steadying hand against the stable wall. "I'm afraid I do. McKinney," he said, his throat tight. "Louisa—Mrs. Harlow was never here. Byron came home on his own."

McKinney paled. "Bloody hell! Then where could she be?"

The question did not yet have an answer, but it triggered

Maxwell into action. He strode over to Fraser's stall, snapping out orders as he went. "Go back inside McKinney. I want a search party organized. As many men as you can muster, dressed appropriately and carrying lanterns. Then come back here. I want you in the saddle. Bring blankets with you as well. George, tack McKinney's horse. I'll see to Fraser myself. And make haste, damn it. Minutes are hours on the moor!"

JUST TWENTY-FOUR HOURS earlier, Maxwell had been seated in the cozy dining room of the Crown Hotel in Sheffield, feasting on tender roasted beef and Yorkshire pudding. While his colleagues had been celebrating the potential success of their new business venture, Maxwell had been pondering his marriage. More specifically, his wife. He hadn't quite figured out how she'd crept into his heart and stolen it without him even realizing.

Now, from atop Fraser's back, he was about to issue orders to a group of fourteen men who had gathered in readiness to search the moors for her.

It was, by far, the most harrowing experience of his life.

The men stood in near darkness and silence at the foot of the path that led up to the moor, each carrying a lantern, some leaning on staffs. Only Maxwell and McKinney were on horse-back. Questions remained unanswered and would till Louisa had been found. Obviously, she'd fallen from the horse, but what had been the cause? Perhaps Byron had shied, catching her unawares, or he'd stumbled, throwing her from the saddle. The other possibility, less likely, was that she'd been attacked or set upon. The first scenario was bad enough for Maxwell to consider. The second, he couldn't even bear to contemplate.

"We cannot know for certain what has become of Mrs. Harlow," Maxwell said, turning a restless Fraser in a circle. "But it's reasonable to assume whatever befell her happened on the moor somewhere between here and Highfield. I suspect, and I pray, that the event happened closer to Northcott, given that her horse found his way back. McKinney and I will lead. The rest of you spread out behind, keeping several feet apart if possible. If some of you get ahead of the others, that's fine, but try to maintain a straight line as you move forward. That said, watch your step. It's almost dark, and this is rough terrain. I don't want to delay the search in order to deal with an injured man. Obviously, if you find my wife, or any clues at all, yell out." He drew a shaky breath, feeling the unfamiliar sting of tears at the back of his eyes. "And in the meantime, please pray for her."

"We'll not give up till the mistress is found, Mr. Harlow, no matter how long it takes," one of the men said, his announcement resulting in a mumble of agreement from the others.

"I appreciate that, thank you." Maxwell pressed his knees to Fraser's flanks. "Let's go."

Aye, without doubt, the most harrowing experience of his life. *So far.* He could only pray the sad achievement would not be surpassed by night's end.

The first few spots of rain hit them as they reached the upper stretch of the moor. A minute later, it fell steadily. Maxwell uttered a worthy curse. Exposure to the elements, especially cold and damp, could be deadly for an injured person. In truth, he had no idea how long Louisa had been effectively missing. Had she fallen from the horse on the way to Highfield, or on the way back? The former would mean she'd been out here for several hours already. Either way, she'd obviously not been able to pick herself up and make her way home. *Badly injured, then, or...* Maxwell bit down, hard, and lifted his face to the rain, allowing it to mingle with the tears that had at last escaped.

Could I live without her? Oh, God, please don't make me find out. Please, let her be found alive. Let me bring her home.

"You were right, Captain," he whispered. "A man must never leave his house angry, lest he may live to regret it."

The gloom of night, combined with the rain, made for miserable progress. Maxwell and McKinney had dismounted and now led the horses along the main track. Even with the lanterns, it was difficult to see, especially in places where the ground sloped away. Wet earth sucked at horses' hooves and men's boots as the rain sneaked its way beneath the tightest collars. With each passing minute, Maxwell's hope of finding Louisa alive ebbed. He sensed a feeling of despondency from the others as well. After a while, he glanced back toward Northcott, curious to know how far they'd come. He couldn't see the place, of course, but he guessed they'd covered at least a mile.

And then, at last, from somewhere off to the left, "Here, Mr. Harlow," a man shouted, waving his lantern. "She's here!"

Fear knotted in Maxwell's gut. He handed the reins to McKinney and stumbled over to where the man stood. There, between two thickets of gorse, lay the still form of his wife, on her back, strands of wet hair plastered across her forehead and cheeks. Maxwell crouched down and lifted the wet strands away, uncovering a face pale as death, a bloodied nose, and a faint bruise on the left side of her forehead. "Please, God," he whispered, probing for a pulse in her throat, her flesh like cold clay beneath his touch. "Please."

At first, he felt nothing, resulting in a rise of sick panic that drew the blood from his head. And then, at last… a faint tap against his fingertips, steady, but alarmingly slow.

"Thank Christ," he muttered, swallowing bile as he lifted his gaze to those standing around. "She's alive."

There followed a collective mumble of relief.

"But not out of danger," he added. "We need to get her home as soon as possible."

McKinney pulled a folded blanket out from beneath his woolen cloak. "Any sign of broken bones, Mr. Harlow?"

Maxwell ran his hands quickly over Louisa's limbs. "Nothing obvious." He gathered her into his arms and stood. "Though it's impossible to be sure till we get her home."

"Give her to me, sir." McKinney shook out the blanket. "I'll hand her to you once you're mounted."

Maxwell did so. "Take a lantern and ride on ahead, McKinney, as quickly as you can without being foolish." He swung into the saddle and lifted Louisa back into his arms. "I want a fire lit in my wife's chamber and her bed thoroughly warmed. And have someone send for the doctor!"

"Yes, sir." The man took up a lantern and went on his way.

The men, lanterns held aloft, escorted Maxwell back along the track. Weighing risk against urgency, and given the conditions, he kept Fraser at a frustratingly steady walk. The rain, thankfully, had eased off somewhat.

Every few minutes Maxwell glanced at Louisa's face, which was partially hidden in the folds of the blanket. So far, she'd shown no sign of consciousness. He gathered her close and pressed a kiss to her forehead, her flesh cold and clammy against his lips. "Hold on, my love," he murmured. "Please hold on."

"Tha'd be best bedding down with the lady when you get her home, Mr. Harlow," the man beside him said. "Never mind them bloody warming pans."

Maxwell regarded the man, wondering if he'd misheard. "*What* did you say?"

The man looked up at him, wizened face lit by lanternlight. "I said to take your lady beside you in the bed. 'Tis the best way to warm a living thing what's chilled to the bone. Slept by the fire many a time with a frozen newborn lamb when I were a lad workin' me uncle's farm. Cuddled them like a babe all night. By morning, they'd be up an' about, right as rain an' ready to feed. Your body has heat to spare, y'see, so you should share it with your lady who needs it." He sniffed. "'Tis the best way, mark my words."

The suggestion sounded shockingly inappropriate, yet oddly made a lot of sense.

"What's your name, my man?" Maxwell demanded.

"Thornthwaite, sir," the man replied. "Reuben Thornthwaite."

Of course. A name Louisa had mentioned on more than one occasion. The memory of her standing beside a smoking bonfire with the man also surfaced. "The gardener," Maxwell said, as much to himself as Reuben.

"These past twenty-six years, aye." Reuben nodded toward Louisa's still form. "Young mistress often comes looking for a chat when she's out walking. Loves 'er flowers, she does."

The innocent statement ignited a heated flush of shame, for it occurred to Maxwell that this gardener probably knew things about Louisa that he did not. He swallowed his blasted pride and asked a question, the answer to which, all at once, seemed incredibly important. "What is her favorite flower? Do you know?"

Reuben tugged on his earlobe and pondered for a moment. "Well, the lady is fond o' roses, like most women, but I'd have to say she has a special fondness for sweet peas. She's filled her flower-basket with them a time or two."

"Sweet peas," Maxwell repeated, not even sure what a sweet pea looked like.

"Aye." The man gave a nod. "She's right fond o' those. 'Tis true they have a pleasant scent."

Maxwell swallowed over a renewed tightness in his throat. He knew the physical attributes of his wife well enough. He was intimately familiar with every sweet curve, every freckle, every dimple. But how much did he really know about *her*? How often had he sat down and chatted with her about the minor stuff? The small details that formed the unique mosaic of a person's character? To his shame, he could probably count the occasions on one hand. Preoccupied with building his empire, he'd presumed to keep Louisa otherwise contented with tokens, such as clothes and jewelry. If she'd asked him for something, he'd provided it. He'd denied her nothing, in fact, except for his time and companionship. Those he'd given sparingly.

He could only pray it wasn't too late to make amends.

MAXWELL HAD WORN a path in the carpet, pacing back and forth outside the bedroom door. Inside, Archer and another maid had supposedly been settling Louisa into a warm bed.

"What the deuce is taking so long," he muttered, glaring at the closed portal as if doing so might fling it open. He'd originally proposed, quite seriously, that he help with the task of undressing Louisa and preparing her for bed. She was, after all, his wife. But the appalled look on Archer's face had stayed his argument.

He'd arrived back under Northcott's roof a half-hour since, wasting no time in carrying Louisa upstairs. A man had already been dispatched to fetch the doctor, but Maxwell knew it would likely be morning before the good physician put in an appearance.

"I need you to go to Highfield at first light," he'd said to McKinney. "Her parents must be told about what has occurred. I've no doubt they'll want to come here, in which case, please wait and return with them." He could only pray they'd arrive at Northcott to find their daughter still alive.

The door opened at last, and Archer emerged, red-eyed and sniffling. "The mistress is as comfortable as she can be, sir. Her nose bleed has stopped. There's a bruise on her left shoulder as well as the one on her head, but I didn't see any other sign of injury."

"She hasn't stirred at all?"

The woman shook her head, pulled a handkerchief from her sleeve, and dabbed at her eyes. "No, sir. I rubbed her limbs and put a liniment on her chest, but she still feels awfully cold to the touch. The bed is well-warmed, though."

"All right, thank you, Archer, that will be all." Maxwell moved to the threshold. "I'll stay with her tonight."

Archer looked dubious. "Are you sure, sir? Perhaps it would be better for me to stay. She might awaken and have need of me."

"Yes, I'm sure," he replied. "If necessary, I'll send for you."

Still looking doubtful, she bobbed a curtsey and left. Maxwell closed the door quietly and glanced about. A fire burned brightly in the hearth, a two-armed candelabra on the dresser held two lit tapers, and a solitary candle flickered on the bedside table. The coziness of the room belied the tragic situation.

Louisa lay on her back, covers pulled up to her chin, the bruising on her face a dark stain on the pallor of her skin. Maxwell moved to the bedside and touched her forehead, wincing at the chill of her flesh. He then drew back the covers and reached for her hand, which felt equally as cold and horribly lifeless.

"All right, Reuben Thornthwaite." Maxwell began to undress. "Let's see if this suggestion of yours works."

Stripped naked, he slid into the bed and gathered her close, the smell of the liniment tingling in his nostrils. The chill of Louisa's skin, seeping through the cotton of her nightdress, alarmed him. The warmth of her breath at the base of his throat gave him reason to hope.

He rested his cheek against her still-damp hair. "I love you, Mrs. Harlow," he murmured, hoping that somewhere in the depths of her unconsciousness she might hear him. "Please don't go."

Sleep, for Maxwell, was out of the question. But, as the hours passed, Louisa's body grew noticeably warmer, and he became less fearful for her life. Even her breath felt stronger against his throat. Still, she had yet to show any sign of consciousness, and he hardly dared consider the repercussions of a head injury. The doctor might be able to tell him more, but Maxwell suspected that time alone would declare the truth of it.

When the first bird shouted a greeting to the dawn, Maxwell left the bed, pulled on his shirt and trousers, and went to the washstand to splash water on his face. Then, somewhat revived, he dragged the armchair from the corner, placed it next to the bed, and sat down to await the physician's arrival. Sitting back, he allowed his gaze to wander around the room, his attention drawn to something sitting atop the armoire, but partially hidden by the cornice. Curious, he went to investigate, and lifted the thing down.

A hat.

He recognized it immediately, for he had held it once before. Dragged it out of a gorse bush in fact, pheasant feathers and all. The memory surfaced with startling clarity, bringing the sound of Louisa's laughter back to him. He hadn't realized, at the time, just how significant the incident had been. It was, as Louisa would say, a trinket. A moment in his life he would never forget.

"Please, God," he whispered, his throat tightening, "don't take her from me. I beg of you, *please.*"

CHAPTER EIGHTEEN

AN ICY DARKNESS, thicker than any fog, held Louisa in its clutches. What felt like a hard, knotted rope twisted and tightened around her head, biting mercilessly into her skull. But she was not alone. Someone was with her in the blackness, comforting her, holding her, the contact gentle and so wonderfully warm. A voice too, familiar, masculine, uttering quiet words she couldn't quite understand. As the chill ebbed from her bones, she tried to speak, to move, to let him know she was aware of his presence. But she couldn't find the strength.

And then, from somewhere in the distance, a bird sang—a thrush—its sweet refrain piercing the blackness. Louisa held her breath, seeking the direction of the sound. She had the impression of floating upwards, as if emerging from the depths of a lake. Above, a golden glow appeared, flickering like flame.

Then, like the vanishing of a dream, the darkness slid away as she opened her eyes.

Candlelight cast shadows across her bed canopy, while somewhere outside the thrush continued with its pretty song. Louisa attempted to gather her thoughts. She turned her head toward the window, wincing at the sudden throb of pain in her skull. *Am I ill? Has something happened?*

She squinted into the candlelight and blinked, unsure of what her eyes beheld.

Max?

He appeared to be asleep in her armchair, which, for whatever reason, had been moved to the side of her bed. He was also in a noticeably disheveled state; shirt hanging loose, hair tousled, jaw shadowed. A vague sense of panic set her heart rattling. Why was he there? Was she dreaming?

"Max?" It came out as a croak. She swallowed over a dry throat and tried again. "Maxwell?" Still a croak, but stronger this time. He frowned in his sleep and then opened his eyes, blinking once or twice as he met Louisa's gaze.

Then his eyes widened, and he sat up. "Louisa!" He leaned forward. "Oh, thank God. How do you feel, my love? Speak to me."

"I…" *My love?* She hesitated, wondering if she'd heard him correctly. *Are those tears in his eyes?* "What… what has happened? Have I been ill?"

"Not exactly." He leaned in and cupped her cheek, his flesh cool against hers. "You came off your horse yesterday. Had quite the tumble. Do you recall any of it?"

Still confused, Louise tried to think. She also tried to move and let out a squeak of pain.

"Careful, sweetheart," Maxwell said. "Try to lie still, at least till the doctor arrives. I want him to examine you before you even think about getting out of that bed. You've acquired a few bruises, but I don't think anything is broken."

She winced. "I have the most awful headache."

"Aye, it seems you took a bang to the head. The shoulder as well. Do you remember how it happened? Anything at all?"

Even as they'd spoken, images had begun to emerge from the fog in her brain.

"I remember… I remember leaving Highfield, and…" She looked inward, an image dancing on the edge of her memory. A gray shape in the mist. "There was someone, I think, hidden by the mist. She startled Byron, but I'm not sure if… I cannot quite remember…"

"She?"

"I think…" The memory blurred and faded. Was her mind playing tricks? Another memory arose, that of birds and the flutter of wings. "Yes, I think so, but I'm not certain. Is Byron all right?"

"Byron is fine," Maxwell replied. "He came home on his own, and thank God he did, or you might have lain up there a good while longer. Scared the hell out of me when I realized what must have happened."

Something didn't quite make sense. "This happened yesterday, you said?"

"Aye."

"So today is… Friday?"

Nodding, he glanced at the window. "Early morning."

"I don't understand."

"What don't you understand, love?"

"Well, I …" She cleared her throat. "Actually, could have a sip of water? I feel as though I've swallowed a bucketful of sand."

"Of course." He filled a glass from the jug on the bedside table. "Not sand, perhaps, but quite possibly a good mouthful of Yorkshire earth. Here, let me help you sit up. Easy, now." He held the glass while she drank. "Better?"

"Much, thank you." Exhausted from the effort, she relaxed against her pillows, still trying to sort things out in her head. "I'm confused. I thought you weren't coming back till tonight."

He cleared his throat and set the glass on the table. "That was the original plan, aye."

"Oh." She frowned, hearing something in his voice that said more than his words. "Things went well?"

"I'm sure they did." Maxwell ran a hand through his hair and sat down again. "I expect I'll get the final report from Finlay when he gets back tonight."

Things still did not add up. "Why did you come home early?"

He heaved a sigh. "Because I realized there were issues here that needed my urgent attention."

A tingle of trepidation ran down her spine. "What issues?"

"Us, my love. You and me. The understanding we had before we married." He sighed. "I realized things have to change, Louisa. And they will, from now on."

Her thoughts whirled in confusion. Had she misunderstood his earlier expressions of affection? Had they merely been used to cushion her against a subsequent upbraiding? Tears of disenchantment pricked the back of her eyes. "I regret embarrassing you at dinner, Max, but I was just so disappointed when—"

"Nay, hush, my sweet, don't upset yourself." He took hold of her hand. "You misunderstand. It's me who needs to apologize."

"For what?

"For the abysmal way I've treated you since we were married." He kissed the back of her hand, his lips lingering there for a few moments. "My priorities have been utterly misplaced, and I intend to do things differently from now on. Or, at least, I intend to *try*, though I must ask for your patience. This… this concept of love is something very new to me."

Love? Her breath caught in her throat. Was she dreaming? Had she heard him correctly? "You… you love me?"

"Very much," he replied, "and last night, when I realized you hadn't come home, I feared I might never get the chance to tell you just *how* much. The fear that I'd lost you…" He shook his head. "Well, God knows, I never want to feel that way again. So, from now on, things are going to be different. Fin is willing to take on more responsibility and will do so unless my presence is specifically required." He grimaced. "Such as for the Glasgow meeting. That one, I'm afraid, absolutely demands my presence, and I deeply regret my oversight with the dates."

"Oh, Max." She smiled through her tears. "I can hardly believe what I'm hearing."

"It's long overdue, sweetheart."

A tap came to the door. "Come," Maxwell called, and Archer entered, her worried expression dissolving instantly.

"Oh, God be praised, ma'am. You're awake and sitting up too. I've hardly slept for worrying."

Louisa smiled at the maid. "I'm rather sore and have a monstrous headache, but I think I'll live."

Archer beamed. "Very glad to hear it, ma'am. May I attend you? Freshen you up a little? Order some tea, perhaps? A bite of toast?"

"Oh, yes," Louisa replied. "That sounds quite lovely."

Maxwell rose. "Then I'll leave you for now. The doctor should be here soon. I sent word to Highfield too, so I imagine your parents will be here before long as well." He leaned in and kissed her cheek. "I'll be back shortly. Do not leave this bed, understand?"

"PULSE IS A little elevated, but not alarmingly so." The physician released Louisa's wrist and snapped his fob-watch closed. "No fever to speak of at the moment, though that might yet change. Your clavicle is bruised, but I don't believe it's fractured. There's not much to be done about it if it is. However, do nothing to aggravate it further. I suggest plain food for the next few days as well. Nothing too spicy or rich. Some broth. Perhaps a little fruit. A glass of wine or sherry is acceptable. Some warm milk and honey at bedtime, if you like."

"Thank you, Doctor," Louisa replied. "When might I leave this bed?"

He grunted. "Not for three days at least, and that's assuming all goes well."

Louisa made a sound of dismay. "Three days? Surely not."

The man peered at her over the top of his spectacles. "You've had a nasty tumble, young lady. You must rest. Give your body time to heal."

Maxwell, who'd been watching the proceedings, folded his arms and arched a brow at Louisa. "Have no fear, good sir," he said, "I'll make sure she behaves."

The man nodded. "Then I'm done here for now. Good day to you, Mrs. Harlow."

"I'll settle with you downstairs, Doctor." Maxwell winked at Louisa as he followed the doctor from the room. "I won't be long, sweetheart," he whispered.

Fresh tears arose in Louisa's eyes, and she quietly berated her foolishness, for her response had been brought about by nothing more than a wink from her husband. But then, her husband appeared to have undergone a startling transformation and, consequently, her emotions were all over the place.

"He loves me," she whispered, and released a happy, but weary, sigh. Although she'd carped about a three-day confinement to bed, she knew she was in no condition to leave it. Archer's administrations—making Louisa as presentable as a lady could be under the circumstances—and the doctor's examination, had left her utterly exhausted.

She closed her eyes and drifted into a sound sleep.

WHEN NEXT LOUISA awoke, it was to the sight of her mother sitting beside the bed, and her father and Maxwell standing by the window, the two of them speaking in hushed tones.

Grace inhaled sharply and reached over to stroke Louisa's hair. "There you are, dearest. How are you feeling?"

"Um." She shifted slightly and winced. "A little bit sore, Mama."

The men's whispered conversation had halted, and her father spoke. "What a business," he said, and moved to stand beside the bed, gazing down at her with obvious concern. "Thank God you're all right. You gave us quite the scare."

"Sorry, Papa," she said, wincing again. "Believe me, it was not intentional."

Her father grunted. "I understand you think Byron was startled by someone. Is that so?"

"Er…" Louisa's eyes flicked briefly to Maxwell, who gave her a resigned smile. "I'm not sure, Papa."

"Aldous, please, allow the child a moment to gather herself," Grace said, frowning. "Are you thirsty, dear? Could you manage some tea? Or some broth, perhaps?"

"Some tea would be lovely, Mama." Louisa winced as she shifted again. "And I should like to sit up a little, please."

"Of course." Her mother leaned over and arranged Louisa's pillows. "Better?"

"Much, thank you."

"Your father and I are going back to where the accident occurred," Maxwell said.

Puzzled, Louisa looked from one to the other. "Why?"

"To see if we can find any clues as to who or what startled Byron," Aldous folded his arms. "I know it's unlikely, but we have nothing to lose by it."

"But I'm not even certain it *was* a person, Papa," she replied, her brain again conjuring up what looked like a figure emerging from a patch of mist, the details obscured. "I can't decide if the image in my head is real or just something my brain created while I was unconscious. I definitely recall some birds flying out of the heather. Grouse, I think. Or pheasant, perhaps. But I don't think Byron reacted to them. He wouldn't usually."

"But surely, if someone saw her fall, they would have remained with her, or at least gone for help," Grace said, frowning. "Truly, I can't imagine what kind of clues you hope to find."

Maxwell shrugged. "Probably none at all, but it won't hurt to look, and it shouldn't take too long. In the meantime, I'll have some tea sent up."

"You know, I never doubted Maxwell's commitment to your union, or that you would be treated kindly," Grace said, moments after the men had left the room. "But I confess I did wonder if he would come to love you in the way you deserve to be loved. Any doubts in that regard have gone. It's quite obvious he adores you."

Louisa released a shaky sigh. "I admit to having a moment or two of doubt myself, Mama," she said. "But not anymore."

MAXWELL STOOD AT the spot where Louisa had lain and glanced about once more. As expected, it had been an exercise in futility. They had found a few items; a rusted belt-buckle, an equally rusted horseshoe, and the moth-eaten remains of a knitted glove. All were found within a reasonable vicinity of the accident, none of which implied anything other than people and animals used the moor road on a regular basis. There were footprints and hoofprints too, of course, their impressions exaggerated in the wet earth, and especially around the spot where Louisa had been found, which could easily be explained. Maxwell hadn't really expected to find anything conclusive, but the lack of an explanation remained frustrating. What troubled him the most was the possibility that someone—man or woman—had been there when the accident occurred and done nothing to help Louisa.

"Well, it was worth a try." Aldous pulled himself into the saddle and gathered up the reins. "Louisa is on the mend, that's the main thing."

Nodding his agreement, Maxwell moved to Fraser's side, intent on climbing back into the saddle. As he lifted his foot to place in the stirrup, something snared in a nearby clump of heather caught his attention. He wandered over and pulled it free; a large feather, its soft white barbs discolored and damaged by the elements.

"Louisa said something about birds," he said, twirling the feather in his fingers as he walked back to where Aldous sat. "Any idea what kind of bird might have shed this?"

Aldous regarded it for a moment. "Given the color, swans and geese come to mind, though it looks too fine to be either one.

I suppose Byron might have been startled by birds, though he doesn't usually startle easily."

"Hmm." Maxwell twirled the feather once more and then released it to the wind, watching as it traveled some distance before it tumbled earthward and became entangled once more. Reaching for the saddle, he swung himself up onto Fraser's back and glanced around one last time. "As you said, Captain, it was worth a try."

THANKFULLY, THREE DAYS later, Louisa was up and out of bed, still a little sore but very much on the mend. Her parents returned to Highfield, and for the next several days Maxwell remained at her side. Then a summons came from the South Shields location, where a labor issue had resulted in the threat of a strike.

"The foreman is demanding my presence." Maxwell waved the letter clutched in his hand. "So as much as I hate to leave you, my love, I'm afraid I have to go. I should only be gone a few days, but I'd like you to stay at Highfield while I'm away. I'll have McKinney drive you. You can take Archer with you, of course."

Louisa, who had been curled up in a chair in her sitting-room, set her book aside. "I don't have to go to Highfield, Max. I'm perfectly fine here."

He regarded her. The bruising on her face had faded to a shadow, but her shoulder still pained her some. Her memory of what had caused her accident remained frustratingly elusive. Though he couldn't explain it, something about the incident still bothered Maxwell, and the thought of leaving her troubled him. "I'd feel better if you were at Highfield, lass."

Louisa shook her head. "I promise I won't leave the house except, perhaps, for a stroll around the gardens. I won't be alone. Archer will take care of me."

He scowled. "Very well, if you insist, but absolutely no riding.

I'll tell McKinney he'll lose his job if he lets you take Byron out. If you *do* decide to go to Highfield, you'll take the carriage. And when you go for a stroll, stay in the gardens and take Archer with you."

She feigned a huff. "How many times must I tell you, Mr. Harlow, I am not made of porcelain."

He suppressed a smile. "Nevertheless, you'll do as you're told, and I'll have your word on it."

"On one condition," she said, cocking her head. "That when you return, we take a trip back to Knaresborough. I'd like to see Jane and also visit Samuel again."

Because of what had occurred during their previous visit, Maxwell's first instinct was to refuse the request. But for what reason? The old man's actions had been bizarre, but not harmful. "There'll be no conditions from you and no promises from me," he replied, hedging. "We'll see how things are when I get back."

Louisa wrinkled her nose. "Then may I at least write to Jane and inquire about another visit?"

"That you can do, aye," he said and held out a hand. "Stand up, will you, love?"

Unfurling her legs, she placed her hand in his, and he drew her gently to her feet before taking her in his arms.

"What's this for?" she murmured.

He kissed her hair and breathed in a hint of roses. "Do I need a reason?"

"No." She parted with a soft sigh. "No, of course you don't."

"Just be careful while I'm gone," he whispered, tightening his hold. "The last time I was away—"

"I'll be careful." She lifted her head and regarded him. "I promise."

"Good."

"Are you leaving right now?"

"In about an hour."

An enigmatic smile appeared. "We have enough time, then."

"For what?" he asked, and then gasped as her hand slid down

the front of his trousers. "No, Louisa, I think not. You're still recovering."

"I have a sore shoulder, that's all." Still caressing him, she stood on tiptoes and kissed the corner of his mouth. "The rest of me is working as it should."

A groan escaped him as he hardened. "Are you sure?"

"Never more so, unless you can think of a better way to pass the time."

"Hmm." He looked away for a moment, as if pondering. "No, my sweet, I don't believe I can."

A little less than an hour later, dressed, packed, and with the carriage waiting, Maxwell bent and kissed Louisa's cheek. "I have to go," he murmured. "Behave yourself while I'm gone."

Still abed, hair tousled, face aglow with the aftermath of pleasure, Louisa gave him a lazy smile. "I love you, Mr. Harlow."

"I love you too," he replied. "I'll be back in a few days."

CHAPTER NINETEEN

THE SECOND VISIT to Knaresborough took place on a day when clouds and a cool breeze conspired to steal sunlight and warmth. Louisa didn't care. She was simply happy to be tucked into the carriage beside Maxwell, looking forward to seeing the Fairburns, and visiting St. Giles House again.

Three weeks had passed since her accident. Other than strolls around Northcott's gardens and a couple of accompanied visits to Highfield, she'd been confined to the house the entire time. Maxwell had continued to forbid her from taking Byron for a ride, insisting she wait a full month before taking to the saddle again. She had argued, sulked, and pouted, but to no avail. He remained firm, making it clear that his reasoning was for her own good, as well as for his peace of mind.

This outing, then, came as a welcome respite from the mundane. She barely suppressed a shiver of excitement.

Immediately, Maxwell reacted. "Are you cold, love?"

She shook her head and snuggled closer to him. "No, not at all. Just excited."

How he fussed over her! After a rather sober beginning, their marriage was evolving into something she had only ever dreamed of. Despite giving more responsibility to Finlay, Maxwell still spent time away from home and likely always would. Yet Louisa no longer felt abandoned or secondary. Quite the contrary.

By the time they arrived in Knaresborough, the breeze had

eased, and the sun had warmed things up a little. Jane was tending her rose bushes when the carriage pulled up to the rectory.

"At last!" The lady waved a greeting and hurried over to open the gate, smiling from beneath a wide-brimmed straw hat decorated with silk roses. "I've been so looking forward to seeing you both again."

"Likewise, Jane." Louisa took Maxwell's hand as she stepped down from the carriage and then hugged her friend. "It's lovely to see you."

"How are you, dearest? Quite recovered from your accident?" Jane stepped back and gave Louisa a critical gaze. "You look wonderful. I trust Maxwell has taken good care of you."

"He has indeed." She gave Maxwell a fond look and linked her arm through his. "I could not wish for better."

"I'm glad to hear it." Jane went to him and offered her cheek for a kiss. "Was Louisa a difficult patient, Maxwell?"

"Horrible," he replied, straight-face. "Absolutely horrible."

Laughter ensued, followed by the sound of Charles' booming voice carrying across the garden. "There you are," he said, striding along the path. "Welcome, both. Luncheon is almost ready."

Louisa waited till they were seated at the table before mentioning the subject that lingered at the forefront of her brain. "I'm looking forward to visiting St. Giles House again," she said. "We'll have to take a carriage this time, though, because we've brought a trunk full of items for the men. Some clothing, and several blankets."

The subsequent silence gave Louisa the impression she'd misspoken. Then Charles cleared his throat. "Thank you, both," he said. "That's very generous of you. The blankets, especially, will be most welcome come winter."

"Yes, indeed," Jane said. "You are both so kind."

Smiling, Maxwell inclined his head in acknowledgement, but said nothing.

"It's our pleasure." Louisa glanced around the table. "How are things at St. Giles?"

"We've lost two residents since you were last here, I'm afraid." Charles said, soberly. "One died peacefully in his sleep, the other collapsed in the garden and died shortly thereafter. The doctor suspects a bleed to the brain caused the latter."

"Oh, how sad." Louisa's hands clenched. "Was one of them… I mean, is Samuel all right?"

"Frederick, the one who died in his sleep, shared Samuel's room," Jane replied, her eyes flicking, briefly, to Charles, "but Samuel is quite well."

"Thank goodness." Louisa fiddled with the pearl pendant at her throat. "I mean, I'm truly sorry about the others, but I'm glad that Samuel is well. I'm looking forward to seeing him again. And what of young Tom?"

"Tom is also fine." Charles frowned and cleared his throat again. "I must tell you, Louisa, that I've given much thought to Samuel's strange reaction to you, and I believe it's probably best that you avoid him when you visit St. Giles today."

"Avoid?" A flush of heat arose in her cheeks. "Why?"

Jane reached over and gave Louisa's hand a squeeze. "He was quite agitated after your last visit, dearest. Hardly ate a thing for three days and wouldn't even play dominoes with young Tom. He's now back to his normal self, but given what occurred previously, he'll be tucked away in his room during our visit today. I'm sorry, but we just don't want to risk another episode like that. We have to consider his well-being. I'm sure you understand."

Louisa's featherlight mood popped like a soap bubble. "I understand, of course," she replied, forcing a smile. "I certainly have no wish to upset him. May I ask if he's spoken since my last visit?"

"Not a word," Charles replied.

"I see." She looked down at the untouched raspberry tart on her plate, which no longer tempted her. "Oh, well."

"Do you want to cancel the visit, Louisa?" Maxwell asked, gently. "We don't have to go if you don't feel like it."

"No, of course we don't." Jane squeezed Louisa's hand once more. "Perhaps we could just take a walk along the river instead."

Louisa shook her head emphatically. "Goodness, no, I don't want to cancel the visit. I'm still looking forward to it."

Though not nearly as much, she thought, her mind continuing to mull as the conversation picked up around her. She listened in with only half-an-ear, while in her head she went over her first meeting with Samuel. His initial reaction, his tears, his lopsided smile, and the utterance of those two little words; one that made sense, the other that surely meant nothing to anyone but him. Perhaps he'd been agitated when she left, but in the beginning, he'd been happy to see her.

Happy.

"I disagree with your decision to keep me away from Samuel," she announced, her interruption silencing all other conversation. "In fact, I believe you are wrong to do so."

"Louisa, please." Maxwell's tone was no longer gentle. "You'll respect Charles' wishes on this issue."

"That's all right, Maxwell, I'll hear her." Charles leaned forward. "I'm always willing to listen to other points of view. Go ahead, my dear. Explain why you think it's wrong."

"Thank you." Frowning, she looked down at the untouched tart again and gathered her thoughts. "I remember something you said the last time I was at St. Giles, Charles," she began, raising her head to look at him. "You'd said you'd always believed there was something going on behind Samuel's mangled face. As I recall, you described him as a wonderful mystery. Forgive me, then, if I fail to comprehend why you choose to ignore what might be a way to solve that mystery. For some unknown reason, Samuel reacted to me in a way he'd never reacted to anyone before. He *spoke* to me. A man who, according to you, had never uttered a word in all the months he'd been at St. Giles. For the short time I was with him, it appears something inside him came back to life. Surely, such an unusual response should be explored rather than ignored. Indeed, I daresay it should be encouraged. Or perhaps you'd prefer he remain in his calm, oblivious state till he, too, simply passes away in his sleep.

Personally, I think that would be a shame, since it seems he still possesses the ability to communicate. I believe I should be allowed to see him, to see if he responds to me as he did before, and to encourage whatever it is he's trying to express. Please consider it. Please." Heart thudding frantically beneath her ribs, Louisa sat back, stuck her hands under the table, and crossed her fingers.

As she'd spoken, the hint of a smile had settled on Maxwell's face. "That was quite the rebuttal, my dear," he said.

"Indeed, it was." Jane regarded her husband. "Charles?"

Bushy brows knitted together, Charles continued to stare at Louisa, seemingly reflecting on what had been said. Then he blinked, lips firming as he inhaled through his nose before releasing a breath. "Very well," he said, startling Louisa when his hand slapped the table. "I'll allow it, but not without some reservation, and I insist upon being an observer."

"As do I," Maxwell added. "You'll not be left alone with him, Louisa."

Relief washed over her like a balm. "I understand, and thank you," she said. "Though I don't believe for a moment that Samuel is dangerous."

DESPITE THE COOLER temperatures, several of the residents of St. Giles House were seated outside, all suitably attired. Samuel was not among them, but Louisa recognized young Tom Ellis from her previous visit. He was seated in his bathchair beside one of the garden benches, a rug tucked around his legs. Tom apparently recognized her too and raised a hand in greeting. A lady sat on the bench beside him, obviously keeping him company. One of the volunteers, Louisa assumed. "I'm just going to have a quick word with Tom," she said to the others. "I'll meet you inside."

Lifting her skirts slightly, she padded over the thick, damp grass. "Good day to you, Tom," she said, as she drew near. "It's a pleasure to see you again. How are you?"

"I'm quite well, thank you, Mrs. Harlow. It's a pleasure to see you again as well." He cast a fond glance at the woman beside him. "This is my mother, Dora. Mam, this is Mrs. Harlow."

"Oh, how nice!" Louisa regarded the woman seated on the bench. Of middling years, she was slightly built, her blue woolen coat well-worn, but neat, her blond hair edged with silver around her bonneted face. "Tom told me about you the last time I was here, Mrs. Ellis. It's a pleasure to meet you."

The woman's cheeks reddened slightly as she dipped her chin. "Likewise, ma'am, I'm sure."

Tom's face lit up with a smile. "Mam lives in Knaresborough now, Mrs. Harlow," he said. "Got a live-in job as chambermaid at the Bridge Hotel, so visits me often."

"Now that is *very* good news." Louisa returned the smile. "I'm so pleased. Well done, Mrs. Ellis."

"'Twas naught I did, ma'am," Dora said, shaking her head. "'Twas all arranged by some kind soul whose name was never told to me. But being able to visit my son like this is the answer to a prayer, for sure. The answer to a prayer."

"I did wonder if you and your husband had something to do with it, Mrs. Harlow." Tom cocked his head. "Mam getting the job, and all? If you did, we're very grateful."

"No, I…" Frowning, Louisa glanced over her shoulder, seeing no sign of Maxwell. Could it be? Had he arranged this without telling her? He did have a penchant for keeping certain things to himself. "I don't believe I can take the credit for it, Tom. But, like you, I'm grateful to whoever it was."

After saying her farewells, Louisa went off in search of the others. The front door at St. Giles House opened with a groan, and she stepped inside, nostrils flaring as she inhaled the indelicate air. From the kitchen came the hollow rumble of voices, one of them Maxwell's.

Louisa paused and shifted her gaze to the corridor, specifically the direction of Samuel's room. The sound of voices faded away when, like a portent, the same feeling she'd experienced on her previous visit crept over her. A touch of breathlessness, and a tingle of raw anticipation that set her nerves on end. This time, however, she couldn't blame it on too much sun.

"Louisa."

Startled, she turned to see Maxwell standing beside her.

"Is something wrong?" he asked, frowning as he peered at her.

"Um, no." She shook her head. "I'm perfectly fine."

"Then why didn't you answer me?"

"I…" Confused, she shook her head. "Forgive me, I never heard you approach. My mind was elsewhere."

"Hmm." Maxwell looked down the corridor toward Samuel's room. "Despite your earlier reasoning, my love, I'm still not convinced this is a good idea; my concern being more for you than Samuel."

Louisa tut-tutted and made an exaggerated show of adjusting her gloves. "I'm quite well, Max, I can assure you," she said. "Actually, I was thinking about the chat I had with Tom Ellis just now. The lady sitting with him is his mother, Dora, who told me she recently secured a live-in position as a chambermaid at the Bridge Hotel here in town, which means she can now visit her son regularly. She also admitted none of it was orchestrated by her, which makes me wonder if you might know something about it."

Maxwell grimaced and rubbed the back of his neck. "I couldn't really say. I might have made a couple of recommendations here and there, but I wasn't sure if they'd actually accomplish anything."

Louisa gave a soft laugh. "Maxwell Benedict Harlow, you are

a wonderful man." She grabbed his lapels, stood on tiptoes, and planted a kiss on his mouth. "Truly wonderful."

From nearby came the exaggerated sound of a man clearing his throat. Louisa let go of Maxwell's lapels and turned to see Charles and Jane standing outside the kitchen door. Jane looked decidedly amused. Charles, perhaps not quite so much. Louisa blushed. Maxwell merely smiled and threaded his fingers through hers.

"If you're ready," Charles said, moving past them, "we can go and see Samuel. He's on his own."

Louisa's heart sped up. "I'm ready," she said.

As before, the door to Samuel's room stood slightly ajar.

"Go ahead, Louisa." Charles pushed at the door, its hinges creaking as it swung open. "We'll stay back but will remain in full view. If Samuel shows any sign of anxiety or agitation, you will leave immediately. Understood?"

Louisa nodded her gaze already fixed firmly on the man who sat in silence at the small table. The dominoes lay on the table before him, placed as if he'd just completed a game with an invisible companion. She glanced down and saw a solitary tile on the floor, by his feet.

Drawing breath, she moved toward him. "Good day to you, Samuel," she said brightly, slowing her step as she approached. "I've come to visit with you again. I hope you remember me."

As before, he showed no indication he'd noticed her. That is, till she bent to retrieve the errant tile. She sensed his awareness while still crouched at his feet and looked up to see his mangled face gazing down at her, his one good eye widening in recognition. A sound escaped him; a raspy groan that surely implied delight, followed by the scrape of his chair as he pushed it back. Then, to Louisa's astonishment, he rose to his feet, stretched out a hand, and waggled his outstretched fingers, the intent unspoken but quite clear.

Here, let me help you.

From somewhere behind her, she heard Jane's soft gasp.

Louisa regarded his outstretched hand, which trembled slightly. The papery skin, mapped with irregular veins, bore the telltale stains of age, but was otherwise unmarked. The fingers waggled again, demanding, encouraging. Long, fine fingers, the kind one might easily imagine dancing across the ivory keys of a piano.

Louisa placed her hand in his, his flesh cool against hers. Then he closed his grip, surprising her with his strength as he helped her to her feet.

"Thank you, sir," she said, as he released her. He said nothing, but merely regarded her through his one blue eye, which narrowed a little, as if assessing her.

"Do you remember me?" she asked, placing the single domino with the others. "I was here not long ago. You spoke to me and asked me to play."

Then he touched her cheek with his fingertips and his lopsided smile appeared. "Gray," he said, and sat down, pulling up his chair before shuffling the dominoes. "Play."

Louisa glanced at the others, her expression a silent request for approval.

"I have no objection," Charles replied. "All right with you, Maxwell?"

Maxwell nodded. "He seems calm enough."

"It truly is remarkable, Louisa, the way he responds to you," Jane said. "Not only speaking but offering you his hand the way he just did. As far as I know, he's never displayed that kind of behavior with anyone else."

They played as before, except this time they played more than once. Samuel remained engaged throughout, constantly encouraging Louisa by making the same, odd little sounds. She, in return, talked to him, encouraging his moves, asking him all kinds of questions, trying to tease another word out of him. But to no avail.

"It seems 'play' and 'gray' is the extent of his vocabulary," she said, after conceding the last game to him. "I wonder if there's something else we can do besides playing dominoes. How mobile is he? Maybe we could take a stroll around the gardens."

"He walks well enough," Charles said, his eyes flicking to the window, "but bright sunlight bothers him. I'm not sure if it's because of his sight or the scarring on his face. Maybe both. In any case, today wouldn't be a good day, since the sun keeps putting in an appearance."

"Play," Samuel said, having just mixed the dominoes atop the table.

Louisa cocked her head. "I should think you'd play all day long if you could, Samuel. Am I right?"

"Have you had enough, dearest?" Jane asked.

"I believe I should be asking you that question," Louisa replied. "If you're all agreeable, I'd like to play one more. He's obviously enjoying himself. Besides, if I win this one, it will make us even. Right, Samuel?"

"I have no objection," Charles said. "I'm more concerned about how he'll react when you leave."

Since Samuel had won the previous game and obviously anticipated another, he'd already picked his first tile; a double four. "Play." His mouth twisted in another smile. "Play gray."

Louisa held up a forefinger. "Just one more. All right?"

He didn't respond other than to regard her expectantly. Though he couldn't communicate with speech, he communicated nonetheless, she realized. His good eye was like a small window, displaying what lay behind it, expressing what his tongue could not. Right now, it was expressing anticipation and a touch of impatience. *What are you waiting for?* it seemed to say. *Get on with it.*

Louisa smiled, chose her first domino, and the game began.

"That makes us even, sir," she announced sometime later as she placed her final tile. "Three games each. I've enjoyed your company, but I have to go now. All right?"

Samuel responded by shuffling the dominoes atop the table again.

"No." Louisa shook her head and placed a hand atop his,

halting his movements. "No more today."

He lifted his head to look at her.

"Louisa," Maxwell muttered, his tone cautioning.

"It's all right," she replied, without taking her eyes off Samuel's face, "I'm just trying to make him understand that I have to go home now."

Smiling, she took her hand from his, pushed her chair back, and stood. Samuel's gaze remained fixed on her.

"I'll visit again soon." She drew a cross over her heart. "I promise."

He blinked but said nothing.

"All right, Louisa." Charles moved into the room. "Just step quietly away."

Louisa scowled at the two men. "You're both behaving as though I'm in some kind of danger, which is ridiculous. Samuel would never hurt me. He's incapable of—"

Samuel's chair scraped back as he got to his feet and held out a hand, which trembled as before.

Louisa heard Maxwell's sharp intake of breath. "Louisa!"

"Stay calm," Charles muttered.

"Unlike the two of you, I'm extremely calm." Smiling, Louisa reached out to take Samuel's hand. "He's saying goodbye to me, that's all."

Still holding his hand, she moved to his side, lifted up on her toes, and kissed his cheek. "Gray," he murmured, so quietly Louisa doubted the others even heard it.

"Till the next time, my friend." Releasing his hand, she stepped back. "Thank you for today."

Samuel stood still for a moment, watching her. Only her. Then he blinked, turned away, and sat down again.

"Remarkable," Jane said, fanning herself as they wandered out into the corridor. "Quite remarkable."

"Indeed." Charles shook his head. "Not what I expected at all. Quite different to his last reaction."

Louisa looked back to see Samuel seated, unmoving, at the

table. A haunting sense of loneliness crept into her heart, as if she could feel exactly what he felt. It was profound, the way he affected her. "With respect, Charles, perhaps you expect too little of him." Moving on, she looped her arm through Maxwell's. "I tend to believe, with more encouragement and interaction, he'd begin to awaken from his silence."

Charles looked dubious. "I'm not sure I agree. And if so, it would take a tremendous amount of time and dedication. He has no family, and I know of no one who would be able or willing to devote that much time. Besides, he's never shown any real interest in anyone but you, Louisa. He's captivated by you, it seems."

"He's not the only one, damn it," Maxwell muttered.

Louisa laughed. "Then I shall just have to visit him as often as I can."

CHAPTER TWENTY

IT WAS SATURDAY, the sixth day of September. Late afternoon sunlight slanted through Louisa's bedroom windows, its mellow glow hinting that summer was drawing gently to a close. A memorable summer, in so many ways.

Thus far, it had also been a memorable day. A day that had, apparently, been marked on Maxwell's calendar since before their marriage, prompted by his initial enquiry into her birthstone. He might have forgotten about Uncle Isaac's birthday, but it seemed he had not forgotten about hers.

That morning, Louisa had awoken in Maxwell's arms; always a rare occurrence given his penchant for sleeplessness. They had made love in the soft light of dawn, and then taken breakfast on the terrace, serenaded by birdsong and the cascade of the fountain.

Mid-morning, they had gone for a ride together and had a light luncheon in the village inn. Upon returning home, and with Maxwell ensconced in his office for a few hours, Louisa had brought her journal up to date before settling down to read.

Now, freshly bathed, hair styled, and clad in a silk *peignoir*, she sat at her dressing table and opened the lid of her jewelry box, seeking a suitable pair of earrings before dressing for the evening event. At that same moment, Maxwell emerged from his bedroom. "Close your eyes, Mrs. Harlow."

Louisa regarded her husband's approach in her mirror, her

heart quickening at the sight. He, too, had been readying himself for the evening ahead, though he had not yet donned his coat. Still, he cut a fine figure. The blue silk of his waistcoat enhanced the rich blackness of his hair and contrasted magnificently with his starched white shirt. His tailored, slate-gray trousers fit perfectly across his hips and tapered impeccably over thigh and calf. The citrusy smell of bergamot drifted into her nostrils, the tang of it subdued by subtle hints of sandalwood.

"You look deliciously handsome, Mr. Harlow. You smell rather heavenly as well." Unabashedly, Louisa gaze drifted to the fall of his trousers. "Do you think my parents would be disappointed if we didn't show up this evening?"

A slow smile appeared as he moved to stand behind her. "What else do you have in mind?"

As if he didn't know! "Well, it isn't a game of dominoes."

"Hmm. Tempting. But I think your parents would be disappointed if Finlay was the only one to show up for your birthday dinner. However, I shall definitely look forward to *not* playing dominoes later tonight. Now, do as you're told and close your eyes. I've been waiting all day for this."

Smiling, she did as bidden, aware of what felt like a fine chain being placed around her neck. She bent her head as Maxwell fastened the catch, his touch at her nape causing a sweet little shiver to run down her spine.

Both his hands then came to rest on her shoulders and a soft whisper brushed across her ear. "You can open them now, my love."

She did so, gasping at the sight of the blue sapphire resting at the base of her throat. The large, faceted stone, oval cut, was set in a notched gold bezel and suspended on a chain of fine gold. It was a simple but elegant design that did not detract from the beauty of the jewel, but rather enhanced it. A flush of delight warmed her cheeks. "Oh, my goodness, it's magnificent. I love it. Thank you."

"We're not quite done yet." He handed her a small, blue

leather box. "But I think it best you put these on without my help."

Another gasp escaped her when she opened the lid to see a pair of sapphire drop earrings, the settings smaller, but identical to that of the pendant. "Oh, Max, they're *perfect*." She reached for him in a silent demand, and he bent to kiss her mouth.

"I'm glad you like them," he said, straightening.

"I adore them." She leaned into her mirror as she put them on. "I was undecided, but now I believe I shall wear my rose taffeta gown tonight. It will look lovely with the blue, don't you think?"

Maxwell's hands returned to her shoulders, his thumbs tracing soft circles on her neck. "I'm sure it will."

"I'm curious," she said, studying him once more, "did you choose that waistcoat to coordinate?"

"Mmm, your birthday gift might have influenced my choice a little," he said, and dropped another kiss on the top of her head. "I'll send Archer in and leave you to finish dressing. Meet you downstairs when you're ready?"

Louisa nodded her assent and continued to gaze at her reflection, her sight turning inward as she fingered the sapphire pendant. Not seven months earlier, on a mild day in late winter, she'd been hurtling across the moor on Byron's strong back. At the time, as she faced another London Season, her optimism for her future had been mired in doubt.

No longer.

These days, her life felt like a dream and the future looked wonderful. Granted, getting to this point had been the result of some questionable decisions, a touch of inappropriate behavior, and perhaps a few misgivings. But now, as far as she was concerned, her life—her *marriage*—was just about perfect. The only thing missing, for Louisa at least, was a child. Every month she waited, hoping, praying she would not bleed. So far, though, it had been one disappointment after another. As for Maxwell, she wasn't even sure how he felt about children. He'd never broached the subject, which in turn made her reluctant to do so. She had yet to find the right moment—or perhaps the courage— to discuss the issue with him.

Certainly, today wasn't the day.

A tap at the door drew Louisa back to the present and she surrendered to Archer's ministrations.

THE PERFECTION OF the day continued into the evening. The first surprise came upon their arrival at Highfield, where they, and Finlay, would be staying for the night. Louisa discovered, to her great delight, that Arthur had come home from school and Josiah had made the journey from London. For the first time since her wedding, all her siblings were back under Highfield's roof.

Louisa's pendant and earrings garnered their merited admiration, and yet more gifts followed. Dinner was a rambunctious affair, with plenty of food, drink, and laughter. Memories, some poignant and some comical, had been resurrected and rejuvenated. Tales of childhood mischief had been shared, some previously told, others confessed for the first time.

"Grace, my dear, it appears we were completely blind to the machinations of our children." Aldous, feigning misery, shook his head. "I can only conclude that we are failures as parents." The subsequent chorus of cheerful denials loudly contradicted their father's statement.

Even Maxwell, who was neither boisterous nor loud by nature, appeared to be caught up in the gaiety. "I can't say I got into too much mischief myself," he remarked, when asked. "My father always kept me busy and consequently out of trouble."

Finlay snorted. "Whoa, not so fast, brother. I seem to recall Mam telling a tale of you putting frogs in the church font. Frightened the life out of the minister at my baptism."

Maxwell laughed. "Aye, right enough. I'd forgotten about

that. Got the strap for it, too."

Later, when bellies were full, and the distinctive odor of cigars drifted through the house, Louisa followed her mother upstairs to light the candle in the rose window.

"What a splendid evening it has been," Grace declared. "Have you enjoyed it?"

"Very much, Mama. It's been wonderful."

Grace smiled. "It gladdens my heart to see my daughter so happy."

Louisa returned the smile and stood in solemn silence till the candle was lit. Then, "I consider my life—our marriage—to be just about perfect," she said, watching as the little flame settled into a steady burn. "There is only one thing missing, Mama. Something I would dearly like to happen but, as yet, has not occurred."

Understanding showed on her mother's face. "These things often take time, dearest." She touched Louisa's cheek. "My suggestion is to set your worry aside and just enjoy your marriage. The fact that you're happy with each other is already a blessing." A ponderous frown appeared. "Mind you, I have to say, we tend to be fortunate with our unions in this family. Fate has a habit of stepping in and arranging things for us in the most unorthodox ways. As you know, your Uncle Isaac first met Eleanor after falling off his horse in Hyde Park. What a fairytale that was! And if not for a snowstorm, your father and I might never have met."

Louisa wrinkled her nose. "And then there's me and Maxwell."

Grace chuckled. "Yes, most definitely unorthodox, but it has all turned out for the best. He seemed very much at ease tonight. One of the family, in fact. I'll be interested to see how he copes with the extended family at Myddleton in a fortnight."

Louisa shrugged. "I have no doubt he'd cope very well if he were there, Mama."

Grace's eyes widened. "What do you mean?"

"He can't go. He has a meeting in Glasgow scheduled for that week and cannot change it. I'd still like to go, though. May I travel with you and Papa?"

"Of course, but can't Finlay stand in for him?"

Louisa shook her head. "Not on this occasion, I'm afraid."

"Well, that is a pity." Grace gave her a sympathetic look. "Are you terribly disappointed?"

"I was." Louisa shrugged. "But it can't be helped. If he could be there, he would be."

"Oh, well, never mind. There'll be plenty of other occasions." Grace looped her arm through Louisa's. "Come on, let's go. They'll be wondering where we are."

THE MIDNIGHT HOUR was well behind them by the time the celebrations ended. Maxwell, having lingered with Aldous awhile before joining Louisa upstairs, now eyed the doll that sat on the chair in Louisa's bedroom. Its scruffy appearance implied that it had been a well-loved childhood toy, but Maxwell found its porcelain stare strangely unsettling.

"Her name is Margery." Clad in some baggy, white garment, Louisa was sitting cross-legged in the middle of the bed, brushing her hair. "There was a time when I wouldn't go anywhere without her."

"Well, I'm very glad you broke that habit." Maxwell unbuttoned his shirt and tossed it onto the chair, covering the doll. "Have you enjoyed your day, sweetheart?"

Louisa laughed. "Poor Margery. And yes, I have. Have you?"

"Very much. I have to say, you're fortunate to have such a close family."

"Of which you are now a part." Louisa frowned and appeared to examine a tangle in a thick strand of her hair. "I'm hoping, one day, you and I will have a family of our own. Is it something you've considered, I wonder? You've never mentioned it."

Maxwell's hands paused on the unfastening of his trousers, and he pondered a moment before he answered. "Being a father wasn't something I ever seriously considered. My lifestyle, I thought, simply did not lend itself to parenthood. I assumed Finlay would be the one to fall in love and produce several offspring, and that Harlow Industries, assuming it still existed, would be transferred to nephews and nieces after my day." He shrugged. "But then I went and got myself in a pickle with this aristocratic Yorkshire lass, who has since stolen my heart. So now, I have to say yes, the thought of having a child is something I have considered. Are you trying to tell me something, Louisa?"

Her eyes widened briefly. "Oh, no. No, it's not… I mean, I'm not with child. I simply wondered how you felt about it."

"If and when it happens, my love, I shall be delighted."

She chewed on her lip. "And if it doesn't?"

"I don't see any reason to worry about that just yet." He continued to shed his clothes. "My parents were married for three years before I put in an appearance, and it was another three before Finlay showed up."

"But, what if it doesn't?"

Frowning, Maxwell settled himself beside her on the bed, and held out a hand. "Give me the brush, lass."

She handed it to him and then turned her back. "Be gentle," she said, tossing her hair over her shoulder, where it tumbled to her waist in a cascade of soft, brown waves.

"To dwell on 'what if' can take the joy out of 'what is'." He lifted a silken handful of her hair to his face and breathed in the subtle, floral scent. Then he set the brush on the bedside table, ignoring Louisa's squeak of surprise as he pulled her into his arms and positioned her beneath him. "And, right now, I'd much rather dwell on what is."

"I thought you were going to brush my hair," she said, feigning a pout.

"No, not what I had in mind at all." Frowning, he eyed her

voluminous attire. "What the devil are you wearing, lass?"

She wrinkled her nose. "It's one of my old nightgowns. I'm in a nostalgic mood tonight. What did you have in mind, then?"

"Well first, I need to get this bloody sack off you." He tugged her nightgown up to her hips and then straddled her bare legs. "Lift your arse up a little. Aye, that's it. Arms up as well, so I can get it over your head. Good Lord, it's a veritable tent."

Snorting with laughter, Louise emerged naked from beneath a couple of yards of cotton. "It's comfortable," she protested.

"It's almost as hideous as that doll," he replied, and tossed the garment onto the same chair as his shirt. "In future, you'll wear the damn thing only when I'm away, understood?"

She laughed again, a sound he had come to love. Her happiness had become profoundly important to him. Making her happy basically made him happy. It was as simple as that. As for children, he saw no reason to believe they would not eventually appear. Maybe even after tonight.

He propped himself on his elbows and lowered his head to take an erect nipple in his mouth. Louisa gasped, her spine arching as he scraped his teeth over the hardened peak. Maxwell's stomach muscles tightened. His desire for his lovely wife had been quietly simmering for most of the evening. Now, the musky smell of her, the natural way she responded to him, and her soft mewls of pleasure, rendered him as hard as steel.

He continued his explorations, trailing kisses down to the triangle of soft curls at the apex of her thighs. Then he laid her open to his tongue, teasing and tasting the sweetness of her. He used his thumb as well, flicking and circling the sensitive nub as she writhed in his grasp.

"Max, please," she whispered, her head tipped back. "I want you inside me."

He answered with a low growl and slid up to cover her body, stifling her cry of pleasure with a kiss as he sank into her with a single thrust. Then, arms braced, he lifted his head to watch her as he ground his hips to hers, thrusting slow and deep.

"I've been wanting to do this all evening," he said.

"Mmm, I know."

"How do you know?"

"The way you looked at me over dinner and afterwards in the parlor."

"Was I that obvious?"

Eyes glazed with pleasure, she smiled lazily. "To me, yes."

Parting with another growl, he slid his hands down to cradle her buttocks, holding her steady against him as he continued to thrust. She matched his movements, her soft moans of pleasure driving Maxwell to near madness.

"Louisa," he murmured. It was a plea for mercy, a demand for her release before he lost all control.

Her responding whisper brushed hotly across his throat. "Yes, Max. Oh, *yes*."

Her body went rigid as her sex pulsed hard around his cock, sending him hurtling into ecstasy.

Later, in the depths of night, Maxwell awoke from a sound sleep and, as usual, his mind began to rove. Had he been at Northcott Manor, he'd have slid from the bed and sought his own or, more likely, wandered downstairs to his office. Here, he could neither, so he lay still and allowed his thoughts to drift.

Beside him, Louisa shifted slightly in her sleep, snuggling closer while parting with a sigh that spoke clearly of contentment. Maxwell smiled into the darkness, acknowledging his own, newly found sense of gratification, which had nothing to do with his commercial success. It was simpler, yet more profound, more rewarding. And it was all due to the woman sleeping peacefully at his side. She had become his priority. He would do anything to make her happy.

That admission brought the upcoming Glasgow trip to mind, which coincided with her uncle's birthday. The oversight was entirely Maxwell's fault, and he saw no way out of it. At least, not entirely. But maybe he could shorten it and still show up at Myddleton for her uncle's birthday, albeit a little late. He turned his head and breathed in the soft scent of her hair.

"I'll try," he whispered. "I promise I'll try."

CHAPTER TWENTY-ONE

A FORTNIGHT AFTER her twenty-first birthday, Louisa participated in the celebration of her Uncle Isaac's eightieth. Myddleton House, the Derbyshire seat of the Earl of Hutton, had seen three splendid days of music, dancing, and parlor games within its stately walls, and a fair amount of eating and drinking as well. For Louisa, however, the best part had been spending time with the family she loved so much.

She missed Maxwell terribly, but successfully hid her occasional attacks of despondency a task made easier by the celebratory atmosphere that permeated the entire house. That, and the occasional amusing moment, like the brief conversation that had taken place when Grandmama Hutton had asked after Maxwell.

"A pity he's not here," the dowager countess had declared. "I was quite looking forward to having another conversation with him. I'll admit I was appalled when I first learned about your marriage to this fellow, but he's actually quite charming for someone of his class."

"I'm glad you think so, Grandmama," Louisa replied, biting back an urge to laugh. Had Maxwell just been complimented, or insulted? "I know he thinks well of you also."

The old lady had looked genuinely puzzled. "Why would he not?" she responded.

Uncle Isaac's actual birthday had been the day before, and the celebrations had gone on well into the small hours. Now, in the late afternoon of this fourth day—a Sunday—things had substantially calmed down, much to Louisa's relief. Some of the guests had departed after luncheon. Of those who remained, the men, with the exception of her uncle, her father, and Josiah, had gone pheasant-shooting, while several of the ladies, her Aunt Eleanor included, had retired for an afternoon nap. Josiah and her uncle were in the billiard room. Everyone else, with Louisa, had gathered in the Crimson Parlor to share conversation, read, or play card games. Partnered with Evie, Louisa had just lost a third game of Whist to her father, who was partnered with Clara.

"Another?" her father asked, shuffling the cards.

"Absolutely, Papa," Clara replied, and pulled a face at her twin sister. "We're on a winning-streak."

Louisa rose to her feet. "Thank you, but not for me. If you don't mind, I think I'll take a little turn around the room and stretch my legs."

"Of course," her father replied, still shuffling. "I'm sure we can find someone to take your place. Catherine, how about you?"

Catherine, Louisa's cousin, reclining on a nearby chaise-longue, stifled a yawn. "Thank you, dear Uncle, but no. I find myself quite lacking in energy today. In fact, I'm of a mind to take a quick nap before dinner."

Louisa, contemplating the possibility of an outdoor walk, moved toward the window to see if the weather would allow for such a venture. But, noting the bleak skies and seeing several loose leaves skipping past the window, decided she wasn't in the mood to battle the elements. A stroll about the room would have to do. Vaguely, she wondered what Maxwell might be doing at that moment.

"Then will you play, Grace?" Aldous asked. "I should like a chance for revenge. As I recall, the last time we played, you and Josiah took every trick."

Startled by a strange and sudden sense of recognition, Louisa turned and regarded her father. His words had certainly come from his mouth, yet she had the oddest impression they didn't belong to him, that they'd been spoken by someone else. The significance of it taunted the edge of her mind but remained frustratingly elusive. It felt like she'd made a discovery. Found the missing piece of a puzzle. The lost key to a locked door.

"All right, yes, I'll play," her mother replied, laughter in her voice. "But you'd better prepare to lose again."

What puzzle? What door?

Desperate, Louisa clung onto the baffling reaction, terrified that the hidden meaning behind it would fade, that she'd lose the answer she sought. Why were her father's words so relevant? What was she missing? She echoed his words in her head, searching for the answer.

'...will you play, Grace?'

The revelation hit her like a gust of icy wind, the shock of it stealing her breath and all but halting her heart. At that same moment, as she struggled to grasp a plausibility that was surely beyond plausible, the figure of a man appeared in the parlor doorway. Had he not been so familiar to her, so beloved, she might have taken less notice of his presence. After all, he was not supposed to be there. He was supposed to be two hundred miles away, in Scotland.

Maxwell?

The secondary shock of seeing her husband dissolved the last remnants of Louisa's shattered composure. The world around her faded into twilight and the floor rose up to meet her with alarming speed. As she tumbled into oblivion, she heard Maxwell call her name.

"No!" Wincing, Louisa turned her head away, her eyes flickering open. Despite her obvious displeasure, her protestation at having a bottle of smelling-salts shoved under her nose came as a relief to Maxwell. Of all the reactions he might have expected upon his surprise arrival at Myddleton, seeing his wife drop to the floor in a dead faint was not one of them.

"Easy, my love." He slid an arm beneath her shoulders and raised her up a little. "I have you."

She blinked up at him, confusion, and perhaps a touch of fear, evident in her eyes as she grabbed at the lapel of his jacket. "Max?"

"Oh, thank goodness," Grace said, fingering the pearls at her throat. "You gave us such a fright."

Aldous spoke. "Move back, everyone, please. Let her have some air."

"Do you hurt anywhere, love?" Maxwell asked. "Did you bump your head?"

"No, I...I don't think so." She touched his face, fingers icy against his cheek. "What are you doing here?"

"At this precise moment, feeling exceedingly guilty," he replied, catching her cold hand in his. "I wanted to surprise you, not cause you to faint."

"It wasn't your fault," she said. "I was... I mean, I've been feeling a little bit tired all day. I'm sure that was the main reason."

"Would you like a drink, dearest?" Grace asked. "Some water, perhaps?"

"No, thank you, Mama." Louisa rubbed her temple, her hand visibly trembling.

Maxwell raised her up a little. "Put your arms around my neck, love. Let's get you onto the settee."

"You don't need to carry me, Max, I think I can stand," she said. "Perhaps just help me to my feet."

"All right. Careful, now. Lean on me." He guided her to a nearby settee. "There. Better?"

"Yes, much." She reclined against the cushions. "Thank you."

"Are you sure?" Maxwell was not at all convinced. Her face was void of color and had a dazed expression, unfocused, as if her mind was elsewhere. He exchanged glances with Grace and Aldous. "I think we should call a doctor."

"I agree," Aldous said. "Can we send for him, Mama?"

"Of course." The dowager nodded to a footman standing by the doorway. "See to it, will you?"

"I don't need a doctor, Papa," Louisa said. "I fainted, that's all. I'm not ill."

"But I've have never known you to faint before." Grace sat beside her and took her hand. "You're still awfully pale, and oh, my goodness, your hand is like ice."

"I'm fine, Mama, truly. I just need a few minutes." She regarded Maxwell again. "I can't believe you're here."

"The result of unforeseen circumstances, but nothing to worry about." He gave her a sympathetic smile. "And I'm in agreement with everyone else, love. The doctor should be called."

Louisa shook her head. "I'm feeling better by the minute. By the time he gets here, I'll be up and about, and he'll have come for nothing."

"Might you be anticipating, Lou?" Clara piped up.

"That's what I was wondering," Evie added. "Women are apparently prone to fainting when they are in a delicate condition."

Maxwell's stomach tightened. Could that be it? Was Louisa carrying his child? He did a quick calculation which left him doubting. Her menses had not been that long ago. It was surely too soon, then, for such a symptom to manifest.

The dowager countess, Lady Hutton, banged her cane on the floor and scowled at the twins. "A little more decorum, if you please! I agree with your Mama and your husband, Louisa. The doctor should most definitely be called, if only to tell us that you're in fine fettle. In the meantime, get yourself to bed. I'll have some chamomile tea sent up to you."

"But I swear I'm not ill, Grandmama," Louisa said. "And neither am I anticipating, Clara. I was up very late last night, and I'm tired. I'm sure that's all it is. I don't deny I need to rest, and some chamomile tea would be very welcome, but please don't bother calling the doctor. I assure you, it's not necessary."

Maxwell narrowed his eyes. He couldn't quite put his finger on it, but for some reason, Louisa's assurances didn't quite ring true. She seemed, for want of a better word, distressed. Evidently, her mother thought so too.

"I'm not at all convinced," Grace said. "I would prefer to have the doctor examine you, Louisa. No argument."

Later that evening, after the doctor had declared Louisa free from any apparent affliction, Maxwell settled into bed beside her. Silhouetted in the soft glow of candlelight, she nestled against him, her voice notably silent.

"Tell me," he murmured, gathering her close.

"Tell you what?"

"About whatever it is that's troubling you."

She fidgeted. "Nothing's troubling me."

He nuzzled her hair. "Well, you definitely have something on your mind."

"It's nothing, truly. Tell me about Glasgow and how come you managed to be here."

Maxwell had the distinct impression that his being there actually took second place to whatever issue presently occupied Louisa's thoughts. He answered, nonetheless. "I'm here because I managed to deal with most of the important stuff in the first two days. The rest I left in Finlay's hands. And also, our German associate never showed due to the fact that his elderly father passed away suddenly. We've rescheduled for another, shorter meeting with him a month from now."

"Oh, I see," Louisa murmured, her gaze aimed at the ceiling and a slight frown on her brow.

"I trust it's been a good week here at Myddleton?"

Louisa continued to stare at the ceiling. "Mmm."

"You've enjoyed yourself?"

"Uh huh."

"Good." He cleared his throat. "And by the way, I'm thinking of shaving my head. Be easier to manage. I can just give it a polish each morning. I trust having a bald husband won't bother you."

Louisa blinked, her frown deepening as she regarded him. "What?"

He gave her an amused look. "Did you hear anything of what I just said?"

"Yes, of course." She wrinkled her nose. "Well, no, actually, not everything. Something about your German associate? Forgive me. My mind wandered."

"Obviously, and I'd like to know where it went."

"Oh, nowhere really." Her brow relaxed and her sigh brushed across his throat. "Make love to me, Max."

"Hmm. A diversionary tactic and a tempting one at that." Parting with a sigh of his own, he propped himself up on an elbow, his free hand stroking the curve of her waist and coming to rest on her hip. "I'm concerned, Louisa. I know there's something going on in that head of yours. I hope you're not afraid to tell me what it is."

Another frown appeared as she traced the line of his mouth with a fingertip. "All right, I'll admit, I do have something on my mind, and no, I'm not afraid to tell you about it. It's just that I'm not quite ready to do so yet, because I'm still trying to sort it all out in my head. I promise you, though, it's nothing to worry about. It's not even about us. Well, not really. Just give me some time, Maxwell, please."

"As you wish." Feeling somewhat appeased, he shifted, half-covering her as his hand slid between her legs. "But how much time? Would an hour be enough?"

"I might need a little longer than that," she replied, lifting an errant strand of hair from his brow. "And I trust you weren't serious about shaving your head."

CHAPTER TWENTY-TWO

THEY'D BEEN BACK at Northcott Manor for two days, and Maxwell had not once pressed Louisa further about what occupied her mind. Now, at breakfast, she nibbled on her slice of toast as her thoughts continued to ruminate. Time after time, she'd gone over every detail, pulling the puzzle apart and putting it together again. And each time, the pieces fit unerringly, turning coincidences into clues that surely provided the answer to a previously unanswerable question.

So why was she so reluctant to voice her conclusions?

Probably because she was as terrified of being wrong as she was of being right. What if all the coincidences turned out to nothing more than a handful of accidental by-chances, even if her instinct—her *heart*—told her otherwise?

No. There was no denying it. There could be no doubt.

None.

She felt Maxwell's scrutiny and met his eyes, her piece of toast pausing on its way to her mouth. She knew he wanted answers and, God knows, he'd been patient enough. By the look on his face, however, the patience had just run out.

"I believe I've given you enough time, Louisa," he said, his expression somber. "We cannot go on like this. *You* cannot go on like this. Something happened while you were at Myddleton, and I need to know what."

Louisa heaved a sigh and set her piece of toast down. He was right, of course. It was time to face it. To bring it out into the open. To make the announcement that would change lives. Drastically.

"You have been very tolerant, Max, and I appreciate it. And yes, something did happen at Myddleton, but I hardly know where to begin. I'm afraid you'll think I've lost my mind once you hear it."

He looked doubtful. "There's nothing you could say that would make me think that my sweet."

"Oh, but there is," she replied, "which is why I need you to swear you'll let me finish without interruption."

He dipped his chin. "As you wish."

"All right." She drew a breath. "I've been preoccupied because I had a revelation at Myddleton. A shocking revelation. It's about…it's about Samuel."

Maxwell's eyes widened briefly, but he said nothing.

"I believe I've solved the mystery of him… no, I'm *certain* I have. I know who he is. His actual identity." Silently cursing the tremble in her voice, Louisa clenched her hands against a mounting surge of long-suppressed emotion. Speaking out at last was akin to pulling a cork from a shaken bottle. "Samuel doesn't respond to me the way he does because he's captivated by me. It's not that at all. At least, not in the way you infer. The reason he responds to me the way he does is because he *recognizes* me."

At that, Maxwell's brows lifted.

"And the reason he recognizes me is because—" she swallowed over the tightness in her throat—"is because he believes I'm someone else."

Maxwell scrubbed a hand across his jaw. "Forgive me, love, but this makes no sen—"

"No, don't you *dare* interrupt," she cried, sitting forward. "Let me *finish*. Samuel thinks I'm someone else because I *look* like someone else. A person from his past. In fact, I look almost exactly the way she would have looked the last time he saw her, which was more than thirty years ago. That's why he cried when he first saw me."

The mention of it prompted her own tears to spill, unchecked, down her cheeks. "Samuel isn't saying 'gray', Max. He's saying '*Grace*'. He thinks I'm my mother. He thinks I'm his *sister*. He taught her to play dominoes when she was a child. They used to play all the time, which is why he constantly asks me to play. It's a memory, one that has somehow remained intact in that poor, damaged brain of his. 'Play gray' actually means 'Play, *Grace*." She laughed through the continuing cascade of tears. "Don't you see? His name isn't Samuel. It's Julian. Julian Frederick Thackeray. He's my mother's brother. My *uncle*. The one who went off to fight the French and never came home. The one we light a candle for every night at Highfield. I've gone over this in my head, time and time again, and I know it's him, right down to the blue of his one good eye. In my heart, I know it! And that being so, we have to bring him home. Back to Highfield. Please, Max, we have to bring him home."

Sobbing, Louisa dropped her head in her hands, startled moments later by a gentle touch on her shoulder. "Come here." Maxwell lifted her to her feet and folded her in his arms. "Hush, now. Don't cry, love. It's all right. We'll sort this out."

Sniffing, Louisa scrubbed tears from her eyes and regarded him, searching his face for some kind of affirmation. "Say you believe me," she said. "Please say you do. It's so important to me that you do."

"It's an extraordinary allegation, but one I'm willing to believe," he said. "That said, I think your conclusion merits a cautionary approach. We can't just arrive on your parents' doorstep and proclaim that we've found Uncle Julian. We can, however, suggest our suspicion of his true identity and take it from there. Likewise, we can't show up uninvited at St. Giles and whisk the poor fellow away without being fully assured of who he really is." He kissed her forehead. "If he truly is who you believe him to be, it'll be a tremendous shock to your mother. Likewise, if it all turns out to be a mistake—"

"But it won't, and it's not a suspicion."

"Nevertheless, you have to consider such a scenario, just in case, and think about the anguish and disappointment that would ensue. I'm on your side, my love, but we have to approach this carefully, with consideration for everyone involved, including Sam—including *Julian*."

He was correct of course; a voice of reason in the midst of Louisa's turbulent emotions. Although she was utterly convinced of Samuel's real identity, she saw the merit in being careful when approaching Grace. "So, how do we proceed?" she asked. "I'm frightened he might die before everyone has had a chance to meet him. Or before he's had a chance to come back to Highfield. It's his house, after all."

"Hmm." Frowning, Maxwell brushed a tear away with his thumb. "Do you happen to know if your parents are at home right now?"

"Yes, they should be."

"Right. Then I see no point in delaying. I'll have the carriage prepared. Go and get ready and we'll head over there."

"Carriage?" Louisa shook her head. "But that'll mean taking the road. It would be quicker to ride across the moor."

"Nevertheless, we're taking the carriage." Maxwell held up a hand as she opened her mouth to respond. "And I'll hear no argument."

Louisa sighed. "All right. But what will I say to them when we get there? I wouldn't even know how to begin."

"We can discuss that on the way over."

"Right. Yes, of course." She raised up on tiptoes and kissed his cheek. "I can't tell you how much it means to have your support in this. I love you so much, Mr. Harlow."

"Then I am the most fortunate man under Heaven," he replied, huskily. "Go on, now. Dress warmly. I'll meet you at the door."

CHAPTER TWENTY-THREE

"THE FAMILY ARE in the music room," Barnes said, having met Louisa and Maxwell at Highfield's door sometime later. "Would some tea be in order?"

Louisa, her thoughts spiraling into fresh chaos, stared at him blankly for a moment. "Er, no, not for me."

"Nothing for me either." Maxwell tucked Louisa's hand into the crook of his arm. "But thank you."

A ripple of sweet piano notes drifted down the hallway. Louisa recognized the piece—Mozart's *Piano Sonata Number 16*—as one of her mother's favorites. She envisaged her mother seated regally at the pianoforte, slender fingers gliding effortlessly over the ivory and ebony keys, a serene expression on her face. The rest of the family would be seated around, watching, listening. A calm and harmonious scene, one Louisa had experienced many times before. Except today, it was about to be hit by a maelstrom of shock and disbelief. None of them had any idea of what was to come, nor could they even begin to imagine it.

Especially her mother.

In a brief moment of gut-clenching panic, Louisa considered saying nothing about her discovery. Leaving things as they were, her mother blissful in her ignorance.

I wonder about him every day, Louisa. Every single day.

The moment passed.

But, as they approached the music room door, Louisa dug her

fingers into Maxwell's arm. "I'm terrified," she said. "I don't know what to say or even how to begin. I've forgotten absolutely everything we discussed on the way over."

He placed a hand on the door handle. "Take a breath before speaking and take your time. Say the words in your head before saying them out loud. Don't worry, love. I'll be with you, beside you. All right? Are you ready?"

She filled her lungs and exhaled slowly. "I don't think anyone could ever be ready for something like this," she replied. "Can we at least wait till Mama has finished playing?"

"Of course." Maxwell drew Louisa into his arms, and she pressed an ear to his chest, the steady beat of his heart mingling with the music. They stood without speaking for a few minutes, waiting till the sonata's conclusion, which was followed by the sound of applause and muffled voices expressing obvious pleasure and approval.

Maxwell released Louisa, gave her a solemn smile, and opened the door. They stepped inside and five sets of eyes turned toward them: Aldous, Grace, Julian, and the twins.

"Maxwell, Louisa!" Grace, who had been placing another music sheet on her stand, paused. "Oh, what a lovely surprise."

"Indeed," Aldous said, rising from his spot on the settee. "Welcome, both of you. A spontaneous visit, I trust?"

Louisa opened her mouth to respond, but hesitated, just long enough for it to be noticeable.

"Is everything all right?" Julian asked, frowning.

"Everything is fine," Maxwell replied. "But no, our visit is not entirely spontaneous. We're here because there is something we feel compelled to impart to you. To *all* of you." The solemnity of his voice had a tangible effect on the atmosphere.

"It sounds rather serious, I must say," Grace said, her expression wary. "Let me get comfortable." She rose from the piano and went to join Aldous, both taking their seats.

"But is it good news?" Evie asked, her eyes wide.

"Or bad?" Clara continued.

"I'm not certain either describes it accurately." Louisa hesitated again, her gaze drifting to her mother. "Shocking, certainly, and extraordinary in the extreme. I'm not quite sure how it might be accepted."

Aldous gestured. "Then sit down and tell us what this is about."

Louisa did as bid, with Maxwell beside her. He took her hand, linking his fingers through hers. "I'll begin if you like," he said.

As she gazed into the dark depths of his eyes, an idea slid into her mind. "Thank you, Max, but it's all right. I know how to begin." She regarded her mother once more, intent on asking a question, already aware of the answer. But it was a gentle first step. "Mama, what color were Uncle Julian's eyes?"

Grace raised her brows. "Blue," she replied. "A bright, brilliant blue, just as they are in his portrait. The same as Josiah's. Why do you ask?"

Josiah. Of course! Why didn't I realize that before? Not only the eyes, but the curly hair too.

Yet more validation. Not that Louisa needed it.

"Do you remember the night we spoke about him, Mama? Earlier this year, on the anniversary of his departure?" She gave Maxwell's fingers a squeeze. "It was the day before Max agreed to take tenancy of the manor. I remember you telling me you *wonder* about Uncle Julian every day. Not *think*, but *wonder*. It sounded like a deliberate choice of word, and it begs a question. Do you believe Uncle Julian died at Waterloo? Or do you wonder if he somehow survived the battle, and just… just couldn't come home because something prevented him from doing so?"

"I don't understand, dearest." Grace shook her head. "Why are you asking me this?"

"I have my reasons, Mama."

"Then share them," Aldous demanded. "You know this subject is upsetting to your mother."

"Yes, I know, Papa, and I apologize. I just want to hear Mama's thoughts before I go any further, that's all."

"Very well. The answer is 'no'." Grace shook her head. "I have *never* believed my brother died at Waterloo and, for the first few years at least, neither did your grandfather. We believed he survived but, for some terrible reason, was unable to come home. Whenever we told anyone, of course, we'd get a sympathetic look, or a remark meant to placate, but which actually implied we were clinging onto the impossible and unwilling to accept the truth. So, we simply stopped mentioning it. And I think, eventually, Papa gave up his belief. But I did not. To this day, I refuse to believe my brother died on that battlefield, though I cannot explain why. It is simply a feeling."

Frowning, Aldous addressed her. "I never knew any of this, Grace. Why did you not tell me?"

"Because I was afraid that I'd see the same expression of sympathy on your face, Aldous," she replied, softly, "and I couldn't bear the thought of it."

"Oh, my love." He raised her hand to his lips. "I'm so sorry."

There followed a moment of silence, then Julian spoke.

"We're waiting for an explanation, Louisa. Why all these questions about Uncle Julian?"

"Because..." Louisa's throat tightened, and the faces of her family blurred behind a sudden veil of tears. "Because I believe I've found him."

Grace's hands flew to her face, capturing a cry that surely came from her heart.

"Bloody hell, Lou." Julian's expression hardened. "You'd better be able to substantiate that claim."

"I would *never* have guessed you were going to say that," Clara murmured.

"Me neither," Evie said.

Aldous put an arm around Grace's shoulders. "I echo your brother's remark, Louisa. You'd better corroborate this outrageous claim with something solid."

Louisa wiped an errant tear from her cheek. "I would never have made such a claim had I not been certain. This is not easy for me either, I can assure you. Not easy at all. I knew it would be a shock to you."

"That's putting it mildly." Grace, her face ghost-white, shook her head. "I hardly dare believe what I'm hearing. In fact, I cannot believe it. What makes you think this person is my brother?"

"And where is this person?" Aldous asked.

"He's in an institution in Knaresborough," Louisa replied. "It's called St. Giles House, and it's run by the Reverend Charles Fairburn and his wife, Jane. They are wonderful people and, as institutions go, it's a fine place."

Grace made a sound of dismay. "But it's still an institution. Is he ill, then? Crippled?"

Louisa hesitated. "He's not exactly ill, Mama, but…"

"At some point in his past, he suffered a serious injury to the head," Maxwell said. "The scarring is substantial and his mental capacity severely diminished. Consequently, he is not at all as you remember him. You must prepare for that."

"If it is actually him," Aldous muttered. "I'm still waiting to hear how you arrived at this unlikely conclusion."

"Is he in pain?" Grace asked, her eyes shimmering with tears.

"Oh no, Mama." Louisa gave her head an emphatic shake. "I don't believe he's in any pain at all. At least, not anymore, though it's certain he suffered greatly at one time."

"Wait a minute." Frowning, Julian leaned forward. "Is this the institution you mentioned to me several weeks ago?"

Louisa nodded. "Yes, it is. And he's also the man I told you about. The one who spoke to me, though at the time I didn't understand the relevance of what he was trying to say. Actually, it was something Papa said at Myddleton that made me realize the truth of the man's real identity. That's why I fainted that day in the parlor. The shock of it—the *certainty* of it—was utterly overwhelming." She squeezed Maxwell's hand again. "Well, that, and seeing my husband unexpectedly appearing in the doorway. It was all too much."

"Something I said?" Aldous frowned. "What did I say?"

"You asked Mama to play cards with you," she replied.

He looked perplexed. "I don't understand."

Maxwell held up a hand. "Please, all of you, perhaps you might allow Louisa to explain without further interruption. I totally understand your doubts, believe me. But we're not getting anywhere, going back and forth like this. Let her speak, hear her out. Try and save your questions till she's finished. I guarantee you'll agree her claim has merit."

"Maxwell is right, we're getting nowhere." Grace drew a shaky breath. "Start at the beginning, dearest, and tell us everything. I want to know all the details. I need to understand why you're so sure this man is my brother. I have to be left with no doubt about his identity before I'll allow myself to believe it, for I'm not certain I could bear the disappointment."

"There will be neither doubt nor disappointment, Mama," Louisa replied, "but there will be heartbreak, and for that, I am truly sorry."

"I understand," Grace said, nodding. "All right. Go ahead. Tell us about him."

Louisa drew breath. "Well, first of all, they call him Samuel…"

CHAPTER TWENTY-FOUR

THE MAN SWUNG his scythe back and forth in a smooth, semi-circular movement, each sweep of the blade slicing effortlessly through the lush grass, taking it down to ground level. The rich scent of his labors, so pleasing to the senses, suffused the air, reminding Grace of warm summer days, picnics, and outdoor games.

A half-dozen apple trees, leaves already dappled with the hues of autumn, added an appealing rural touch to the scene. Some of the gnarled branches still bore fruit, though most appeared to have been harvested. Several wooden benches—a few of them occupied on this fine October morning—had been placed here and there. Grace regarded the occupants with interest, though she'd been told Samuel wasn't among them.

Samuel?

Or Julian?

She turned her attention to the building itself, St. Giles House, which was exactly as Louisa had first described not quite a fortnight since. Grace had wept as the story had unfolded, for in describing Samuel, Louisa had also described Julian: the curly hair, the brilliant blue gaze, even the two words he uttered. *Play, gray.*

Play, Grace.

According to Louisa, it was a case of mistaken identity that could be attributed to a mother-daughter resemblance. But Grace still harbored doubt. Could it truly be him? After all this time? There was only one way to be sure. She would have to see him.

And so, here she was, having just arrived at St. Giles House with Louisa, Maxwell, and the Fairburns. And Aldous too, of course, who couldn't quite hide his fear that this was all a terrible mistake. That the man Grace was about to meet was not at all who Louisa believed him to be. And that the subsequent disappointment for everyone, but especially for Grace, would be heartbreaking.

"Whenever you're ready, Mrs. Northcott, we can head inside," Charles said. "We've made sure he's on his own."

How could one ever be ready for something like this? There was no way to prepare for it, no matter the outcome. What if it wasn't him? What if it was?

Dear God, I want to believe. I want to believe it so much.

Grace nodded her assent and followed Charles, Jane, and the others into the building. It was a silent procession that felt oddly ceremonial, Grace thought. Like a visitation to some hallowed place. The outside scent of cut grass sweetened the less agreeable air within. Grace paused just inside the door, aware of the sudden quickening of her heart, and an odd prickle that wandered over her scalp. She turned and looked down the hallway to her left.

"You feel it, don't you, Mama?" Louisa said. "As do I. Every time. Cannot explain it, though."

"Feel what?" Aldous asked, but Louisa merely shrugged. Grace said nothing.

"It's this way." Charles gestured and then headed off down the hallway, where sounds of human occupation could be heard: muted conversation, a spate of coughing, a man's laughter. Following, Grace kept her eyes ahead, a hard lump of emotion already forming in her throat. It had been agreed that morning, before coming to St. Giles House, that she would enter Samuel's room alone, while the audience, such as it was, would remain nearby. What happened after that had yet to be determined.

Charles paused by a door that stood slightly ajar, and regarded Grace, inclining his head. Words were not necessary. Grace nodded her understanding, lifted onto her toes to kiss Aldous' cheek, and then pushed the door open.

Taking one hesitant step and then another, she halted and regarded the profile of the man seated at the small table. He was obviously tall and plainly thin, his clothes hanging loose on his frame. A halo of white curls softened the edges of a face—what she could see of it—touched by time, the flesh sallow, as if it had not seen sunlight in a good while. Standing quite still, she took in the man's every detail: the tilt of his head, the slope of his brow, the line of his nose and jut of his chin, the shape and movement of his hands. Even the way he sat.

The man paid Grace no mind at all. He was too busy playing his silent game of dominoes, setting up the small rectangular tiles with hands that trembled a little. Even as she watched, a single tile slipped from his fingers and bounced to the floor with a clatter. He appeared not to notice, but simply carried on with his game. And, as she continued to observe him, a transformation took place in her mind.

His shoulders broadened and his arms grew strong, filling the loose sleeves of his jacket. His thighs thickened, smoothing out the bagginess of his trousers. The white curls adorning his head darkened to a rich chestnut, glinting here and there with hints of gold and copper. His finely sculpted hands ceased their tremble, long fingers confidently adept as they continued to set up the dominoes. And his countenance sloughed off the years—ten, twenty, thirty or more—till his face glowed with youth and vitality. Then, in her mind, he turned to look at her, eyes bright and blue as a summer sky, smiling as he spoke. "Will you play, Grace?"

The clatter of another discarded domino shattered the image, and the silent white-haired man returned. But no matter his age, no matter what time and war and suffering had done to him, Grace would have known him anywhere. Her gloved hand flew to her mouth, stifling a sob, yet unable to prevent her acknowledgement of his true identity.

"Julian."

From behind her came a couple of soft gasps and a distinctly male mumble, though she did not dare to look back. To do so, to see the expressions on the faces of those she loved, would be her undoing. Instead, recalling what Louisa had described, she moved forward and crouched to pick up the dominoes, readying herself for what was to come. Almost immediately, Julian's hands stilled, and she felt his gaze upon her. Keeping her eyes lowered, she rose to her feet and set the errant tiles on the table. Then, for the first time in over thirty years, she looked into her brother's face.

And her heart broke.

Tears blurring her sight, she touched his scarred cheek. "Oh, my beloved brother," she said, her voice tight with emotion. "I knew you were alive; I just knew it. I never stopped believing. May God have mercy, how you must have suffered. I am sorry. So sorry." The tears escaped, rolling down her cheeks. "Do you know me, Julian? I am Grace. I am your sister."

Julian blinked and opened his mouth as if to speak but made no sound. Rather, he appeared to study her, tilting his head slightly as he did so. Did her words mean anything to him at all? Did he even recognize his own name? She had the impression he was puzzled, and assumed it was because he was seeing someone who looked like Louisa but was more than twenty years older.

"I am Grace," she repeated, placing a hand atop her heart. "Your sister."

He blinked again and looked down at the dominoes as if expecting them to provide the answer he sought.

And perhaps they did, Grace thought. Perhaps they held the key that opened his mind. She settled onto the opposite seat and reached over to touch his hand. "Will you play, Julian?"

At that, his head came up and a soft sound escaped him. She thought she saw it then, reflected in that brilliant, blue eye. *Recognition.* She held her breath.

A moment later, he smiled a beautiful, crooked smile, pulled a folded handkerchief from his pocket, and leaned over to wipe the tears from her cheek. "Play," he said, nodding his encouragement in exactly the way she remembered. "Play, Gray."

Grace laughed through yet more tears and looked toward the door to see she was not the only one weeping. Even Aldous was decidedly watery around the eyes.

"Julian's coming home, Aldous," she said, and began to choose her dominoes. "My brother is coming home at last."

CHAPTER TWENTY-FIVE

O N A DAMP afternoon in early November, the carriage carrying Julian Frederick Thackeray, Baron Westerdale, pulled up to the main door of Highfield Hall. Grace, seated beside him, placed her hand atop his.

"Are you ready, Julian?" she asked, not expecting an answer.

He looked down at their hands for a moment and then returned his gaze to the window, the contents of his mind known only to him.

Grace was under no illusion that the weeks and months ahead would be easy, but her decision to bring her brother home had never been in question. He belonged at Highfield as much, if not more, than she did. Despite his terrible injuries, he was still the true heir. He was born here and would, inevitably, die here. But, till that day came, the time he had left would be spent in as much comfort as possible.

Preparations had been made over the past few weeks. The little-used parlor next to the library had been set up as Julian's apartment, complete with bed, a seating area and, of course, a table with a set of dominoes already in place. Aldous, with his military connections, had interviewed and hired a man by the name of Geoffrey Singleton. A retired army orderly, the man had also lost an eye while in military service but was still relatively young and quite physically able. Acting as a *valet de chambre*, he would be attending to all and any of Julian's needs, as required.

The household servants had been told what to expect, as well as what was expected of them.

The rest of the family had also been thoroughly prepared. Grace had prayed that everyone would see past Julian's terrible deformity. That they would understanding it was not something to be feared, but merely a mask disguising a gentle soul who had suffered terribly.

Already, news of Julian's identity had spread as far away as London, and perhaps farther. It could hardly be avoided, of course. Aldous had naturally contacted the relevant war departments, advising them that a lieutenant, thought lost at Waterloo, had been found in a Yorkshire institution. How Julian had ended up in a variety of institutions would never be known. "War is chaotic," Aldous had said, simply, when Grace had asked the unanswerable question.

As for today, it had been decided that Julian's return to High-field Hall should be done quietly and without fuss. It was, after all, a monumental transition, and Grace wanted as little stress as possible placed on him. Consequently, only she and Aldous had accompanied him in the carriage, and the rest of the family, including Louisa, had been asked to wait till he had settled in before making themselves known.

So far, though, he'd shown no sign of stress at all.

As the carriage door opened, Grace looked to where Aldous sat, on the opposite seat. He smiled at her. "Ready, my love?"

"As I'll ever be," she replied, swallowing over the lump in her throat.

Aldous descended first and then turned, holding out a hand to Julian. "Come on, my old friend," he said. "Let's get you settled."

Julian regarded Aldous' hand for a moment, and then reached for it and stepped down from the carriage. Grace followed, watching as her brother gazed up at Highfield's ancient façade for the first time in over thirty years. He stood stock-still, as if transfixed by what he was seeing.

"Welcome home, Julian," Grace said, fighting the ever-present threat of tears as she looped her arm through his. "Oh, how I wish I could see inside your head, to know your thoughts. Do you recognize anything, I wonder? Anything at all?"

As Julian continued to stare, she felt a shudder pass through him. He turned and looked at the gatehouse for a moment, and then shifted his gaze back to Highfield, specifically the rose window. Then his chin lifted slightly, and his mouth formed its familiar, lopsided smile.

"He knows, Grace," Aldous said, quietly. "He knows."

"It's in the *Illustrated London News* and the *News of The World*." Louisa sighed, set the papers aside, and picked up her teacup. "Papa and Mama will not be at all pleased. They really did not want all this publicity."

"Unavoidable, I fear," Maxwell said. "A veteran lieutenant—a Baron, no less—found alive in a humble institution thirty years after supposedly being lost at Waterloo? Stories like that don't stand a chance of remaining a secret."

"He wasn't a Baron at the time." Louisa took a sip of tea. "And the way they describe his injuries is dreadful. In one paragraph he's presented as a long-lost hero, and in the next, they make him sound like a monster."

"Hyperbole sells, my love. As much as people like to read happy tales, they are also drawn to the gruesome side of things. Don't despair. Your uncle's story will soon be old news. You'll see."

"I hope so." Louisa set her cup down and poked at her scrambled eggs.

The past fortnight had been an exercise in emotion. Though her Uncle Julian still only spoke the same two words, there was little doubt at all that he knew he'd come home. His happiness bypassed his external scars and manifested in the sparkle of a brilliant blue eye, and a frequent lopsided smile. He had become used to the family members, all of whom spent time with him regularly, mostly playing the game he loved. Geoffrey Singleton, the orderly, had turned out to be a blessing, taking care of Julian's needs. His return and subsequent acclimatization to life at Highfield had, in fact, been easier than expected.

And Louisa had been at Highfield two days ago, when Julian had received a letter from his regiment commander, a man whose name was already a legend in military and civilian circles. In it, he had given thanks for Julian's sacrifice and bravery, as well as wishing him peace for the remainder of his life. Grace had read the letter to him, though it was beyond doubtful he understood any of it. She'd also shown him the signature at the bottom of the page, determined he should see it even if it meant nothing to him. It consisted of a single name only.

Wellington.

One thing had not changed, that being the nightly ritual of lighting the candle in the rose window. Grace had insisted it continue, to serve as a reminder that many sons, brothers, and fathers, never came back from the war. And, of course, it also continued to provide a beacon for those who might have need of one.

A solitary candle. A light in the darkness.

CHAPTER TWENTY-SIX

AUTUMN SLITHERED ALONG in a generally damp fashion. It was Louisa's least favorite season, for it stripped the trees and wasted the gardens. She had to admit, however, that the rich blue of an autumn sky was unlike any other. On such a day, Louisa was chatting with Reuben, the sun having created a summer-like atmosphere in the greenhouse where they stood. The old man was telling her about the time, as a young man, he'd been bitten by an adder that had been curled up in a woodpile. "Got me on the wrist when I reached in," he said, showing her the two, tiny white scars. "Arm swelled up so much, I had to tear my shirt sleeve to get my shirt off. Still have a bit of numbness in these fingertips, even after all these years."

Louisa suppressed a shudder. "Ugh. How awful. Have you ever seen any in the garden?"

"Nay, not adders. Seen the odd grass-snake, but they do no harm. They just make a stink or play dead if you mess with 'em."

"Still, I hope I never—" She paused, frowning at the sight of a woman wandering through the garden toward the fountain. "Who's that?"

She doesn't look like a beggarwoman. Maybe she's collecting for some charity or other.

Yet something about the woman's behavior seemed odd, especially when she paused by the fountain and gazed up at the house.

"Lass looks a bit familiar, Mistress," Reuben said, following Louisa's gaze. "I think I've seen her before. Back in the summer."

Louisa's eyes widened. "Here, in the garden?"

"Nay. Walking in the lane, yonder." He nodded vaguely toward it. "A pretty lass. Bid me a good morning, she did. Scottish accent."

Louisa gave him a dubious look. "Are you sure it's the same woman?"

He scratched at the white bristle on his chin. "Aye, looks like. That's to say, the lass in the lane was wearin' a hat a bit like the one she's wearin' now, with a bunch of feathers flapping about. White feathers, though, as I recall. Made me think of a circus pony. Could be a coincidence, o' course."

Louisa bit back a smile at the old man's description. "Well, I'd better go and see what she wants. Maybe she's looking for work."

"Could be." Reuben touched his cap. "Please give the captain my regards, mistress."

Louisa nodded. "I will, Reuben. Thank you."

She and Maxwell had planned a visit to Highfield that afternoon to see the family, and especially her Uncle Julian. There were times when she still couldn't believe all that had happened. The odds, after all, were surely incalculable. Much of the public clamor had eased, thankfully. And, so far, the experts had sadly been proven right, in that there had been little change in Julian's communicative ability. But Louisa took comfort in the fact that he'd at least be spending his final years in his home, surrounded by people who loved him.

Temporarily lost in thought, Louisa didn't notice that the strange woman had gone till she drew closer to the fountain. She glanced about to see that her standing on the lawn nearby, still staring up at the house. The continued odd behavior stirred a flutter of unease in Louisa's stomach, and she slowed her step as she approached, taking in more details in an attempt to ascertain what this stranger's purpose might be. The woman stood with her back to Louisa, her green wool coat enhancing a rather pretty figure. A matching hat, complete with decorative blue and green feathers, sat at a jaunty angle on her head. Though the woman did not give an overall impression of wealth, she certainly didn't appear to be impoverished.

"May I help you?" Louisa asked.

The woman flinched visibly, parting with a soft gasp as she turned around, the shocked expression on her face quickly dissolving into a smile. "Och, gracious, you startled me," she said, a gloved hand pressed to her chest. "I didnae hear you approach. I'm guessing you are Louisa, aye?"

Louisa was momentarily taken aback, and not just by the woman's casual greeting. Reuben had said the woman was pretty. An understatement. She was, quite simply, a vision, with golden ringlets framing an exquisite face, skin like cream, and eyes the color of fine jade. And, if her Scottish accent was anything to go by, Reuben had been correct in his assumption. Whoever this woman was, it seemed she'd been here before.

The flutter of unease persisted.

"I am Mrs. Harlow," Louisa corrected, with emphasis, "and you are on private property. May I know your name, and what you are doing here?"

The woman stood a little taller. "My name is Flora MacNally, and I'm here to see Max."

Max?

Louisa frowned and fiddled with the silver locket at her throat, a gift Maxwell had brought back from his recent trip to Glasgow. "For what reason? Are you a relative?"

"Och, nay, not a relative." The woman gave a slight shrug. "And my reasons are personal. Is he home?"

Louisa drew her wool shawl tighter around her shoulders as a faint smell of alcohol drifted into her nostrils. She regarded the woman more closely, noting the tell-tall glaze in the eyes and, instead of answering the question, asked one of her own. "You seem to be on very familiar terms with my husband. May I know why that might be?"

"I've known Max a long time,' she replied, pursing her lips as she pondered. "Five… nay, six years."

"In what capacity?" The beginnings of a horrible suspicion had crept into Louisa's mind. "I find it odd that you know my name, yet I've never heard of you."

"Well, I cannae really blame Max for not telling you about me. 'Tis not something a wife might easily accept." The woman shrugged. "Some do, mind."

Louisa stared blankly at her for a moment, fearful of asking a question that begged to be asked, dreading the answer. But it could not be avoided. "And what is it that a wife might not easily accept?"

"Finding out that her husband has a mistress."

Like an invisible punch to the stomach, the response momentarily stole Louisa's breath. She shook her head. "No, that's not… I mean, I don't believe you." Her voice grated over a sudden ache in her throat. "My husband does not have a mistress. He does not *need* a mistress."

The woman gave a soft laugh. "Why, of course he needs a mistress. He's hardly ever home, is he? I serve a purpose and an important one at that, keeping him satisfied when you cannae. In return, he provides me with a house and money, which is actually the reason I'm here. I didnae get my allowance for October and I want to know why. We have an agreement, after all."

"A house?"

"Aye. It was a gift from him." She gave the manor a quick glance. "No' as grand as this, mind. But it serves."

A gift? Louisa shivered. "Where is this house?"

"Glasgow."

Only one grim question remained. "And when did he last visit you?"

The woman answered without hesitation. "September. Dinnae recall the exact date. Somewhere in the middle of the month. He had a big meeting in the city."

The world swam before Louisa's eyes. Shaking her head, she

took a step back and gave voice to her thoughts. "No, that's… that's not possible. He wouldn't. He loves me."

Flora hiccupped. "Told me he doesnae."

Louisa blinked. "What?"

"Love you. He told me he doesnae. But then, Max has never loved any woman." She laughed again. "Not even me."

"SOUTH SHIELDS IS barely keeping up with demand." Maxwell, seated at his desk eyed the report again. "And I don't see any sign of that demand dropping in the near future. We need to take a look at increasing output. An expansion of the current location, possibly, or a completely new site. Something to put past the shareholders at the next meeting."

The responding silence drew his attention to the window, where Finlay stood, looking out over the garden.

"Any thoughts, Fin?"

Finlay shifted on his feet. "Aye, I think you should come and take a look at this."

"Sounds ominous."

"I suspect it might be."

"What is it?" Maxwell rose and went to the window.

Finlay gestured. "Not exactly sure," he said. "But I'm fairly certain you won't like it very much."

Maxwell looked out across the lawn to where Louisa stood in apparent conversation with another woman. "Who's that with her?" he muttered, even as a sickening recognition crept into his mind.

Finlay scratched his head. "Well, I sincerely hope I'm mistaken, Max, but I do believe it's—"

"Flora." Shock, like an ice-cold hand, squeezed his stomach. "What the bloody hell is she doing here?"

"Good question," Finlay muttered. "I assume you didn't

actually tell her where you lived."

"Of course not." He scrubbed his jaw. "Christ, I don't believe this."

"What are you going to do?"

"To echo your comment, good question." He blew out a breath. "I have to get out there. I have nothing to hide, Fin. I haven't seen the lass since April."

"I know that, but I'm not sure if Louisa will believe it. Depends on what's been said, I suppose. Want me to come with you?"

"God, no." Maxwell went to the sideboard, half-filled a glass with whisky, and downed it in one gulp. "I'll handle it."

LOUISA CLUTCHED AT her shawl when she saw Maxwell striding toward them. If she felt anything at all, it was fear, for she was about to face a terrifying moment of truth. An affirmation that Maxwell knew this woman, and that they did, indeed, share an intimate relationship. And, if that were the case, Louisa's life with Maxwell, her belief in their *perfect* marriage, would be forever destroyed. Surely, he could not be that deceitful, that cruel. Yet already his swift pace across the lawn seemed to indicate some kind of foreknowledge.

Her teeth began to chatter and she bit down to stop it.

The direction of Louisa's gaze obviously alerted Flora, who turned and, at the sight of Maxwell, smiled and fiddled with some of her curls. "Och, but he's a braw man, aye?"

Louisa said nothing, but kept her gaze fixed on Maxwell, trying and failing to gauge his demeanor. But then, he was an expert at hiding his true emotions, which did not bode well, either. The thought that she'd been fooled this entire time was utterly nauseating.

He drew near, his gaze fixed on Louisa before it shifted to

Flora. "What the bloody hell are you doing here, Flora?" he demanded.

The woman's name on his lips was like an arrow to Louisa's heart.

"Well, obviously I've come to see you, Max," Flora replied, pouting. "I believe you owe me some money."

And still, Louisa needed to hear him say it. "Do you know this person, Maxwell?"

"Aye, I do," he said, scowling at Flora. "And I owe her nothing."

"Aye, you do," Flora retorted. "I didnae get my allowance this month."

Louisa gave a bitter laugh. "I see."

Maxwell groaned. "No, you don't, Louisa. This is not what you think. She has no cause to be here. Just let me expl—"

"What I *think* is that you should get your drunken whore off my lawn and away from my home," she said, moving past him. "You bastard."

"No, wait, please." He grabbed her arm. "We need to sort this out. I swear it isn't as it appears."

All at once feeling strangely calm, Louisa looked down at his hand and then into his eyes. "Let go of me, Maxwell."

"Aye, leave her be, Max," Flora said. "You can sort it with her later."

"Shut your mouth, Flora," Maxwell snapped. "Louisa, please, just let me—"

"Take your hand off me," she said, each word annunciated through gritted teeth.

"Christ," he muttered, releasing her. "You really have got this wrong, love."

Louisa huffed and then glared at Flora. "If I ever see your whore here again, I'll have her arrested for trespassing. I want her gone, Maxwell. Immediately. See to it."

She concentrated on controlling her pace, but it took all she had not to lift up her skirts and bolt to the house. Once inside, she closed the door behind her and leaned against it, chest heaving beneath the weight of shock and disbelief.

"Louisa." Finlay's voice startled her. "Are you all right?"

He stood in the office doorway, his expression one of concern. Undoubtedly, he'd observed the goings on from the office window.

Louisa had always liked Maxwell's brother. Had come to love him, even, like a brother of her own. But now she looked at him with suspicious eyes, wondering how much about he knew and had kept hidden from her. Everything, probably. *God help me.* As if the anger and hurt were not enough, she also felt naive and foolish.

So bloody foolish.

"Louisa," he said again, and stepped toward her.

"I'm quite all right, Finlay." Giving him a scathing look, she pushed herself upright and headed for her sitting-room. "Everything is fine."

The sitting-room door closed behind her with a quiet click, and again, seeking support, she leaned against it, harsh questions continuing to torture her mind. Had Maxwell's declarations of love all been lies? Had he merely been playing a game all along? Had he really said that he didn't love her? Did he prefer bedding Flora McNally?

The last question in particular clawed viciously at her heart. Louisa treasured their intimate moments, never so happy as when she lay in her husband's arms, feeling loved and special. The thought of him being intimate with another woman was simply too much to bear.

Tears burned her eyes, demanding release, but she blinked them away. She would *not* let him see her pain. She would *not* cry. There would be time for that later, in the silent, dark hours of night.

Drawing breath, she drew herself upright, went to her desk, and wrote a short note to her parents, excusing herself from the planned afternoon visit to Highfield, due to a headache. Not a lie.

Certainly, her mind was agonizingly chaotic. Having summoned a maid and dispatched the note with instructions, Louisa went to stand by the window. She would stay there till he came to her, as she knew he eventually would. The window offered a pleasant view of a private side garden, not that it really mattered. She merely needed something to occupy her gaze, so she didn't have to look at him. She would have to listen, of course, as he denied and pleaded.

Disbelief and pain bore down on her again, crushing her resolve, and she bit her lip against a fresh threat of tears. "How could you," she whispered. "My God, how could you!"

SICKENINGLY AWARE THAT untold damage had been done, Maxwell watched Louisa walk away. He then turned to Flora, who stuck out her bottom lip. "She's no' as bonny as me, Max," she said, sniffing.

An urge to laugh, Maxwell realized, was not at all contingent on there being a humorous situation. It could also manifest when faced with a circumstance so unthinkable that it lacked any kind of attributed response.

Oddly, along with his urge to laugh came an adverse and unfamiliar compulsion. Not once had he ever laid a rough hand on a woman. Not once had he ever even thought of doing so. Till that moment.

He didn't laugh, however. Nor did he give in to a desire to shake Flora McNally till her brains rattled. Instead, he uttered a command. "Come with me."

She sniffed again. "Where to?"

He didn't reply, but headed toward the stables, setting a rapid pace, attempting to burn off some of his anger. Flora followed, complaining the entire way that she couldn't keep up. He ignored her till they entered the stable yard.

Then he halted abruptly, causing her to stumble against him. He placed his hands on her shoulders and set her back from him, frowning at the telltale smell of whisky on her breath. "Who told you where I lived, Flora?"

Her mouth opened, though she said nothing for a moment, then, "Um, I cannae remember."

Maxwell scoffed. "No, of course you can't. No matter. I'll find out who it was. In any case, you had no right to come here. None."

"But I didn't get any money last month."

"Because there is none due, and you know it. I told you back in April that the money would be enough to cover your expenses for six months only, which—"

"But I—"

"*Which* should have given you more than enough time to get yourself a job and become self-sustaining. If you've wasted the chance I gave you, then you're a fool. There'll be no more money from me, Flora. Not a damn penny. Is that clear?"

She clasped her hands, prayer-like, beneath her chin. "But, Max, if you'll just—"

"What I will do, though I'm in no way obligated, is put you in a carriage and have you taken to the nearest coach-stop. After that, you're on your own. And if I ever see you back here again, it won't be my wife who'll have you arrested for trespassing, it will be me. Understand?"

"Max, please listen." She touched his sleeve. "Truth is, I thought... I thought I could just let you go and get on with things, but it hasnae been easy."

Maxwell thrust her hand away. "So, you decided to come here and upset my wife? That, I cannot—*will not*—tolerate."

A sullen look came to her face. "You're happy with her, then, your Sassenach?"

"Very happy, aye."

"Do you love her?"

"More than anything."

She flinched. "You once told me you couldnae love any woman."

"Well, I was wrong. I only hope I can fix the damage you've done, and that begins with getting you off this property. Wait here while I arrange for a carriage." He began to turn, but she caught his sleeve again.

"I dinnae have enough money for the coach, Max."

"Damn it, lass." Maxwell pulled himself free of her grasp, dug into his pocket, and pulled out some coins. "This is all I have on me," he said, dropping them into her palm. "It should be enough. Now, wait here."

Once again, she caught his sleeve. "I love you, Max. Have done since the first night I saw you at Buchanan's."

"That's enough!" He jerked his arm away. "I mean it, Flora. You have to—"

"I never told you before, because I reckoned it wasnae something you wanted to hear, but I'm telling you now because it needs to be said, for my sake at least. See, I always had this hope that one day you'd consider me as more than just your mistress. So, when you told me you were getting wed… well, to be honest, it broke my heart." A smile appeared and then faltered. "But, despite what you said about being faithful to your wife, I kept hoping you'd still seek me out once in a wee while. Then I heard you'd been in Glasgow in September, and my heart broke all over again knowing you'd been there and not come to see me. Part of the reason I came here was to see if your marriage was a happy one. And I'll be honest, I hoped it wasnae, that you'd have cause to come back to me. I hope your wife knows how fortunate she is."

"I'm the fortunate one," he said. "Now, wait here."

A short while later, having given instructions to McKinney, he returned to where he'd left her. All he found was a scatter of coins on the ground; the same coins he'd dropped into her palm. Cursing, he retraced their steps back to the garden, only to find the lawns and pathways empty.

"She left by yon side gate," Reuben said, gesturing as Maxwell approached. "Appeared to be in a bit of a rush, skirts hoisted up an' all. Cryin', too, she was."

Maxwell uttered yet another curse under his breath, wondering if he should send someone after her, to make sure she found her way to the coach stop. He suspected, however, that going after her was exactly what she was hoping he'd do and decided against it. She'd found her way to Northcott Manor on her own and could surely find her way home.

"If you see her again anywhere on or near the property, please let me know," Maxwell said. "Or tell McKinney, if I'm not here."

Reuben nodded. "Aye, will do."

After informing McKinney that the carriage was no longer required, and asking him to also be vigilant, Maxwell made his way into the house. He paused in the hallway, feeling the solid thud of his heart beneath his ribs. But, other than the pronounced tick of the nearby grand clock, not a sound could be heard.

The clock indicated it was ten minutes after eleven. A mere half-hour earlier, Maxwell's marriage—his *life*—had been as damn near perfect as it could possibly be. Not anymore. Everything had since changed, although the amount of damage inflicted by Flora's visit had yet to be ascertained. He wondered if he should wait before finding out, perhaps allow some time for emotions to settle. No, he decided, there'd be no waiting. A wound to the heart, to the *soul*, merited no less immediate attention than a wound to the flesh. Often, the former took longer to heal.

"Where are you, lass?" he whispered, his mind travelling, searching through the house. The small sitting-room seemed the most likely choice. It was her favorite spot. Her quiet retreat.

He made his way to the door and paused again, ear cocked, hearing nothing from the other side. Sucking in a breath, he tugged at his cravat and reached for the door handle, his hand hovering over it for a moment. What would he say? What *could* he say? A declaration of his innocence, though essentially true, would be expected and, most likely, disbelieved. Perhaps a passive approach would be better. Let Louisa speak first. He placed his hand on the door handle and gripped it hard, steeling himself for whatever was to come. Then, releasing his breath, he opened the door and stepped inside.

At first glance, the room appeared to be empty. But then he saw her, standing by the window gazing out, arms folded, a beautiful silhouette against the morning light. He assumed she'd heard him enter, though she showed no sign of it.

He moved to her side and studied her for a moment, trying to determine her mood from her stance and the profile of her face. If anything, she appeared calm, brow smooth, cheeks free from tears, arms loosely folded. Yet, somehow, he found the apparent lack of emotion to be more worrisome. He had the impression she was oblivious to what lay beyond the window, that her sight was turned inward. Was she even aware of his presence? The answer came a moment later.

"Has she gone?" she asked, without looking at him.

"Aye, she has."

The fingers of Louisa's left hand, where they rested on her right arm, tightened slightly, sunlight glinting off her engagement ring. "How embarrassing for you, Maxwell, having your mistress show up at your marital home," she said, her voice now laden with contempt. "Exposing all your nasty little secrets to your wife. I should imagine you are more horrified than I am."

Maxwell suppressed a sigh. "I have no secrets, Louisa. Flora McNally ceased being my mistress the moment I placed that sapphire on your finger. I swear on my life, I have been faithful to you."

"On your life?" Louisa gave a bitter laugh and turned to him, anguish now evident in her eyes and expression. "It seems there is much about your *life*, sir, that I do not know. Yet your Scottish whore appears to know a great deal about mine. My name, for one thing, and even where I *live*. Explain that, if you will. What other snippets about your wife have you shared with her?" Her lip trembled. "How she compares in bed, perhaps?"

He groaned. "Damn it, lass, of course not. I haven't seen or spoken to her since April, when I told her I was getting married. At that time, she asked what your name was, but I only gave her your Christian name. As for where we would be living, I said it would be in Yorkshire, but gave no specifics. I don't know how she found out about the manor. I can only surmise she got the address by asking around at the Glasgow office, and believe me, when I found out who told her, they'll be looking for another bloody job."

Louisa turned her gaze back to the window. "She said you visited her when you were there in September."

"She's lying."

"I don't believe you."

He winced slightly. "Well, it's the truth, whether you believe it or not."

Louisa huffed. "If it's all as innocuous as you imply, why didn't you mention any of it to me before?"

"Because I saw no reason to do so," he replied. "The relationship I had with Flora is in the past. She is no longer relevant in my life."

Louisa gasped and turned to him once more. "How the hell can you say that when she's living in a house you gave her, and surviving on a monthly allowance that you provide? Tell me, Maxwell, is she the only whore you're supporting, or do you have others hidden away in Sheffield and South Shields as well?"

A burst of anger flared within, burning through the last few threads of Maxwell's composure. Fists clenched, he opened his mouth, ready to berate and defend. But, at that same moment, a fleeting expression crossed Louisa's face, there and gone, like the shadow of a bird swooping past a window. And it gave him the unmistakable impression of a cornered soul, snapping and snarling in order to hide its fear and pain.

She was merely lashing out, he realized, desperately trying to make sense of a harrowing situation that should never have occurred, none of which was her fault. Even so, her current mood did not lend itself to reason. To continue bickering in this manner served no purpose.

Maxwell ran a hand through his hair. "The ugliness of this conversation is not getting us anywhere. I swear my conscience is clear, but given what has occurred, I don't blame you for doubting me, hating me, and probably wanting to kill me right now. That being so, I'm going to retreat till, hopefully, things settle down a little. For the next while, I'll be in my office, where I intend to avail myself of a generous measure of whisky. Beyond that, I have no real plans. If, at some point in the near future, you decide you'd like to give me a reasonable chance to explain about Flora, and why things are the way they are, I'll be more than happy to oblige. That is, of course, if you'll at least *consider* believing what I have to say." A sigh escaped him. "I love you, Louisa. *Only* you. I would give up everything I own to keep you at my side. Everything."

With that, he headed for the door.

"Yet you told her you didn't."

He paused and half-turned toward her. "What?"

Louisa gave him a disdainful look. "You told Flora you didn't love me."

Maxwell gave a soft, bitter laugh and scratched his jaw. "Christ, she really went for the throat, didn't she?"

"Are you denying you said it?"

"No, I am not. I said it because it was true at the time. I made it clear to her just now, however, that things have changed." He gave her a grim smile. "Don't let the irrelevance of the past poison our future, love. We have too much to lose, you and me. I hope you'll come to see that." Again, he moved toward the door.

"Are you aware that she's been here before?"

Once again, he halted and regarded her, an odd little prickle lifting the hair on his neck. "Did she tell you that?"

"Reuben did. I was with him in the greenhouse when we first spotted her wandering in the garden. Said he'd seen her in the lane this summer. Apparently, he'd bid her a good morning, and she'd responded."

"Is he sure it was her?"

Louisa parted with a short, bitter laugh. "I take it you're denying any knowledge of it."

Maxwell hissed through his teeth. "Yes, I am, damn it. Answer me. Is he sure it was her?"

"Why don't you ask him? He told me he recognized her hat. Or, at least, it reminded him of the one she'd been wearing, except the feathers were white, not green. He also mentioned her Scottish accent and how pretty she was. Seems to be more than a coincidence, don't you agree? I'm wondering, then, if these visits will be a regular occurrence."

Maxwell stared at her for moment, his blood chilled by the image of a white feather tangled in a clump of heather. "No, they will not," he replied. "I guarantee it."

Louisa shrugged. "Forgive me if I harbor doubts about your ability to control her."

Maxwell's eyes narrowed, his mind playing out a scenario he could barely comprehend. He couldn't even muster up a reply, but simply turned on his heel and left.

He needed to speak to Reuben.

CHAPTER TWENTY-SEVEN

"YOU CANNOT STOP Louisa from visiting Highfield," Finlay said. "She'll want to know why, and I wouldn't want to be in your shoes if you tell her about your suspicions. Things are bad enough as they are."

Maxwell frowned. "I don't want to stop her from visiting Highfield. I just don't want her going over the moor alone."

"And I repeat, she'll want to know why. You're over-reacting, Max. The feather could have come from anywhere. You have no proof it has anything at all to do with Flora, or Louisa's accident. Besides, the lass won't come back here. Not now. She wouldn't dare."

"I wish I was as certain. Given what Reuben said, I have no doubt it was her he saw several weeks ago. It makes me wonder how many other times she's been here."

Finlay huffed. "Then maybe you should hire men with dogs to patrol the grounds."

Maxwell, who'd been gazing at some vague spot on the far wall of his office, straightened in his chair and regarded his brother. "Actually, that's not a bad idea."

"Bloody hell, Max, I was being sarcastic."

"Hmm." He pondered. "Then how about I hire someone in Glasgow to keep an eye on her? To let me know if she shows any sign of heading back here?"

"And then what? You hire the man and the dogs at that point?

No, sorry, brother. It's not only extreme, it's underhanded, which is the last thing you need to be right now. When the time comes, simply tell Louisa of your suspicions and ask her to be vigilant. That's all."

Maxwell regarded Finlay for a moment. "When did my little brother become wiser than me?"

Finlay laughed. "Most of what I know I've learned from you. In this case, since I'm looking at this situation from the outside, I suspect my view is somewhat clearer than yours."

"You don't say." Maxwell pinched the bridge of his nose. "I can barely think straight."

"Hardly surprising. Have you slept at all these past two days?"

"Not much."

"You look like death."

"Thanks."

"Are you still planning to leave for Sheffield tomorrow?"

"Certainly." He shrugged. "I'm of a mind that leaving for a few days might be a good idea."

"I'm not sure I agree."

"I'm not sure about anything." He slumped back in his chair. "What a devilish mess, Fin."

"She'll come around. It's only been a couple of days."

"Aye, but I fear the damage is done. Trust, once broken, is a damnably difficult thing to repair." He winced and rubbed his temple. "The way Louisa looked at me in her sitting-room the other day, as if she despised me. I just cannot get that image out of my head."

"She hasn't given you a chance to explain yet. Once she does, she'll see how things are, which is precisely how they've always been."

Maxwell didn't respond. Since their ugly exchange in her sitting-room, Louisa had taken great pains to avoid him, day and night. A pall had settled over the entire house, deepening the shadows and amplifying the silence. There had been moments when he'd been tempted to seek her out, to demand she sit and listen to him. But so far, he'd resisted the urge, a little voice telling him it was yet too soon, to wait till she'd be more amenable to hearing what he had to say. If that day should ever arrive.

As for his suspicions about Flora's involvement in Louisa's accident…well, perhaps he was over-reacting a little. But it seemed almost certain that Flora had been there before and wandered around the vicinity of the manor unnoticed. Might she have seen Louisa riding out on that summer's day and followed the path up to the moor? Had she been the obscure figure in the mist? Had she startled Byron? If so, it meant she had then left the scene without giving aid to Louisa, or even summoning someone to help. It was all conjecture, but Maxwell's stomach tightened at the mere thought of it, nonetheless.

Gritting his teeth, he rose and went to the sideboard. "Want one?" he asked, lifting the whisky decanter from its tray.

Finlay glanced at the clock on the mantel. "It's not even ten o'clock, Max"

"So?"

"So, it's a little early for imbibing, don't you think?"

"Not when you've been up since half-past-three." He poured himself a good measure, downed it in three solid gulps, and then frowned into his empty glass. "Here's the funny thing, brother. Marriage was never something I'd considered. Was never something I even *wanted*. Then Dent approached me, offering me his aristocratic, undowried daughter for a price. And I thought, why not? Being shackled to Miss Chessington would be at least tolerable and not completely without benefits. Our feelings, or lack thereof, were mutual after all. But then I botched everything up at Richmond's party, and found myself married to a girl who, despite all my efforts to the contrary, somehow managed to turn my well-ordered world upside down."

Finlay sighed. "Stop it, Max."

Maxwell grimaced. "I have to admit, I resented it at first. The effect Louisa had on me I mean. I even fought against it. But then

I came to realize that I'd actually acquired something terribly rare, something so damn *perfect*, it defied description. Marriage, of all things, was actually turning out to be my greatest investment, and had the potential to be my finest achievement. And now, God *damn* it…" He hurled the glass at the opposite wall, where it shattered in a hailstorm of shards. "I've buggered that up as well."

SEATED AT HER desk, Louisa lifted her head, wondering at the noise she'd heard, like a crash of crockery or glass. Perhaps one of the servants had dropped a tray. She listened for a few moments longer and then, hearing nothing more, turned her attention back to her journal.

The last two entries had taken little time to write.

On one page: *I met her today.*

On the other: *Everything has changed.*

More than enough to remind her of what had occurred over the past two days. As if she'd ever need reminding.

For now, she was all at sea, eyes gritty from crying, heart and mind in torment. Not a word had been spoken between her and Maxwell since the confrontation in the sitting-room. Part of her longed for him to come to her, to explain everything in such a way that she was left with no doubt about his fidelity and his love. But she also feared his words would not be enough, that doubt would remain, tainting their marriage and their future. It had all been so special, and now she ached with anguish, no less than if she'd taken a physical blow to the ribs. At times, she also burned with resentment, her spine stiffening as fierce little outbursts of fury replaced her grief.

Heaving a quick sigh, she closed the cap on her inkwell, set her pen in its stand, and went over to the window to observe the weather. By now, most of the leaves were off the trees, and today were being scattered by a vigorous breeze. But the skies, despite having a few clouds, did not look overly threatening. It was, in fact, a fine day for a ride. And she hadn't been out in several days.

Sometime later, having summoned Archer to help her prepare, and issued instructions to have Byron saddled, Louisa descended the stairs and headed for the door.

"Where are you going, Louisa?"

She turned to see Maxwell standing in the doorway to his office, the sight of him momentarily stalling her response. Outside of the bedroom, she had never seen him so unkempt; hair ungroomed, jaw dark with growth. He looked exhausted besides, and perhaps not quite sober. A sudden ache squeezed her heart, and, for a moment, her misery and anger were replaced by a surge of compassion. But only for a moment. His suffering was not because of anything she'd done.

She shrugged. "Well, quite obviously, I'm going for a ride."

"Over the moor?"

"Yes."

His expression didn't change. "I'd rather you didn't."

Louisa's eyes widened. "Are you *forbidding* me?"

"No. I'm merely asking you not to go."

"And may I know why that might be?"

He hesitated for the briefest of moments and then glanced at the transom window above the front door. "The weather is not suited to it."

She scoffed. "It is bound to be preferable to the climate within these walls. I need a change of air."

He opened his mouth as if to respond and then closed it, his gaze dropping to the floor for a moment. Then, "Will you be visiting Highfield?"

"Why do you ask?" she snapped. "Is it of some importance to you?"

A sigh escaped him. "I wish only to know how long you'll be gone, Louisa."

She searched for yet another retort, something scathing and sharp to throw doubt on the validity of his concern but stopped herself. Such churlish behavior went against her nature and served little purpose. Still, she was far from feeling amiable toward the man she'd married and kept her tone austere. "I'm not sure," she replied. "An hour, maybe two."

He nodded. "Please be careful," he said, and turned from her, closing the door.

Sometime later, Louisa reined in atop the moor, cheeks tingling, the tears in her eyes solicited solely by the wind. She breathed deep, her gaze traveling the landscape, pausing briefly at the spot where she'd first seen Maxwell back in February. Only a matter of months since that day, yet it felt much longer. Then she looked toward Highfield Hall, the house itself not visible from her vantage, its distant location marked by an ancient tree and equally ancient watchtower.

She longed to visit but didn't quite trust the stability of her battered emotions. It would only take one family member to ask how she fared, and the tears would come unchecked, prompting questions she had no desire to answer. She'd give it a little more time. Maxwell and Finlay were leaving for Sheffield tomorrow and would be gone for the better part of a week. Perhaps then, she might find the wherewithal to visit Highfield, and maybe even spend a night or two there.

Not long after, when the clouds began to thicken, Louisa returned home. It had been a shorter ride than usual, but she felt less stale than she had earlier. And, while she'd been unable to eat a bite at breakfast, the thought of some tea and toast now set her stomach growling. She dismounted at the block and handed Byron's reins over to young George, who'd hurried out to meet her. Then, brushing off her skirts, she headed toward the door, her attention caught by movement at one of the library windows. Maxwell, she realized, who acknowledged her return with a dip of his chin before turning away.

For the rest of the day, she stayed in her sitting-room, curled up on the settee with a book and a blanket, listening to the rain, which now pelted the windows. There had been no tears, just a terrible feeling of emptiness, as if something had reached inside and torn out her happiness.

The tap on her door came around supper time, and Finlay poked his head into the room.

"I wonder, Louisa, if I may speak with you."

Louisa regarded him warily. "Did Maxwell send you?"

The reply came without hesitation. "No, he did not, nor would he even think of doing so. You know, as well as I do, that delegating personal responsibility is not one of his traits."

"I'll grant you that," she said, "but I must assume you're here because of him."

"I'm here because of you both, if you would just spare me a few minutes."

"I'm not sure this is any of your business, Finlay."

"Perhaps not, but I feel compelled to speak anyway. Whether or not you'll pay any mind to what I have to say is, of course, entirely up to you."

Louisa regarded him, seeking signs of duplicity in his earnest expression, and finding none. "Very well." She unfurled her legs, settled herself more regally on the settee, and clasped her hands on her lap. "I'll hear you."

The slight frown on his brow cleared. He closed the door quietly and perched himself on a nearby chair, leaning forward as he spoke. "How to begin," he said, and cleared his throat. "Well, I suppose, basically, I'm here to tell you that Maxwell is telling the truth."

Louisa sighed and shook her head. "What else would you be likely to tell me? You're his brother, obliged to stand in his corner."

The frown returned. "This is not a boxing match, Louisa. I'm not standing in anyone's corner or under any kind of obligation. I'm merely a spectator to misconception, watching two people I love being torn apart by pretense. And the tragic part is, neither of you are to blame for any of it."

"Neither of us?" She gave him a dubious look. "Your brother

lied to me, Finlay."

"Are you sure? What falsehoods has he told you?"

"Well, to begin, he denied having a mistress while admitting he's been supporting her for the entire time we've been married."

Finlay tutted and shook his head. "Things are not always what they seem. It's not my place to explain it all, either. Maxwell must do that, if you'll let him. I beg you, please give him the chance to do so, before this union is damaged beyond repair."

Louisa gasped. "Things are not always what they seem? How can you possibly say that? His mistress was *here*, in my garden, staring up at my home. And not for the first time, it seems. She even knew my name!"

"Aye, I know, and none of that should ever have happened." He shifted in his seat. "Forgive me, Louisa. My intention was not to upset you more. I merely urge you to look beyond what has occurred and examine the reasons behind it. Ask yourself *why* Flora McNally came here. I mean, assuming a mistress is in good stead with her lover and reliant on his support, why would she risk any of that by showing up at his marital home?"

Frowning, Louisa glanced down at her hands, her weary mind stumbling over Finlay's words, seeing the rationale, but fearful of being falsely appeased. She found it easier to capitulate to her curiosity. "I assume you know the woman. That is, you've met her."

He shifted again. "I've met her a few times, aye."

"Do you like her?"

His brows lifted. "Does it matter?"

"Not really. I'm just curious."

He shrugged. "I had no reason to dislike her till recently. I never once considered her as a potential sister-in-law, however, if that's what motivated your question."

"She said Maxwell didn't love her. Is that true?"

He laughed softly. "Maxwell is in love with only one woman, who just happens to be sitting across from me right now. And my answer surely begs another question. Why would my brother, having married a lass he'd give his life for, risk it all by keeping a mistress? Think about it. Think about *him*, how he operates. Aye, he takes risks in his business ventures, but none that have the potential to destroy everything he's achieved. My brother is not a frivolous man. He takes life seriously. He takes his marriage seriously. His only mistake was…" Finlay shook his head. "No, I'll say no more about that. I'm not even sure it *was* a mistake. It's just Maxwell's way and for him to explain. I simply came here to ask that you give him the chance to do so. This blasted silence and avoiding each other serves no purpose at all."

Louisa heaved a shaky sigh. "I'll think about it," she said, fingers pressed to her temple. "I'm just so confused right now, Finlay. It's as if the ground has opened up beneath my feet and I'm still trying to claw my way out of the hole."

"I sympathize, believe me." He rose. "Thank you for listening, Louisa. I'll leave you to think about what I've said and please, at least consider giving Max a chance to explain. He could insist you listen to him, of course, but he's not willing to pressure you. Said he'd rather you approach him when you're ready, and I'm hoping that will be sooner rather than later. For both your sakes."

Finlay left her with much to consider. Indeed, she spent much of that night considering it before drifting off into an uneasy sleep. When next she opened her eyes, it was to profound darkness and the sound of carriage wheels on gravel. No doubt Maxwell and Finlay were leaving for Sheffield at their usual time, with sunrise, at this time of year, still a couple of hours away.

The sounds of the carriage leaving reminded her of another morning earlier that year, one that had also followed a miserable night. On that occasion, she'd gone tearing down the stairs, half-dressed and barefoot, desperate to stop Maxwell from leaving without some kind of reconciliation between them. She had successfully stopped him, too, quoting her father's words in support of her action.

A man must never leave his home angry lest he might live to regret it.

Uttering a soft cry, Louisa sat up, listening as the sounds of Maxwell's carriage faded into silence. Had he left angry this time? No, anger was probably not an accurate description of his mood. But she knew he had not left unburdened. And she had let him go without giving him an opportunity to lighten that weight.

"I should have given him a chance," she whispered, burying her face in her hands. "Please, God, don't let anything happen to him. Please."

Any further sleep was out of the question. Louisa left her bed, tugged on her dressing gown, slid her feet into slippers, and headed downstairs, her sitting room being the intended destination. At the foot of the stairs she paused, a draught of cold air biting at her ankles. It came, she realized, from the front door, which stood slightly ajar. An oversight, surely, given that the carriage had only left minutes before. Then she saw a valise sitting on the floor nearby and recognized it as Maxwell's. Had he forgotten it? Tugging her dressing-gown closed, she padded across the marble floor and pulled the door open, parting with a squeak of alarm at the sight of a dark figure on the driveway. The figure spun around, and Louisa took a couple of steps back.

Maxwell?

"Louisa." Frowning, he entered, removed his hat, and closed the door behind him. "Forgive me. I didn't mean to alarm you."

A single candle, flickering on a hall table, cast his face in a low light. He'd shaved since the last time she saw him, but evidence of fatigue lingered beneath his eyes. He was dressed for travel, hands gloved, the hat clasped in his hand matching his black topcoat. So, what was he doing here? Why hadn't he left?

"Well, if you'll excuse me, my dear," he said, moving past her. "I shall bother you no longer."

It was a response to her silence, she realized, which had obviously been taken as a rebuff. She remedied it. "You're... you're not going to Sheffield?"

He paused and half-turned to face her. "No."

"But I heard the carriage."

"Finlay has gone on his own." He came back to her, the lines of fatigue around his eyes becoming more apparent. "I fully intended to go with him. Even went so far as to get into the carriage. But I was reminded of something you once said and decided it would be better if I stayed behind."

His familiar scent permeated Louisa's senses, causing her fingers to tie themselves in knots at her waist. "Something I once said?"

"Aye. Well, actually, I believe you were quoting your father. Something about a man not leaving his house angry—"

"Lest he might live to regret it."

A brief look of surprise crossed his face. "Exactly. Not that I *am* angry. But things here are not as they were. Or as they should be."

"No," she whispered, "they are not."

A muscle in his jaw clenched visibly, and he looked down for a moment. Then, "I wonder, Louisa," he said, lifting his head, "if you might consider taking some tea with me."

"Tea." She blinked. "Now?"

He fiddled with his hat. "Aye."

Hugging herself, she glanced about. "The servants are not yet awake."

"Not a concern. I can make it."

Her eyes widened. "You?"

"Certainly." The beginnings of a smile appeared. "It is not beyond me to do such things."

"Well, um…" She ignored a mulish impulse to refuse. "I suppose that would be acceptable."

"Excellent." The smile showed itself a little more. "Where shall we take it? In your sitting-room? I can light the fire for you. It'll warm the place up while I'm preparing the tea."

"All right, but I'll light the fire." She dropped her hands to her sides and lifted her chin. "It is not beyond me to do such things, either."

A short while later, Louisa knelt at the hearth and set a burning taper to the kindling. The flame caught with enthusiasm, flaring quickly as it consumed the fragile tinder before poking its yellow tongue between the pieces of coal. Louisa stood, set the fireguard in place, and then retired to her settee to wait.

While nibbling on a fingernail, she pondered the rather remarkable fact that she and Maxwell had shared the same thoughts that morning, specifically the mutual recall of her father's adage. She dared to consider it an orchestrated coincidence. That Maxwell had acted as a result of it certainly touched her heart. His request to take tea with her was, undoubtedly, a tactful request for an exchange of dialogue, which she'd been totally at liberty to refuse. As Finlay had stated, no pressure, no demands.

But she was willing to give Maxwell the chance to unburden himself. However, she resolved to neither prompt nor question him as he spoke. She desired only to listen, hoping to find integrity in his words. More than anything, she wanted to believe that her vision of their marriage had not been an illusion. That Maxwell's love for her was real and vital.

The soft chime of the mantel clock pulled her from her musing and, with some dismay, she regarded the fingernail she'd just destroyed. At that same moment, the door opened and Maxwell entered, balancing a loaded tea-tray on one hand with all the adeptness of an experienced servant.

"Tea is served," he said, setting the tray on a small table. "Milk for you, but no sugar, correct?"

Louisa straightened. "Yes, thank you."

"I stole some biscuits." He poured her tea and set the cup on the table beside her. "Want one?"

Her eyes widened. "Biscuits for breakfast?"

He held out the plate. "Why not?"

"Perhaps just one." She took it, placed it next to her teacup, and then sat back, watching as Maxwell poured himself a tea before sitting in the same chair Finlay had occupied the day before. Then she waited, in silence.

He took a sip of tea and looked briefly to the fire, which now burned vigorously, before his gaze met hers once more. "Will you allow me to explain, Louisa?"

She nodded. "Yes."

He released a breath, his shoulders visibly relaxing as he set his cup down. "Thank you. And I pray, when all has been said, you'll understand my reasons for doing what I did. You may, of course, ask questions as you wish. I ask only that any discourse we share remains within the confines of decorum. I have no desire to argue or fight."

"There will be neither questions nor discourse, Maxwell," she said. "I wish only to hear what you have to say."

And to believe it.

He appeared to study her for a moment. "I swear, on all I hold dear, that I will not lie to you."

She flinched inwardly. Had he read her mind? In any case, she didn't respond, her continued silence prompting him to begin, preceded by a clearing of his throat.

"After leaving you in London, I went straight to Glasgow, specifically to tell Flora of my engagement. I'd last visited her in January, and had no contact since, so she was surprised to see me. It was dark when I arrived at the house, but I had no intention of staying the night. I was there only to tell her of my intent to marry you, and that, consequently, my relationship with her was over. I admit to having some apprehension, simply because I knew I was about to injure someone I cared about. But there was never any doubt about my decision. In fact, she was made aware of it within minutes of my arrival. I explained that my marriage— *our* marriage—was important to me, and I wanted things to be right and proper. As I mentioned the other day, she then asked me your name, so I told her, but *only* your Christian name. She also asked where we'd be living, and I mentioned Yorkshire, but gave no address. Then she asked if I loved you, and I said..." His voice faltered, and he reached for his teacup, cradling the vessel in both hands as he took a sip. "I said I did not. She put up a bit of a fight after that, suggesting I maintain my relationship with her despite being married to you. I refused. She then asked how long she had to find a new place to live, or if I intended to evict her immediately. That's when I told her the house belonged to her. I'd made certain arrangements with my solicitor beforehand, you see." His gaze flicked briefly to the fire before returning to Louisa once more. "My decision to give the house to Flora was made after some warranted consideration. First, I could not, in good heart, evict her. The house might have belonged to me, but I had never actually lived there, whereas it had served as Flora's home for five years. But, since I was to be married, continuing to maintain a house where my ex-mistress was living was not something I could rationalize. In giving her the house, I also removed myself from the responsibility of maintaining it, which leads me to explain about the allowance she mentioned. In a final gesture, I left a single sum of money with my solicitor, along with instructions for it to be paid out in monthly increments, enough to tide Flora over to this past September, but nothing beyond that. I did it that way to prevent her from being too frivolous, while giving her time to find employment. Her claim that I owed her money for October was completely false. A pretext, I assume, to justify her presence here." He set his cup down with a bit of a clatter. "My generosity, if you can call it that, was not entirely selfless, either. The truth is, I did these things to ease my conscience, to compensate, in some way, for letting Flora go. I cannot apologize for it, Louisa. It felt right at the time. But I left it at that. I never expected to see her again, and I certainly did not visit her in September when I was in Glasgow, nor did the thought even cross my mind. Seeing her here came as a complete shock to me, so I cannot begin to imagine what a shock it must have been for you. You have every reason to be upset, but please believe me, I have been faithful to you and will always be faithful to you. I would never risk destroying what we have. Never. My marriage, my life with you, means everything to me."

Tears pricking at her eyes, Louisa regarded him for a moment, and then looked down at her lap. More than anything, she wanted to believe him, to reignite the trust they had previously shared. Finlay's assurance came to mind. *My brother is not a frivolous man, Louisa. He takes life seriously. He takes his marriage seriously. His only mistake was...*

His only mistake, it seemed, was attempting to make amends to a woman who'd just been told she was no longer a part of his life. Few men would have done as he did, and Louisa could hardly condemn him for it. He was, by nature, altruistic. Yet still, she hesitated. It was not easy to simply emerge from the cold depths of despondency and resume life as it had been, all within the space of a few minutes.

"Though nothing would make me happier right now, I'm not expecting you to leap into my arms and tell me things are back the way they were," Maxwell said, rising to his feet. "All I can do is hope you'll see the truth of the matter. And even then, I realize it might take some time before you feel comfortable in my presence again. For now, I'm just grateful for the opportunity to explain things to you. It's a start, is it not?"

Louisa lifted her head, her heart touched by his perceptive words, which more or less echoed her thoughts and feelings. "I think so, yes."

For a moment, she thought he was about to speak again, for he hesitated. But he apparently thought better of it and departed, leaving Louisa feeling oddly—and frustratingly—bereft. The idea of actually leaping into Maxwell's arms had sent a tingle down her spine. Despite her uncertainty, she missed him terribly and longed for his touch.

A glance at the mantel clock told her it was almost a quarter-to-six. Still early. Still depressingly dark. She hadn't drunk her tea, she realized, but since it had likely gone cold, it didn't appeal anymore. Neither did the biscuit, though Maxwell's boyish comment about stealing them caused her to smile.

She curled her legs onto the settee and grabbed a nearby embroidered cushion, hugging it as she pondered all that Maxwell had said. It helped that he had not taken a defensive stance, demanding an answer then and there, but had simply stepped away, allowing her time to consider. And, as she did so, the doubts and fears, little by little, began to dissipate. After a while, lulled into sleepiness by the flicker of firelight, she stifled a yawn and stretched out on the settee, still hugging the cushion.

AFTER LEAVING LOUISA, Maxwell retreated to the sanctity of his office, where he lit a fire to dispel the chill from the room. For now, as far as pouring the proverbial oil on troubled waters, he'd done all he could.

Some things he had not spoken of, like how the sight of her in the hall that morning, recently risen from her bed, braided hair ruffled from sleep, had made him weak with longing. The desire to take her in his arms, to inhale her sweet scent and feel her mouth against his, had been nothing less than torturous.

Those things, he had kept to himself.

Several hours passed, much as they would on any other day. Maxwell took coffee and luncheon in his office, went through his mail, and even managed to write a couple of business letters. The rest of the time he spent pacing back and forth from his desk to the window, wondering.

Hoping.

It wasn't till late afternoon, when the curtains had already been drawn and firelight and shadows flickered across the walls, that Louisa came to him at last. Maxwell rose and moved out from behind his desk, studying her as she approached, though her expression told him nothing. She halted a mere handspan away and stared up at him, a slight frown on her brow. Then she heaved a sigh, wrapped her arms around him, and rested her head against his chest. "I believe you," she whispered.

He groaned, folded her in his embrace, and buried his face in the scented softness of her hair. "Oh, my love," he muttered, his lips brushing over the shell of her ear. "I was so afraid I'd lost you."

"I was afraid too." Tears shone in her eyes as she regarded him once more. "I've been so desperately unhappy, Max. These past few days have been terrible. I just want to put them behind us."

"They're already behind us." He stroked her hair. "That said, there is something else I need to speak of, before we go any further."

She stiffened. "Should I be worried?"

"No. In fact, Finlay is convinced I'm overreacting, and he's probably right, but I still think it's something you should be aware of. Come and sit with me and I'll explain." Taking her hand, he led her to the settee. "I almost mentioned it this morning but decided it could wait."

Frowning, she sat beside him. "I knew there was something else you wanted to say."

"Well, first, I have a question about your accident, one I know you've answered before, but I'm wondering if you can remember anything more about the figure you believe you saw. Any detail at all."

"Why do you—?" She gasped. "Do you think it was Flora?"

Maxwell blew out a breath. "I don't know what to think. But the day your father and I went up there looking for clues, I found a large white feather tangled in a shrub. I thought little of it at the time, but then the old gardener said the woman in the lane was wearing a hat with white feathers on it, which is why I'm asking if you can recall any specifics."

She shook her head. "None, I'm afraid. It's more of an impression than a memory, actually. Like a dream."

Maxwell gave a nod. "Nevertheless, I want you to be extra vigilant from now on. Keep your wits about you when you're out on the moor, or anywhere alone for that matter."

Louisa pondered. "Is that why you tried to stop me from going out yesterday?"

"Aye."

"Do you really believe she's capable of doing me harm?"

"If I really believed that I'd have you watched night and day. So, my answer is no, I don't, nor do I think she'll dare to return here. But I'd rather err on the side of caution. I just need you to promise you'll be careful, that's all."

She settled back and snuggled into him. "I promise."

"Thank you." His arm tightened around her. "Tired, sweetheart?"

"Just a bit off-kilter." A sigh escaped her. "I fell asleep on the settee this morning and didn't wake up till one o'clock. Archer should have woken me but said she didn't have the heart."

"She's been worried about you, no doubt. Have you eaten?"

"A little. I already told the staff we'd be eating dinner together tonight, by the way."

"Good."

"So, it seems the rest of the afternoon is ours."

Aware of the implication buried in her statement, Maxwell smiled inwardly. "It is indeed, my love, and I'm quite happy to spend the rest of it sitting here with you, unless you have something else in mind."

"You know I do, Max." Pushing herself upright, she regarded him, eyes once again glinting with tears. "After all that has happened, I need more than your words. I want your touch. I need to feel your love. I need us to be together completely."

Maxwell leaned forward, cupped her cheek, and stroked his thumb lightly along the line of her cheekbone. Then, without another word, he stood and held out his hand, which she took, rising to her feet. In continued silence, he led her upstairs and into his bedroom. And, sometime later, no doubt remained. Only love and trust.

MAXWELL'S FEARS THAT Flora would return to Northcott Manor came to an end a few weeks later when he received a letter from Alexander Blair, his Glasgow-based solicitor. He read the letter several times, absorbing the information while allowing the initial shock to lessen. A while later, when he felt ready, he went in search of Finlay and Louisa, asking them to join him in his study.

"Sit, please," he said, gesturing to the settee. He remained standing, his back to the hearth, the letter clasped in his right hand.

"What's this about, Max?" Finlay took his seat, his gaze flicking briefly to the letter. "Is there a problem?"

Louisa sat beside him, her questioning expression echoing Finlay's concerns.

"It's probably easier if you read it for yourselves," Maxwell said, handing the letter to Finlay. "And then, share your thoughts by all means."

Silence fell as their heads bent over the paper. Maxwell glanced toward the window, which displayed clear blue skies, and an empty lawn glittering with an early December frost. A peaceful scene. Unlike the one in his head, which showed a chessboard-tiled hallway and Flora McNally's lifeless body at the bottom of a flight of stairs. An accident, they'd ascertained, likely due to being intoxicated. No foul play suspected. Death had been instant; a broken neck. Maxwell wondered how long she had lain there before being discovered. The letter didn't say. Not too long, he hoped.

A soft gasp from Louisa implied her shock and drew his attention back to the matter in hand. She was looking at him, eyes wide, lips slightly parted.

Finlay spoke. "Sad news, brother, but I hope you don't feel in any way responsible. You gave the lass every chance."

"I agree." Louisa handed the letter back to him. "But I don't understand why Mr. Blair is asking how you want to handle the estate. I thought you'd given the house to her."

"I did, but there were a couple of temporary conditions attached, both of which she was made aware of when she signed the papers." He set the letter on his desk. "One, she couldn't sell the house for three years, and two, if she died, the house came back to me. The first condition was to prevent her from doing something foolish or being coerced into it by a third party. The second was always meant to be negotiable. Had I died first, or if she married, that condition would have been expunged immediately."

"She had no relatives?" Louisa asked.

"No."

Finlay cleared his throat. "I suppose this means you'll be going to Glasgow."

Maxwell shrugged. "I don't have to. Alex sent me all the relevant documents. All I need to do is sign and send them back. He'll take care of the rest. As the letter states, the burial has already taken place. Despite all this, however, I still intend to find out who, at the Glasgow location, told Flora where I lived."

"What will you do with the house?" Louisa asked.

"Well, I don't want to keep it. I'll sell it and perhaps donate the proceeds to charity."

Louisa nodded. "That's a fine idea."

"Maybe you could help me decide where the money should go," he said. "St. Giles House is an obvious choice, I suppose, but there'll be enough to make donations elsewhere."

"Of course," she said. "You said she'd been buried already. Does she have a stone? For the grave, I mean."

Maxwell had already considered that but hadn't been sure how to mention it to Louisa. Deep down, he wanted to provide one, yet as much as it felt right, it also felt wrong. "No, not as far as I know."

"Then perhaps some of the money from the estate can pay for one."

He gave a solemn smile. "Yes, perhaps."

"Obviously, I'd like St. Giles House to be considered for a donation," Louisa continued. "But I think, given Flora's circumstances, it might be appropriate to donate the majority to a charity for women. Preferably one in Glasgow, since that is where she's from."

"I'll ask Alex Blair to provide some suggestions," Maxwell said, deciding, at that moment, there was no limit to how much he could love his wife.

EPILOGUE

Florence, Italy,
May 1846

LOUISA OPENED THE double windows with a dramatic flourish, flooding the room with the sound of church bells, their ancient cacophony summoning people to worship. A mild breeze intruded as well, rippling the ivory silk of her peignoir and molding it to her body.

"Oh, Max, it's such a beautiful morning," she announced, with equal flourish. "Come and see."

He slid from the bed and went to her, wrapping his arms around her waist from behind. "What a bloody racket," he said, adhering his body to hers.

"It is loud, but also magnificent." She heaved a sigh. "It makes me want to cry."

"It does stir the soul, I must admit." Maxwell inhaled deeply, absorbing the pleasant and not-so-pleasant smells of the city. Above, a flock of pigeons wheeled through the air before settling on the roof across the way. It appeared to be their regular roost, judging by the unsightly evidence caking the terracotta roof-tiles. Below, the paved streets were quieter than usual. This being Sunday, the shops and cafes were closed, windows and doors shuttered.

They had arrived in Florence the night before, planning to spend several days in the city before beginning their three-week journey back to England. Thus far, they had completed almost six weeks of travel through France and Italy, mostly by coach, though utilizing the train where available.

The lengthy trip had taken some planning and had been a surprise for Louisa. Maxwell had handed her the itinerary at midnight on Christmas Eve, when they'd been sat by the fire doing nothing more than enjoying each other's company. "Merry Christmas, my love," he'd said, and was all but knocked flat moments later as she'd hurled herself into his arms with a squeal of delight.

Finlay had been left in charge of Harlow Industries and, so far, Maxwell had managed to contain his apprehension about abandoning his empire for so long. After all, Finlay had proven himself more than capable of handling things. At least, that's what Maxwell kept telling himself.

Besides, Louisa's happiness and well-being had become his priority. Over the past year, the lass had endured one emotional upheaval after another. He also knew, though she had mentioned it only the once, that she longed for a child. Perhaps this journey, with all its wonderful distractions, would provide the perfect environment for conception to take place. In any case, he'd been left in no doubt about her enjoyment up till now. Her on-going enthusiasm was infectious.

"You look incredibly beautiful this morning." He trailed a few kisses across her shoulder. "I especially like what the breeze is doing to this flimsy thing you're wearing. Very arousing."

She wriggled against the tell-tale evidence. "Mmm, so it seems."

"Give me strength," he muttered, his hands moving up to cup her breasts.

"Maxwell, I'm not sure groping me in full view of passers-by is proper. Especially since they're likely on their way to church."

"Then close the window and come back to bed."

"You're insatiable."

"Yes, I am. Bed. Now."

She laughed, and did as bidden.

A while later, utterly sated, he flopped back on his pillow, one arm behind his head, the other cradling Louisa against him.

"I've been trying to figure out when it happened," he said, "and I think I might have narrowed it down."

"When what happened?"

"When I first fell in love with you."

"Ah." She snuggled closer and trailed a fingertip down his breastbone. "It was when you were away and I had my accident, wasn't it? That's when you first told me, at least."

"Aye, but I think it might have happened before that."

"You're not sure? I know the exact moment I fell in love with you."

"And when was that?"

"You first."

"No, ladies first."

"All right. It was the night of Lady Richmond's party, when we were dancing. You asked me if I was enjoying the season, and I told you I wasn't. Your fingers, at that moment, squeezed mine. And that's when I fell in love with you."

His brows lifted. "Because I squeezed your fingers?"

"Not *because*, necessarily, but that was the moment I realized what I felt. Truth is, it's also partly why I ended up in Lord Richmond's parlor. Seeing you with Miss Chessington was just a little too much to bear. Well, that, and the fact I'd just told Mama I was willing to marry Mr. James Barclay. I was in dire need of a quiet place in which to contemplate my sad fate."

"Good Lord," Maxwell muttered. "I knew you were attracted to me, but I had no idea it was that bad."

Her fingertip ceased its journey. "You knew?"

"From the start. You gaped at me when we first met in the stables."

She snorted. "I did not gape, Maxwell."

"You certainly did, my sweet. And blatantly. Your father noticed it as well."

"Hmm, all right. Maybe I did gape a little." Her fingertip drew circles on his breastbone. "So, when *did* you fall in love with me?"

He grimaced. "I can't believe you agreed to marry Barclay."

"Maxwell!"

"Hmm. Actually, I think it might have been before we met."

Louisa chuckled. "Don't be silly."

He frowned. "I'm not. I'm fairly sure it was on a breezy day back in February, when I'd ridden up onto the moor from the village, following a suggested short-cut to Highfield Hall. Didn't see a soul at first, and then, all at once, I spy this horse and rider flying across the moor at an all-out gallop. A woman, no less. Intrigued, I stopped to watch, only to see her hat fly off. I expected her to stop, but instead she let out a joyous squeal of laughter. That sound stirred something within me that I'd never felt before. It was a moment I'll never forget."

"Then how come you've never spoken of it till now?"

"I put it down to fanciful thinking, which is not something I generally entertain, and chose to ignore it."

"Oh. Well, in any case, it doesn't mean you fell in love with me. You can't love someone you've never met, Max. Even my fanciful imagination doesn't go that far."

"Nevertheless, something inexplicable took hold of me that day, which is why I went to retrieve your hat. Much like the prince and the glass shoe, I was determined to find its owner. I had no idea you were a Northcott till you appeared in the stables."

"Looking rather the worse for wear, I'm afraid."

"Aye, like you'd taken a tumble in the heather." He kissed the top of her head. "Still beautiful, though."

"I still have the hat."

"I know. I noticed it atop your armoire."

Louisa fell quiet for a moment. Then, "And now, here we are, all because we were discovered alone in Richmond's off-limits parlor."

"I have no regrets, my love."

"Me neither. Not a one." She chewed on her lip. "But there's something about the parlor, and more specifically the artwork, that I haven't told you."

Maxwell's brows lifted. "And what might that be?"

"Before I tell you, you have to swear not to tell anyone else."

He looked down at her. "I cannot remember the last time I was this intrigued."

"Swear it," she said.

"All right, I swear."

She winced as she spoke. "I know who the artist is."

"You *what?*" He pulled his arm from beneath her, propped himself on his elbow, and stared down at her. "And how, pray, do you know that?"

"Because he told me."

"He told….? You've actually *met* this person? When did that happen?"

She grinned. "Why, I do believe you're gaping, Mr. Harlow."

"Come on, Louisa. Who the bloody hell is he?"

"Well, obviously, he's an artist. He's also someone I'm rather fond of. Very fond of, actually. You've also met him a couple of times."

Understanding dawned. "Josiah," he said. "Good God, your *brother* is the artist? How long have you known?"

"Since he confessed to me on our wedding day. I was suitably shocked at first, but I now think it's rather amusing. He uses a pseudonym, apparently, and is masked when he works, so no one knows his true identity. It's all very *risqué* and wonderfully mysterious. Quite typical of Josiah. He's always forged his own path."

"Unbelievable," Maxwell muttered, "and no doubt lucrative."

Louisa chuckled. "Yes, he said he'd received several commissions as a result of our little scandal."

"Hmm, interesting. Might be something worth investing in."

Louisa gasped. "Maxwell Benedict Harlow, don't you dare!"

He laughed and pulled her into his arms again. "Are there any other scandalous family secrets I should know about?"

"Nothing comes to mind at the moment." She chewed on her

lip again. "I do have a question for you, though. It's about something you said when we were discovered in Richmond's parlor."

"What did I say?"

"Well, that's sort of the point of my question."

He frowned. "I don't understand."

"Maybe I'll just ask it."

"All right. Go ahead."

"What does 'fuck' mean?"

LATER THAT DAY, Louisa stood in the *Piazza della Signoria* and gazed up at Michelangelo's *David*. She had seen the statue on her previous visit, but that did not diminish the familiar sense of wonder she felt in the presence of the masterpiece. It had taken the young artist more than two years to extract Goliath's young adversary from the massive lump of marble. But then, worthwhile endeavors often took time to achieve perfection.

As she continued to gaze at the statue, her hand fell, casually, to her abdomen. Perhaps she did have another secret to tell. For the past ten days she had waited for the expected onset of dull pain, low down in her belly, usually accompanied by a gush of sticky warmth between her legs. So far, neither had occurred. Her calculations, checked again and again, were correct. And, as each day passed without incident, little by little, she dared to hope. For surely, there could only be one reason for the delay. She had said nothing to Maxwell, nor would she till she was certain.

His voice—the voice she'd come to love above all others—meandered into her ear. "He's rather magnificent, isn't he?"

She regarded the man she'd married. There had been a few doubts at the start of their life together, but then, just like now, she'd dared to hope. It had taken a little time, and presented a challenge here and there, but had since become something exceedingly worthwhile.

Perfect, in fact.

"Yes," she said, sliding her hand into his, "he certainly is."

The End

Bits and Pieces

Thank you so much for reading 'Doubts and Desires', book one of the six-book series, The Highfield Chronicles. I do hope you enjoyed it!

The Waterloo Medal was conferred by the Prince Regent on every officer, non-commissioned officer, and soldier of the British Army who took part in the Battle of Waterloo. It was also the first campaign medal awarded to the next-of-kin of those killed in action.

Grace's advice to Louisa on the morning of her wedding-day is, verbatim, the advice my mother gave to me on mine. As I was getting ready at my parents' home, my mum urged me to set my nerves aside and simply enjoy the day. Which indeed I did (though maybe the glass of sherry I drank before going to the church helped a little). In any case, I often dwell on the wonderful memories of that special day.

Keeping the honeymoon location secret was apparently a thing during the Victorian era, which is why Louisa was reluctant to reveal the destination to Josiah.

William Wordsworth, who is undoubtedly best known for his daffodil poem, became Poet Laureate of the United Kingdom, (an honorary position appointed by the [current] monarch) in 1843. His house, Rydal Mount, does exist and is open to the public. He really did have a "writing hut", which can still be seen in the garden at Rydal Mount.

The poet was known as a benevolent man but, had Maxwell Harlow been real, I'm not sure they would have got along quite as well as implied in my book. Fearful of the potential harm a large influx of people might do to the pristine landscape, Wordsworth was strongly against anything that encouraged tourism in the area, including the railway. The poor man must now be turning in his grave! These days, his beloved Lake District is a designated National Park and a World Heritage Site, with well over 16 million visitors a year.

The Lady of the Lake steamer, as mentioned in the book, was real. She was launched in 1845 and was the first steamer to operate on an English lake. Driven by a 20-horsepower steam engine, she had a length of 80 feet and a depth of 6.4 feet. The launch ceremony was reported in the *Illustrated London News*, and included some celebrity guests, such as William Cavendish, (7th Duke of Devonshire), and Harriet Martineau, a lady often referred to as *the first female sociologist*. Harriet was also one of the few women of her time to make a decent living from her writing! (She has a wiki page, if you're interested to know more about her.)

The Lady of the Lake carried 200 passengers and was apparently quite luxurious. Her hull was finished in black and gold, and sported a white figurehead, and the first-class saloon was fitted with mirrors and carpets. She continued in service for twenty years. William Wordsworth was fiercely opposed to the launch for the same reasons as mentioned earlier. There is now a fleet of steamers on the lake.

Samuel/Julian and his love of dominoes was partly inspired by memories of my father. At the age of seventy-six, while driving his car, Dad had a clot rupture in his brain. He went unconscious and crashed the car, giving himself some nasty bruising but no broken bones. Fortunately, no one else was involved.

While the clot had apparently been extremely small, the rupture had left tracks and done damage. Dad recovered up to a point, still able to speak and function physically. But mentally, he lost all concept of time and date. He remembered things with remarkable clarity from years before but couldn't remember what he'd done that day. Like Julian (Samuel), he especially loved to play dominoes, his playing ability unaffected by the damage to his brain. Just like Julian (Samuel), he would play over and over.

Michelangelo's **David** is now located in the *Galleria dell'Accademia*, in Florence. These days, too, he is also in his full naked glory, with nothing left to the imagination. In 1846, however, *David* stood outside the *Palazzo Vecchio*, which was the seat of civic government in Florence, located in the *Piazza della Signoria*. And in those days, modesty prevailed in the form of the cliché fig-leaf.

In later years, the Victorians didn't have to travel to Florence to see *David*. A full-scale plaster-cast and fully naked replica of the statue was put on display in the Victoria and Albert Museum, which was officially opened by Queen Victoria in 1857. Interestingly, the queen was shocked at the statue's nakedness and, as a result, London's *David* was provided with a removable "fig-leaf" to be used whenever the royals visited.

Other books in this series:
Book 2 – Charades and Chivalry
Book 3 – Passion and Principles
Book 4 – Pride and Propriety
Book 5 – Obsession and Obligation
Book 6 – Vices and Virtues

Other books connected to this series:

A Solitary Candle
(Written under my other author name, Avril Borthiry.)

To keep up to date with my book releases, please follow me on:

Facebook:
facebook.com/Wrenbooks
facebook.com/borthiry

Amazon:
amazon.com/Charlotte-Wren/e/B08FFBR14W
amazon.com/Avril-Borthiry/e/B006RNN04W

About the Author

Charlotte Wren writes heartfelt historical romances set in the Regency and Victorian eras.

You can find Charlotte at the following social media sites:
Facebook – facebook.com/Wrenbooks
Amazon – amazon.com/Charlotte-Wren/e/B08FFBR14W